Dear Reader,

I hope you enjoy *Elusive Love*. This story is more
than just a tale to tell for me, because I have lived
so very much of it. Though all my stories are
written from my heart, this one was written from
my soul. So many of you have contacted me,
expressing your feelings about the kind of story you
would like to read, and I suppose, in my way, this is
my return letter. I want to thank all of you for your
heartfelt comments and the parts of your lives and
thoughts you have shared with me. I value both
your warm wishes and prayers.

Fondly,

Catherine Lanigan

What reviewers say about Catherine Lanigan:

"Catherine Lanigan's books…represent the
changing—and booming—genre of
women's fiction."
—*Chicago Tribune*

"Catherine Lanigan is in a class by herself."
—*Affaire de Coeur*

"Catherine Lanigan is a master storyteller."
—*Rave Reviews*

Also available from MIRA Books and
   CATHERINE LANIGAN

DANGEROUS LOVE

Watch for

TENDER MALICE

MIRA Books
March 1998

CATHERINE LANIGAN

ELUSIVE Love

MIRA BOOKS

MIRA

ISBN 1-55166-286-8

ELUSIVE LOVE

Printed in U.S.A.

To: J.D.A.
From: C.D.L.

Only if we believe strongly enough
And are lucky enough,
Will we discover that even on this side of Paradise,
Dreams do come true.

This human needed a flock of angels to make her dream come true. Gratitude and appreciation only skim the surface of my deep respect for all your hard work, support and belief in me.

Charlotte Breeze
Kimberley Cameron
Dianne Moggy
Amy Moore
Ilana Glaun
Jodee Blanco
Katherine Orr

Prologue

The dream was always the same.

It began with Susannah looking out over a charcoal ocean. A thick fog crawled over the water, blurring the division between sky and earth. As it surrounded her, she felt her will dissolve, as though overtaken by a supernatural force. Then an eerie foreboding emanating from the sea, fog and sand enveloped her like an invisible cocoon. Flooded with anxiety, she desperately began searching the seashore for something, but didn't know what.

As the dream continued, Susannah would become so frightened, she would awaken screaming for her mother. Susannah was six years old when the dream first appeared. Her mother had reassured her there was nothing to fear and that dreams were not real.

The dream returned two or three times a year. Frightened and a bit embarrassed, Susannah never mentioned it again to anyone. She carefully locked away the experience in her subconscious and went on about her life.

Not until the week before spring break her freshman year at Indiana University did Susannah Parker allow the dream to alter her plans.

That night the dream changed drastically.

Through her childhood, the dream continued in the same way. Frantically she paced the shoreline. Anxiety riddled her mind as she mumbled to herself. "Have I missed the appointment? What will I do if I'm not on time?"

Then she stopped and wondered what exactly she was afraid of missing. She'd never understood the significance of this particular place.

It made no sense that she should be standing by an ocean. There was no ocean in Indiana, though Lake Michigan, at the very northern tip of the state, was quite vast. Powerful whitecapped waves and strong currents told her this was surely an ocean. But which one? Just as she was at her wit's end, *he* would appear.

He rose from the sea wearing ink blue robes. Adorned with sapphires and amethysts, the garment appeared to be made of water, not fabric. He possessed majesty and an overwhelming presence. The fog masked his face, making it impossible for her to discern his features. She wanted to ask his name but was too awestruck to speak. He beckoned her to join him. Terrified that if she walked into the sea she would die, Susannah shook her head in refusal.

Sometimes he would give up his plea, transform into seawater and blend into a wave that crashed at her feet. As she grew older, the only change in the dream was that his visits with her lasted longer and longer. Though he never spoke, she could feel his pleas with her heart. As time passed, his urgings became more sincere and were marked with profound sadness.

In her young mind, Susannah empathized with the sea king. Though he appeared to be made of water, she believed he was out of place somehow. They were alike that way, because she'd always felt she was a misfit.

* * *

Susannah's mother, Kate, was from Atlanta and had carried her Southern accent, manners and generosity with her to Indiana when she married Stu Parker, a pharmacist.

Susannah adored her mother's stories about the Old South and the life of gentility that existed before the Civil War. When the family went on short trips in the summer, Susannah always begged to go anywhere south of the Mason-Dixon line. Strolling through antebellum mansions on the banks of the Mississippi transported her back to a time she wished she'd been born to. More than an affinity for the architecture and the furnishings, she felt an eerie familiarity with these homes. The fragrance of night-blooming jasmine, tea roses and camellias sparked Susannah's imagination. She envisioned herself walking, dressed in hoopskirt and straw bonnet, among early spring dogwoods and enormous magnolias. The deeper into the South the family traveled, the more Susannah felt at home. Humid gulf breezes along the coastline of Alabama and Mississippi filled her mind with visions of turn-of-the-century resort hotels and fabulous carriages. The only way she could bring the South with her to Indianapolis was by filling her pockets with Gulf Coast sand and seashells. Every time she rearranged her crowded bedroom shelves to add a new sand dollar or dried sea horse, her curiosity about the dream grew.

By the time Susannah was twelve and the dream came to her again, she mustered the courage to ask the sea king which ocean it was. Again, he never spoke, but when she looked at her feet, drawn in the sand was the word *Atlantic*. In the dream, she placed her hand in an oncoming wave and found it was cold, as the Atlantic should be. She'd hoped it would be warm like the water along the Gulf Coast of Alabama and Mississippi.

Disappointed that the sea king was not from the South, nor even remotely resembled Rhett Butler, she vowed never to ask him a question again.

A freshman at Indiana University, Susannah had planned to spend the week of spring break on campus to get caught up on her research papers. Putting in a few extra hours waiting tables at the Steak Shack would help pay off her Ayers department-store bill and her gasoline charge card. Her Alpha Phi sorority sisters had offered a variety of invitations ranging from spending a week at Alyson Baker's parents' horse farm in Kentucky, to going to Charisse Claybourne's vacant Fifth Avenue penthouse while her parents were in Paris, to joining the majority of the girls in Daytona Beach and Fort Lauderdale.

Susannah was too practical to blow what little savings she had on, what she considered, a frivolous trip. She steadfastly refused every lure her sorority sisters cast her way.

Such was her thinking until the Thursday night before everyone left when she dreamed about the sea king again.

From the beginning, Susannah knew something was different. The fog was not as thick as during previous visits. The sea itself was a radiant crystal blue marbled with streaks of an incredible turquoise green. This time she was not a little girl but nineteen, as she was now. Rising out of the water, the sea king dispelled the remaining fog, bringing the landscape into focus. It was the first time Susannah thought her dream could be real.

Now that the fog was gone she could see his face. His straight hair was light sandy brown worn back from his face to reveal a high forehead. His cheeks and sharp jaw-line created a heart-shaped face, making him seem vulnerable at one moment, yet determined and purposeful the next. He was tall and slender, though his shoulders were wide and his arms looked strong. His hips were narrow and the muscles in his lean thighs and calves reminded her of an athlete's. To her, he appeared able to swim across the ocean with ease.

She waited for him to beckon to her, but he did not. Instead, he walked toward her, the waves lapping against his calves. For years she'd wondered if he was half fish, with fins for feet. Standing next to her, she knew he was all man.

Afraid he might be some kind of sea monster, she expected his eyes to be a cold fathomless blue and refused to look into them. He waited patiently as she screwed up her courage. She was stunned to discover they were a warm honey brown with golden flecks and glowed like candlelight, offering refuge.

When he put out his hand, she took it. She was amazed to feel real flesh and the rhythmic beat of his pulse at his wrist.

"I expected you to vanish like smoke," she said with awe as she smiled at him.

"Never again," he replied in a thick Southern drawl.

She gasped when she realized he was the embodiment of her childhood musings about the South.

This is impossible! she thought to herself. *Silly fool, this is only a dream. He's not real. I'm not here, and when I wake up I'll be in my room at school and everything will be normal.*

"You are a silly girl," he said. "Dreams are meant to become real."

He'd read her thoughts! She wondered if she could read his mind as well. As she was about to ask him another question, he moved closer, putting himself only a breath away. He gazed at her.

"Your eyes are the color of the Caribbean," he said as he placed a strong arm around her back and pulled her body against his. "Look into my eyes when I kiss you. Then you will be mine."

Chills blanketed her. *What if his kiss changes me somehow? What if I die from his kiss?* As a child she'd feared he would transform her into a mermaid and she'd never see her family again.

As an adult, her curiosity urged her to put an end to her questions. She was all too willing to throw caution aside.

Maybe he's my guardian angel come to take me to heaven.

"I assure you, my dear, I am no angel." He pulled her closer to him. "You must kiss me so that you will know me when we meet."

"When we meet? You're not just a dream?"

"Only for now," he said, moving his lips over hers.

Tentatively, Susannah gave in to the kiss. Had she known that kiss would alter her life, she never would have consented.

As he explored her lips with his mouth, shivers trickled down Susannah's back. Possessively, he increased the pressure of his lips until her body shook with delicious chills. She could feel his passion building as he slanted his mouth over hers again and again. Her skin tingled with millions of tiny electric shocks. Slumbering emotions awakened her heart. Tears seeped through her closed eyelids, and joy rang through her soul.

The sea king was breathing life and love into her.

She put her arms around his neck and pressed her breasts into his hard chest. A rush of warmth swept away her goose bumps and she felt as if she were melting into him. They were becoming one person, she thought.

"We have always been one," he whispered lovingly.

Slowly, his flesh transmuted into a ghostly image and Susannah was no longer human, but spirit.

Overwhelming love filled Susannah's mind, heart and soul. Love banished all her fears. Like the rushing tides of the sea, she was washed clean by its power, every atom in her body, every cell in her brain purified by his love. She realized she could never describe this feeling, this experience to another human being for the rest of her life.

More incredible was that Susannah found the same unconditional love in her own heart for him. Never had she known a human could give love divinely.

I want this kiss to last for eternity.

Those words had no more than skittered through her head when she realized that the closer she held him, the less she felt the press of his body. She opened her eyes to see him slowly vanishing while still in her embrace.

"Don't leave me!" she pleaded.

She tried to touch him, but he was like vapor. She wanted to tell him that she loved him, but he couldn't hear her.

"I'll leave the earth! I'll stay with you here...in the dream. Just don't go!"

Standing alone on the seashore, sadness consumed her heart like a voracious parasite. She almost hated him for showing her how hollow she could be. Loneliness clung to her as she scanned the horizon one last time.

The fog rolled in, erasing all clarity to the landscape. Tears flooded her eyes, making it more difficult to see.

"Why have you done this? Why are you torturing me?

All these years you have haunted me only to abandon me! Come back! Please, come back!"

Susannah awoke staring at the ceiling. She held her breath as hot tears rolled down her cheeks and dampened her pillow. She swiped a hand across her face and found the hair at her temple soaking wet. She'd been crying for quite some time.

The light from the full moon outside illuminated the glistening tear on the pad of her finger. *I don't understand any of this.*

She recalled her roommate Marilou's words as she'd urged Susannah to go with all of their friends to Fort Lauderdale.

"We'll have a blast, Susannah. You can't stay stuck behind a book all your life. That's not living! You've gotta go!"

Susannah looked at the moon and then she knew. *The sea king was in Florida! I must go to Fort Lauderdale with Marilou and the others.*

It was a crazy notion, but even her father had recounted stories of researchers discovering new drugs or cures on the impulse of a dream.

And both her parents had always told her that nothing in the world was impossible, if only she would believe.

If dreams were meant to come true, then maybe, just maybe, the sea king would come back to her.

1

Bloomington, Indiana
1976

Susannah was nearly crushed by her sorority sisters as they barreled down the stairs three and four abreast carrying bags packed with suntan oil, bikinis and fake ID.

"I've been looking all over creation for you, Susannah. I want to know what's going on. Leavin' me a note sayin' we're goin' to Florida together, after all. Why, just yesterday you told me to leave with Pam Mayard," Marilou drawled. Susannah loved the soft melodic sound of her friend's voice. "Pam's already left! You better not be lyin' to me!"

"Don't get your Memphis dander up, Marilou," Susannah replied with equal frustration. "There will be plenty of Harvard men left on the beaches to see that Brazilian bikini of yours."

"Strings are the latest thing in Rio. I could have bought a much skimpier one while I was there, but I was being thrifty. *I* love it," Marilou replied with a haughty upturned nose.

"What there is of it, you mean. Lord save those poor unprepared boys from what they are about to see." Susannah loved teasing Marilou because her platinum-haired, blue-eyed, buxom Southern friend took man-hunting seriously.

"Oh, hush up, Susannah, and tell me where you've been."

"You're awfully bossy for someone who is without a car or money right now," Susannah teased as Marilou glared back. "Since it's my car we're taking and my credit cards we're using to make this trip happen at all, I figured I'd better gas up and check the oil and tires." Susannah hoisted a stack of books from her left hip to her right.

"The Department of Highways will commend you, I'm sure."

Susannah stepped out of the way as a trio of girls wearing sunglasses and baseball caps came running down the stairs singing the Indiana University fight song.

Marilou shot her friend a censorious look. "We're gonna be left in the dust if we don't hurry!"

Susannah tossed a hunk of flaming auburn hair over her shoulder as she gave Marilou a warning look. "Working overtime at the Steak Shack plus studying for midterms on my breaks has not put me in a good mood."

"I can see that!" Marilou said as they dodged another onslaught of girls headed for the front door. "Mercy, Susannah! If we don't hurry, we *will* miss all the fun."

Susannah took advantage of the break in traffic on the staircase and dashed up to their second-floor room. She put down her books and pulled out a packed suitcase from under the bed.

"Lord! When did you do that?" Marilou exclaimed.

"Early this morning." Susannah grinned happily. "I'm just as anxious to get out of here as you are." She put on a pair of sunglasses, grabbed her purse, the suit-case and a portable radio. "What are we waiting for?"

Marilou's pert mouth turned up in a smile. "Not a damn thing."

Susannah's Chrysler LeBaron convertible had been in a major wreck so she'd gotten a good deal on it. Believing she only needed transportation from Brownsburg to Indianapolis where her parents still lived, she hadn't paid much attention when the salesman had told her never to take the car over fifty-five.

"It'll top out at sixty before it gets the shakes," he'd told her.

"I don't worry about that. I'm a very safe driver. Never had an accident in my life!" she'd said proudly.

"You're only eighteen. Wait'll you've been driving twenty years."

As they drove down I-65, Susannah admitted he'd had a point. He'd also been right about the "shakes."

"We'll never get to Fort Lauderdale if you insist on drivin' the speed limit," Marilou said. "God! I hate these new laws. I used to do eighty-five on roads like this."

"Yeah? Was that before or after your daddy took the Mercedes away?"

Marilou crossed her arms over her chest defiantly. "How many times do I have to tell you, it was a Porsche!"

"Whatever. Listen, Marilou, the frame was bent on this thing, so it's never sat right on the wheels. It isn't a Porsche and it shakes a bit, but it'll be cool when it counts."

"How's that?"

Susannah's eyes flashed mischievously. "When we're

cruising along the beach with the top down, they'll be looking at us, not the car."

Marilou grinned widely. "I almost hate that you're so smart."

"What a ridiculous thing to say. Nobody hates me because I use my brain."

"The hell they don't. And you have such a bad habit of using every brain cell you've got. It certainly isn't the Southern thing to do."

Susannah was curious. Because she'd fallen in love with sorority life during rush week, she'd had to take a job to pay the house fees. Juggling work hours, a full class schedule and homework left little room in Susannah's life for dating. "You mean, the boys don't like me because I make good grades?"

"I can't believe this is news to you, Susannah. You yourself told me that no boy in high school ever asked you out past the second or third date."

"True. I got bored with them."

"My point exactly. But the sorority's not complainin'. They love that you're the lead contender for valedictorian of our class—it would boost the overall GPA. Not to mention that you look like a *Cosmo* cover girl, all that hair, those turquoise eyes and legs long enough to reach to the moon. I heard there was not a single vote cast against you. In fact, half the house is still tryin' to find something wrong with you."

"This is the craziest thing I've ever heard," Susannah replied as they crossed the Kentucky state line and drove into Tennessee.

"I'm your roommate and I told them not even to look for a zit...a freckle! There aren't **any** to be found. Let me put it this way. They love you for being perfect, and they hate you for it, too."

"Look, my parents are not wealthy like yours and most of the sisters'. They've saved since I was a baby, sacrificing vacations and things they wanted and needed for themselves. And it still wasn't enough to pay my house fees. I work my butt off at the Steak Shack so I can be an Alpha Phi."

"And I'm not sayin' you shouldn't be one. But what good is it if you don't go out with anybody? That's what sororities and fraternities are for...weeding out the riff-raff and matching up socially equal men and women. Backgrounds count for a lot, Susannah."

"Do you really believe that?"

"If you don't, you should. God, I shudder at the up-bringing you've had!"

Susannah raised her chin. "I'll stack my upbringing against yours any day."

Marilou patted Susannah's hand, which was tightly clenched on the steering wheel. "I'm not criticizing you. I'm trying to help. Gracious, you can be so testy."

Susannah remained silent.

"Background is important for a long-term relationship of any kind, especially a marriage," Marilou went on. "Could you see me even dating a garage mechanic?"

"Emphatically no."

"That's right. I'm better suited to a senator, a Wall Street tycoon or a shipping magnate like Onassis."

Susannah started to laugh at her lovable but often-times addle-brained friend. "You don't think that you just might be setting your sights a bit high?"

"Not in the least. I'm thinkin' long term. That's your problem, Susannah, you don't consider the entire ex-panse of your life like I do."

Marilou's words hit their target dead center. Susan-nah had never thought about the "entire expanse" of her life. All through grade school and high school she'd saved her baby-sitting and waitressing money for college. She'd kept her goal of becoming a teacher, not so much because she loved teaching—she'd never been in front of a classroom of children—but because it was a secure profession. Once she had that license in her hand, she could always rely on teaching. That's what her mother had told her.

The truth be known, Susannah hadn't considered a thing past graduation day in three years. She'd been so intent on taking her required courses that she hadn't thought about what majoring in education actually entailed. So far, she found the curriculum boring. Because she loved literature, music and art, especially all blended together in a theatrical play, she'd declared dramatic arts as her minor.

In high school Susannah had tried out for and captured the role of Maria in *The Sound of Music*. Julie Andrews, Susannah was not, but her voice was passable and trainable. The seventy-five dollars she spent on voice lessons two months before the play paid off handsomely. Susannah was a hit. But this was Indiana. There were no jobs for aspiring playwrights, directors or actors. No one noticed.

What daydreams she'd ever had about matching her natural talents with her college studies died back in Indianapolis. Like her mother, she would be practical and acquire skills that could support her all her life. But for Susannah, teaching was more palatable than cutting, perming and coloring hair.

Practicality had played an even bigger part in Susannah's social life. She did not care about going to movies and fast-food restaurants with boys who couldn't carry a conversation and who only wanted to screw her before taking her home. She told herself that boys were a bore, and as a result, she'd never had a serious relationship. So, when it came to matters of the heart, she was still inexperienced.

Susannah could never tell Marilou or anyone else that she simply believed Prince Charming would come to her some day, much the way the sea king had appeared to her in her dreams. Mr. Right would show up and he would be nearly a clone of herself—with the same wants and needs—and they would marry and have beautiful talented children. Her mother and father had told her that was the way it happened to them. They'd been together twenty-two years and were blissfully happy.

She believed she would be as lucky.

"Okay, Marilou, you tell me what you think I should do."

"Okay." Marilou mused thoughtfully to herself for a moment, started to speak and then closed her mouth. She tapped her perfect oval-shaped fingernail against her sparkling white front tooth. It was a habit Susannah abhorred. She should tell Marilou that Harvard-trained future senators wouldn't consider tooth-tapping an asset.

"Given the fact that you are too tall for easily half the men in America, too smart for another forty percent, and too beautiful—which translates to *intimidating*—for anyone who is left, I think you'll have to wait 'til you're forty for the men to catch up to you."

"Shit."

Marilou shrugged her shoulders and gave Susannah a meek apologetic grimace. "Sorry."

Susannah laughed. "You're not telling me anything I haven't already heard."

"Oh, yeah? When was this?"

"In high school. That's what the boys said about me then."

"See? That's the trouble right there. They haven't grown up. Maybe you should consider older men."

"Oh, barf!"

Marilou faced her friend seriously and put her hand on her shoulder. "Susannah, I think you've got a problem."

"I think you shouldn't worry about me," Susannah advised. "I'll be fine, as I've always been."

"Sure, when you were a little kid. We all were, but the stakes are different now. The competition is heatin' up every minute."

Susannah took off her sunglasses now that the sun had completely set. "This isn't a game, Marilou."

"Life is the biggest game of all." Marilou took in her friend's expression. "I can see I'm not convincing you. Fine. Have it your way! Me? I'm playing every day as if this just might be the day I win!"

"I do that, too," Susannah said, defending herself.

"Right. That's why you never go to the mixers and study instead. You barely made it to the home games, for God's sake! Susannah, you act like a hermit."

"I don't care. I know that somewhere out there, the right man is waiting for me, and when we meet he'll know I'm the one and I'll know it's him."

Marilou appeared to be beside herself with frustration. "I suppose you're just going to open the front door and there he'll be..."

"Yeah." Susannah smiled wistfully, thinking of the sea king.

"Delivering pizza!" Marilou blasted.

"He will not. He'll be tall with hair the color of a sandy beach and light brown eyes so sparkling they look as if they've been studded with gold. He's got that same Southern drawl you do...well, similar, at least. And he'll kiss me..."

Marilou's eyes were suspicious slants. "So, I was wrong about you. You've been lyin' to me all along."

"What? I have not!" Susannah protested.

"The hell you haven't. Where did you meet him? How old is he? Do I know him?"

"Who?"

"Mr. Right you've been describing. From the moony look on your face, I can tell this isn't just some ordinary guy from Munster, Indiana. What's his name?"

Susannah stared at the oncoming stream of head-lights. "I wish I knew."

"He's kissed you and you don't know his name?" Marilou clucked her tongue as she shook her head wea-rily. "I thought I trained you better than this. Get their names! Get their phone numbers! Addresses! License plates. Something, for God's sake, so you can track 'em down!"

"I didn't mean it like that. I haven't actually met him. I'm hoping I will, though. God, I hope I will..." Her voice trailed off.

Marilou slapped her cheek with her hand. "I'm losin' it." She leaned over and began shuffling the road map, empty paper cups and hamburger wrappers that were strewn on the floor.

"What are you doing now, Marilou?"

"Lookin' for my brain. It's down here somewhere. I wouldn't have left it all the way back in Bloomington."

"Would you knock it off?"

"Pardon *moi*? You're the one who isn't makin' sense. I know the look on a girl's face when she talks about being kissed by someone special. Rapture. That's what was all over your face just a minute ago. Don't try to fool me anymore, Susannah. I know *all* about these things."

Marilou folded her arms over her chest and waited patiently.

Susannah let five minutes pass. She put a tape in the player. Then she turned it off. "Okay. But you're going to think this is the craziest thing you've ever heard."

"Try me."

"I met him in a dream."

Marilou slapped her cheek again. Slowly, her splayed fingers slid down the side of her face to her neck. "You're right, I think you're crazy, but don't stop now."

"I've had this dream dozens of times since I was six. It's always the same dream. I see this man rising out of the sea and coming toward me. Last night was the first time I'd seen him in a long time. Years maybe. Anyway, he stood on the beach with me. Then he kissed me. It was the most incredible experience of my life. I had no idea love could be that unconditional, that joyous, that exhilarating."

"Knocked your socks off, huh?"

"He made the earth quake, the sky tumble. It was unreal."

"*That* is exactly right. Unreal. As in a dream. A fantasy. A...wait a minute. A guy in the sea. On the beach! So that's why Miss Priss Practical decided this morning to cry uncle, pack up and go to Fort Lauderdale."

Susannah glanced quickly at Marilou's animated look of surprise. She gripped the steering wheel tightly as she admitted the truth. "I think I'm going to find him, Marilou. I *know* I am," she said with determination.

Marilou roared with laughter. "As my daddy says, 'Don't that beat all?'"

2

Fort Walton Beach, Florida
1976

Repeated blasts from an antique horn and a trio of bois-
terous voices yelling his name brought Michael West out
from under the Jaguar convertible he'd spent two days
repairing.

"Hey! Michael! Get yer butt in gear! We're ready to
take off!" Sam Tonn stood on the hot plastic seat of his
neon orange Jeep and leaned on the roll bar.

"What the hell you doing, Michael?" Pete Simmons
called from the back seat. "You're not ready at all."

Jim Callaghan tugged on Sam's T-shirt. "He's not going."

Michael pulled a blue cotton towel out of the back
pocket of his work overalls, wiping his grease-covered
hands as he walked toward the Jeep. "That's right,
guys." He looked back toward the garage. "See that row
of cars over there? Those are the ones I promised would
be ready by today. See those in that row over there?
They have to be finished by Thursday. My dad hurt his
back yesterday, and Jerry's only good at pumping gas. I
can't leave Dad in a bind like this."

"Hey, man. We figured this trip on a four-way split.

The gas, the room, the babes..." Sam grinned widely as Pete slapped him on the back.

Jim, always the more serious of the four, leaned closer to Michael. "Are you sure about this? You're the one who planned this trip, got the triple-A maps and guides for us. You booked the reservations, got the fake ID. You've talked about Lauderdale since...junior high!"

Michael looked thoughtfully across the road to the white-sand gulf beach. "Yeah, I guess I *have* wanted to go there that long." After a pause, he looked back at his friends. "I *still* want to go. I don't know what it is. I feel as if something is pulling me there."

"Then do it, man!"

"Yeah, Michael, think of all those bikinis. Whoa!"

Michael laughed and nodded. "Guys, we grew up on this beach. Cut our teeth on bikinis." *This is something different. Something I can't describe even to myself.*

Michael remembered that as a child he'd wanted to travel, see new places and meet interesting people. Though he'd spent his life on the Florida Gulf Coast, his biggest fantasy was to own a sailing yacht that he would sail to the Florida Keys and farther to the Virgin Islands. As he got older and began working at his father's gas station, Michael met travelers from all over the country. His observations and inquiries over the years revealed that the richest travelers were from New York City. They drove expensive foreign cars and wore incredibly beautiful clothes. Living on the beach all his life, Michael had only one suit in his closet. Shorts, jeans and T-shirts were the extent of his high-school wardrobe.

Michael had been sixteen when a brand-new black Testerosa with an overheated engine was brought in. That was the day Michael knew what he wanted.

"I think I can fix it," Don West, Michael's father, told

the owner, a Wall Street broker. "The radiator hose has a slit in it. Manufacturer's defect. It'll take some time..."

"All right, give me the bottom line. How long and how much?" the man asked, sliding his hand into his pants pocket and pulling out a thick wad of hundred-dollar bills.

Michael's father coolly glanced away from the money roll and replied, "I can have it ready first thing in the morning. We've got a crackerjack parts house that's never let us down."

"Wonderful. Listen, could I use your phone to book a hotel room? And I really need to call my office in Manhattan. If I reverse the charges, would that be all right with you?"

"Certainly, sir," Don West said and motioned for Michael to show the man to the phone in the office.

Michael filled the nearby soda machine so that he could eavesdrop.

"Do you have a suite available? I get cramped easily. And if possible, I need two phone lines. One is just never enough," he joked smoothly. "Good. Some fresh flowers always make me feel at home, if you wouldn't mind. Do you have a wine cellar? Very good. A bottle of Le Montrachet burgundy. And could you recommend a seafood restaurant?" He jotted down the name in a leather-and-gold-embossed notepad.

Then he placed the call to New York.

"Charles! I've had a bit of bad luck and I'm stranded in Fort Walton Beach. It's in Florida, Charles. No, Lauderdale is on the other side of the state. I won't be there for two days. Is Margaret flying down tonight? Good, she can check the boat for us and make certain it's well stocked with caviar... Yes, Charles, I know what's riding on this deal. I never scoff at seven- and eight-figure deals."

Michael's jaw dropped when he realized this man was talking millions of dollars! His ears didn't miss a single word.

"I told you that I got a hell of a deal on the car. That's why I'm doing this. Look, it's just got a few bugs to be worked out, but the fellow here seems to know what he's talking about. She's a beaut, Charles. You're going to want one. Black, of course. Classic black. Nothing but the best for Margaret. Excellent. I'll see you all the day after tomorrow then. Ciao."

The man finished his call, then left the office.

"Michael, take Mr. Van Buren to his hotel and make sure you don't scratch that nice suede luggage he's got there in the trunk," he heard his father call a few minutes later.

Michael exited the office, took the keys to the Testerosa from his father and carefully opened the trunk. Michael inhaled the scent of new car leather. He'd seen expensive cars all his life, since their garage was the only one in town that serviced foreign cars, but he'd never seen anything like this. Michael knew then that just fixing another man's car would never be enough for him. He wanted—needed—to *own* the car, the yacht in Fort Lauderdale and have a job in New York City.

"Thank you very much, Mr. West," Mr. Van Buren said, and followed Michael to the pickup truck he'd bought two months before.

Michael's curiosity was killing him. They had driven less than two blocks when he asked, "What kind of work do you do, Mr. Van Buren?"

"I'm a stockbroker," he replied proudly. "I work for a

large firm on Wall Street. My grandfather's firm, actually."

Michael nodded his head. "A family business. Like my dad and me."

"Yes. Perhaps you've already discovered that it isn't as easy as it seems. Most people think inheriting the family fortune is a piece of cake. At least some of my so-called friends do. The truth is, sometimes I actually believe it would be less work to simply start from scratch rather than struggle to correct my father's mistakes, my grandfather's mistakes and his before him."

"If they made so many mistakes, how could there be a company left to inherit?"

Mr. Van Buren smiled appreciatively. "How old are you, Michael?"

"I'll be seventeen in September."

"Well, you're a very sharp young man." He reached in his pocket and pulled out a thin gold box. He took out a business card and handed it to Michael. "If you ever decide to enter the world of finance, give me a call."

"And how do I do that? Enter the world of finance, I mean?"

"Get a college degree in finance. Then obtain your stockbroker's license by passing the SEC exams, which are damn tough, by the way."

"I've made straight A's all my life. Tests don't bother me. So, I do what you said and that's all there is to it?" Michael didn't know his face was filled with expectation.

"Not quite, I'm afraid. A certain measure of talent is required."

"What kind of talent?"

"Instinct. Discernment. Quick thinking. Fearlessness. God, I wish I knew what to call it. But the best of the best on Wall Street have it. They can smell good deals a continent away. They intuitively know when to push the client and when to pull back. They're never fooled by phonies and they don't need shortcuts. They are the movers and shakers. They can make the capitalist world rock."

"How will I know if I have 'it'?"

Mr. Van Buren slapped Michael on the shoulder. "That, my boy, can only be accomplished by throwing yourself to the sharks. Make a few deals and see how good you are, in other words."

"I'll make great deals," Michael assured him as he pulled the truck to a stop in front of the hotel. "I'll call you when I get my license."

"You do that, Michael West," Mr. Van Buren said as he shook Michael's hand and got out of the truck.

"You can bet on it!"

Three years had passed since Michael met Mr. Van Buren, and he still kept the stockbroker's business card in his wallet. Every so often Michael pulled it out and remembered the conversation. His junior year in high school, Michael switched all his electives to math courses and excelled.

He'd breezed through his first semester of college at Ole Miss. With half the spring session behind him, he'd proven to himself he was a natural at accounting and economics.

Michael began subscribing to the *Wall Street Journal* so that he could track the rise and fall of the stocks he'd researched. It was a real test of his wit and talent. After six months of scoring himself, he had chosen only one loser. But as far as Michael was concerned, the jury was still out.

Michael had planned all year to go to Fort Lauderdale.

He wanted to look up Mr. Van Buren, check out his yacht and remind his mentor that he was working on making his dream happen.

Michael had many great dreams about Fort Lauderdale but, unlike his friends, none of them involved a bikini-clad coed.

"Sorry, fellas," Michael said.

"Lauderdale isn't the same as here and you know it! It's spring break. These Yankee girls are ripe for the pickin'. We'll never see them again, they'll never see us. Who's to know what we do?" Sam asked.

It was hard for Michael to get excited like his friends, because Michael didn't believe in searching for the girl of his dreams. She'd just be there when the time was right.

"C'mon. Y'all are pissed because without my share this trip is going to cost each of you more," Michael countered.

"Damn straight," Pete said honestly.

Adjusting his baseball cap over his sandy-colored hair and putting on his sunglasses, Michael dug into his back pocket. "I'll give you my share. That way, nobody's out anything. How's that?"

"Cool," Sam replied with an approving smile, and took the money. "Guess we better get on the road," he said, backing away.

"Have a great time, guys!" Michael waved as two cars simultaneously pulled into the station. One was a LeBaron convertible needing gas. The other was a 1960 Ford Fairlane driven by elderly Mrs. Hart. Michael had a soft spot for the old woman he'd known since childhood. She lived in a small cinder-block house down an unpaved road a mile from his home. She barely had enough money to feed herself, much less pay for gas or car repairs. He knew she would be looking for him because Michael always paid for her gas and small repairs out of his wages.

"Hello, Mrs. Hart," he said, walking over to her car and opening the door for her. "You sure do look pretty in that blue dress."

The white-haired woman's watery blue eyes twinkled. "Oh, Michael," she said, chuckling. "You'll flirt with anybody, won't you?"

"Just you, Mrs. Hart. You know you're the only girl for me. Let me treat you to a Dr Pepper while I fill up your car and check the oil."

"You know all my weaknesses," she scolded playfully.

"You wait inside where it's air-conditioned. I'll come get you when I've finished."

While Mrs. Hart shuffled away, Michael nodded to Jerry, one of his Dad's employees, who was all too eager to wait on the two pretty girls in the convertible.

The hot-looking blonde and the auburn-haired beauty were arguing over whose fault it was that they'd gotten the wrong directions. Obviously, they were on their way to Fort Lauderdale, too. Michael had heard the same kind of argument a hundred times before over the spring break. He chuckled to himself and raised the Fairlane's hood.

Susannah smiled at the attendant who asked if she wanted regular or premium gasoline. "Regular, and would you clean the windshield? It was pretty dusty along that last stretch in Alabama." Turning a scowling expression to Marilou she said, "And never mind we weren't supposed to be in Alabama in the first place."

Marilou opened the car door. "Alyson Baker told me we take I-65 to Florida. So that's what we did!"

"But we're on the wrong side of the state! We're losing a good six hours!"

Marilou got out of the car. "This is all your fault, you know. If you hadn't been so wrapped up in that damn dream of yours, you would have paid more attention, too." She put her hands in her shorts pockets. "I'm getting a Coke. You want one?"

Expelling her frustration with a deep sigh, Susannah realized it was futile to be mad at Marilou when she was just as guilty for not buying all the maps she needed and carefully charting their route before they left. She *had* been too wrapped up in her thoughts to think clearly about anything. "Yeah, thanks."

Running on adrenaline for the past eighteen hours had strained her nerves, she thought as she cocked the rearview mirror to look at her face. This bit of misfortune wasn't the end of the world and it was wrong of her to take it out on Marilou.

Pulling off her baseball cap, she grabbed her hairbrush and worked it through the snarls in her hair. As she did, in the corner of the rearview mirror she watched a tall, slender young man, wearing a baseball cap and sunglasses, lower the hood on an old Ford. He wiped the headlights and cleaned the windshield wipers. Then he went to the door of the office and held it for a woman who looked to be in her eighties.

Gently he placed her arm through his as he helped her back to her car. She could tell they were familiar with each other because of the fondness in the woman's eyes. Susannah liked the way he patted her arm, held the door for her and with a smile reassured her that everything was fine with her car. She overheard the woman protest that someday she would pay him for the gasoline.

"Don't you worry about a thing, Mrs. Hart. That little

bit of gas isn't going to break the bank. You just take care of yourself for me."

"I will," she replied.

Fully aware of how many cars awaited servicing, Susannah noticed there was nothing hurried about the young man's movements as he made certain the elderly woman didn't close the door on her skirt.

Such a gentleman, she thought. *I hope I find someone like him.*

"Are we ready, doll?" Marilou asked, practically jumping back into the car with two Cokes.

Jerry had just finished cleaning the windshield. "That'll be nine dollars," he said.

Susannah handed him the exact amount, started the engine and pulled out of the station, never noticing she had the attention of both station attendants.

Stopping at the curb, the driver of the LeBaron convertible looked both ways before easing into traffic. As she did, a gust of wind lifted a long lock of auburn hair away from her face. Michael watched as the morning sun spun through her hair, illuminating it like wildfire. He noticed the gentle but strong curve of her jaw and the graceful tilt of her head.

I've never seen anyone that beautiful. She must be a goddess. She couldn't possibly be real.

Glancing at her license plate, he said to Jerry, "Ever been to Indiana, Jerry?"

Watching the LeBaron move into traffic and drive out of sight, the attendant answered, "No, but if there's any more like that up there, maybe I should think about it."

Michael was barely breathing. "I don't think I'll ever find anyone like her."

Jerry slapped Michael on the back good-naturedly.

"You just did, but you let her get away!" He laughed as a bell rang, signaling another car to be serviced.

Did I? I thought she was just a dream. And I can always hold on to a dream.

3

Driving for twenty-four hours straight, living on coffee, colas, cookies and cheap hamburgers left Susannah and Marilou exhausted and cranky. Susannah looked in the rearview mirror and exclaimed, "I need some sleep. I look like dog meat."

Marilou yawned and waved the air dismissively. "On your worst day, you look better than the rest of the female population."

"I'm not so sure about that..." Susannah gestured with her head to the right, where small groups of beautiful, tanned, lean girls strutted down the sidewalks wearing bikinis as small as Marilou's Brazilian string. "We're a long way from Indiana."

Marilou's optimistic bubble burst. "Where did *they* come from? Hollywood?"

"Who cares? This isn't a competition. We're here to have fun," Susannah replied with an upbeat smile.

Marilou slid down in the seat, her lower lip in full pout position. "Fun? Not for me. I'll be spending the entire time tryin' to pound reality into your head. The Major League playoffs aren't as tough as Fort Lauderdale at spring break. God! I thought you Yankees were smart, but you've been more sheltered than any Memphis belle I've ever known!"

"I guess I'm your cross to bear," Susannah quipped.

She wasn't interested in anything but finding her sea king. But now that she was actually here, driving down the palm-lined streets with restaurants and clubs overflowing with college kids, she was very unsure about what she was doing.

Maybe Marilou is right. I've sent myself on a wild-goose chase. He's just a dream.

The Holiday Inn where Marilou had booked a room was swarming with college students. Susannah stood in the registration line digging in her purse for her credit card while Marilou zealously scanned the lobby. The line moved quickly and within minutes they flopped onto two single beds in their room. Sleep came instantly.

Their first days were filled with sunning on the beaches and dancing at the bars. Marilou was having the time of her life; Susannah was beginning to tire of her quest for the man of her dreams. She'd come to feel like an idiot searching every crowd for a sandy-haired, golden-eyed man who would fall instantly in love with her.

Tonight they were yet again among the throng at a popular local bar. Susannah knew that Marilou could—and would—dance until dawn. Between band breaks, Susannah told Marilou she was going for a walk on the beach. She would meet her back at the room. Marilou barely paid attention.

It was a balmy tropical night with a full moon gleaming down on the ocean. The floral-scented breeze slapped palm fronds against each other. *It's a night meant for romance,* Susannah thought.

Filled with anticipation, Susannah gazed intently at the water. She stood for a long time, waiting, hoping. A lone man stood farther down the beach, but she was oblivious to everything except the ocean.

Susannah realized that the absence of fog was the only missing part of the dream. Everything else—the warm wind, the rushing waves, the moonglow—was perfect.

If ever I were to meet him, this is the night, she thought. *I will wait.*

Dawn found Susannah wide-awake sitting on the sand still staring out to sea. She'd rationalized that until the morning fog rolled in, he wouldn't appear. But because it was unseasonably warm that year, no fog appeared. By eight o'clock, Susannah had given up and returned to the Holiday Inn. Marilou was sound asleep and Susannah tried not to wake her.

A few minutes later, Marilou pushed herself onto her elbows and asked groggily, "Didn't find him, huh?"

"No."

"I told you it was a stupid idea."

"I'm going back tonight."

"God, you're stubborn," Marilou groaned, and turned on the bedside radio. The announcer was giving the weather report.

"...and by Thursday, we'll be experiencing a drastic drop in temperature. Expect early-morning patches of fog. And for all of our spring-breakers, you'll need jeans and sweaters through the rest of the weekend."

"Rats!" Marilou moaned. "I'm hitting the beach now. There's no way I'm going back to school without a tan." Marilou grabbed her bikini and towel. "You coming?" She looked at Susannah. "What are you smiling about?"

"Didn't you hear that? Fog! That's the missing piece of the dream. There wasn't any fog this morning. I was too early, was all."

"God, you're hopeless," Marilou groaned.

"So what? It's my life!"

Marilou put her hands on her hips and glared up at her tall friend. "Yeah, and you're fucking it up. However, it is only because I love you that I put up with you. When your fella doesn't show up, I'll still be here to pick up the pieces."

"He'll be there. I can *feel* it."

Marilou grabbed Susannah's arm. "C'mon. Let's work on your tan. Later, you'll find the right guy who won't care that you've got a few bolts loose upstairs and will love you for your tan and glorious body, the way it should be."

"Marilou, you're incorrigible!"

4

The fog drove most of the couples inside as night shifted into morning. Susannah nearly had the beach to herself except for the same lone man who'd been there the night before leaning against a palm tree smoking a cigarette. Without the moon to light the beach, she couldn't tell much about him except that he was tall and was as obviously immersed in his thoughts as she was in hers. She watched as his glowing cigarette fell to the sand and he crushed out the butt with his shoe. He turned and retreated into the hotel, leaving Susannah alone.

The fog curled over the waves, which gave the beach an unearthly quality. Susannah rose and entered the ethereal mist. She listened for the sound of his voice. She couldn't call out to him because she didn't know his name. She zipped up her hooded sweatshirt and hugged herself to stay warm. This was the first night in her life when she knew she was not dreaming. She was no longer a child waiting for life to happen to her. She was forcing her dream to come true.

Where are you? I'm here. Why aren't you?

Believing in the power of the mind all her life, Susannah was convinced she would find him. She moved closer to the water and noticed that the change in weather had made the sea angry. The waves were black and powerful as they rushed to shore and slapped her bare feet.

She couldn't understand why the waves were pushing her farther back toward the beach. Why weren't they beckoning her as they had in her dreams?

Though she strained her eyes to see through the fog, still there was no sign of him. "Where are you? I couldn't have come all this way for nothing!"

Relentlessly, she stood her ground. She refused to give up her fight. She would wait till hell froze over before she'd give in.

Hadn't she read about recurring dreams in *Psychology Today*? Such phenomena are considered by many dream analysts to be harbingers of the future. They are meant to warn, to instruct, to lead one through life's journeys. Even her psychology of education professor told the class that they should take a child's dreams seriously. Children were open to the mysteries of the deep subconscious. Adults, on the other hand, tended to override the subconscious with their logical mind.

Susannah had seldom been passionate about anything in her life, except the antebellum South, her high-school plays...and her dream. She was guilty of utilizing her rational mind at *all* times. Heartfelt issues were rare to Susannah, but when she *did* commit to believing in something, she jumped in with both feet.

How could she give up on her dream when it had reappeared just a few nights before? There had to be a logical, albeit cosmic, reason why sensible Susannah was here tonight on this Atlantic beach.

"I'm waiting for you," she said into the fog.

No one answered.

As dawn lanced through the fog, Susannah's optimism began to fade. *I've been a fool.*

Looking at the sun rising above the horizon, she realized she was crying for the second time that week. Angry at herself, she mashed the tears into her cheeks with the palms of her hands.

"I'm so stupid...stupid..." She pulled her knees to her chin and dropped her head. "How could I kid myself this way? How could I have let myself spend all this money to come here? I hope I can get more hours at the Steak Shack to make up my losses."

Balling her fists, she pummeled the sand, taking out her aggression. She wished now she'd never told Marilou about the sea king. She'd be lucky if Marilou ever let her live this down. What if her friend told their sorority sisters...?

Susannah didn't even want to think about the repercussions. They'd all have a field day. Sensible Susannah chasing phantoms. Sensible Susannah falls in love with King Neptune.

"Well, they can tease me all they want, I'll make sure it doesn't happen again," she said as she bolted to her feet. With shoulders back and head held erect, she stared into the diffused sun rays as she formulated the vow to herself.

"I will never again believe in things that aren't real. Dreams are for children. From this day forward, I will act like a responsible adult. There are no sea kings. There are no magical kisses. And I will never allow myself to be a fool."

Scooping up a handful of sand, she walked to the water's edge and threw it into the sea to seal her vow.

She turned her back on the Atlantic Ocean. It was now a part of her past.

Thick swirls of fog concealed Susannah as she moved away from the shore.

"Hey, there! Better watch where you're going."

Lost in thought, at first Susannah only saw a flame and heard a man's voice. *How odd. There's a candle in the middle of the fog,* she thought. Then she saw a man's smiling face. He was lighting a cigarette. "Sorry."

"No apology necessary," he said. "It seems you've been here much longer than I. I guess that gives you squatter's rights. Or maybe it would simply be possession is nine-tenths of the law."

"Huh?" The haze in Susannah's mind was more dense than the fog.

"What I meant to say was that you've been out here all night, haven't you?"

Suspicion knit her eyebrows. "How would you know?"

"I've been watching you," he replied.

Fear cleared Susannah's head instantly. *Was he a stalker or just a plain old mass murderer?* She glanced sidelong down the beach, but all she could see was fog and sand. They were alone. "Terrific! Well, I gotta go!"

She tried to sidestep him but he blocked her path. "I'm harmless, really. Except on a tennis court. So I've been told."

Susannah stepped back as she gazed at him. "I don't play tennis."

"Is there anything I can say to pique your interest in me?" He chuckled with the kind of melodic male laugh that probably turned a lot of women on. Susannah wondered if the laugh was natural or practiced.

"My name is Greg Walton. I'm in law school at Harvard," he said.

"That's nice."

He leaned toward her and when he did, a beam of

sunlight sliced through the fog to reveal a pair of sparkling blue eyes. "Aren't you interested in Harvard
men?"

"I haven't given it much thought as we have so few in
Indiana."

"Indiana? I thought I detected a bit of a drawl in your
accent. I thought you might be from around here," he
said, tossing his half-smoked cigarette in the sand.

"My mother is from Atlanta. A couple of days in the
South does that to me."

"Brings out the worst, you mean?"

"Brings out the best." She beamed proudly.

"I love it here, too. My parents keep their sailboat here
and..."

Susannah nodded knowingly. "I suppose they have a
condo, too?"

He laughed. "And a house in Westhampton. Am I
bragging too much?"

Susannah noticed his face was quite near hers and she
wondered if his imperceptible movements were as cal-
culated as they seemed. "A bit, but it's okay."

"And your name is?" he asked in a low seductive tone
as he put out his hand to her.

"Susannah Parker." She slipped her hand in his, waiting for the magical tingling she remembered from the
dream. His hand was warm and callused from tennis.
Sadness flitted through her heart, but she banished it. At
least Greg was real flesh and blood.

"Tell me, Susannah Parker, from Indiana, why have
you been staring out to sea every night?"

She remained silent, knowing he'd think her nuts if
she told him the truth.

"I'm curious," he continued. "Are you melancholy or
contemplative?"

"A bit of both, I think." She glanced back at the ocean.

The sun had baked off most of the fog. Though it was much colder today, groups of students wearing sweatshirts emblazoned with their respective college logos began covering the sand with blankets. A trio of already tanned boys wearing Ole Miss caps and matching windbreakers tossed a football back and forth. She chuckled, watching them aim passes more at the girls lying on beach towels than at each other.

"Hey! Sam! This is gonna be a long one," the deeply tanned tall boy called.

As she watched it spinning through the air, Susannah suddenly realized the football was aimed at her. She grabbed Greg's hand. "Duck!"

Sam leaped in front of Susannah, snagging the ball only inches from her face. "Wow! That was some catch, huh?" Sam asked her, pointedly disregarding Greg's presence. Sam's face was filled with appreciation as he gazed at Susannah.

"Don't you think this is just a bit obvious?" Greg suddenly asked icily.

Susannah didn't like the proprietary tone in Greg's voice. Nor did she like the way he moved possessively to her side as if he was protecting her. She didn't think she needed protection. She liked Sam's honest and open face.

Sam ignored Greg. "You're the most beautiful girl on this beach. Hell, any beach! And I grew up on beaches!"

"So, that makes you an expert?" Susannah taunted playfully.

"Yep." He tossed the football in the air between them and caught it without taking his eyes off her. "My name's Sam Tonn. I'm from Fort Walton Beach. You don't sound like a Yankee. Where y'all from?"

"I'm from Indianapolis and a freshman at I.U." She

stuck out her hand. "Susannah Parker. Nice to meet you, Sam."

The second her hand touched Sam's, his friends came running. Susannah felt as if the starting whistle for hunting season had just been blown.

"I'm Pete!"

"I'm Jim." The last one nudged his way in front of Greg, practically pushing him aside. "I'm the oldest and smartest."

"Yeah? Says you!" Sam argued, then turned a beaming smile on her again. "We go to Ole Miss. We're all Pikes. Are you in a sorority?"

"Alpha Phi," she answered.

"What's your major? Here by yourself? Do y'all ever get down to Fort Walton Beach?"

"No, I don't know where it is," Susannah replied brightly as the three boys jockeyed for position, each wanting to be close to her.

Greg politely placed his hand on Susannah's shoulder. "I have to go. Look me up when you finish playing around," he said, and walked away.

"Gosh, you're pretty," Pete said. "I've never seen hair like yours."

Susannah almost didn't catch Greg's caustic tone. When she turned to face him, he was gone.

Vanished. Just like the sea king. But if you're really him, why don't I feel the way I did in the dream? And why would you walk away?

5

Oxford, Mississippi
May 28, 1976

Michael rubbed his bleary eyes as he sat at his desk studying for finals. The temperature was eighty-nine degrees and the air conditioner in the fraternity house was undergoing repairs. So when his three friends burst into his room, they did not find him in the best of moods.

Pete flopped onto the unmade bed and folded his arms beneath his head. "This is your last chance, Michael."

"Yep," Sam replied as he slapped Jim on the back. "This is the bicentennial Indianapolis 500 we're talking here."

"Look at it as history in the making," Jim urged.

Michael pinched the bridge of his nose, hoping he could stay awake for his next exam. Ever since spring break, he'd driven back to Fort Walton Beach on weekends to help his father at the station. The eight-hour drive after his afternoon class on Friday, the twelve-hour shifts on his back beneath cars and the eight-hour drive back late Sunday night to Oxford had not given him a moment to catch up on his homework. He couldn't complain to his father, because it was the money from the gas station that paid for his schooling.

Michael was grateful for every minute of class time he had.

He looked up at the giant poster of New York City over his desk and the "I love NYC" coffee mug in front of him. "I'm not going, fellas."

"Jesus! Y'all are *such* a bore, Michael! When are you ever gonna have some fun?"

Michael glared at Sam. "When I'm forty. Now, will you buzz off? The only history I'm interested in making is on this exam—" he checked his watch "—which is in less than twenty minutes."

Pete winked at Sam. "Remember that fantastic redhead we told you about? And Marilou? We're gonna look them up when we get to Indianapolis."

Michael kept reading his textbook. "I don't like redheads. Brunettes, either."

Sam nodded to Pete. "These girls are special."

Michael looked at Sam. "I know you've been calling Marilou. I know she writes you and that you've been to Memphis to see her. You've staked your claim. Jim's dating Melody now and that leaves Pete with the redhead. So, why would you want me around?"

"We always do everything together, Michael," Sam said, and looked at the others who nodded in unison. "We're just trying to keep the group together..."

"I know, but things are changing. My dad's health isn't what it was. He's spent the years since my mom died building the station's clientele and now he's overloaded. If I don't help him, I can't stay in school." Michael's eyes were serious as he leaned back in his chair. "All of your parents have plenty of money. I'm glad you can see the 500. But I have to tell you that next year isn't going to be any easier for me. Or the next. Maybe when I'm on my own in New York, I can do all these things.

But not now. Someday I'll be in your league, financially, I mean. Maybe you should find another friend who—"

"Michael!" Sam cut him off. "It's not the end of the world, you know. It's just a weekend!"

Michael suddenly felt a hundred years old. It was as if some great hand had removed him from the carefree world of his youth and forced him to see life through new jaded glasses. "I think my life is going in a different direction, is all. I don't want to hold you back from asking somebody else, thinking I'll get mad or get my feelings hurt. It's okay, fellas. Really."

Sam's chuckle was meant to be lighthearted, but it clattered sadly as everyone fell silent. "If that's the way you want it..."

"It's the way it is," Michael said in a low voice.

Sam shoved his hands into his jeans pockets as he motioned with his head to Pete and Jim. They left in silence.

Michael looked up at his New York poster. "I'm gonna make it. I *know* I am."

Indianapolis, Indiana
Memorial Day, 1976

Susannah stood in the kitchen making hamburger patties as her mother went bananas. Kate splashed tea over the rims of the tall ice-filled glasses. While she mopped the mess with a wad of paper towels, she accidentally knocked over the watermelon boat she'd spent hours carving the day before.

"Oh, God! Look what I've done!" Kate wailed. "I ruined it!"

Susannah patted her mother on the back. "It's fine!" she soothed and picked up the watermelon. Carefully she scooped up a handful of perfectly round cantaloupe and honeydew melon balls. "No one will know the difference."

"I can't believe you did that! They were on the floor!"

"Mother, if you ever worked at the Steak Shack, you'd know this is nothing compared to what I've seen those cooks do."

Kate clapped her hands over her ears. "I don't want to hear it!"

"I'll rinse every last strawberry," Susannah offered.

"That's better." Kate sighed.

Susannah took the watermelon to the sink and turned on the faucet. "I've never seen you like this, Mom. It's just a family picnic. We have them every year. Why are you so...nervous?"

Kate pushed a thick clump of auburn hair off her face. "We've never had a lawyer here. And especially not one from New York!"

"Oh, Greg you mean." Susannah looked out the kitchen window to see Greg wiping off the seat of a folding chair before he sat down next to her father.

"My God, Susannah. I can't believe your luck in meeting him. It's as if it were...kismet."

"Kiss what?" Susannah hoped Greg didn't blow cigarette smoke in her father's face. She knew her father despised smokers.

"Kismet, dear. Fate. Destiny. You know," Kate said as she blended plain yogurt into the dressing for the potato salad.

Susannah watched as Greg flicked an ash off his blazingly white tennis sweater that matched his expensive white summer slacks. Even his shoes were white kid leather. "You think fate had something to do with it?"

"I certainly do," Kate replied with a smile. "I always knew you'd do well in life, Susannah, but to have someone so accomplished and from such a good family...heavens! I just can't believe your luck!"

Susannah turned to see the enthralled look on her mother's face. "I thought you said it was kismet. Luck had nothing to do with it."

Kate wasn't listening to Susannah. She was obviously too busy spinning daydreams of her own. Susannah knew her mother took the fact that Greg had flown to Indianapolis for the weekend as a sign that he was serious about her. Greg had told Kate that he'd passed up an invitation to visit his Harvard friends in Hyannis Port, and that he'd told his parents he would not be going to Fort Lauderdale because he wanted to see her daughter. Susannah had seen the look of speculation, and hope, in her mother's eyes.

Kate clapped her hands together. "Susannah, you do like him, don't you?"

"Greg's okay," she replied, still looking out the window.

"Just okay? What does it take to make you happy? He's been absolutely everywhere—Europe, Cairo, Tokyo. His friends are among some of the oldest families in America. Think of the invitations you'd receive! Fox hunting in Maryland—"

"Mom, I think you're getting a little carried away with all this. After all, I hardly know the guy. I met him in Florida. He tracked me down at the sorority house and called me a few times. I mentioned this weekend in passing. I had no idea he'd take me up on it."

"See? A take-charge kind of guy. I like that in a man. It reminds me of your father," Kate replied dreamily.

"Sometimes I'm not too sure about you, Mom. You're still a hopeless romantic. And you're married!"

Kate shook her head. "Marilou is right. You are naive."

"Speaking of whom..." Susannah remembered she'd been in the shower when Marilou called that morning. She wiped her hands with a towel and went to the wall phone to dial the sorority house in Brownsburg where Marilou was staying. After the holiday, she planned to fly home for the summer. Following what seemed like a hundred rings, the Alpha Phi phone was answered by one of the girls. Susannah counted the costly minutes until Marilou picked up the phone.

"Oh, it's the traitor," Marilou said derisively.

"Are you still on this kick?"

"You stole my guy!" Marilou hissed.

"Greg was never yours. You didn't even know his name until I told you. And I never encouraged him. He got the house number from information, for God's sake."

"I put in my order for someone just like him and you got him," Marilou whined.

"Order? Sorry, Marilou, I'm not aware of this cosmic Sears store. Besides, you have Sam now."

"Oh, Sam's not serious. He's just for fun."

"Does Sam know this? He calls you every other day. He's coming up to see you this afternoon. I think you should level with him, Marilou. It seems to me that he's very serious."

Marilou huffed dramatically. "Talk about the pot callin' the kettle black! No one is as serious as Greg. Flying first-class to see you? God!"

"I haven't seen him since Fort Lauderdale. He called me a couple of times and then practically invited himself here. I haven't even kissed the guy! It's too soon to be serious."

"He flew—"

"If you were back in your daddy's good graces," she interrupted, "would a plane ticket be a big deal to you?"

"Well, no. But you're missing the point. Only serious-minded people fly to see other people—what do you mean you haven't kissed him?"

Susannah slapped her forehead with her palm. "Marilou, I don't want to talk about this anymore."

Marilou ignored her. "You don't understand people like Greg, but I do. I'm only saying this because you're my friend. The truth is, he's out of your league, Susannah. Greg and I have similar backgrounds. We've been to the same places, move in the same circles. We even drive the same car, damn it!"

"*Did* drive." Susannah couldn't resist the jab, especially when Marilou's class-conscious claws were out.

"Oh, hush! I get the car back when I get home. I wish I'd never told Sam I'd wait around this boring old campus for him. I could be in Memphis having a gay old time. Or even...in Indianapolis," Marilou hinted.

"What are you gonna do? Have Sam drive you here so you can ogle Greg? Well, go ahead, I don't care."

Suddenly, a loud crash made Susannah jump. She whirled to see her mother standing amid a gooey glob of red Jell-O and broken crockery.

Kate was aghast. "Are you crazy?" She stepped over the mess and glared at her daughter. "Hang up!"

"Mother!" Susannah matched her mother's damning look. She put her hand over the receiver. "I know what I'm doing."

"I doubt it," Kate mumbled, then turned to the task of cleaning up the Jell-O.

Marilou was quick to pick up on the invitation. "You're kidding. You'd let me take your boyfriend?"

Susannah groaned to herself. "He's not my boyfriend and if you think you can make any more impression on him than you did in Florida, be my guest."

"Okay! Okay! So my approach was slightly off with him..." Marilou hesitated and when Susannah did not respond, she said, "My approach was totally wrong. Go ahead and say it. He doesn't like me."

"Between you and me, Marilou, I think he likes tall women," Susannah admitted. "But if you want to bring Sam and the gang, you're welcome here."

Susannah looked at her mother who paused from mopping up the last of the sticky jelly to roll her eyes. Susannah finished her conversation and hung up.

Kate looked at Susannah and seemed to be choosing her words carefully. "After this, I promise I won't say another thing on the subject."

Susannah nodded and folded her arms over her chest, waiting for the onslaught.

Kate continued, "Consider this. You're an intelligent, hardworking, dependable and giving person. Except for your IQ, which comes from your father's side of the family, I taught you the rest. I want you to take a long hard look at me, Susannah. I'm thirty-nine years old and I've had to work hard since I can remember. I've been juggling work at the salon, this house, you and your father, long before anyone ever heard of Gloria Steinem. It doesn't have to be that way for you."

"What are you saying? That you don't love Dad?" Susannah felt her face flush with shock.

"Not at all. He's been my life. And it's been a good life, but it could have been better. You are so beautiful, sugar. You could have any man you want. Rich, intelligent, sophisticated men admire smart women. They want nothing more than a beautiful woman with manners and wit. Lord knows I taught you social graces even Melanie Wilkes didn't know. You're as polished as they come, darlin'." Kate placed her hand on Susannah's cheek.

"Mom..."

"Hear me out. I'm not telling you to marry a man you don't love. But there are all kinds of love, and sometimes I think you've believed a bit too long in fairy tales. Men have never been knights. I have to agree with these women's libbers that most men have more faults than we do. Think about your future. Kindergarten teachers don't make as much as I do with tips. Make your life more exciting and rewarding, Susannah. You have advantages I never had. The fact that Greg is sitting out there on our patio right now is one of them."

"I dunno, Mom. Maybe it's the way his lip curls when he looks at our house." Susannah's shoulders shook at the distasteful thought.

"Can you blame him? His parents live in a mansion on Long Island. Their friends live the same way. I overheard him ask you to visit for the Fourth of July—I want you to go. Just for the experience. Maybe you won't like Greg, after all, but you might meet one of his rich friends."

Susannah broke into laughter and put her arms around her mother's shoulders. "You're hopeless!"

"I love you, sugar. I just want the best for you. The best."

Susannah hugged her tightly. "So do I, Mom. I just wish I knew what that was."

6

Michael tightened the lug nuts on a brand-new white-walled steel-belted tire. The expensive tires were the fifth set he'd sold since coming home from college. Convincing the owner that his four-year-old Cadillac deserved the best tires money could buy had been a cinch. What Michael didn't understand was the fuss the other mechanics and his father were making over the sales.

"Our sales double when you write up the orders, Michael," his father told him.

Michael countered. "It's not such a big deal."

Don West shook out a clean utility cloth and wiped his sweat-soaked forehead. "You're a born salesman, son. I don't know what happened this year at school, but you've sharpened your sales pitch."

"All I did was study, and work here on weekends." *And cross off the days until I move to New York City.*

Don slapped his son on the back. "You're focused, all right, son." He laughed. "Whatever it is, this business sure needs you."

Michael put the ratchet wrench back in the toolbox and lowered the hydraulic lift to set the Cadillac back on the clean concrete floor. How many times in his life had he swept and hosed that floor, keeping the station up to his father's immaculate standards? How many times had he spent Friday nights crouched over a cantankerous engine instead of at his high-school football game? How many times had his father made it clear he wanted Michael to carry on with the "family business"? *About as many times as I've kept silent about wanting to become a Wall Street broker.*

"Hey, Michael!" his father called.

Michael shoved his musings to the back of his brain. "Yeah!"

"The mail's here. There's something from Ole Miss." Don waved the envelope in the air.

"My grades!" Michael wiped his hands on his overalls. He didn't want a greasy mechanic's smudge to mar the envelope. He took the letter from his father, extracted his pocketknife and slit the flap.

Michael read the grades aloud.

"History...an A. Calculus...an A. Business law... Oh, God. Oh, Jeeezuzzz! They're all A's!"

Don smacked his lips as he grinned and then gave Michael a bear hug. "Of course they're all A's, you dummy! Why would they be any less?"

"Dad! This is college not high school. This was a bitch, I don't mind saying!" Michael looked at the stack of grades to be absolutely sure they were real. "Nope. I read them right. A four point O!"

Michael glanced at his father and his heart warmed at the pride he read on his face. Then he saw a tear creep around the corner of the older man's eye. He knew exactly what he was thinking. "I wish Mom was here, too, Dad." Michael wrapped his arms around his father's large frame.

Don West had always been a man of few words when

it came to his emotions. He'd chosen to bury his grief over his wife Emmy's death with her. He'd told Michael that life was for living and not mourning. Don had released his emotions by attacking his small business like a relentless hurricane. He'd painted the exterior white, navy and sky blue. He'd installed new gasoline pumps, added a car wash and built four new garage bays. Don had worked night after night to pound nails into every shingle on the roof. And the business had profited from his work.

After Emmy's death, Don lost twenty pounds he'd been trying to shed during what turned out to be the hottest summer in Fort Walton Beach's history. He'd taught himself how to sleep on Emmy's side of the bed and brought himself to donate her clothes to the church. He'd removed everything that reminded him of her except the silver-framed picture that he kept beside his bed.

Don was so busy healing himself that he wasn't aware of the anger that festered in his twelve-year-old boy. More than he missed his mother, Michael hated the hit-and-run drunk driver who killed her.

There were no witnesses to what occurred on the moonless night when Emmy had crossed the highway headed for a walk on the beach. And the police never found her killer. However, they felt certain that the man had been driving without headlights. Otherwise, over-cautious Emmy would never have crossed the road.

Michael thought of all the "ifs" that could have kept his mother alive. If she hadn't been so petite, she might have survived the impact. If she had worn pink that night instead of her favorite deep-sea blue, the driver might have seen her. If she hadn't been so obsessed with building her seashell collection... Michael's list of "ifs" grew every day until it finally broke down the wall that caged his anger.

That day, eight years ago, the outdoor thermometer had read one-hundred-and-one degrees. Michael had just finished filling the Dr Pepper machine. He'd looked up to see a battered pickup truck careen into the station and slam to a halt, narrowly missing a brand-new gasoline pump. The door opened as a filthy-looking, thin, middle-aged man staggered toward Michael.

Michael balled his fists as he marched toward the drunk. "How'd you wreck that front bumper, mister?" Michael asked as he sank his fist into the man's face. The drunk dropped like a stone. "Are you the bastard who killed my mother?" Michael screamed at the immobilized man. Spittle rained out of Michael's mouth as he stood over the man, still cursing him.

"Michael?" Don looked up from the bent rim he was pounding. The hammer fell from his hand as if it were red-hot. "Michael!" He lumbered across the pavement in less than a half-dozen long strides.

Don quickly checked the unconscious man's condition before placing his enormous hands on his son's thin shoulders. "It's all right, son." Don turned Michael around to face him.

Michael and his father gazed into each other's identical honey brown eyes. Then Don put his hand on the back of his son's head and pressed his face into his enormous chest. "I miss her, too, Michael. I miss her so much."

Michael hugged his father as tight as he could. He never knew it was possible for a person to cry so hard and for so long.

Michael was barely aware that his father's employees carried the drunk to his pickup, shoved him inside and drove him to the police station where he would spend the night sobering up.

Michael was only aware of the unusually loud sound of his father's heart. That was when Michael realized that breaking waves sounded much like breaking hearts.

"Great going, son," Don slapped Michael on the back, ending his bone-crushing hug. "Take a break and give your friends a call. They can't be more proud of you than I am," he said with a trace of emotion Michael knew his father found embarrassing.

"Thanks," Michael replied, and walked inside the air-conditioned office. As he stuck his utility towel in his back pocket, he felt his wallet. Suddenly, he knew whom he'd call first.

Carefully and with the respect one gives an icon, Michael withdrew Mr. Phillip Van Buren's business card from his wallet. Holding it between his fingers almost reverently, he placed a long-distance call to the number on the bottom right-hand side of the card.

"Mr. Phillip Van Buren," Michael said to the receptionist when she answered the call.

"And whom may I say is calling, sir?"

Michael stopped as if he'd been shot. *Whom?* Michael knew that Phillip Van Buren, man of the world, Wall Street tycoon, would never remember a skinny kid from Fort Walton Beach. And certainly not after three years. "Michael West...from Fort Walton Beach."

"Thank you, sir. Please hold."

Michael shifted his weight, folded and unfolded his arms. He thought about hanging up. This was ridiculous, calling Mr. Phillip Van Buren to tell him about his grades. The man would think him insane. He'd be lucky if Phillip Van Buren didn't answer the call at all.

Jesus, Michael. This was really stu— "Hello? Mr. Van Buren?"

"Forgive me," Phillip Van Buren began, "but are you the young man who worked on my car?"

Michael threw his head back in surprise. He felt his cheeks stretch, his smile was so broad. "Yes, sir! I can't believe you remember me."

"It wasn't difficult. I've only been to Fort Walton Beach once in my life, Michael. And it was not a pleasant layover."

"I'm sorry about that, sir."

"What can I do for you?"

"Sir, I just wanted...well, I called to tell you that I just got my grades from my first year at the University of Mississippi. I wanted to let you know I'm doing just what you told me to do, sir."

"And that was?"

"I'm majoring in finance. And I got a four point zero, sir. I've been researching stocks like you told me, and so far, I've been picking eight out of ten winners."

There was a long pause on the other end of the line. "Say that again? I was signing some papers."

"My average is about eight out of ten. I just wanted to thank you for encouraging me—"

Phillip cut him off. "Did you invest your own money in these stocks, Michael?"

"Uh, no, sir. I'm still trying to pay for my tuition and..."

"It's always a different feeling when real money is at stake. Putting your own money on the line sometimes disrupts your intuitions."

"I understand that, sir, but I can't do that right now."

"Do me a favor and call me in a week with four stocks

you'd invest in if you had the money. I'll put up a couple hundred dollars and let's see how good you really are."

"Oh, I couldn't do that, Mr. Van Buren," Michael replied nervously.

"*That* is exactly what you'll be doing if you become a broker. You see, Michael? Your fear is already blocking your intuition."

Michael was stunned. Phillip Van Buren was absolutely right. Four points didn't count for shit in the *real* world of finance. His view of life turned another one-eighty. His college courses were no more than grade-school basics.

"I'll call you next week same time with my selections," Michael promised.

"That will be fine, Michael. I'll talk to you then."

Michael hung up the phone wondering if Phillip Van Buren knew how much he'd altered a young man's life.

By the end of June, Phillip Van Buren had been more than a little impressed with Michael's choice of stocks. The telephone conversations and letters he'd received from Michael were concise and intelligent, and his ideas were sound. If he'd personally molded a protégé, he couldn't have done any better than Michael West.

Often flattered by ambitious young men in the firm, Phillip was surprised that Michael considered him a mentor. Michael West had no reason to buff an older man's ego, Phillip thought. Unless...Michael was sincere.

Phillip Van Buren was fifty years old, divorced and childless. He was the bane of his autocratic, aristocratic mother, Adele, who thought he should remarry and sire heirs to the Van Buren fortune. Fortunately, Phillip's younger brother, Bartholomew, had produced two girls and two boys, giving Phillip not only room to breathe, but a houseful of children for all national holidays. The bicentennial of the nation's country was considered by all the Van Burens to be a "family reunion."

For years, Bartholomew had lorded his passel of brats over Phillip's head, touting their academic conquests and artistic achievements as personal victories.

Phillip had never been able to surpass his brother on this score. Now, however, Phillip had created the next best thing to a flesh-and-blood son. Michael West would be his "son," if not in name, then in spirit.

With each telephone call, Phillip noted the reverence in Michael's voice when he spoke the Van Buren name. Much attention was given to protocol in his letters. It was Phillip's bet that somewhere in Michael's lineage there were more than a few Southern aristocrats.

"Breeding tells." Phillip smiled to himself as he gazed out onto the manicured English gardens of his Long Island estate.

He turned back to his two-hundred-year-old Chippendale desk, which had belonged to the third generation of Van Burens during the Revolutionary War, and lifted a small leather notebook. He flipped quickly through the pages and dialed Michael's number at the garage.

When Michael came to the phone, Phillip came to the point. "I'd like to see you over the Fourth of July holiday, Michael. If I were to send you a plane ticket, have a driver fetch you at the airport and give you lodging here at my home, could you arrange the time off from your work?"

Dead silence echoed over the line a few moments before Michael spoke. "Not a problem, Mr. Van Buren. I'll get the time off. Just tell me when you'd like me there."

7

Staring at her nautical-patterned bedroom wallpaper, Susannah wondered if she'd been wrong about Greg. She plumped the pillow beneath her head and swung one leg over the edge of the bed and considered the matter.

In the month since Greg had come to Indianapolis, he'd called her twice a week and, though he didn't write, he'd sent her a bouquet of red roses. *For no reason at all!* she reminded herself. Maybe he *would* turn out to be the man she'd been looking for.

All things considered, there wasn't much *not* to like about him. He was handsome enough to make any woman drool. He was more than a perfect gentleman and treated Susannah with respect. Admittedly, it was a bit of an adjustment for him learning to get along in her family's small ranch house without a maid or gardener. But once he learned her routine chores of kitchen cleanup, garbage detail and laundry duty, he pitched in willingly.

He spellbound her parents with stories of the Broadway plays he'd seen, his favorite and "frightfully expensive, but worth every dime" restaurants, the Fort Lauderdale condo and his obsession with entering every sailing regatta on the Cape. Not once did he press Susannah for any future commitments, nor did he anxiously urge her to spend time alone with him. He appeared content with her parents' uneventful weekend plans. He complained very little about his cramped quarters in her mother's sewing room/guest room. Though Susannah knew he tossed and turned on the aggressively uncomfortable Hide-A-Bed, Greg made a point of mentioning how well he'd slept.

When she drove him to the airport on Tuesday morning, she knew he intended to kiss her. However, traffic had been a nightmare on the loop, making Greg late for his plane. He dashed out of the car, assuring Susannah that dropping him off curbside was all she need do. She had leaned over and touched his hand. He'd smiled back, promised to call her soon and then raced inside the airport.

Being truthful with herself, Susannah would have to admit she was afraid to kiss Greg.

Remembering the vow she'd made in Florida had not quieted the small voice in her head that kept asking, *"Could Greg be the sea king?"* He had been standing there on the beach. His eyes weren't honey brown, but his hair was close enough to the sea king's sandy color. Greg was tall and athletically built where the sea king was lean and slender. He was older than she'd imagined the sea king, but what dream was perfect?

There was only one sure way to find out. She had to kiss him. *But what if he is the sea king? Then what?*

This was a predicament she hadn't considered. She still had three more years of college ahead of her. All her life she'd promised herself a college degree. Even though her mother liked Greg, Susannah knew both her parents would be crushed if she didn't fulfill her promise to herself. Unfortunately, she'd been so focused on her goal that she hadn't considered any other options.

Greg would finish law school next June, study for his law boards and once he passed, he'd immediately go into practice. While he met beautiful and sophisticated New York women in droves, she'd be stuck in Bloomington. She'd lose her sea king!

Clamping her hands on her flushed cheeks, Susannah berated herself for being overly dramatic. Conjecture and supposition were no proof Greg was the man of her dreams. She'd done pretty well with her life so far by thinking things through and being practical. The *only* impetuous act of her life had been the trip to Florida. And then she'd found Greg. Or rather, he'd found her.

The phone rang, catching Susannah arguing with herself over the issue of who found whom. "Hello?"

"Susannah," Greg said.

She reminded herself that Greg hadn't a smidgeon of Southern accent. *He's not the sea king*, she finally decided. "Hi, Greg. How are you?"

"You sound rather down. Anything the matter?"

"No," she replied, sitting up against the white-painted headboard. "I was just thinking..."

"About what?"

"You, actually."

"Well, that's a good sign, isn't it?"

Absentmindedly, Susannah tugged on her earlobe. "I guess," she mumbled. "How's your week been going?"

"Incredible, if I do say so myself. As you know, Susannah, my family is making a big show about the Fourth. The house is practically overrun with caterers and florists. I don't know where Mother plans to put everyone. My Aunt Gloria flew in today from Monte Carlo and in her usual way, she's turned the house upside down."

Susannah thought she'd never get used to the careless way he flung foreign locales into his conversation. She still hadn't figured out if he was trying to impress her or simply being himself. Since he'd always been wealthy, she supposed he thought nothing of it. Her father had told her once that doubts were like tiny black spiders. They could hide beneath a dust mote in an open room, but sooner or later they'd bite.

Susannah cradled the receiver between her chin and shoulder and closed her eyes to the spiders. "Monte Carlo? I'd love to go there...someday."

"Don't tell that to Aunt Gloria! She'd take you back with her."

Susannah opened her eyes. "I don't have a passport anyway."

Greg chuckled and then took a long breath. "Well, you don't need a passport to fly to New York... Susannah, I would very much like for you to be a guest in my family's home. Just think of it this way, it will be something you will tell your children and grandchildren about. Being in the nation's largest city for the bicentennial." He chuckled. "I just thought of something funny. You could tell them that I threw the biggest party in two centuries trying to coerce you to see me."

"Is that what you're doing, Greg?"

He stopped as if realizing he'd allowed himself to be too liberal with his feelings. "I suppose I am."

Susannah had debated too long about the Greg issue. It was time to discover the truth. "I would love to attend your party, Greg. What should I wear?"

Susannah sat on the plane thumbing through recent copies of *Town and Country* and *Vanity Fair*. She groaned aloud at the prices of the fabulous Halston dresses. The white-linen Yves Saint Laurent walking suit at more than a thousand dollars made her light-headed. She'd never seen clothes this beautiful even in the phone-book-size August edition of *Seventeen*. There was no question about it, she was about to step into the twilight zone.

She shoved the magazines into the pocket holder in front of her and turned her face toward the window, gazing solemnly at masses of clouds.

What a moron I am! she chastised herself. Greg had told her, "Leave anything with a bell-bottom in Indiana. Mother has no appreciation for radical styles." Susannah had laughed and explained that was all she owned.

She remembered now he'd displayed little humor at the time. With that single statement, Greg had brought into sharp relief the dissimilarity of their backgrounds.

Though Susannah had seldom rubbed shoulders with hippies or even met a political subversive, she considered "bells" and "hip-huggers" as nothing more than a young style. She owned scads of halters, granny dresses, jeans and T-shirts, which she wore for knocking around. However, being graced by good fortune with a long neck and elegantly slender body, Susannah could wear classic styles with an aplomb and flair that shorter girls envied. Because turtleneck sweaters, blazers, wool skirts and dressy suits were "out," they were always reduced to rock-bottom sale prices. So Susannah had rounded out her wardrobe with a few inexpensive classic pieces, making her wardrobe adequate...for Indianapolis.

Sympathy for her predicament hit a shallow well when Susannah went to her mother.

"How many times did I plead with you to buy more sensible clothes, hmm?" Kate asked while she folded the laundry.

"I bought these at a two-for-one sale!" Susannah held up a fistful of flowered and patterned slacks.

"My point exactly. For what you spent, you could have bought one nice skirt."

"Oh, Mother. Must you always be right?" Susannah slumped on the bed next to the pile of towels Kate had just folded.

Kate took her daughter's chin in her hand and peered deeply into her turquoise eyes. "Don't worry, sugar. You're so beautiful, no one is going to be looking at what you're wearing. I'd lend you some of my things, but since you're six inches taller than I am, I don't think they'd fit. But..." Kate stood and motioned with her forefinger for Susannah to follow her.

"What?" Susannah was intrigued with her mother's mysterious grin.

"I have something I want to show you." Kate pulled open the top drawer of her lingerie chest and rifled through the contents. "Ah! Here it is," she said pulling out a small antique vial.

Susannah examined the long bottle etched with roses. "What's that?"

Kate's eyes were wistful and her voice was softly reverent when she spoke. "This perfume was blended by my mother for me. She told me the recipe was created in Paris especially for your great-great grandmother, Kathleen, before the Civil War. Every generation of O'Shea women have worn this perfume, on our wedding days and other special occasions. Your father makes it for me now since he can get the oils through one of his suppliers."

Kate lifted the tiny cork from the vial and passed it under Susannah's nose. She inhaled the familiar floral blend.

"Mother, you always told me you wore Emeraude. Shame on you for lying to me," Susannah teased.

"That's for every day. *This* is special. I never told you about it because it's expensive. Knowing you and your girlfriends, you would have gone through my entire bottle at one of your slumber parties. What a waste that would have been. No, sugar, this perfume needs to be appreciated by a man. I want you to take it with you to New York."

Gingerly, Susannah took the vial from her mother, realizing the importance of this exchange. For the first time, Kate was admitting Susannah was a woman. Susannah hugged her mother and thanked her. "I'll only wear it when I *feel* it's going to be a special night."

Kate smiled at her daughter. "I wish all your nights will be just that, sugar."

"Thanks, Mom," Susannah replied. When she got to the bedroom door she turned around and asked, "By the way, Mother, what *is* it that makes this perfume smell so...divine?"

"Southern night jasmine. It used to grow in thick blankets on the O'Shea plantation before the Civil War. Very few people recognize anything more than the tea rose and vanilla. Only a true Southerner with family roots reaching as far back in the past as mine would recognize that fragrance."

Susannah remembered the many family stories her mother had told her over the years. As a girl, she'd so often imagined herself in the old family mansion outside Atlanta that she felt she'd spent half her childhood in the Old South. The descriptions of the gala parties and balls attended by her gentrified ancestors remained foremost in her mind despite hearing about the horrific burning of the O'Shea mansion and lands by the Yankees during General Sherman's March to the Sea. Kate told hundreds of stories over the years, but in all that time Susannah had never known about the Southern night jasmine perfume.

She glanced down at the precious vial in her palm. "Yes," Susannah whispered, thinking of the sea king's sweet drawl. "Only a Southerner would know."

Susannah noticed the cloud masses breaking up under the plane's wing. The fasten seat belt sign blinked on and the sound of the bell shook Susannah out of her reverie.

She wiped her forehead with the back of her hand and found she was perspiring in the air-conditioned plane.

God, Susannah! You've really bitten off more than you can chew this time. You're headed for elegant, wealthy Westhampton and about as prepared for this as a trip to the moon.

As the plane circled La Guardia Airport preparing to land, Susannah snatched the magazines out of their resting place and quickly memorized every designer detail. Kathleen O'Shea had possessed a thousand times more class and style than any of her Civil War contemporaries. No Westhampton women would have intimidated Kathleen. Susannah would not let her down.

8

Greg was not at the airport as he'd promised. Susannah scanned the thick throng of people deplaning and realized that half the world had flown into New York for the bicentennial celebration. She was nudged, pushed and shoved into the constantly moving flow of holiday revelers. She felt as if she were riding the crest of a rushing river without a bank on which to stand. She strained to search the crowd for Greg. Children carrying fistfuls of helium balloons and older kids twirling fluorescent-colored strips of plastic overhead obstructed her view. If she hadn't been so tall, she never would have seen the signs directing her to the baggage-claim area. A break in the mass of summer suits, blue jeans and sneakers looked like Mecca. She slipped through to the other side and slammed her back against the wall.

"God! Have you ever seen anything like this?" she asked the sandy-haired man in the Ole Miss shirt who stepped through the crowd and stood next to her.

Simultaneously, they exhaled a sigh of relief.

The man shook his head.

For a brief moment their eyes met and held. Feeling eerily off-center—as if time had stopped—Susannah quickly looked down.

He cleared his throat. "No," was all he said before

darting back into the swarm of people around the luggage carousel.

Susannah tried to follow his movements, but lost sight of him. Then she scanned the crowd again hoping to catch a glimpse of Greg here. Suddenly, she wondered if they'd gotten their signals crossed. She'd expected him to be at the gate. Now that she reflected upon their conversation, all he'd told her was that he'd meet her at the airport. She kept one eye on the carousel for her bags and the other on the people as they pushed past her toward the door.

All the luggage from her flight had long since been claimed as Susannah clung to the hope that perhaps Greg was caught in traffic. She hoped he hadn't been in an accident. She knew all kinds of things could and did happen in New York.

Wiping away the sheen of nervous perspiration from her forehead, Susannah looked up to see a man dressed in a chauffeur's uniform holding a cardboard sign with her last name on it. He was staring intently at her. He moved the sign a bit as if she should know what to do.

She smiled at him and glanced away.

He continued to stare at her.

The extent of Susannah's world travel had consisted of road trips with her parents, one trip to Florida with Marilou and two plane flights to Atlanta for O'Shea family weddings when she was in grade school. She understood very little about airport protocol. All she knew about New York was what she read in the papers. It was filled with sickos and weirdos. The last thing she wanted was an incident with a pervert.

Lord! But she was getting tired of this man staring at her. Giving up hope of finding Greg and anxious about how to hire a taxi to Westhampton—not to mention the cost of such a ride—she approached the chauffeur.

"My name is Parker. By any chance, are you here for me?"

The thin middle-aged man glanced at the very tight new shoes she wore. He sniffed and made no attempt to hide the disdain in his voice. "I'm looking for Susannah Parker," he said in a clipped British accent Susannah immediately pegged as fake.

Susannah had heard better accents than his in her high-school play. She wondered how he thought he could be fooling anyone. "I'm her! I mean..." She ran her hand through her thick hair to keep it out of her face. "I was afraid Greg had forgotten about me." She chuckled hollowly.

"Susannah Parker? From Indianapolis?"

"I'm here to see Greg Walton," she replied, relieved that Greg had not forgotten her and that she would not be forced to hire a taxi.

"Mr. Walton begs your pardon. He's been unavoidably detained. I am to take you to him."

Whenever Susannah was nervous, she had a habit of nodding her head very quickly, which made her look like a bobbing drinking-glass bird in fast motion.

The chauffeur cranked a bushy eyebrow to its apex. "Shall I fetch your luggage, miss?"

Susannah snapped her head to a standstill. "Thanks..." *Ever so? Very much? Yes, James? Please do so?* Susannah was in a quandary. She'd never addressed a servant in her life, and certainly not a chauffeur.

"And what kind might that be, miss?"

Susannah stared blankly at him. A vision of Marilou's expensive Gucci purse flashed across her mind. "Oh!" she blurted out. "My hanging bag is just a navy blue zippered thing...and my train case is a white American Tourister."

Turning away from her, he sniffed again.

Sheepishly, Susannah glanced around to see if anyone else noticed her gauche and unstylish luggage.

The chauffeur's haughty manner was making her even more anxious. Deciding she would take the bags herself, she turned to see him emerge from the new wave of passengers surrounding the carousel.

"This way, miss," he said, walking briskly through the door.

Susannah got the distinct impression he was trying to leave her behind. In her rush out the door, she bumped into the same sandy-haired man she'd seen earlier.

"Sorry," she said, barely having a chance to glance at him.

"Excuse me." He was looking in the direction of the two double-parked stretch limousines. One was white, the other dark blue. Without looking back, he walked toward the dark blue car.

Susannah's chauffeur was putting her bags down beside the white limousine. She rushed up to him and he held the door for her. Once she was inside, she noticed him slip a nearby policeman a twenty-dollar bill. He put her hanging bag and train case in the trunk, closed it and got in the car.

Susannah noticed how the driver dusted off his hands before he clutched the steering wheel, as if her bags had been coated with filth. She pretended to search the interior of her purse for lip gloss, but she did not miss the sharply abhorrent glance he shot her in the rearview mirror.

Never had Susannah met with such unwarranted derision. She had no idea if this man didn't like her in particular, all Greg's girlfriends or just people from Indiana in general.

   She chose to remain silent as they drove through the city streets and out to Long Island. She'd only been in New York ten minutes, and without having met a single Walton family member, she had managed to get off to a bad start.

9

No antebellum mansions, no Indianapolis turn-of-the-century palaces could ever have prepared Susannah for the Waltons' opulent 1920s granite and marble Westhampton mansion. As the car slowly bent around the circular brick driveway, she gaped at the three-story structure with its verdigris copper roof and admired the ancient maples, oaks and hickory trees that surrounded it. She felt like Daisy going to meet Jake Gatsby.

Patiently, she scanned every window, looking for a sign of Greg, but they were heavily draped. *Surely he must have heard the car as we drove in,* she thought as the chauffeur opened the door for her. She smiled at him, but he failed to warm up.

On either side of dark wood double doors, two fierce-looking gargoyles watched menacingly over the plush lawn and symmetrical flower beds that were newly planted with red geraniums, blue stocks and white petunias.

She heard the sound of the trunk closing. *Where was Greg? Maybe he'd gotten the dates mixed-up. No, silly, that's impossible. He sent the driver.* She looked at the monstrous stone carvings realizing their expressions weren't angry so much as deeply sad. "Don't take it so badly, guys. At least you haven't been stood up," she muttered to the statues.

The chauffeur carried her luggage as they walked up the stone steps. With all the sleepless nights of the past week and her mounting anticipation of seeing Greg again, she had to admit she'd let her imagination create an unrealistic arrival scene.

Though the chauffeur had to unlock the front door, Susannah still held out hope that Greg would fling open the door, take her in his arms and kiss her right in front of the tight-faced driver.

"After you, miss," he said with a perfunctory bow.

Susannah's ears pricked to attention as she entered the tomblike silence of the vestibule. *Now*, she thought as she turned toward the immense staircase, *Greg will come dashing down the stairs shouting my name, and take me in his arms....*

Afraid her thoughts were louder than the ticking grandfather clock, she forced herself to face reality. Greg was not at home. Whatever it was that had taken him away this particular afternoon had been more important to him than she.

She was guilty of building her hopes too high. Her elation plummeted. She was unaware of the slump in her shoulders as she glanced at the chauffeur.

A smug grin flitted over his lips. "I'll take these to your room."

She barely heard him as her eyes adjusted to the dim light. *So, this is Greg's home.*

The interior of the house was dark and immense. The charcoal slate floors were scattered at intervals with red, black and deep gold Persian rugs. Huge mahogany beveled mirrors sought but never found any sunlight to reflect. From the intricately hand-carved staircase to the collection of predominantly Oriental antique wooden furniture, it was evident to Susannah that the Walton family had spent generations of fortunes acquiring ugly and uninviting pieces for their home.

Not in the vestibule, living room, nor long, narrow dining room did she see a single photograph of Greg, his mother or father. She could have been in a museum, for all she knew.

Just as she shivered, the front door slammed behind her. Her hopes soared again. She whispered, sensing that in a house like this loud voices were never used. "Anybody home?"

She heard feet shuffling in the shadows. "Greg?"

A voice answered her, but it was only the butler who instructed her that the guest room was at the top of the stairs, three doors down on the left.

During Susannah's first hour at the Walton estate, she met Taylor, a very ancient butler who spent most of his time asking Susannah to repeat herself; Carrie, the upstairs maid, who, despite her impressive mass, insisted on unpacking Susannah's bags and sending the majority of her clothes to be pressed; and Penny, who appeared to be the maid-of-all-trades.

Penny stood next to a pink marble–topped console next to a bank of windows that overlooked a private courtyard below. "You'll have a wonderful view from this room, miss." She fluffed the down throw pillows on the window seat, then turned back to Susannah. "Perhaps you'd care for a soda? Iced tea? Lemonade. Mrs. Walton insists we use only freshly squeezed lemon, powdered sugar and cracked ice, never cubed. It's lovely, actually," Penny said, parting thick lips over uneven white teeth. Her dark eyes looked like raisins in her very pale young face.

Susannah tried not to burst into laughter. "Does everyone who works here have the same accent?"

Penny clasped her hands in front of her, clumsily attempting a proper stance. Her square, stubby fingers refused to interlock. Finally, she stuck them behind her back. "Yes, miss," she replied, not budging an inch from her British dialect.

"And you have to speak like this all the time?" Susannah asked, incredulous.

The maid nodded.

"What on earth for?"

Penny glanced quickly over her shoulder, then put her hand over the side of her face and whispered conspiratorially, "In case any of Mrs. Walton's friends was to hear us, miss. She wouldn't want to be embarrassed. If we was to be caught without our accents, she'd kill us!" Penny snapped her stubby fingers for emphasis, her British accent suddenly gone.

Susannah howled. She couldn't help it. She put her hand over her mouth to stifle herself, but it did no good. "I'm sorry. I've just never heard anything so ridiculous."

"This your first time to New York?" Penny asked.

"Yes, it is."

"Then you don't know what you're talking about. There's a lot more ridiculous things here. Unemployment is one of 'em."

Susannah sobered instantly. "You have a good point. May I call you Penny?"

"That's acceptable."

Susannah smiled at the slender young woman. "I must admit you do a better job with your tonality than the chauffeur."

"Marty? He's not the chauffeur. There is no chauffeur.

He's the gardener. Mrs. Walton makes him put on that outfit to pick up guests every once in a while."

"He's *not* the... Why, that...giving me those creepy looks like I was dirt under his feet."

"Yeah, that's Marty, all right. Slimy sort of guy, isn't he?" Penny laughed.

Susannah hugged her ribs as she roared with laughter. "What did you do, Penny, go to acting school?"

Penny grinned even wider. "Yes, miss. Been goin' over a year and a half. I've got a part in an off-off Broadway comedy. I play an English dairy maiden. I get banged up in the first act."

Susannah stopped laughing and sat perfectly still on the bed. "You are an actress," she said matter-of-factly.

"Hope to be. If the play's a hit, I can tell Mrs. Walton to go to hell!"

Susannah laughed good-naturedly as Penny left the room, once again acting the role, speaking in that incredibly bad English accent.

The fact that Penny was only two or three years older than Susannah was not lost on her. Penny's manner had been flippant about the subject of her job as a maid, but when she talked about acting her tiny eyes had burned with an emotion Susannah did not understand. Whatever it was, it seemed to help Penny put up with her employer's nonsensical rules until she got her break. Penny was going after her dream.

Just as I am. My college diploma is a sensible dream. And then there's Greg. Maybe he's my dream man.

Within the sliver of time she'd spent with Penny, Susannah realized she herself didn't have fire in her eyes. She could only wonder how to get it.

* * *

Formality was the watchword in the Walton home that evening as family and guests were called to dinner. Susannah wore a figure-skimming buttercup yellow cotton dress with low-heeled white pumps. Sleeveless, with a square neckline that revealed what little tan Susannah had acquired in her backyard over the past week, the dress hung to midcalf and was buttoned up the front with quarter-size white buttons.

She didn't realize she was the last to be formally called when the folded white note was slipped under her door announcing the specifics of the evening's agenda:

Cocktails on the terrace at seven. Dinner in the formal dining room at eight. Nightcaps in the library at eleven for those who so choose.

Susannah wished someone had thought to attach a map to the note since she did not know where any of the appointed gathering places were located. She had expected Greg would knock on her door and escort her to dinner. He would introduce her to his family. Instead, she had not seen nor heard from him. She was on her own.

Looking in the cheval mirror and examining her freshly shampooed hair that fell in lush ripples down her back, and the light application of blush, mascara and lip gloss, she congratulated herself on achieving *Town and Country* status.

She was about to place a precious drop of her mother's perfume at the base of her throat and then thought better of it. She might have looked the part but she didn't feel at all "special" tonight. In fact, she felt overlooked and ignored. She put the cork back in the vial and carefully replaced it next to her cotton nightgown in the bureau drawer.

Susannah was nearly to the bottom stair when she heard voices coming from the back of the hall. She was led by the sounds down a long hallway through the center of the house, into a conservatory filled with tropical plants and black wicker furniture, through a pair of opened glass doors to the veranda.

"Susannah!" Greg nearly shouted. "You're here!"

"I've been here a while." Her smile was a struggle as she felt herself being pulled into his arms. Her face nestled in the crook of his neck. He smelled like tropical spices and rum. It was divine. "Why didn't you come to see me?" she whispered.

"It's not done," he whispered back through a wide smile. "Mother!" He kept his arm around Susannah's shoulder and turned her to face a crowd of mostly women, each more exquisitely dressed than the next. With not a hair out of place, nor a smidgen of too much lipstick, they advanced upon her like a well-prepared army.

"Susaaaaaannaaaaaaah," they said in chorus as they fell upon her.

Greg introduced her to each of them, announcing their names and family placements as if they were royalty. "My father, Jack Walton. My mother, Bettye Banning Walton. My great-cousins, the misses Nora and Nell Walton, and lastly, my great-aunt, Gloria Banning Smythe Chilton."

Susannah shook hands, asking how-do-you-do's of everyone until the words ran together and sounded like howdy doody. "You and your father are the only men in the family?" Susannah asked guilelessly.

"Lord have mercy!" Gloria slapped her white-gloved hands together. "What a refreshing child! You are going to marry this one. Aren't you, Greg? Hmm?" Gloria's blue eyes were the size of half dollars, Susannah thought as she struggled to hide her surprise.

"M-marriage is hardly apropos at this moment, Aunt Gloria." Bettye grabbed the older woman's arm, turning her away from Greg and Susannah.

"Take your hypocritical hands off me!" Gloria blasted, and jerked her arm back.

Bettye glared at Gloria, who stuck out her tongue at Bettye. Then she advanced upon Susannah again. "You're absolutely breathtakingly beautiful. If my grand-nephew doesn't ask you to marry him, I can only conclude he's gay!"

Jack Walton rolled his eyes and stood to make a quick exit. "I need another drink." He signaled to Penny, who brought a silver tray with a tall scotch on the rocks. She gave Susannah a quick sidelong glance as if to say, "What did I tell you?"

"Gloria! Please mind your manners," Bettye scolded her.

Gloria waved Bettye away with her hand. Conspiratorially, she led Susannah out to the terrace. Greg followed silently behind. "Bettye doesn't have the slightest notion about good manners. You'd think she wrote the book, not Emily. Good friend of mine, Emily."

"You knew Emily Post?" Susannah gasped.

"Her book was just out then. That's when Father and I built this house. Mother died when I was twelve. This house was her dream. Father and I finished it just the way she would have wanted it. I tolerate the rest of my family because without me they'd have no place to go."

"Now, Aunt Gloria," Greg said warningly.

"Do be a sweet boy and bring Susannah and me some champagne."

As Greg started to walk away, Gloria touched his

sleeve. "And darling, don't bring me that crap your mother buys. You know where to find my favorite in the cellar."

"Yes, ma'am." Greg winked at Susannah as he left.

Susannah looked out over the lawn that sloped down to the water's edge. The long golden fingers of willow trees tickled the ground as an evening breeze cooled the air. Susannah hugged herself and inhaled the scent of the sea.

Gloria smiled. "You like the sea?"

"I love it." She chuckled. "I suppose that sounds rather odd coming from someone who has never lived by the sea."

"Not at all, my dear. That view is the one thing I love about this house."

Susannah nodded and then looked back at the forbidding house. "You say your mother wanted it like this?"

Gloria's eyes grew round again. "Heavens, no! She was a woman of style and grace. She, as do I, had the lightest touch. She furnished the house with delicate French antiques and gilded mirrors. Back then, every room boasted a minimum of three Austrian-crystal chandeliers. Some small. Others quite large."

Susannah was shocked. "But what happened? I mean...oh, God. I've stuck my foot in it."

Gloria laughed heartily. "Bettye thought Mother's things trivial and gauche, which, of course, they were nothing of the sort. Instead, Bettye wanted 'important' pieces to impress her Manhattan friends. When Jack made a killing in the stock market—and the housing industry and the hotel business and whatever else he's done to keep the money rolling in here by the cartload—Bettye went shopping."

"What happened to all your mother's lovely things?"

Gloria clamped her hand around Susannah's wrist and smiled. "I took them all to Monaco, the *only* civilized society on this planet."

"Really?" Susannah had never met anyone so worldly, yet so honest and open as Gloria.

Greg returned with Penny following him bearing a silver tray on which sat three exquisite crystal flutes filled with bubbling vintage champagne.

Gloria toasted them. "May every minute of your life be filled with happiness."

"And money," Greg reminded her as he touched the rim of his glass to Susannah's flute.

Gloria shook her head. "Money doesn't buy happiness, Greg."

He laughed. "How would you know? You've always had money."

Susannah watched as the look in Gloria's eyes became very distant. "Back in the twenties, my dear, my father and I threw parties here that would curl your hair. They would last for days. We drank the best French wines and ate delicacies you would swear were prepared by the angels. We never worried about money, that's true. But all the money in the world could not bring my mother back to life. All I wanted for my father was to see him happy again. Truly happy."

Gloria took Susannah's hand in hers. "I've lived a wonderful life, doing whatever I wanted and going wherever I felt like going. When my father died, I gave the house to Bettye and moved to Europe. I've been married twice, but only once was I in love. And it wasn't with either of the men I married. You're beautiful, Susannah. I can tell you have a good heart, too. I also know that if you hang around Bettye too long, she'll drive you nuts. I'm lucky. I fly off to Monaco when I've had enough of her social climbing." She patted Greg's arm and looked over at Bettye who was watching them from the conservatory.

"I know she's your mother, Greg, but she can get on one's nerves. She wants everything she can't have or doesn't deserve. She can be grasping and jealous. She doesn't mean to be that way, she just is." She turned back to Susannah. "Bettye is already jealous of you. I see it in her eyes and the way she pretends not to watch your every move. She'd like to criticize your dress or speech, but she can't. You're perfect. And I'm very happy to have you in our family."

Greg cleared his throat but remained silent.

Susannah stifled a gasp as Gloria leaned over and kissed her cheek. Out of the corner of her eye, Susannah saw Penny watching them from behind a potted topiary. The maid lowered her eyes, turned and disappeared into the house. Susannah remembered how she'd admired Penny's resolve to become an actress, but just then she'd seen a flicker of envy in Penny's eyes. Yes, Susannah admired Penny, but she did not envy her. Intuition told her she needed always to remember there *was* a difference.

Dinner was good, although an inordinately formal affair. After dinner, Susannah sampled Napoleon brandy and discovered she loved it, though Greg refused the drink, stating it was too strong for his taste. Susannah thought she could sit for hours and listen to Gloria's stories, but when the grandfather clock struck midnight, everyone retired for the night.

Susannah slipped beneath what looked like brand-new designer sheets, faintly disappointed they weren't the hand-tatted Belgian linens Gloria had described. She crossed her arms beneath her head and looked at the moonlight flooding through the open window.

So, this is how things stand with Greg and me. The family assumes we are to be married.

She'd had no proposal, no ring, no asking if she loved him. He'd never said that he missed her so badly he couldn't eat or sleep. Greg hadn't mentioned any wildly passionate dreams about her. Worst of all, he had not even tried to kiss her the way she knew her "sea king" would.

Greg had been a perfect gentleman, but Susannah was expecting more.

A lot more.

10

Susannah stood on the front steps of the house waiting for Greg to bring around the Mercedes. She couldn't believe the turn of events the morning had brought. Greg planned to spend the entire day and evening showing her around Long Island. They were going to be alone at last!

"Susannah," Bettye said, opening the front door. "I thought you might need a scarf for that lovely hair of yours." She handed Susannah a pink-and-brown-printed square of silk. "It's Pucci, dear," Bettye said as an aside.

"Thank you," Susannah replied, wondering if Bettye deliberately chose something that would clash with the navy-and-gold walking shorts and matching blouse she wore.

Bettye smiled placidly, but made no sign of leaving. "Greg has a terrible habit of driving fast, and the sea spray on Fire Island is murderous on hair color."

Susannah smiled to herself, turned her face to the wind and tied the scarf around her hair. Bettye thought Susannah dyed her hair. Susannah wasn't about to fall for the bait. "Fire Island. It sounds so romantic." *Two can play this game.*

"Public beaches are all the same to me. I haven't the

slightest notion why Greg would take you there this weekend especially."

"Really? He told me you suggested it. You don't think I'll like it?"

Bettye's blue eyes darted under her thickly mascaraed short lashes. "He misunderstood me. I told him *not* to take you there."

"Oh." Susannah bit her bottom lip to keep from laughing.

Greg rolled up to the front steps in a shiny red Mercedes convertible with tan interior. Flashing her an incredibly bright smile, he hoisted himself out of the bucket seat and leaped over the door. "Cinderella, your carriage awaits." He bowed theatrically, then, chuckling to himself, he took her hand and led her around the front of the car to the passenger's side. He kissed her cheek as she got into the car and then closed the door for her.

"We're off, Mother! Don't wait up!"

Bettye's eyes narrowed. "Greg Walton, you've lost your mind. Have you forgotten the party tonight at the Van Burens'?"

Greg jumped over the driver's seat and lowered himself behind the wheel. "I was just teasing. We'll be back in plenty of time to dress for the ball." He leaned over and kissed Susannah's cheek again. "Won't we, Cinderella?"

Susannah couldn't help the crimson blush that covered her face and neck. "Absolutely!"

Greg waved to his mother as he hit the gas. "Ta-ta, Mother!"

Bettye folded her arms tightly across her chest as she watched them speed away.

Though only a half mile wide, Fire Island ran for thirty-two miles, giving Susannah and Greg a chance to relax and talk. It was a glorious day, Susannah thought as she placed the hideous scarf in the glove box. She ran her fingers through her hair and let it blow in the sea breeze. Though it was nearly eighty degrees, a strong cool wind blew in off the ocean. Voluminous snowy clouds scudded across an azure sky.

"What a great day for a sail. I hope the weather is the same tomorrow," Greg said as he put his hand over Susannah's and squeezed it. "I want to take you sailing."

"We're going to sail? Tomorrow? But I don't know anything about it."

"You don't have to, gorgeous. I'm an expert, if I do say so myself." The wind tousled his thick hair. "You'll be safe with me." A sensual gleam sparkled in the corner of his eye when he glanced at her. There was no missing his double entendre.

"Maybe I don't want to be safe," she replied with a pert lift of her chin.

He squeezed her hand tighter. "Don't say things you don't mean."

"I know exactly what I'm saying."

He grinned mischievously and pressed harder on the gas. "I have something I want to show you."

They passed children and young couples on bikes and drove farther west. "Ever hear of Sailor's Haven?"

"Only in the mythical sense," she quipped, enjoying the sparring words and double meanings they tossed back and forth.

"Touché," he said, laughing. "It's some of the finest beach on Fire Island, I think. When I was a kid I used to ride my bike just like those kids are doing and walk the nature trails that weave around the dunes. If you're real good, I'll show you the Sunken Forest."

"How good?"

"Really, really good," he said, pulling the car into the Fire Island State Park parking lot. Once the ignition was off, he leaned across the seat and slipped his arm around her shoulder. "Come here. I've wanted to do this since the moment I laid eyes on you..." His blue eyes turned a smoky amethyst color. His nose was nearly touching hers. "And that's been a very long time..."

"I know," she whispered, lowering her eyes to watch his full lips as they parted.

"I doubt you have any idea. I saw you the first day you arrived in Fort Lauderdale. Every night I watched you sit on the beach, staring at the moon...as if...you were looking for someone."

"I was."

His breath was warm and sweet on her mouth as his lips touched hers. "Was it me?"

"I don't..."

His lips were soft as they claimed her mouth. She felt the muscles in his arm flex as he drew her closer to him. He placed his other hand on her cheek, holding her as if he was afraid she would leave. He slid his body closer to her and pulled her into his chest.

"God, Susannah, you taste even better than I imagined," he groaned, and kissed her again.

When his tongue slipped between her lips and plunged into the interior of her mouth, she heard him moan. Then his breath quickened. She could feel his heart beating wildly. He slanted his mouth over hers again and again. His breath came in quick, shallow pants. Beads of perspiration spread across his forehead.

Susannah caught his excitement and kissed him back. She slipped her hand around his nape and pulled him closer. Her heartbeat accelerated. Heat caressed her body as she let herself slip deeper into the kiss.

"Hey, mister! Go for it, will ya!" one of the young boys on the bicycles yelled.

The outburst made Susannah jump. She bit her own lip. "Ouch." She looked at Greg who was having a very difficult time reorienting himself.

His blond lashes hid the passion in his eyes. "I'm sorry. I should have waited, but I just couldn't..." He kissed her lightly, and reluctantly sat up straight in the seat. He shook his head as if trying to kick start his brain. "Whoof! What do you put in those kisses? Opium?"

Susannah rubbed her bottom lip thoughtfully with her fingertips. "You liked it? I mean, do I kiss differently than other girls?"

"God, if you only knew!" he said, shoving his hands between his legs and pushing on his erection before leaving the car. "I haven't felt like this since high school."

"Really? What was her name?" Susannah asked teasingly as she opened her door, ready for their walk on the beach.

"Miss February," he said, and took her hand to lead the way across the dunes.

By two o'clock Susannah was famished.

They'd spent the morning wandering around Fire Island and then driven back up the coast to East Hampton, where, she knew, people who had even more money than the Waltons lived. Greg did not choose a people-watching restaurant for lunch like East Hampton Point, though it was touted as the most beautiful spot on Long Island. Instead, they went to the Maidstone Arms. He told her he liked the country-inn atmosphere, and because it was situated on Main Street in East Hampton, there was no breathtaking sea view to take her attention away from him.

Susannah thought the clientele overly dressed for lunch and worried that her walking shorts would not be accepted. Greg assured her that there would be no problem since he knew the owners quite well, which proved to be accurate.

Not only was Greg received with a warm handshake, but they were given a very private and quiet table in the far corner.

"Do you always get your way like that?" she asked.

"Usually," he replied as the waiter approached. Greg ordered a bottle of French cabernet and a grilled-seafood platter they would share.

After the waiter left, Susannah stared thoughtfully at the cluster of red, white and blue carnations on their table. "You're so different now. When I arrived yesterday..." She looked at him. "You weren't there to meet my plane. I've never had a chauffeur pick me up. I didn't know what to do. If only you'd told me."

"I'd planned to be there, honestly. I've still got a dozen roses in the kitchen cooler I'd bought for you. I told Penny to put them in your room today while we were gone."

"Oh," she said, still unable to shake the disappointment she'd felt. "But I didn't see you until happy hour or whatever it is you call it."

"Cocktail hour," he corrected. "We had a very important family meeting with our estate attorney and our investment banker yesterday afternoon. It seems that everyone was scurrying to finalize business matters before the long holiday began. You can understand that, can't you?"

"I suppose. But, couldn't you have done all this last month or something?"

Suddenly, Greg smiled. "Why, Susannah. I do believe you are beginning to care about me." He reached out for her hand.

"I am?"

"Admit it. You were disappointed when I wasn't there. How sweet of you!" he said merrily. Then his voice was barely audible when he said, "I don't think that's ever happened to me before."

"What happened?"

His eyes peered deeply into hers and for a brief instant, Susannah knew what it was like to see someone's soul. A light poured forth from within him. It was clear silver, like the purest seawater. Then the opening closed again.

"Someone cared," he whispered.

The wine steward presented a bottle of red wine to Greg, breaking the intensity of the moment with his crisp professional manner. "The cork, sir."

Greg sipped the wine, sloshed it around in his mouth like mouthwash and nodded. "It's fine."

The waiter arrived, placing fresh garden salads on brass charger plates. Black pepper was cracked, Parmesan cheese was sprinkled and croutons were offered. By the time they were alone again, the mood had lightened.

Susannah stuck her fork into the salad. "When were you going to tell me that we're going to a ball tonight?"

"Huh?" Greg chuckled. "Oh, the Van Buren party. It's not a ball. Just an East Hampton garden-party thing."

"Will it be anything like what your great-aunt described?"

"Not a chance," he said, gulping his wine. "Nobody entertains like Phillip Van Buren. Even Aunt Gloria bows to his superiority. Considering this is the bicentennial, Phillip will make doubly certain *his* garden party will not only be the party of this century, but will be talked about for another hundred years to come."

Susannah felt her stomach drop to her knees. Quickly, she mentally inventoried her wardrobe again. Nothing had changed since she'd packed. No fairy wands had produced a suitable dress for her to wear. While she scrambled for a plausible excuse she could give Greg for not being able to attend the party, she continued to ask him a barrage of questions about the Van Burens.

"Your family has known them a long time then?"

"Only since the 1920s when Aunt Gloria and her father built the house. The Van Burens have been around for centuries."

Centuries. Susannah swallowed. *Centuries of Van Buren women had worn appropriate dresses to the appropriate parties.* "I suppose your parents and great-aunt will be going, too." She shoved another forkful of salad into her mouth. *Any idea what they're wearing?*

"No, it'll just be us."

"Just us?" She lifted her wineglass and drained a third of it.

"My family has never been accepted by the Van Burens. We're nouveau riche to them. You and I are going because one of my Harvard friends just happens to be Phillip's nephew, Karl Van Buren."

Susannah was still digesting the fact that the Waltons were not rich or powerful enough to be included in the Van Buren circle. It was hard for her to imagine Bettye Walton with even more money. Then suddenly it struck her. It wasn't the wealth; it was how it had been achieved. To the Van Burens, the Waltons were not in their league. People like the Waltons were insignificant to old wealth.

Susannah began laughing. The more she thought about her situation, the more hilarious the whole thing seemed.

"What's so funny?" Greg asked.

She put her hand over her mouth and forced herself to bite her lip. "I'm sorry. I just couldn't help thinking how the illustrious Van Burens are going to react when they see small-town-Indiana me crashing their party of the century!"

Greg did not laugh with her. His blue eyes were darkly serious as he placed his elbows on the table. "They're going to drop their jaws just like I did when I first saw you."

"Thank you for the lovely compliment, but I can't go tonight."

Greg jerked back in his chair. "Why on earth not?"

She expelled a deep sigh of frustration. "You wouldn't understand."

"Try me," he challenged, folding his arms over his chest.

"Greg...I have nothing to wear!"

His shoulders instantly relaxed. He picked up his wineglass and swirled the ruby liquid against the sides. "Oh, that. I realized that might pose a problem. It's been taken care of."

Susannah cast him a befuddled look. "Don't tell me, you waved your magic wand."

He smiled. "Sort of."

"What are you?" She laughed. "My fairy god-mother?"

"No. Your Prince Charming."

11

The light from the setting sun failed to awaken Susannah from her afternoon nap. Caught in her dreamworld, she hurried across the warm sand to the water's edge. This time he was waiting for her, and rushed toward her as if there wasn't a second to spare. "Susannah." He groaned her name heartachingly. "I almost lost you."

He kissed her in that thrilling, soul-wrenching way he had, forcing her to believe in him once again.

"Susannah?" a voice whispered. "Susannah. It's time to wake up. We must hurry. You don't want to be late for the ball," Gloria said, caressing Susannah's forearm, easing her back into consciousness.

The dream tried to pull her back, weighting down her eyelids with sleep. "I'm up," she said as she forced herself up to a sitting position. She rubbed her eyes, then blinked. On the bedside table sat the bouquet of red roses Greg had told Penny to bring up to her room. "I was dreaming."

"It must have been a wonderful dream, dear. You were smiling in your sleep." Gloria put her hand on Susannah's hair and moved a lock away from her face. "It's hard for me to remember being so young that I would smile in my sleep."

Susannah had come fully awake. She touched Gloria's hand. "What a sad thing to say."

Gloria clucked her tongue. "Don't you waste a single ounce of your energy pitying me. I've had my dreams. Now it's your turn." She put out her hand to Susannah. "Come."

Gloria's eyes sparkled with impish mischief as she tip-toed across the room to the cheval mirror. "Now, you stand right here, dear, and close your eyes. I want to surprise you."

Susannah put her hands over her eyes. She loved this game as much as the elderly Gloria. "I promise not to look until you tell me..."

"Look!" Gloria squealed.

"Oh, my God!" She reached out to touch the elegant white-crepe dinner gown and then snatched her hand back. "Is it real?"

"Of course it is, darling." Gloria giggled. "It's mine."

"Yours? But..." Susannah eyed the slender lines of the gown and the impeccably draped folds that gathered from the bias cut over the abdomen and bodice. "I've never seen anything so incredibly designed." She touched the fabric, wondering if this creation could be totally seamless.

"And you never will. No one of your generation will ever know clothes like I owned when Madame Greff made this gown. I wore it to a Fourth of July party my father and I gave in this house in 1927."

"It's magnificent." Susannah was awestruck as she inspected the low-cut neckline and long sleeves. "I can't wear this...it's too perfect."

"You can and you will," Gloria insisted. "Back then, I knew only one woman as beautiful as you, Susannah. She was a model in Paris, the toast of the town. Erté must have sketched her a hundred times. She worked for all the best houses and, as famous as she was, as pursued as she was by Prussian princes and wealthy Americans, there was still that hint of fishing-village background she could never shake.

"I see what Greg sees in you. Even if you don't realize it now, you have an air, a look in your eye that is what my generation called 'class.' No one would ever guess you weren't born to money. Perhaps that is what upsets Bettye so much. She'll never reach your stature. Do you understand any of this?"

"Not really, but I'm trying."

"You will as you mature. But for now, I want you simply to enjoy the natural grace and beauty God has given you." Gloria's look was winsome as she motioned to the gown. "I want you to know what it's like to wear a garment so exquisitely made it becomes your body. I want you to feel like liquid when you descend a staircase with all eyes in the room on no one but you. The night I wore this beautiful creation a man proposed to me," she said in a hush.

Susannah noticed the faraway look in her eyes and she was wise enough not to break the spell.

"That was a long time ago," Gloria whispered, glancing down at the gown. "Now, I won't bother you while you dress, dear."

"Aunt Gloria." Susannah put all the affection she felt for this sweet woman into her voice. "This dress is part of you and your life. Not mine. Besides, I'm much taller than you, and I—"

"Nonsense. Back then, hems draped on the ground in puddles. I'm a very good judge about such things. My calculations have seldom been wrong. The hem will break at the top of your instep. Give the dress another story to tell, Susannah."

Gloria started for the door, put her forefinger to the

side of her mouth thoughtfully and faced Susannah again. "My father told me always to remember that we all put our pants on the same way. The Van Burens are no better than you."

"Thank you, Aunt Gloria."

Gloria blew Susannah a kiss. "You're welcome."

Within the first thirty minutes of wearing the gown, Susannah realized the impact of Gloria's words. The crepe fabric felt unbelievably sensual against her bare skin. For that evening, underwear had been left in the dresser because the crepe was so sheer, it clung to every dip, curve and mold of her body. The tiny rim of her belly button showed through the dress, as did the round swells of her breasts and the slope of her slim hips. As she gazed at her reflection in the mirror, she could hardly believe her eyes.

Gone was every trace of the young coed she'd seen this morning, and in her place was a woman with fiery turquoise eyes and flaming auburn hair. Her shoulders were square, proud and responsible. Her neck moved elegantly as she turned her head. She'd never paid much attention to the fact that her high cheekbones, square jaw and rounded forehead gave her a look of quiet strength. Had it not been for the upturned end of her nose betraying her youth, she could have been a woman of indeterminable age—who'd been magically suspended in time.

Susannah could feel the importance of this night descend upon her like a warm mantle. It was a wonderful sensation, as if tonight she would begin the rest of her life.

She glided to the dresser and took out the vial of perfume her mother had given her. Carefully, she dabbed the heavy oil behind her ears, at her temples and down the length of her exposed breastbone. She lifted her skirt and placed a single drop behind each knee and on each ankle. Putting the perfume away, she turned once again to see her reflection in the mirror and found herself enveloped in a heady cloud of mesmerizing fragrance.

"God, no wonder the O'Shea women had their pick of suitors!" Susannah marveled as she left the room.

Descending the staircase, Susannah indeed moved more gracefully knowing the fabric swirled cloudlike around her feet.

Greg was dressed in a summer white tuxedo dinner jacket, black slacks, black Italian crocodile shoes and white bow tie. His skin looked tan next to the snowy white shirt. He was speaking with his father, adjusting his cuff links and jacket cuff when his father nudged him.

Greg followed his father's appreciative gaze to the top of the stairs.

"Son, I think there isn't a Van Buren alive who can hold a candle to our Susannah," Jack said proudly.

Greg's eyes lit up the room as he half walked, half stumbled toward the newel post and reached out his hand to her. "I've never seen..."

Gloria peeked out from the living room, walked up behind Greg and put her arm around his waist. "Our plan worked perfectly, didn't it, dear?"

"Maybe too well...I...I..."

Gloria squeezed his waist. "You needn't say a word, dear. Just look at her."

Susannah saw the warmth in Greg's eyes as he put his arm around his aunt. *They adore each other.* Then she saw Jack place his hand on Greg's shoulder. He winked at Gloria, who beamed up at Jack. Until this moment, Susannah had not felt any closeness within the Walton family. But now she realized she and this special gown had brought magic back into their lives. She had known something of great importance was going to happen to her tonight. This was enough.

"You're stunning, Susannah," Greg said with reverence in his voice.

For the rest of her life, Susannah wanted to remember every breath, smell, word and expression of this moment. When she glanced at Gloria, she knew the older woman was reading her thoughts.

"Thank you, Greg," Susannah responded. "You look very handsome."

He took her hand and placed it in the crook of his arm. "I hope you still think so when every man in East Hampton tries to steal you away from me."

She smiled at him, basking in the attention he gave her. She didn't know if it was the perfume or the look in Greg's eyes that made her feel light-headed, as if she'd had too much champagne. "Don't be silly. I'm not going anywhere."

After all, you are my sea king, aren't you?

12

———▶◀———

Michael rolled his head as the dream pitched him into a sea of unfamiliar emotions. He was standing on a bridge or dock, he couldn't tell which because it was dark. He knew he shouldn't be there and that Phillip was waiting for him in the library where they would continue their conversation about his future.

"The future," Michael mumbled aloud just as he had before he'd fallen asleep.

From the far end of the bridge he saw the outline of a woman walking toward him. He couldn't tell if her face was obscured by mist or moonlight as he squinted trying to see her. He called to her, "Who are you?"

"Don't you know me?"

"No..."

And then he inhaled her perfume. It was the kind his mother had worn. He would know that fragrance anywhere.

His heart skipped a beat. He held his breath. *This is too good to be true! Mother, I've waited so long to see you. Why didn't you try to come to me all those times when I needed you as a kid? And Dad needed you?*

"I'm not your mother, Michael. She is the past. I am the future."

Still, he could not see the woman. "But you smell like

her. You give off warmth and...love, like her." Michael reached out his hand to her.

She stopped walking toward him. She also reached out.

No matter how he strained to touch her, their fingertips would not connect. It was as if they were both rooted to their spots. "I don't understand this!" He felt himself grow frantic. He kept looking over his shoulder as if someone was trying to stop him. He had to touch her. Then he would know the truth. There was still a chance she was his mother.

"Michael! Touch me!"

"I'm trying. I swear I am!"

"Try harder! There's not much time!" Her voice was filled with panic.

"Not much time for what?"

"For us, Michael. For us!" Her long fingers nearly touched his.

Leaning practically out of his shoes, he struggled to close the distance between them. "I don't understand this. Why can't you come to me?"

"But I have, Michael. I have," she said, standing straight.

Like beacons in the night, her turquoise eyes flashed at him. He felt as if he'd been hit with a bullet and reeled backward from the intensity of the love she'd sent him. It was as if she had drained her heart and soul and given her life to him. Never had he felt so incredibly loved and cherished. Not even by his mother.

Then she started to fade away.

"No! Don't go! Come back!"

"It's time, Michael..." She faded completely from sight.

Michael felt a gentle nudge on his shoulder. "It's time, Master Michael," the butler, Reynolds, said.

"Time..." Michael awoke slowly. The room was dark now, the sun had completely set. Orienting himself to reality proved more difficult than usual. Never having been much of a dreamer, Michael was uncertain about what had happened in the dream, much less what it meant. Pete had talked a great deal about the dream analysis he had studied in one of his psychology classes, but Michael had thought it all sounded like bunk. This dream was so hauntingly real, he wished now he'd paid attention to Pete.

"I've prepared your bath, sir. And your dinner suit arrived from the tailor just in time, as Mr. Van Buren promised."

Just in time. Time. What time is it? Michael blinked his eyes. They were heavy with sleep. "How long have I been here?"

"Two hours, sir."

Michael bolted upright. "Two hours! Holy cats! Mr. Van Buren..."

"Is in the library, dressed and waiting for you, sir," Reynolds said with an urgent tone.

Shit! Michael swung his legs over the side of the bed and dashed to the bathroom. "Tell him I'll be down in twenty...no, fifteen minutes!"

"Very good, sir."

"That's not a mansion! It's a kingdom!" Susannah gasped when she and Greg drove past the thick row of white-birch trees that obstructed her view of the Van Buren estate. It was four stories tall and easily triple the size of Greg's home, she thought. Gothic arched doors and windows blended with stone, granite and marble to create a building intended to endure for centuries. Massive columns topped with soaring leaf capitals lined the arcades where guests walked from the canopied driveway to the front doors. Angels floated at the apex of a massively carved stone arch that formed the cathedral-style front doors. At the very top of the half-dozen three-story leaded-glass windows facing the front gardens were pinnacled gables and arched balustrades copied from Paris's Sainte Chapelle.

The grounds were equally impressive, patterned after the neoclassic baroque style that swept Europe in the 1770s. The neoclassic architecture that influenced the building of Versailles was utilized in the formal gardens, enormous reflecting pool, Romanesque marble statuary and rich mosaics of Tuscan-stone terraces. Greg explained that, though the Van Buren family bought the land in the late 1690s, the house took thirty years to complete. Bankrupting the family coffers, subsequent generations of Van Burens patiently rebuilt and expanded their holdings to include shipbuilding, shipping, trading and banking. During this time, very little was added to the house except necessary furnishings. By the American Revolution the family was enormously wealthy again.

"The Van Burens hired an apprentice of Bernini," he told her as if he expected her to know who Bernini was.

"Really?" Susannah inflected the proper amount of awe in her voice. She promised herself to look up Bernini in the encyclopedia. That and anything else she heard tonight that she didn't understand.

White-jacketed young boys raced toward the serpentine line of imported cars nudging each other away from the fastest, most exotic cars.

"Good evening, sir," a dark-haired valet of about sixteen said as he opened the door for Greg.

Trepidation scoured Greg's face as he reluctantly
handed the boy his keys. "No dings, no scratches on it
now," Greg instructed the boy.

Rapaciously, the boy eyed the car as if it were his first
lover. "No, sir!"

Greg extended his hand to Susannah and they joined
the throng of guests entering the house.

To Susannah, the vestibule looked like a cathedral rotunda, with hallways leading off in a half-dozen directions. Each arched entrance was festooned with gar-
lands of English ivy, white carnations, blue delphinium
and red roses. The sound of Gershwin's "What'll I Do?"
filled the air, making the night reverberate with romance. Greg pointed to small stereo speakers nestled behind the gilded capitals.

Susannah couldn't take in the details fast enough as
her eyes darted from the arched dome overhead to the
radiating halls. Bronze busts of Van Buren men were
prominently displayed in curved lighted niches in the
vestibule walls. Susannah peaked over the heads of the
people in front of her and noticed that every hallway
was lined with marble pillars, each topped with similar
Van Buren busts. She glanced into the living room.
Looking surprisingly warm and friendly with overstuffed sofas and chairs in dark green and gold brocade,
the portrait over the mantel was of yet another Van Buren male. Quickly checking each room, she could not
find a single portrait or photograph of any of the Van
Buren women. Surmising that the Van Buren men must
have been married to unattractive women or worse,
were vastly chauvinistic, Susannah decided she didn't

much care for the Van Burens. She squeezed Greg's arm, thinking how lucky she was to have him.

Greg did not acknowledge Susannah's first overt display of affection. She'd expected a whispered comment or a brush of his lips against her temple. Instead, he was rigidly preoccupied with the slow-moving line.

"I swear," he finally said, "if it weren't for the butlers directing us, no one would know where to go. Have you ever seen such a disastrous floor plan?"

Susannah looked around her. She liked the very French and feminine dining room with its ice blue silk walls, deep royal blue velvet Louis XVI chairs encircling a half-dozen round linen-covered tables. It was elegant and classic, yet intimate. She especially liked the carelessly arranged bouquets of fresh roses because they had none of that mundane floral-shop look. It was easy for her to imagine the lady of the house crossing cool, dawn-dew-covered lawns and filling a straw flower basket with whatever blossoms the new day had brought.

Susannah sighed, imagining herself clipping roses. "I like this house."

"I don't. None of the Waltons that I can recall has ever liked this house."

"I thought your family had never been here."

"They haven't," Greg said, keeping his bent arm so perfectly aloft, Susannah wondered if he'd get a cramp.

"Then how could they—"

Greg interrupted her by giving his name to the butler, who then instructed them that their table was number thirty-nine. Greg thanked him as he took the red-white-and-blue program from a young girl standing next to the butler.

"They have a program for a party?" Susannah asked.

"Yes, Susannah." Greg smiled patiently but his voice held a hint of annoyance at her ignorance.

Sensing Greg's stress level, she realized there was something more important to him about this party than her or the magic dress.

They walked out through a pair of clear-paned glass doors onto a terrace that seemed to be the size of half a football field. White-stone balustrades afforded guests an incredible view of the formal gardens, swimming and reflecting pools, cabana, tennis courts and a huge blue-and-white-striped tent where dining tables were set. Beyond the lawns and flower gardens was the sea. Susannah could see a pier the length of Washington Bridge to which nearly two dozen sailing yachts were moored.

Suddenly, Susannah understood Greg's tension. This was the kind of wealth Greg aspired to. If ever there was a carrot on a stick to taunt Greg, the Van Buren version of Xanadu was it.

This was perfection. Every guest was more richly dressed than the next. Susannah guessed that the cost of the shoes alone on the partygoers could rock Fort Knox. An army of waiters in long tails, black slacks and starched white shirts carried empty silver trays like shields, working their way through the throng of champagne-thirsty guests. A thirty-piece orchestra played hit tunes from the prewar years as young and old danced on a second terrace below them. Susannah gazed down at the swirl of summer tuxedos and brightly colored silk dresses, feeling as if she'd peered through a bewitched kaleidoscope into another world and time. Susannah marveled at these carefree, beautiful people who lived like princes and princesses in fairy tales.

"Humph, no Beatles. Come, Susannah." Greg's voice

broke her reverie as he held her hand and urged her toward the tent. "There's someone I'd like you to meet."

Susannah was so busy taking in the white-silk-draped ceiling of the tent, dozens of crystal chandeliers and the four-foot-tall silver epergnes spilling over with white roses that she remained a few steps behind.

Suddenly, Greg halted.

"Hello, Greg," a seductive woman's voice said.

"Hello, Kristen," he answered.

Susannah felt the heat build in his hand. He tightened his grip. His palm grew moist. She nearly stumbled into Greg's back, which kept her out of sight from the woman he was speaking with.

"It's been a long time, Greg," she purred.

Susannah didn't wait for another word to pass. She drew up next to Greg still holding his hand. She felt the hem of her gown whirl around her ankles. She smiled at the most beautiful blond girl she'd ever seen.

"Kristen, I'd like you to meet Susannah, my fiancée."

"Fiancée?" Kristen was clearly shocked.

But not as much as Susannah. "I'm pleased to meet you, Kristen." Coolly, Susannah held out her hand.

Kristen made a show of trying to balance her cigarette, champagne and a rhinestone-studded evening bag in the shape of a red apple. The young woman smiled then tipped her head and lifted her chin haughtily. "It's nice to meet you, Susannah." She looked down at Susannah's hand as if it were a dead fish too long out of water.

Susannah got the distinct impression that Kristen's reason for not shaking hands had little to do with her full hands. Kristen would have acted the same toward anyone Greg had brought to the party.

Kristen's pale blue eyes seared Greg's face with anger. When she finally turned her gaze away from him, showing an aristocratic profile and elegant neck, her precision-cut shoulder-length hair shimmered as it fell perfectly into place. It was a practiced move; Susannah would bet on it.

Kristen's flawless creamy skin blushed slightly at her jawline but not on her cheeks, where her emotions would be apparent. Kristen gave Susannah an intrusive once-over. "You're quite lovely, Susannah. I don't remember seeing you at rush last fall. Where on earth did Greg find you?"

"Fort Lauderdale," Greg replied before Susannah could speak.

"One of the boat girls?" Kristen hurled the sharp dagger.

"Not at all." Greg had replied a bit too coolly, Susannah thought.

Glancing sideways at Greg, Susannah saw his blue eyes turn to ice. But beneath that she saw burning rage. It was now clear. Greg and Kristen had been lovers.

Susannah felt as if the earth had swallowed her up. How long ago had they broken up? Why hadn't he told her about Kristen? Was his crack about everyone in his family not liking the Van Buren house directed at Kristen? How far did his anger take him? Was she part of some kind of revenge? And what of Aunt Gloria and the magic dress? Were they all in on the plan and, if they were, did they volunteer?

Suddenly, Susannah didn't feel special at all. She felt used. Her hand slipped limply down the side of her hip, skimming over the exquisite crepe. She wanted to run from here. Hide. Anything except deal with the deception she believed she'd been dealt. *Oh, magic dress. Can't you save me?*

"I think I'll get some champagne," Susannah said, but neither Greg nor Kristen was listening. She left them alone.

13

Sitting in a burgundy-leather wing chair opposite Phillip Van Buren's desk, Michael was pleasantly surprised at how comfortable he felt in his new tuxedo and soft black-leather shoes. This was nothing like the tight jacket and overly starched shirt he'd worn to his senior prom. He couldn't resist touching the thin summer wool, which felt like silk. It was amazing how well he fit into the kind of life Phillip lived. It was the lifestyle he intended to create for himself.

Impeccably dressed in a white dinner jacket, black summer-wool tuxedo slacks, white-silk tuxedo shirt with pearl and onyx studs and matching cuff links, Phillip stood at the French doors watching his guests arrive.

"Shouldn't you see to them?" Michael asked, feeling guilty for having spent nearly every waking minute with Phillip since his arrival at La Guardia two days ago. Michael still couldn't believe the deluge of people to the city. Thank God Phillip had been a stickler about giving Michael precise travel instructions.

Phillip had made certain that Michael not only knew about the chauffeur who would be picking him up, but also about the color of the limousine and the exact exit where the midnight blue car would be waiting. *Hell! He'd still be waiting at the carousel like that girl...*

"That's the hell of it, you know, Michael?"

"Sir?"

"Here I'm giving the party of the century, as the columnists are calling it, which is nowhere near the truth but sensationalism sells newspapers...and not one of my guests has come looking for me."

"Are they supposed to?" Michael was confused.

"No," Phillip answered resignedly and turned back to Michael. "But it would be nice to know someone cared."

"Maybe your family isn't here yet," Michael offered.

Phillip flipped the top of a leather humidor and surveyed his collection of expensive cigars. "They're here. Every last one of them." He lifted a particularly fat cigar and inhaled the length of it. He frowned and then replaced it and closed the lid.

Now that Michael had gotten to know Phillip and his mannerisms, he could tell from Phillip's tone of voice that he was about to make Michael his confidant again.

Phillip sat down in the swivel desk chair. "Fate is a funny thing, Michael."

"Yes, sir. It is."

Phillip silently chuckled to himself. "Take you and me, for instance. The way we met. I'd never been to your part of the country in my life. Probably never will be again. I'd never experienced any sort of problem with a new car and certainly not with one the caliber of the Testerosa. The mechanics always see to it that these cars are in perfect condition."

"Yes, sir. I know that's a fact," Michael interrupted, but when Phillip didn't answer, he realized his mentor hadn't been expecting any response. Michael folded his hands in his lap and remained silent.

"Yet, ironically, some hose or belt goes haywire and as a result I meet a young boy to whom I give some advice and my card. How was I ever to know you'd take my words to heart? Make me into an idol of some sort. I hadn't the slightest notion what was going on in your head, the plans you'd made for yourself. And frankly, nor did I care. I had my businesses to run. My own family."

Phillip glanced out the window and quickly turned back to Michael. "Ever since you arrived I've run you through your paces, haven't I, Michael?"

"It wasn't all that bad, sir," Michael quipped with a smile. Phillip had questioned, probed and tested Michael's knowledge, moral character and level of drive. To what end, Michael still did not know. As far as Michael was concerned, Phillip Van Buren wanted to see him and that was enough.

"One thing you'll learn about me is that I am a deliberate man. I'm a plotter and a planner. I think my decisions through very carefully. Life has taught me that much," he said, lowering his voice. "As I've told you, I have no children of my own. My wife didn't care for the 'idea' of children, she told me. I, on the other hand, wanted a dozen. The only thing we seemed to agree upon in our four years together was that we disagreed. I gave her a small fortune and she's been happy ever since."

Michael shook his head. "Do you mind my asking why you didn't discuss the issue of children before you got married?"

Phillip laughed derisively. "I wasn't thinking too clearly back in those days." He steepled his fingers and regarded them as he spoke. "I didn't love my wife is the truth of it. She knew it. I knew it. I suppose it's accurate to say that I was on the rebound."

"If this is too personal, you don't need to—"

"Not at all, Michael. In fact, you'll find this information necessary later on."

Michael hadn't the slightest idea what Phillip had in mind for him "later on," but for now all he could do was listen.

"As a young man I had the misfortune to fall in love with an older woman. An unsuitable older woman, so my mother told me. I allowed my parents to control my life because not to obey them would have meant being disinherited. They used the Van Buren fortune like puppet strings on both myself and my brother, Bartholomew. In his case it was a good thing, because Bart hasn't the wit to get himself out of a dark room...with a flashlight."

Michael put his hand to his mouth to stifle a chuckle.

"Since I was the eldest and the smartest, with an inherent talent for making money, I believed I could do anything I wanted. I courted with passion. I moved heaven and earth trying to make my parents realize that I was truly in love. I went so far as to become engaged without their consent. I made the wedding plans without them, foolishly believing they would come around when they got to know...my fiancée. But it never happened. Behind my back they arranged a scandalous trick, which I won't go into, but suffice it to say my fiancée took one look at me in a very compromising situation and called off the wedding.

"Her parents sued my parents for breach of promise and my parents paid them off...handsomely. For years I believed my mother that the money went to my fiancée and that she'd never loved me, after all. I believed them when they said she'd moved to Europe just to be away from me. I believed everything except the truth."

Never having been in love himself, Michael could not

empathize with Phillip, but knowing how much he'd missed his mother, Michael imagined his pain must have been similar to Phillip's sad experience.

Phillip cleared the emotion out of his throat. "All of that brings me to my relationship with you."

Michael was stunned. "How?"

"Bartholomew took full advantage of my lack of attention to business and my parents' disapproval of me at the time and did *everything* my parents wanted. He married Frances, the cream of the debutantes that year, sired four children and took over the management of a newly formed utilities company along the mid-Atlantic states that my father had spearheaded with the approval of Roosevelt just before the end of the war."

Michael nodded. "There was no way he couldn't make money once the war was over."

Phillip nodded in assent. "That's about the size of it. He's been Mr. Perfect Asshole ever since."

Michael burst into laughter at Phillip's uncustomary language. When they both stopped laughing, Michael asked, "Why didn't you go back to the woman you loved?"

"It was too late."

"She's...dead?" Michael asked timidly.

"No, she's still alive."

"I don't understand. You've obviously devoted your life to loving this one woman, and you're still in the prime of life. I wish I was half as fit as you, even now," Michael said seriously, knowing that Phillip swam two hundred laps twice a day, played a hard game of tennis and worked out in the indoor gymnasium next to the all-glass hothouse.

"That's pushing it a bit, Michael. I'm sixty-seven years old. Too old for...marriage."

I wonder if it's his pride, Michael thought, looking into Phillip's stony eyes.

Phillip seemed to swipe his melancholy thoughts aside. "As I said earlier, fate is a mysterious catalyst in life. Most people must rely on the luck of the draw when it comes to their children. And vice versa, the child with the parents. I believe in making my own luck. Therefore, I have decided that you, Michael, will be my heir."

Michael was so shocked he gulped in a mouthful of air and choked. "You c-can't be serious!" He coughed and stared wide-eyed at Phillip who remained intractable. "Are you dying or something?"

"Healthy as a horse. Nor have I lost my mind. I've come to realize I can't give my wealth to either of my two nephews. Karl is now in Harvard Law School, and his brother, Max, already has his MBA in finance."

"I don't get it. They sound as if they have a lot going for them. Why me?"

"Because Karl and Max haven't a sliver of integrity in their bodies. They jump as high as their father asks because they've watched Bart leap for Mother all his life. My nephews are greedy, vicious people who would kill each other if they thought there was any money in it. I have nightmares about those two dancing on my grave.

"My greatest fear is that the Van Buren family has endured for hundreds of years and those two con artists could wipe us out in a decade. Bartholomew wants to retire to the Fiji Islands—with or without Frances, who probably doesn't care what he does as long as he leaves her the charge cards. And Mother, she'll probably outlive them all as long as her powerful position in New York society is secure. Basically, what I'm saying is that I have no one I can trust, Michael."

"I'm beginning to see that."

"I'm not asking you to be my son. I'm asking you if you would consider becoming my partner. If I had a right arm to watch my companies, my investments, someone who looks at the profit-and-loss statements with the same concern for longevity that I do, then I feel I could make this family endure for another hundred years. Without that..." Phillip shrugged his shoulders and dropped his palms on the desk.

The enormity of the responsibility lodged in Michael's throat like a boulder. Phillip's proposal had not only come out of the blue, but it had an impact on Michael's life like colliding planets. Phillip was offering to give Michael everything he'd ever dreamed of and more. The clothes, the cars, the house and, most importantly, the opportunity to make his life into anything he wanted.

No more struggling to find an hour to study the fascinating subjects he craved to learn. No more long weekends under a lost-case wreck of a car. No more seeing his dad's hopelessness at not being able to pay Michael's tuition. Michael was not yet twenty and he was already the master of his own destiny.

Phillip had just offered Michael the moon.

Michael was going to take it. "What do you want me to do first?"

"Finish your education. You can stay where you are or you can transfer up here to New York. Or, with your grades and my connections, I can get you into Harvard. Anyplace you like. Nothing against your school, but the quality of education you would receive up here..."

"Say no more!" Michael raised his palms to stop him. "I understand. But I'll have to think about it."

Phillip rose and walked around the desk. He put out his hand to Michael. Michael looked at it and smiled broadly. Then he threw his arms around Phillip's shoulders. "I won't let you down, sir."

"I believe you...*son*."

14

—▶ ◀—

With her shaking hands wrapped around a crystal champagne flute and her head preoccupied with doubts and questions about Greg, Susannah did not hear the woman talking to her.

"I don't believe we've met, dear," the beautiful elderly woman said. She was a half foot shorter than Susannah and she used the difference in their heights to stand directly under Susannah's nose. Then she repeated her question.

Startled at the woman's sudden appearance, Susannah stepped back. "I'm sorry. I was daydreaming."

"I know," the elegantly dressed, blue-eyed woman replied. She held out a fabulously bejeweled hand. "I'm Adele Van Buren. Welcome to our party."

"Oh, my gosh!" Susannah took her hand and shook it. "I'm Susannah Parker from Indianapolis and I'm very pleased to meet you." Susannah had heard Gloria's stories about the imperious Adele, always describing her as a controlling, nearly militaristic tyrant. Susannah had envisioned a witchy woman complete with warts. Knowing that Adele was eighty-five made the reality of the woman even more difficult to believe. A thin smattering of gray in the woman's soft cap of chin-length hair proved that it was natural. Her blue eyes were clear and youthful as they sparkled under heavily mascaraed lashes. Her faintly lined skin had been well tended over the years. *Both costly cosmetics and a bit of plastic surgery are one of the rewards of the rich I could learn to live with,* Susannah thought.

"Are you aware you've caused quite a buzz?" Adele inquired with a haughty lift of her chin. She leveled a commanding gaze at Susannah.

"Me?" *I just got here! I couldn't have done anything wrong already!*

"My friends seem not to be able to talk about anything but you. 'Who is she, Adele?' 'Where did she come from, Adele?' 'Is she one of your secret protégées, Adele?'" She shrugged her small rounded shoulders. "Since even my grandson doesn't know you, I had to ask if perhaps you crashed my party."

"Goodness, no! I would never...I mean...I wouldn't be here if not for—"

"Adele darling!" a raspy woman's voice caught Adele's attention.

Susannah followed Adele's gaze to see a tall, strikingly attractive middle-aged woman sweep up the terrace steps, dressed in a flowing hand-painted floral chiffon gown, arms outspread like a hawk circling its prey.

Protectively, Susannah inched back a step as the woman swooped across the terrace, anxiously twisting her head, searching the crowd.

"Hello, Magda," Adele replied.

Magda effusively exhaled, "Darling! You've found her! And my gawd they were right, weren't they?"

Reed-thin Magda scrutinized Susannah like a jeweler studying a diamond. "Turn around," she said commandingly.

"Excuse me?" Susannah scowled as Magda took Susannah's right hand and held it away from her body, inspecting every curve.

Magda halted instantly and dropped Susannah's hand as if she'd been burned. She turned to Adele. "You didn't tell her?"

Adele shook her head. "I didn't have time. Magda Martin, may I introduce to you Susannah Parker."

Susannah's face broke into a wide, awestruck smile. "Not *the* Magda Martin? The owner of Magda's Models—the big modeling agency?" She shook Magda's hand. "I read about you in *Seventeen* and *Glamour*. They say your agency is second only to Eileen Ford. Gosh! When I left Indianapolis, I had no idea I'd meet anyone famous here."

Magda basked in Susannah's praise, but she was quick to turn the compliment around. "Have you looked in a mirror lately?"

Susannah's confusion was evident.

Adele patted Susannah's arm. "Magda has a very bad habit of getting ahead of herself, especially when her competition is only twenty feet away eyeing us like an eagle. My dear, you must be aware that you are without comparison. Look around you. Do you see anyone else with your natural kind of beauty?"

Magda's eyes shot to a petite woman dressed in Italian designer silk.

Susannah followed her gaze. *It's Eileen Ford!* Susannah could only wonder at how many other influential people she'd overlooked.

Magda possessively put her hand on the back of Susannah's waist. "Let's go inside where we can talk business."

"Business?" Susannah's heart skipped a beat as she realized what was happening.

"Yes, dear. Magda intends to make you a star."

"That's right. You'll be bigger than Candy Bergen or Cybill Shepherd," Magda told her. "Bigger than Farrah ever thought of being." She glanced over her shoulder as Eileen Ford advanced toward Susannah. "I haven't seen a woman wear a dress like yours since my mother stopped F. Scott Fitzgerald dead in his tracks in '25 in Paris. Maybe it was 1926. I forget." She gently pushed Susannah through the French doors into the living room.

Quietly closing the doors behind them, Adele's eyes sparkled with excitement as she instructed them to sit on the silk sofas flanking the marble fireplace.

With concern in her voice, Magda said to Adele, "Darling, you needn't stay with us if you don't want to. Your other guests need tending."

Waving away Magda's suggestion, Adele lowered herself onto the sofa. "They know their way around. Besides, it's Phillip's job to entertain his clients and friends, although he's been in a business meeting for hours. No, dear, I wouldn't budge if the house were on fire. I haven't felt this kind of exhilaration since I don't know when."

At that moment, Adele looked like a young girl on Christmas morning, Susannah thought.

"It's rather like kismet, isn't it, dear?" Adele asked Susannah.

"Kismet?" *Mother told me Greg was my fate.* But Susannah knew Greg was still with Kristen. After what she'd witnessed between them, her emotions had bounced from anger to pain to a need for revenge. It was as if God had tipped her world upside down, then spun it, like riding a Ferris wheel and roller coaster at the same time. The worst part was that she seemed to have no control over the events affecting her. Not moments after her illusions about Greg had been shattered, Adele and Magda were handing her a fortuitous opportunity. She was only nineteen, yet she was learning how destiny balanced the scales of life.

Susannah felt overwhelmed. But as she glanced above Adele's head at her own reflection in the tall Austrian mirror, she saw fire in her eyes.

"I don't know anything about modeling, but I'd be interested in hearing more."

A self-satisfied smile curved Magda's lips. "In my business, beauty will get you only so far. Desire, persistence, professionalism—those are the qualities that will set you apart. The hours are long and even painful."

"I'm not afraid of hard work," Susannah said. "I've worked ever since I can remember. Last semester I carried a full load of courses and often worked over thirty hours at the Steak Shack." Susannah hesitated as she thought about the sacrifices both she and her parents had made over the years to save for her education. "This wouldn't interfere with my college classes, would it?"

Magda was firm but gentle when she spoke. "Susannah, the kind of career I have in mind for you would take nearly every minute of your time. I want to start you with a splash. Get you a major contract right off the bat. To do that I'll have to invest a great deal of time and money into grooming you. That'll mean hiring the best photographer in Manhattan to shoot your portfolio. You'll need ballet lessons to improve your walk—despite your natural grace—a work-out instructor, acting classes..."

"Acting?" Susannah's face was ablaze with interest.

"Ah! You've done some acting. High-school play no doubt," Adele observed.

"Yes. I love it. I've been told I was...rather good," she tempered her high-school reviews.

"Wonderful," Magda was unimpressed. "A friend of mine is a great acting coach. She'll tell me in less than five minutes if you have talent."

Talent. Just the way Magda said it, as if it were something more precious than money, more rare than fame, gave Susannah chills. She had no idea if she had talent. She'd planned her life around becoming a school-teacher, being with children and having children of her own someday. Doubts and fears turned her skin icy cold. To even consider not getting her degree was not like her.

How very odd it all was—sitting here in this fantastic mansion where two women she'd never met before wanted to be a part of her life...perhaps even more than Greg did. They were forcing her to ask difficult questions of herself and in the process Susannah was finding a person she'd never known existed. Did she have talent? Could she dedicate herself to fulfilling Magda's goals for her when she'd had much different dreams in mind? Why was all this happening to her? And why now?

Self-consciously she slipped her icy hands under her legs. "Talent. I'm not sure about that. I'm studying to be a schoolteacher. Kindergarten, maybe."

Adele's intense gaze pierced the distance between them. "Youth has never understood the precariousness of life and that's a shame. Without being degrading, Susannah, I feel I must point out to you that you come from a loving, but unsophisticated family. What the people in my world can do for someone like you is offer an opportunity that was meant to be. I still don't know at whose invitation you're here and I don't care. I'm too old to question things like that. Please pardon my bluntness, dear, but you're no more the schoolteacher type than I am. You have a way about you that bespeaks impeccable breeding. Whatever forces brought you here know better than you or I what is right for you. Let me ask you, last year at this time did you think you would even be in New York, much less at a party like this?"

"No. My imagination is good—" she glanced around the room, past Magda's eager face and back to Adele's wise eyes "—but not this good!"

"Precisely," Adele said. "You're an intelligent girl. However, you're uninformed about people like me and my kind of lifestyle. It's simply a matter of proper education."

Magda picked up on Adele's drift. "Look at this experience as your education. I will give you more than a college degree. I will teach you how to be self-sufficient. How to live out your dreams. You'll travel all over the world. Meet fascinating and powerful people. Modeling will open up worlds you never dreamed existed. Darling, you're at the prime age for a model. By the time you went back to school and graduated, you'd be too old to train and develop as a superstar. By the time you're twenty-one I intend for your face and that incredible body to be known around the world. I can do all that for you, but you have to want it so badly you can feel it, taste it, smell it, breathe it."

Holding her breath as she digested every word Magda was saying, Susannah felt as if she'd been lifted out of herself and was looking down from above. It crossed her mind that she might be bargaining with the devil. She was suffused with doubts. What would her parents think? What if she failed? Would she be able to go back to school if this didn't work out? She'd always considered it essential to follow through with her goals. But now she was changing her life midstream. She looked at Adele, at her small, aged, delicate hands folded demurely in her lap. What if she didn't take this chance? What if she walked out of here and never saw these women again? What if she'd been wrong about her future all this time? Was that why things like this happened to people?

CLICK!

The sound in her brain was inaudible but distinct, and for the rest of her life Susannah would remember that click. Sounding like the switching of railroad tracks, it signaled to her that the decision was being made for her. Or perhaps it was her inner voice telling her what her heart already knew.

Suddenly, she felt herself slip back into her body. She knew now she was going to stay in New York.

"I'll do whatever it takes," she told them.

Adele and Magda nodded in unison. "Excellent."

Susannah sensed the interlude was over as Adele rose silently and gestured toward the doors. Magda pressed her business card into Susannah's hand and followed suit. "Call me first thing in the morning. We'll continue then." Susannah nodded in assent.

Just as they walked onto the terrace, Adele halted Susannah. "You must forgive me, dear, my mind isn't what it used to be. Did you tell me how you came by your invitation?"

"Karl invited my date, and I came with him. Greg Walton. The Waltons are almost neighbors of yours, in Westhampton."

Magda seemed to stiffen, but Adele simply sniffed in

that same haughty manner Susannah attributed to nearly everyone she met on Long Island. "Walton? I'm afraid I don't know them. My grandson knows your friend?"

"Yes. They're in law school together."

"Ah!" Adele nodded knowingly, but still without a trace of recognition in her face. Adele looked at Magda. "School chums," she said dismissively.

Instantly, Susannah knew that her presence on the Van Buren estate would never happen again.

Just then, Greg walked up with Kristen and a tall, male clone of herself whom Susannah knew instantly could only be Karl Van Buren.

"There you are, Grandmother." Kristen brushed Adele's cheek with a kiss.

Susannah didn't miss the censorious glare Kristen flashed her. The young woman purposefully slipped her arm around Adele's waist with a casual possessiveness. Her rival obviously wished to establish her blood alliance, thus accentuating the distance between the Van Buren upper class and Susannah's world, several rungs lower.

"Grandmother, I'd like you to meet Greg Walton." Kristen's honeyed words did not reduce the antipathy in her blue eyes.

Greg extended his hand to Adele. "I'm pleased to finally make your acquaintance, Mrs. Van Buren. Both Kristen and Karl have sung your praises so often I feel I know you already."

"I hardly believe that is possible," Adele replied with the same tone Kristen had used.

Clearly taken aback, Greg nevertheless smiled charmingly. But he did not respond, and let Karl take over the conversation, explaining their acquaintanceship at Harvard.

Susannah didn't know what to make of the situation. Only moments ago, Adele was not only warm toward her, but had volunteered to become Susannah's mentor. When Greg and Kristen had seen each other earlier tonight, their eyes had ignited. Now, Kristen's demeanor toward Greg was perfunctory. Susannah couldn't help wondering what in the genetic structure of the very rich allowed them to turn their emotions on and off so effortlessly.

Greg introduced Karl to Susannah and, though Karl was polite, he barely acknowledged her. Karl quickly ushered his grandmother and sister over to another group of guests. Magda waved to a friend, excused herself and breezed away.

Greg tried to slip his hand into Susannah's. "Where did you go? I turned around and you were gone."

Susannah saw a waiter bearing a tray of champagne glasses. "My glass is empty." She walked away, grabbed a glass off the tray and continued toward the end of the arcade where a line of potted conical topiaries closed off the rest of the house to visitors.

"Susannah, what is the matter with you?"

Susannah turned her back to the topiary and faced Greg. "No wonder you couldn't wait for this party. Is Kristen what I'm all about?"

"What the hell are you talking about?"

"Me! This dress! Am I supposed to be the ticket to make her jealous?"

"This conversation is ridiculous!"

"Oh, really! Well, I guess I've jumped to all the wrong conclusions. Funny, I got the impression we were practically, though not officially, engaged! Guess I was wrong!"

"Oh, you're correct. You *have* jumped to conclusions, Susannah. When I introduced you to Kristen, you practically bolted. I made an apology for you and then looked everywhere for you."

Just then, a group of four walked out of the house, their laughter and loud conversation intrusive. Greg took her elbow and together they slipped through the bank of trees.

"I love you, Susannah. You. Do you understand? I don't want Kristen. I want you. I..."

Susannah's back was rigid as she listened.

Obviously frustrated with Susannah's lack of response, Greg took her in his arms and kissed her passionately.

He took her mouth repeatedly, forcing her to respond to him. She did. He inhaled her perfume as he slipped his hands down to her buttocks and pressed her hips into him.

"I'm sorry, Susannah, for any pain I've caused you. It's you I love, truly. You must believe me."

She was breathless from his kisses. "I believe...you," she replied as his lips captured her mouth again.

"The way you smell, the way you feel...God almighty, Susannah. You can drive a man wild!" He pushed his erection into her pelvis. "There's no one here I need to see. What do you say we go home?"

She smiled at him. "I'd like that a lot."

Greg put his arm around her and led her away from Phillip Van Buren's study doors.

15

Michael finished his champagne and placed the glass on the silver tray the butler was holding. Phillip followed suit and then dismissed the butler.

"I can't thank you enough, sir. In fact, I'm speechless."

Phillip slapped Michael on the back affectionately. "No need for blubbering speeches, Michael. Just keep me as proud of you as I am now."

Michael's smile radiated confidence. "That I will."

"Why don't you join the others at the party. I have one more appointment waiting for me and then I'll join you. And if you wouldn't mind, please use the French doors over there."

"Certainly," Michael replied, and crossed the room. Not until he placed his hand on the brass handle did he realize his hands were shaking. He opened the doors, walked through and carefully closed them. Hearing the sound of the band and the cacophony of happy voices, he took a step around the barrier of conical-shaped topiary trees, when he stopped dead in his tracks.

The scent of Southern night jasmine and tea-rose perfume transported Michael back to his dream. He remembered the emotions he'd experienced when he'd looked into the woman's love-filled turquoise eyes and how incredibly drawn he'd been to her. She'd told him that she had come to meet him. He had convinced himself he'd been visited by a ghost. Smelling the perfume, he was now convinced his dream had been a premonition.

I must be nuts! But if she's here, I'm going to find her!

Weaving through clusters of people, Michael felt like a fool sniffing the air like a narcotics dog. He passed the elaborate buffet of crab, clams, oysters, fish and lobster. He barely noticed the faces of famous senators, Broadway stars and Wall Street moguls with whom he'd dreamed of working, as he scanned the room for a pair of turquoise eyes. One young brunette turned his way so that their eyes happened to meet. He quickly crossed to her table. Just then, she and the man next to her stood up.

She's pregnant! Very, very pregnant! Michael stood aside as the woman's husband led her to the dance floor. As she passed by, he realized her perfume was laden with spices and musk.

She's not the one!

Disappointed but not defeated, he walked down the terrace steps, across the lawns and out to the pier where dozens of guests were disembarking from their incoming yachts.

If only I really knew what she looked like.

Finding only three young women all with dark eyes, he instantly left the pier and returned to the terrace. He leaned on the balustrade and watched the couples dance, but found no one who made him believe in his dream. Suddenly, the sun began to set and a bevy of waiters lit hundreds of hurricane candles, Japanese lanterns and walkway luminaries. Michael shoved his hands in his pockets and walked across the arcade and through the open French doors that led into the living room.

The mesmerizing fragrance filled the room. Michael filled his lungs with the scent, his hopes soaring again. Then he heard her crying.

On the very end of the sofa sat a petite blonde facing away from him, her shapely legs resting on the down cushion. Her head was bent as she sniffed, then her shoulders shook as a new wave of sobs overtook her.

His heart went out to her as he reached into his tuxedo pocket for the Irish-linen handkerchief Phillip had provided. He walked over and held it out to her. "It can't be all that bad, can it?"

Her back straightened as she glanced over her shoulder to look at him.

A dark rim of tears and mascara enhanced her blue eyes.

He met her gaze. Were her eyes the same color as the ones in his dream? Perhaps...

She snatched the handkerchief from his hand. "I must look like shit!" She immediately wiped her eyes while watching herself in the floor-to-ceiling gilded mirror opposite her. She blew her nose and started to hand the handkerchief back to him.

"You keep it. In case you need it again and I'm not around to be of assistance," he drawled.

She smiled wanly at first, but as her eyes swept from his Italian shoes, over his tuxedo to his face, her lips spread to reveal straight pearl white teeth. "Are all the knights in shining armor from the South?"

"I must apologize that I don't know any other—"

She snapped her fingers, interrupting him. "Aha! Just as I thought. You're one of a kind, aren't you?"

Michael shook his head. "Any gentleman with half a brain would come to your rescue."

Kristen had pulled some outrageous pranks in high

school, including being caught by the East Hampton police for skinny-dipping. She was not the blushing, virginal type, but at that moment, her pale ivory cheeks blazed crimson red. "I guess I've never met a gentleman then," she said.

Stunned at her beauty, Michael was half-dazed as he crossed the short distance between them. Myriad questions plagued his mind. Was their meeting simply chance or was it destiny? Not only did her fragrance remind him of his mother, but her delicate bone structure was almost identical to Emmy's. Draped over the luxuriously upholstered sofa, she reminded him of his grandmother in an old photograph from the turn of the century, lounging on a white-wicker settee and gazing out at the Gulf of Mexico. On impulse, Michael picked up her hand and kissed it. "Michael West from Fort Walton Beach, Florida."

When he raised his head, she was watching him carefully. "Do you have family here, Michael?"

"I'm afraid not. I've never been to New York before."

An imperceptible twitch pinched Kristen's smile, rendering it faintly less natural. "I see."

"You must not have family here, either," he said comfortingly.

"Why do you say that?"

"Because they would save you from your tears. It's their job," he teased.

She crossed her arms defensively over her chest. "They'd kill me if they knew why I was crying."

Slowly lowering himself onto the sofa, Michael moved closer. There was no mistaking the scent of jasmine and rose on the sofa cushions. "Did he break your heart or is it just a temporary wound?"

Kristen bit her lip. "It was just a misunderstanding between...my brother and myself. No big deal," she said dismissively.

"Bullshit," he drawled. "Somebody hurt you." He touched her hand, caressing the length of her forefinger with his own. "I'd never do that."

"Don't worry, Michael," she replied smoothly. "I won't put you to the test."

He gazed into her eyes. "God, you're beautiful." He lifted his fingertips to her face and gently touched her cheek. "You have the softest skin. Like rose petals. Creamy white rose petals..."

Michael was entranced. He still kept thinking that this vision of fragile beauty would vanish any instant. He felt like a child trying to catch a bubble, knowing that it would be destroyed the moment he captured it. He pulled his hand back and chuckled. "I'm sorry. I guess I got carried away."

She shrugged and started to get up. "No big deal," she said flippantly.

"Please don't go. I haven't had a chance to get to know you...I mean, you don't know me. And I—"

"Look, you were really nice giving me your hanky and all, but I should get going." She stood.

Michael bolted to his feet and put his hands possessively on her arms. "You can't leave yet!" he said urgently.

Kristen cocked her chin to the left and glared at him. "Michael, I don't like macho guys..." She looked straight at the firm, though not painful hold he had on her arms.

"I'm sorry," he said, dropping his hands. "It was just that I felt like I'd come a long way to find you."

Confusion crumpled her forehead. "What have you been smoking?"

"I know this sounds really crazy, but I..." Michael stopped himself the minute she expelled a heavy sigh filled with the kind of exasperation a parent has for a whining child. "Never mind. It was silly, I guess."

"I guess." She looked away anxiously as if she'd been caught doing something wrong. "I need to go."

He stepped aside to let her pass, waiting for her perfume to fill his nostrils. But her fragrance had faded.

She was just about to the French doors when Phillip walked in.

"Michael, there you are!"

Kristen appeared shocked. "You know him?"

Phillip laughed heartily. "Know him? I brought him here. He's my guest."

Michael looked at Kristen, who now seemed in no hurry to leave. "You know Phillip?"

"He's my uncle," she replied sweetly.

Michael's eyes popped open. All he could think about was his dream. It had been precognitive, all right, and, more than ever, he knew now that someday he would marry Kristen.

16

You can't choose family. Kristen had always understood the sentiment behind that saying. Observing the peculiarities of her relatives had proven both entertaining and insightful to Kristen since early childhood. Although only nineteen, she believed she could read people almost as well as her Uncle Phillip. Lord knew, her father didn't know a damn thing about human nature. Kristen agreed with Phillip that Bart was a buffoon. Bart would never be the businessman her uncle was. He'd even told all four of his children he was living vicariously through them. If they excelled in anything in life, he would take credit. She wondered if her father was intelligent enough to realize that the only life goal he and Adele had set for themselves was to marry and have children.

Stud service was all Bart was good for, Kristen thought apathetically.

Phillip was the only Van Buren Kristen came close to admiring; he had cunning, intuition and balls. And knowing Phillip was a genius at concealing truths, she didn't trust the gleaming smile he flashed at Michael as they stood in the living room. His expression held a bit too much intensity for Michael to be just anybody.

Kristen was determined to find out what kind of game Phillip was playing. Every time she pressed either of them for information regarding the circumstances of their initial meeting or the reason for Michael's extended stay in Phillip's house, they evaded her. Skillfully hiding the truth behind compliments and inanities, Phillip changed the subject by maneuvering Kristen into agreeing to dance with Michael. Phillip would then have a chance to visit with his other guests.

Cracking an international spy code would be easier than this, Kristen thought as she let Michael lead her out to the terrace.

Romantic moonlight dancing bored Kristen to tears, but Michael was clearly enraptured by the melancholy strains of the violins. He held her body close to him, moving his hips to the music. His arms were strong as he swept her along the edge of the terrace. Because she was much shorter than most men, she was used to them bending down for their cheeks to meet. She noticed that Michael never leaned toward her. His chin nearly rested on top of her head, making her feel small. She didn't like being made to feel like a child, so she pushed away from him whenever he got too close. Michael simply spun her around again, executing another smooth segue.

"I suppose you took dance lessons in grade school like I did," she said, looking up at him.

"No."

"Liar. Nobody dances like this naturally."

"Well, I do," he said, and chuckled as he spun her around again.

Kristen knew this was just another ploy on his part not to reveal himself. "I like disco better. I go to Studio 54 and Elaine's a lot," she said nonchalantly.

"I don't know much about where to go in New York, but I think I can hold my own on any dance floor," he replied with a smile.

"Cocky, aren't we?" she taunted him.

Michael grinned confidently. "No, just truthful, ma'am," he drawled, and pulled her even closer.

He cupped his hands around hers and brought her fingertips to his lips. He lifted her chin so that he could look into her eyes. "How many fellas have told you that your eyes are beautiful?"

"Hundreds," she replied. It was nearly the truth.

"I'll bet you don't remember their names," he teased.

Only one, she thought. "You're right about that, Michael. I'll bet you have lots of girlfriends back in..."

"Fort Walton Beach," he reminded her. "No girlfriends."

"What's the matter with those Florida girls?"

"Nothing. I'm just picky, is all."

Kristen was more intrigued than she cared to be. Who was this alien person whom Phillip favored? "So, what were you doing when you met my uncle?"

"Fixing his car."

Kristen stopped dead still. "You're joking!"

Michael shrugged his shoulders but kept his hold on her. "Serious. My father owns the best garage in town. We're the only ones who work on imports. Phillip's Testerosa had broken down. He and I talked while I drove him to a hotel."

Indignantly, Kristen nearly sputtered her question, "And when was this?"

"Three years ago." He smiled as the music stopped and the other dancers vacated the terrace, leaving Michael and Kristen alone in the moonlight.

Her eyes narrowed suspiciously. "He must have invited you to Fort Lauderdale to sail and fish? To the condo?"

Michael kept shaking his head. Then he went into a

detailed account of how he and Phillip got reacquainted and the circumstances surrounding his invitation for the Fourth of July.

Shock kept Kristen's mouth closed while he explained. This was too unbelievable. Michael was a car mechanic! He wasn't rich at all. And his family background was light-years removed from hers. She must have mistaken Phillip's level of interest in Michael. Maybe he was on some new kind of Good Samaritan kick. Maybe he was going through a midlife crisis. Maybe he got a kick out of playing with Michael's life. She understood that. She liked doing the same thing with people.

Goddammit! she chastised herself. *I should have gone after Greg like I wanted to. He was practically begging me to come on to him. But no! I had to play it tough…cold. He would have dumped that brunette…or was she a redhead? Oh, who cares? I'm smarter than this.*

Three years… It had been three years since she and her girlfriend Hadley crashed a fraternity kegger at Harvard. Back then, they'd lied to the half-drunk, half-stoned boys they met, telling them they were freshmen at Columbia up for the weekend. Kristen had met Greg and it had been an instant turn-on for her. He was so damn gorgeous she couldn't imagine any girl not wanting him. But he wouldn't have anything to do with her, only telling her his first name. But later that night they'd sat on the front lawn of the frat house and talked. She was nearly gone on pot, she remembered, but she would never forget the round of twenty questions he flung at her.

She also remembered it wasn't until she told him her name that he got truly interested.

"Van Buren? From Long Island?" he'd asked pointedly.

"Kristen Van Buren." Her head flopped back and forth like a rag doll. "From East Hampton. My father has an apartment in the city, too. Sometimes I tell people I'm from Manhattan. To throw 'em off...you know!" She'd laughed and slapped his arm.

Suddenly, she'd felt him grab the back of her hair very tightly, hurting her. Then he'd yanked her head back and covered her mouth with a kiss meant to defile.

"So, what are you doing, Kristen Van Buren? Slumming? You come up here for kicks, don'tcha?" He'd kissed her again, ramming his tongue into her mouth, forcing her to take it. She remembered she could barely breathe and had gasped for breath.

"Slumming? Whazat mean?"

He shoved his hand underneath her sweater, unhooked her bra and squeezed her full, round breast until she cringed in pain. "How old are you, Kristen? Why do you lie to me? You think I'm some kind of ignorant fool that I don't know who you are and what you really want?"

He yanked on her hair again and pinched her nipple.

She felt herself get wet between her legs. "No. Not...fool..." She tried to answer but he plunged his tongue into her mouth again. She threw her arms around his neck and pulled him deeper. She didn't know what was happening to her, but she knew she wanted to see it through to the end. "Sixteen," she finally said, panting between kisses. "I'm sixteen."

"But are you sweet?" His voice was demonically seductive as he pulled her hair again. "Are you?"

One part of her wanted him to stop hurting her, the other part wanted his tongue pushing and probing...

It was as if he'd read her thoughts.

His hand let go of her breast and instantly shot down inside her jeans. His hand was like ice as he pressed and teased her hardening bud. His finger felt thick and cold when he stuck it inside her. Mercilessly, he pumped her until she could feel her own juices all over his hand and trickling down her inner thigh.

Greg had her pressed down against the grass, his body nearly on top of hers. She could hear cars honking as they passed. She heard the sound of laughter as a drunken couple stumbled down the frat steps then out to the street. But Kristen didn't care who saw her. She'd never been so turned on, never knew she was capable of such raw feelings.

"Sweet, aren't you?" he said roughly, withdrawing his hand abruptly.

Pitched to the edge of hungry lust, Kristen craved satisfaction. "Why did you stop?" she asked, her eyes dilated and her breath coming in a rush.

He sneered at her as he bit her lower lip and then suckled on it. "Because you're a virgin, aren't you?"

"I...yes." Kristen was covered in sweat and she thought she'd explode.

"You ever been fingered at all?" he demanded as he grabbed her breast again and pinched it very hard and very long.

"Yes...but not..."

"Not like I do it, huh?" He unzipped his jeans. "That's what you want, isn't it? To go slumming with somebody you wouldn't speak to on the street? Give your virginity to a stranger? Get your kicks out of knowing your fat-cat daddy can't do a goddamn thing about it?"

She held her breath.

"That's it, isn't it?" He yanked her jeans down. She

could feel the autumn-cold ground bite the soft flesh of her hips.

"Yes!" To her own ears her voice was animalistic. She grabbed his incredibly handsome face and riveted him with an angry gaze. "I want to do it with you."

"What do you want, baby girl? You want me to fuck you? Is that it?"

He moved over her. His face was dark and menacing like a devil. She'd never felt so frightened yet so thrilled in her life. "You ever have anybody eat you?"

"No."

"Ever hold a cock?"

"Yes...not really." She shook her head as his words gripped her loins. Kristen didn't know she was capable of the thoughts she had or the tremendous power she felt. Greg was the aggressor, but her intuition told her that he was as caught up in the excitement as she was. In the moonlight she could see the sheet of sweat covering his face, exposed neck and chest as she ripped at the buttons on his shirt. His heart slammed against his chest wall like a tiger in a cage. He wanted her as much, maybe even more than she wanted him.

"Then feel my cock, little girl." He shoved her hand onto his erection and showed her how to squeeze him. "It's the biggest thing you've ever felt, isn't it?"

"Y...yes." She couldn't believe her fingers nearly did not fit around him. She was scared that he might rip her apart, but she was more afraid of not knowing what he felt like.

"Now you put me inside you. That way, you can't yell rape to your daddy later on when you sober up."

"I'm more sober than you are," she hissed, tightening her fingers around him and pulling forcefully.

"Shit! Not so rough!"

"Yeah? I thought you liked it that way," she taunted.

He hovered over her, searing her eyes with his. "I do. You do anything you want with me. Put me wherever you want," he said suggestively. "Before the night is over, we'll do them all, little girl. I'll show you how much fun I can be. Now..."

He pushed himself inside her and when she started to cry out, he covered her mouth with his hand. He put his mouth to her breast and took her nipple between his teeth, biting and nibbling. She didn't know which part of her hurt the most or exactly where the tremendous waves of lust originated. She was more than euphoric, she was instantly addicted.

She grabbed at him and sunk her nails into the fleshy crease between his upper thighs and buttocks.

He jerked back against her hands as if he wanted more. He pushed his hands beneath her hips and brought her up to him. After her hymen quickly broke, he continued pumping her until she climaxed. Before she'd barely caught her breath, he hoisted her off the ground and nearly dragged her to his room. Being a man of his word, he showed her all the other things he'd said he would.

Kristen had sneaked off to see Greg a month after that. The sex had been even more incredible than the first time. Then she discovered that his family was from Long Island. She'd never heard of the Waltons, but she intended to find out about them. When she asked her mother and grandmother about the Waltons, they emphatically told her that most everyone in Westhampton was not in their social milieu. The Waltons were inferior and she was never to consider being friends with any of them.

Kristen observed that when she mentioned the Walton family, Phillip ground his jaw, making a nerve twitch in his cheek. Adele clamped her mouth shut like a clam. Her mother and father ignored her questions altogether.

Still, Kristen dreamed of sex with Greg too often for her own good. When she called Greg at the fraternity house, invariably he was "out." Finally, he told her that she was too young for him. He was pinned to another girl. Devastated, Kristen promised herself she'd never have anything to do with Greg Walton again.

Then he'd walked into the party tonight. He was about the last person she expected to see. In less than five seconds, she could feel the heat rising in her body. She wanted him as much now as she had when she was sixteen.

It was two o'clock in the morning before all the guests left Phillip Van Buren's house. The family sat in the living room sipping brandies and cordials as Phillip formally introduced Michael West to everyone. When Phillip informed them that he planned to subsidize Michael's education and give him the Van Buren seal of approval, the only person still breathing normally was Kristen.

She had to give it to Phillip, he'd never played by Adele's rules and never would. How interesting the next few years were going to be...especially for her brothers who had self-righteously believed they had the Van Buren millions sewed up for themselves. Since Phillip controlled the greatest amount of the family's operating capital and was responsible for making nearly every dime of income in this century, Kristen knew Phillip could damn well do what he pleased, with whom he pleased and when he pleased.

Kristen stole a glance at Michael seated in an heirloom Chippendale chair. Just as she thought, Michael was watching for her reaction. She obliged him with her sweetest and most charming smile.

Look at him! He's practically broken out in hives! Kristen, you're going to have fun with this one.

If Phillip hadn't been looking on, she would have given Michael the seductive look he wanted. Now that she thought about it, perhaps it was best not to show her hand too soon. If fate twisted their lives in knots the way it was known to do, then Michael might become more than a protégé to Phillip. This Southern boy could very well be the new crown prince, edging out both Karl and Max. Should that happen, her own financial security could hang in the balance.

She watched as the rest of the family congratulated Michael with hypocritical words and false smiles. She could almost see them sharpening the knives they planned to stick in his back. Poor Michael hadn't the slightest idea what was happening around him.

Kristen waited patiently while the rest of her family left the room. Phillip was quietly speaking with Adele near the doors when she went up to Michael.

"That was some surprise you and Uncle Phillip cooked up for us," she said. She touched his lapel, then peered up into his face from beneath her long-lashed eyes.

"Don't get the wrong idea...I didn't..."

"Never you mind. I think it's just great."

"You do?" he asked.

"I'll be able to see more of you...especially if you change schools."

"I was going to wait until my junior year. My dad needs me at the garage on weekends."

She pressed the pads of her warm fingers next to his shirt. "Your heart's beating a mile a minute, Michael. Why's that?"

"I think you know."

"Maybe we should find out," she said, mustering her most-seductive tone of voice. "Say, tomorrow? We could go for a sail, just the two of us. I'd like to spend more time with you, Michael." She stepped a bit closer.

"I'd like that."

She winked at him. "I know." She turned around and walked over to her grandmother. "C'mon, Grandmother. I'll drive you home."

Adele looked up at her granddaughter. "Thank you, dear. How very sweet of you to offer."

"No problem."

Kristen took Adele's arm and, after brushing a kiss on Phillip's cheek, she left the room without looking back at Michael. As she drove away from the largest of the Van Buren mansions, she believed Michael had already fallen in love with her. If there was the slightest chance he was simply infatuated with her, she would make sure that he returned to Florida totally in her power.

As a Van Buren, Kristen didn't believe in love. She believed in getting what she wanted. And she wanted Michael West.

17

Trash and filth was Susannah's first impression of uptown Manhattan the day after the bicentennial holiday crowds had left. Double shifts of city crews swept, scooped and speared refuse, making clear the way for Greg's Mercedes as they wove their way toward Magda's office. Susannah watched the workers, thinking how she'd always envisioned a glamorous city. Having her fantasies of New York dispelled by its realities suited her thoughts about the recent turn of events in her life.

Something is out of sync, she thought as she glanced at Greg. *My entire trip has been like a dream come true. Even dreams I'd never dared to have are materializing for me. And so quickly!*

"We're almost there," Greg said as they turned a corner and pulled in front of an office building. He leaned over to kiss her cheek. "Magda's office is on the tenth floor. I've decided to go over to the club and see some of my friends."

"I thought you were going with me..." Susannah gulped, suddenly feeling intimidated by the marble-and-glass skyscraper.

"This is no place for a guy. Least of all me. I don't know this Magda person at all. She obviously likes you a great deal." A wan smile barely curved his lips.

"You think I should have blown this off, don't you?"

He shrugged and stared straight ahead. "Like I said before, I wasn't aware you harbored any secret ambitions about becoming a model, that's all," he answered in a clipped, terse tone.

"I haven't, not really. But I want to at least go this far. What if I had a chance to do more with my life than teach and then didn't go for it? I'd always wonder what could have happened to me," she explained.

Greg did not look at her. "I guess I don't understand the purpose in deviating from one's set goals. After all, isn't that why we set goals in the first place? What if I got a wild idea to go off to Africa and shoot pictures of tigers instead of following through with law school? Wouldn't that be just dandy?" He ground his jaw, making a vein in his neck twitch.

"It's not the same thing," she replied quietly. *Maybe all this time I haven't set my sights high enough.*

"It's exactly the same," he countered as he looked at her sharply. "I was attracted to you because you're beautiful, yes. But it was more than that. I thought you had a head on your shoulders. You impressed me as a down-to-earth person. You knew what you wanted and you were willing to work diligently to get it. Meaning, your degree. I love the fact that you love children. I want a family someday...to carry on the Walton name. I don't want a wife who's traipsing all over the country just to have her picture in some magazine. This, this whole kind of life...models and clothes and...and flashy men is so shallow, so false, it just doesn't fit you at all!" he stammered as his insecurities spilled out.

"I've never been shallow and I don't believe a career could change my basic nature," she countered. "Besides, if this works out for me, I can always go back to college.

This is a chance that I have to take now while I'm young."

Greg did not argue with her but chose to remain sternly silent, which made his point even more eloquently.

Susannah was shocked over his condemnation. She couldn't help wondering what he would tell her if they were truly engaged. She didn't want to upset him. She didn't want to lose him. She reached over and caressed his hand, hoping to reassure him. "Don't be angry with me."

"I'm only stating my opinion," he said coldly.

She glanced up at the building, now seeing it as a powerful sentry who would champion her as she took this step into her future. One part of Susannah couldn't wait to rush into the building. The other part felt Greg's hand turn clammy as though with fear. She'd never thought of Greg being afraid of anything. He was too sophisticated for that, wasn't he?

Flashy men, his words echoed in her head. *Greg is afraid he's going to lose me!* The realization stunned her. Greg was more in love with her than she'd thought. Her heart went out to him.

"I won't go if you don't want me to," she offered.

His smile was too quick not to be honest. Then he shook his head. "Oh, no! And have you blame me for never having tried this?"

"I wouldn't do that!"

"Of course you would. I know I would if the positions were reversed."

"Really?" *I need to remember that.*

Greg pointed to the building. "Now, you go in there and get it over with." He reached in his pocket and pulled out one of his personal cards and scribbled a number on the back. "This is the number at my club. I've got a squash game in half an hour. Then I'll have lunch there, maybe get a rubdown. You call me when you're finished."

"But what if it only takes thirty minutes?"

Greg laughed and pointed up the street. "You *are* from Indiana, aren't you? This is Fifth Avenue. I know girls who spend eight hours shopping in this block alone. Bloomingdale's is down that way. You can call me from there if the agency kicks you out." He leaned over and kissed her tenderly. "Knowing my luck, I will have lost you the minute you walk through that door."

"Never." She smiled and got out of the car.

Susannah waited as Greg pulled out into traffic and was swallowed up by a school of yellow taxis.

Two-dozen girls from ages fourteen to twenty-four lined the walls of the Magda's Models reception area. From pasty-faced waifs to statuesque cosmopolitans, the women manipulated their looks to fit a wide range of client accounts.

Susannah's insecure knees wobbled as she approached the receptionist sitting behind a large cherry desk. A headset creased her punked purple-and-red short hair while her black-lacquered nails clicked rapidly over a huge telephone system. With nearly every light on the board blinking, Susannah feared it would be a long wait. She no more than finished her thought when the girl lifted her green-lashed eyelids.

"You're Susannah Parker, right?"

"Yes."

"I saw you when you came through the door. I've already sent for Magda's assistant to show you to a fitting room."

"Fitting room? I thought I was meeting Magda to-day."

The girl answered two incoming calls and made their connections while Susannah finished her statement.

"She's across town on her way in."

Checking her watch, Susannah naively blurted out, "But I'm ten minutes...early." She grinned sheepishly as she realized her blunder.

The girl answered another call, but never missed a beat. "Don't worry, honey. You'll get the hang of it around here." She answered one intercom call and patched through another three calls before Susannah could form her next question.

"Susannah Parker?" a tall, chubby woman of about thirty-five asked from the door.

"Yes?" Susannah looked up at the woman's unsmiling face.

"I'm Harriet Blane." She reached out her hand. When Susannah shook it, the woman immediately used the contact to whisk her quickly through the door.

"I've got everything set up for you," she said as they trotted down the hall. "Fritz is the best photographer there is—even if he is gay. You must be pretty special for Magda to be going to all this trouble." Harriet's long strides covered ground like a gazelle's. "How long have you known Magda?"

"We just met, at a Fourth of July party." *Jeez! I'm going to get winded before I even get started!* Susannah thought as they wove around a corner and dodged people coming in and out of offices.

"Unreal. What exactly did you do to get to her?" Harriet asked sharply.

"Excuse me? I don't understand the question," Susannah replied as Harriet abruptly stopped at a set of double doors. Susannah nearly smashed into her. "Sorry." She looked away timidly.

Harriet's gray eyes pierced her with an icicle glare. "Nobody makes this much headway with Magda without a great deal of planning, hard work and a bit of...conniving."

Unprepared for Harriet's character assault, Susannah's jaw dropped open. Fortunately, anger shut it quickly. "I guess I got lucky."

Harriet frowned. "I don't believe in luck. We make our own luck. I just wanted to know how you made yours."

Susannah didn't understand why this woman was attacking her. She hadn't done anything personally to Harriet to upset her. As far as Susannah was concerned, the woman made no sense at all. "I do believe in luck and it always seems to find me," Susannah said with a megawatt smile.

Harriet rolled her eyes as she pushed the door open. "Where *are* you from?"

"Indianapolis," Susannah answered, believing the woman expected an answer.

Harriet's long legs sped her ahead of Susannah, who nearly ran into a rippling swath of white silk suspended from the high ceiling. A labyrinth of rainbow-colored silks kept Susannah from finding her way. Huge fans created crosscurrents of air that whipped the material, making it look like gyrating phantoms around her.

"Fritz! Where are you?" Harriet called out.

Susannah followed the sound of voices as she extricated herself from the ribbons of silk. She walked onto a carpeted area encircled with brilliant spotlights and silver umbrellalike contraptions that she soon realized were used to bounce the light.

Fritz was a tall, slender man with a deeply lined, interesting face and arrestingly green eyes. His hair was uncombed and stood up on his head in thick clumps like platinum cotton candy. Had it not been for his incredibly muscular body and his sleek, pantherlike movements, Susannah would have pegged him for a clown. When he reached down to pick up a heavy light and then mounted it easily on a tripod stand, his biceps bulged beneath the flowing white silk shirt he wore.

"Magda needs her goddamn head examined," Fritz ranted while he adjusted the light, still with his back to Susannah. "Calling me in from Martha's Vineyard like this. Jesus! I had that place booked three years ago. I'd still be in bed with..."

Harriet was nodding at Fritz's words when she saw Susannah out of the corner of her eye. She nudged Fritz with her elbow. "Fritz, this is Susannah Parker," Harriet said flatly as she motioned toward Susannah with her hand.

Fritz glanced at Susannah over his shoulder and nearly dropped the light. "Huh?" Then he spun around to face her.

Susannah was not prepared for the explosion in his eyes when Fritz saw her for the first time.

He threw his hands together. "God bless you, Magda!" Fritz advanced upon Susannah in a single leap. He grabbed her hands and brought them up to his lips, but did not kiss them. Instead, he pulled them over her head and used them to spin her around like a top.

"Excellent. Fucking excellent. Needs to lose three, no, four pounds. Some isometrics will tighten up her ass, but all in all...not bad." He dropped her hands and stepped away. He rubbed his chin thoughtfully and spoke to Harriet without taking his eyes off Susannah. "What do you think, Harry?"

Harriet shrugged. "Magda's calling this one. I think it's a mistake. This one's not in the business, no training, no work experience and, obviously, no sense of flair or personality. It's a long shot."

They're talking about me as if I weren't even here!

Fritz continued scrutinizing Susannah. "You're just pissed because Magda got this one first."

"Bullshit." Harriet clomped out of the room. "I'll be in my office when you're done."

These are the craziest people I've ever met, Susannah thought, not understanding half their repartee. Now Fritz was staring at her again. She stared back.

She'd never been treated like an object before. Fritz talked about her as if she were made out of clay, something he could pinch, mold, make into whatever he wanted. Like quicksilver, his demeanor altered from objectively appraising to passionately enthusiastic. At one point he even licked his lips as though she were lunch!

The whole situation was utterly confusing. Harriet was blatantly combative toward her; Susannah's Georgia-bred mother wouldn't have let her get away with bad manners like that for a single minute. Susannah didn't know either of these people well enough to ask if she was supposed to call Harriet "Harry," like Fritz did. And was there a particular way she should treat Fritz since he was homosexual?

A thousand uncertainties spun inside Susannah's head, causing her to reevaluate the wisdom of her decision to come here at all. Unable to withstand the intensity of Fritz's eyes any longer, she asked, "Isn't this Magda's business?"

He jerked like a somnambulist who has suddenly

been awakened. Turning back to the business of mounting the spotlight, he answered her. "Of course it is. Why do you ask?"

"Then why would Harriet be angry that her boss wants to hire me?"

Fritz barely let Susannah finish her question when he interrupted her with a flick of his hand. "Go strip."

"What?" Susannah asked, horrified.

"The dressing room is over there...behind the dark backdrop."

"What'll I put on?"

He cranked his head around. "Where are you *from*?"

"Indianapolis."

"Jesus Christ. You *are* a virgin, aren't you?"

Susannah crossed her arms over her chest indignantly. "I don't see that my virginity is any concern of yours."

He rolled his eyes. "I meant that you don't have any experience in our business."

"Oh."

His sigh was rife with frustration. "There's a robe on the back of the door."

"Thanks." She glanced toward him as she quickly walked away. "I'll only be a minute."

"Good, cuz that's all you ever get around here."

Only in the showers at gym class in high school had Susannah ever felt so exposed. The robe might as well have not existed for all the good it did. Not once was she ever certain that both breasts were covered with fabric at the same time. She couldn't help wondering if this place wasn't a front for a pornography ring like she'd read about in the newspapers.

Frantic heavy-metal music blasted out of a half-dozen

Bose speakers while Fritz positioned Susannah on the floor. Twisting her arms into pretzel-like configurations was not half as difficult as the balancing act she'd had to perform on a Bauhaus chair.

At times, he cooed at her like a mother to an infant. At others, he ordered her about like a general. Still others, he spoke to her with an incredibly deep sexual voice that made her want to melt.

"You're like a mirror of my soul," he'd said poetically, and then barked more orders.

She wanted to ask him how he could be mean and sweet to her at the same time. What made him so quixotic? But there was no time or space for Susannah to ask questions. There was only room in the enormous studio for Fritz's voice and commands.

Susannah flipped her hair, twisted her body, pouted her lips, smiled, frowned and glared. Once she became used to the strobelike flashing of the camera, the music and the sound of Fritz's voice, she seemed to move outside of herself.

Her body flowed rather than jerked from movement to stance. She pretended she was making up a dance as she reacted to Fritz's commands. She was the doll attached to his puppet strings. No longer did she see the flashing lights or the austere room with the hanging silk filters. At one point, she could no longer hear specific words or directions. She felt turned inside out, her emotions guiding her body. She could no longer think. She was one with her feelings.

"*Fantastique! Merveilleuse!* Wonderful! Divine!" Fritz seemed unable to hit his camera button fast enough.

When the shoot ended, Susannah was ushered by the hostile Harriet to Magda's office.

"Come in, my dear!" Magda greeted her with open

arms. "Fritz tells me you did splendidly. Took to it all like a pro."

"He did?" *When did he even talk to her? They must have walkie-talkies in this place.*

"Of course, we won't know anything really until the proofs come back. Most important, the clients have to want your kind of style. I have this feeling they will."

Magda motioned for Susannah to sit in the chair opposite her desk. Pacing while she talked, Magda explained her responsibilities, commission and relationship with Susannah should they sign a contract. Susannah listened intently, taking mental notes. Suddenly, Magda stopped in front of the expansive window and peered out over the city. "Tell me, Susannah, if you could be anywhere in the world, do and be anything or anybody, what would that be?"

"That's easy." Susannah's nervous tension from the unfamiliar experience caused her to blurt out an impulsive answer. "I'd want to be right here in New York, acting on Broadway." She surprised herself with her words but, once they were out, she realized how true they were. Perhaps pursuing the modeling fantasy had released other dreams that she had long suppressed. She continued to spin her fantasy. "I suppose I could act in films, but the whole idea of being a movie star doesn't grab me. I don't want to be a personality. I want to act. Then, if I became rich enough, I'd have a cottage by the water. The Gulf Coast... Deep South." Suddenly she stopped, realizing she'd been rambling as if to herself.

Nodding, Magda said, "I thought as much. Modeling is a great segue into acting, you know. Candice Bergen is a prime example. Everyone has to start somewhere. Look at some of these hot new stars—Jaclyn Smith, Farrah Fawcett. They all started out as models, then went into television commercials." She paused. "If your photographs show anything close to what I think we've got, you'll be bigger than any of them."

"Bigger?" *Do I want that?* she asked herself fleetingly. *What about my other dreams—Greg, children...*

"You could blow them away. I promise you. There's only one thing they have that I don't see in you, at least not right now."

"What's that?"

"Desire and a bit more determination," Magda answered honestly. "It's the toughest business there is. It takes aggressive courage."

"I'm not afraid of hard work. I'm up to it," Susannah reassured her.

Magda smiled thoughtfully at Susannah for a moment, then clapped her hands together. "Great! That's just what I want to hear." She stretched her arm out to Susannah, signaling that the meeting was over. "I'll call you if we land you an assignment. Make sure you leave all your numbers with Harriet."

"I will. I can never thank you enough, Magda. You're like an angel, making dreams come true for girls like me," she said sincerely.

Beaming at Susannah, Magda replied, "Don't thank me yet. I also know a few people who'd like to shoot me for raising their hopes." She walked Susannah to the door. "I'll be in touch."

"Bye and thanks again. I'll be waiting," Susannah called as she left.

18

New York City
September, 1976

Lining the walls of Magda's beige, camel and black–
appointed office were gold-framed photographs of
every face she'd made famous for the past twenty-six
years. Strewn across her glass-and-brass desk were
eight-by-ten glossies of every pose Susannah Parker had
struck for Fritz's camera. On top of the illuminated light
board on the far left of the desk were the composites of
Magda's favorite models from the inception of her
agency.

Harriet sat in a leopard-print chair holding a stack of
thick manila folders, crossing then uncrossing her swollen, aching legs. Fritz rubbed his bloodshot eyes with the
balls of his palms then flopped his head back on the
black silk sofa. His neck cracked.

"I've never been through anything like this in my
life," Magda groaned wearily as she glanced at the
quartz desk clock that read midnight.

"Don't say I didn't warn you," Harriet said smugly.

"Oh, shut the fuck up!" Fritz growled, punching a fist
into a fake-leopard-print throw pillow.

"I told you both that girl was too hayseed for our clients." Harriet folded her arms confidently over the stack

of rejections they'd received since the first photographs of Susannah had gone out.

"You're down on everyone who isn't one of your 'pets,' Harry," Fritz retaliated. "Not one of their entire portfolios even compares to Susannah's outtakes. If it weren't for your string-pulling, they'd be nowhere."

"I don't ask for favors they didn't earn," Harriet said defensively.

"Oh, I'm not saying they didn't work hard...in your bed..." Fritz bored the attack in slowly.

"Knock it off! Both of you." Magda rose and crossed to the window. With the city ablaze with lights, she felt suspended within a galaxy of stars—just the way she liked to think of herself. "Negativity doesn't bring in the money." She scowled as she turned back to them and leaned against the windowsill.

Harriet obviously took the reprimand as meant for Fritz and not herself. "Facts are facts," she said. "I've spent weeks contacting everyone from the A-list on down through the Z-list. No one will hire her! She's an albatross, Magda. Let her fly off into the sunset and forget it."

Magda shook her head. "Something's not right. I don't know what the hell is wrong, but my gut has never been wrong."

"There's always a first time," Harriet chimed a bit too proudly.

Fritz bolted off the sofa with renewed energy and nearly flew to Magda's desk. He grabbed a stack of Susannah's glossies and shoved them under Harriet's nose. "Once in a damn lifetime somebody like this comes along. Not twice, but once! You're so left-brained you haven't an inkling what Magda and I are talking about."

"Neither do our clients. Like Magda said, 'Negativity doesn't bring in the money.' Nobody's paying, pal." Harriet batted Fritz's hand away.

Magda was too tired to argue or referee. "It's late. Why don't you go home, Harry? Thanks for staying so late."

"Sure." Harriet sniffed at Fritz then rose from the chair. She deposited the files on Magda's desk knowing Magda would go through each one before she went home.

When Harriet was gone, Fritz put his hands on Magda's shoulders and rubbed the tight spot between her shoulder blades.

"That feels great," Magda said appreciatively. "Sometimes I feel like you and I are alone on this planet."

"So, get rid of Harry."

"She's good at organizing the office and putting out fires with the clients. She serves her purpose." Magda allowed Fritz to ease the tension out of her neck and back while she sorted out her thoughts.

"We both believe Susannah is ten times, no, a hundred times more beautiful than any model we represent. Yet, for some very weird reason, we can't sell her to a single soul in New York."

"Are you kidding? No one in London, Paris, Milan or Rome wants her, either. That's what doesn't make any sense."

Fritz glanced down at Susannah's face staring up at him from dozens of different poses. "She's perfection. Just look at those eyes! She could sell the mayor every bridge in this city."

Nodding in agreement, Magda picked up one of the photographs. "I've built this business by listening to my intuition, Fritz. This girl is so incredibly beautiful I knew for the first time I could throw intuition out the window. All that mattered was that the camera saw what I saw. Not only is she photogenic, she's a master at expression. She told me she's wanted to be an actress since childhood and that she landed the leads in her high-school plays. She's got the creativity. Just look at these..." Magda flipped through the stack for the hundredth time. "It's more than natural talent, you know."

"Mmm." Fritz nodded. "Soul-fire. That's what Susannah's got."

"Yes, and everyone will always want a part of it."

Suddenly Magda slammed Susannah's pictures on the desk. "That's it!" She grabbed Fritz's upper arms. Her eyes were blazing as she stared at him.

"I'm not following you, Mag."

"The reason Harriet reacted so intensely to Susannah. Practically hating Susannah on sight." Magda dropped her hold as she pensively looked away.

"Harry wants her," Fritz suggested with a chuckle.

"Yes, but it's more than sexual. She wants Susannah's inner fire, her power. Harry was intimidated by her. Not just her beauty, because Harry sees gorgeous girls every day, as we all do." Her thoughts forming as quickly as she could voice them, she continued, "Susannah is *too* perfect. Granted, it's not there every second of every day, but it's *there*. She's got something Harriet and people like her—common, ordinary, everyday people— could never understand. It's almost like a human struggling to understand the mystery of the universe."

A light went on in Fritz's head. "That's why the advertisers turned her down!"

"Yes!" Magda smiled. "Who buys their products? Common, ordinary people. The bottom line is all that matters in the end."

"Jesus! What a waste!" he said, piling Susannah's photographs into his arms. "She could have taken me to the moon."

Magda touched his arm sympathetically. "Not this time around. I know I've said this before, but if it's not in the cards right now, it will be later."

Grasping the last vestiges of his quickly evaporating dream, Fritz clutched the eight-by-tens to his chest as he left Magda's office. "Another time. Another place," he mumbled under his breath.

"There will always be another girl, Fritz."

He paused as he was about to close the door. His lusterless smile reflected hers.

"Not like Susannah," they said in unison.

"I hope I'm there when it happens for her," Magda said.

"Me, too," Fritz replied and quietly closed the door.

Bloomington, Indiana
September, 1976

Munching on a carrot stick, Marilou watched Susannah unpack last year's fall wardrobe into the minuscule closet they shared in their room at the sorority house. "Let me get this straight, Susannah. Not only have you met the entire Walton family who think you and Greg are getting married, but Magda thinks you're the next Candice Bergen. And you're back here in Bloomington?" Marilou shook her head violently as she grabbed a handful of sweaters out of Susannah's hands.

"What are you doing?" Susannah demanded.

"What does it look like? I'm repacking!"

"Why?"

"Because if I don't get you back to New York where

you belong, the authorities are going to come for you with a straitjacket.''

Susannah frowned and yanked her clothes out of her suitcase for the second time. "It's like I told you. Magda and Fritz thought I'd do very well. I knew it was a long shot from the beginning. I mean, I didn't have any training and other girls know just how to pose and look in the camera. I told Magda I knew how hard it was to be a model and it's even worse trying to get into acting. She told me she'd call me if she found work for me. I guess she didn't." She shrugged her shoulders. *That's dream number two I can put on the shelf. When am I going to learn that dreams are for children...and fools?*

"I came back home just as I'd planned and I haven't heard a word from her. It was fun while it lasted, but the reality is..." Remorse flooded Susannah's face as she looked down at the pile of clothes she'd worn since her junior year in high school. She couldn't help comparing them to the magical dress she'd worn that special night.

It's not the clothes, she thought. They were only pieces of fabric. It was the genius and talent it took to make the gown. It was the light in Aunt Gloria's eyes when she'd worn the dress. It was the feeling that something should have happened and didn't.

Every day and night since she'd returned to Indiana, Susannah kept trying to put her finger on what *exactly* had and *had not* happened to her during her days in New York. She could specifically remember thinking her life had turned a corner. She was *sort of* engaged to be engaged to Greg. She believed his family loved and accepted her, except for his mother, but she hoped they could work that out in time. She'd glimpsed the fantasy world of the Van Burens. Until her return to school, she'd believed a divine force was showing her the way to a new career. She'd allowed herself to conjure visions of herself living in Paris, working with high-fashion designers from all over Europe. She just knew her parents would freak-out the first time they saw her face on a magazine cover. Later she'd get into television commercials and maybe, if she was talented enough and lucky enough, real acting. Her fantasies had run wild for nearly two months, but now it was time to come back to earth.

She smiled to herself as she remembered every detail of every minute on Long Island. How strange it was, she thought, that when real events turned into memories they became dreamlike, as if they'd never happened. Her blue-green eyes were slightly wet when she turned away from Marilou and began pulling toiletries out of a cardboard box.

"Their world is very different from mine. I'm not crazy enough to think they can't see that. The elegant party, all of Magda's fantastic plans for me, even the day with the photographer—it was an adventure. But that's all. I guess they realized I don't fit in there."

"Bullshit! We've only been back at school a few hours and Greg has already called to say he's worked it out so he can come for the homecoming game in October. You're right, though—you're not nuts. You're just plain stupid!"

"I'm being practical."

Marilou rolled her eyes. "I thought you said Greg was 'the one,' you know..."

Susannah stacked the hair spray next to the shampoo on the closet shelf. *I wish there was some kind of sign so I could really be sure,* she thought, remembering his kiss at the airport. *Shouldn't I be missing him more than I am?*

Shouldn't I want to get on the next plane to Cambridge just to be with him?

"He is. It's just that for a while there in New York, it was like my life was filled with all kinds of possibilities. I'd never thought about what it would be like to travel to foreign countries and work with glamorous people. Magda talked about acting lessons from famous coaches! You of all people know that's been one of my secret dreams. I couldn't help getting caught up in the excitement. I even dreamed about seeing my name in lights on a Broadway marquee and I actually believed it could happen. I *felt* it could happen. Then I flew back home and everything was just as it had been before I left. Greg called me a few times each week, but there was no news from Magda."

"It does sound like a bummer," Marilou said, morosely flopping into her study chair.

"Exactly. A real bummer." Susannah sat on the end of the unmade twin bed. "You know, Marilou, I've got to quit doing this to myself."

"Doin' what?"

"Deviating from what I know is the right thing for me, like getting my teaching degree. When I was a kid and in high school, it was okay to daydream about acting and what it would be like to be a movie star, but I'm grown-up now. I can't waste any more of my life on fantasies." She pounded her fist into her palm. "I *know* better than that. I was a fool to put any stock in what Magda said."

Marilou looked up at the *Gone With the Wind* movie poster hanging over Susannah's bed. "If it was me, Greg would be all I'd ever want."

Susannah gazed thoughtfully at the poster she'd owned for more than ten years. "You're absolutely right.

I don't want to end up like Scarlett. No home, no man, no children."

"Me, neither," Marilou replied, tossing her half-eaten carrot into the wastebasket. "I'm sick of this diet. Let's splurge at the House of Pies."

"Great idea," Susannah agreed, ignoring the echo of Fritz's advice to lose a few pounds.

As they walked across campus, seeing the familiar buildings and waving to old friends, Susannah felt oddly misplaced. Though she could find her way around campus blindfolded, she felt that something had changed. The maple trees were just as broad and tall as they were last year. The sound of honking horns and boys whistling at the girls were just the same. Even the rush banners strung across the sorority- and fraternity-house porches were no more creative than before. Admitting to herself that she had metamorphosed because of her experience in New York was too much for Susannah. She wanted to believe she was content in Bloomington. She hadn't lost her love of children, nor her desire to be a wife and mother someday. She believed Greg would marry her, after both their graduations.

All her life, Susannah had believed that her dreams were simply fantasies. The summer of '76 had revealed, if only for a short time, that dreams were possibilities waiting to happen. But when nothing happened, Susannah learned she would be wise not to dream. It was safer that way.

19

***

Fort Walton Beach, Florida

Michael tossed his duffel bag onto the already over-flowing seat in his pickup truck.

"You got everything, son?"

"I think so," Michael replied, knowing his father had spent weeks making an exhaustive list of clothes, supplies and small pieces of furniture he was certain Michael would need in New York.

"Maybe we should double-check everything," Don suggested.

"Dad, we've triple- and quadruple-checked. I've got enough stuff to last me until my own kid goes to college," Michael said, and chuckled.

Sheepishly, Don glanced down the street at the yellow school bus as a group of children boarded. "I guess I'm having a tougher time with this than I thought I would."

"It's okay, Dad. I'm going to be fine."

"I know you are, son. It's not that. It's that I'm going to miss you." Don looked away.

"I miss you already, Dad." Michael hugged his father. "We never planned on something like this happening to me. I mean, I always hoped I'd get to New York, but things have happened so fast this summer."

Don gave a tight bear hug before he slowly released

his son. "I could never dream of sending you to someplace like Columbia. Guess I'm guilty of not dreaming
big enough."

"I hope I'm not guilty of dreaming too big." Michael
laughed as they both mashed their tears with the palms
of their hands.

Abruptly, Don stopped. "Don't ever say that, Michael.
You dream as big as you want. See how things happen?
A couple of months ago, I was driving myself crazy trying to think of how I'd get you through the year because
business hasn't been good—thanks to my bad back.
Then Phillip Van Buren not only offers to pay for your
education, but makes a couple of phone calls and gets
your records transferred in the blink of an eye. I still
don't know how he did that..."

"Connections," Michael said under his breath, not
wanting to interrupt his father.

"...and to top it all, he gets you accepted in less than a
week! I know, don't tell me, connections."

They laughed together.

Don's face fell serious. "You did tell him we intend to
repay him for the tuition? Helping me through a tough
spot is one thing, handouts are another."

"I told him," Michael assured his father.

"You got that city map he sent you? I don't know that
I'd ever learn my way around a place that big. You sure
it's not far from the school to your apartment?"

"It's not far." He took out the map and pointed to the
penciled area around the university. "Here's the school
off Morningside Drive and One Hundred and Sixteenth.
Here's my brownstone on Ninety-fifth Street. I can jog it
every day and stay in shape. I'll have the small loft
apartment and there's even an old carriage house in
back for the pickup. Phillip told me that the first floor is

rented to a married couple and the second-floor apartment is occupied, as well. There are other people around, so I won't be totally alone."

Don frowned. "If you say so." He shoved his hands into his overall pockets. "You going to be seeing that Kristen girl when you get there?"

"Yeah. I guess," he replied, wondering how to tell his father that in the space of one short weekend his life had changed in more ways than one.

Only in the movies did a guy like him find a girl as beautiful as Kristen. Incredibly, she wanted him as much as he wanted her. Just thinking about the way she kissed him made him break out in a sweat. Being used to Southern girls who'd learned for generations how to flirt and tease, Michael thought he'd been prepared for anything a girl could dish out. There was no doubting that Northern girls followed an entirely different set of rules.

Once he and Kristen were alone the night after the big party at Phillip's, she'd come on to him at warp speed. She'd parked near a dense grassy area in the dunes where she assured him they would find absolute privacy. He'd discovered that as far as Kristen was concerned they didn't have time for moonlight walks on the beach or hand-holding. Their first kiss was all lips and tongues and hands everywhere. His and hers.

Boldly clamping her mouth over his, she'd pried his mouth open with an insatiable lust. Holding his face in both her hands, Kristen interspersed her kisses with nibbling bites that gave him the fastest, hardest, most wonderfully painful erection ever. Panting like animals, he pulled her underneath himself and she let him fondle her breasts. Because she seemed like a delicate little bird to him, he was astonished at their size and unusual firmness. She told him she worked out at a club.

Kristen was anything but dainty, he learned as she pressed her fingertips onto his buttocks, crushing his erection into her pelvis. Michael knew he would explode and he did.

It was embarrassing trying to hide what seemed like a gallon of semen, but his reaction to her had pleased Kristen to no end. She'd reveled in it.

Every time she telephoned him from Long Island over the rest of the summer, she never failed to talk dirty to him, then asked him if he'd gotten an erection. He always did.

Michael looked at his father watching the school bus deposit the neighborhood kids and then drive off, knowing he was remembering Michael's grade-school years. This wasn't the right time to mention things like erections and wet kisses.

Don shook his head. "A girl calls you long distance from New York City nearly every other day for two months and you're not sure if you're going to see her?"

"I mean, yeah. She said she wants to take me to Greenwich Village on Sunday. She said that's the best day to bum around down there. Try different dishes at different places. You know, stuff like that." Just talking about Kristen, thinking about her, made him horny.

"It's good you know someone in the city who can show you the ropes."

Michael wanted to laugh aloud. If his father only knew what kind of ropes Kristen had in mind, he'd want to let the air out of the pickup's tires. Michael was sure it would take a lifetime to do even a fourth of all the things she'd suggested over the phone. "Everything's going to be great, Dad. I couldn't ask for a better school than Columbia." *Except Harvard, perhaps. Phillip had offered, but the tuition was too far out of sight. He'd never have been able to repay it.*

"I know you, Michael. You'll make everything great. You always have."

"Thanks, Dad." Michael hugged his father. *Thanks for letting me go.* "I love you, Dad."

"I love you, too, son. Now, you call me as soon as you get there. I want to know that you arrived safe and sound."

Michael smiled warmly. "I'll call you from the road tonight. How's that?"

"Even better. Well, you'd better get a move on."

Michael hugged his father once more before getting into the truck. When he pulled out of the driveway, he waved, honked and waved again. When he looked in the rearview mirror, he saw his father still waving and then wiping a tear from his cheek.

He thought, *I'll always remember this...always remember you, Dad. Always.*

After a day and a half on the road, Michael arrived in New York shortly before midnight. He was exhausted and wanted only to go to sleep. However, when he pulled his truck up to the brownstone and saw two stoned young men and a bedraggled-looking girl hanging all over both of them, he suddenly felt wide-awake. Eyeing them as intensely as they watched him, he noticed they paid a bit too much attention to the mound of furniture and boxes underneath his blue plastic tarp.

"Y'all live here?" Michael asked.

"Y'all?" they chorused, and looked at each other.

"Where you from, bro?" the tallest one with the tight muscle T-shirt asked as he stood up.

Michael was tired, but he was neither drunk nor

stoned. He watched the guy addressing him waver in his high-top basketball shoes. "Florida. Where're you from?" he asked, putting a harder edge to his voice. Michael guessed his opponent was no more than two inches taller and carried an extra twenty pounds, max. Michael could take him.

"Right fuckin' here," the other one said, hoisting his jeans to his waist as he stood.

"In this house?" Michael asked.

"None the fuck other."

"Good. Then we're neighbors. I'm Michael West. I'll be going to school at Columbia this year."

The girl lit a joint and blew the smoke at Michael. She laughed loudly, slapping her bare leg as she took another drag. Suddenly, she seemed to realize no one else had made a sound. Sensing the malevolence in the air, she called, "I'm outta here!" and took off down the street, the joint still in her hand. She didn't look back.

Michael watched her for a minute. "Seems like a nice girl." He smiled.

The two young men glared at him.

Michael clapped his hands together. "Well, since you're my new neighbors, I think it would be right neighborly of you to volunteer to help me move in."

"Huh?" Their heads wobbled as they looked at each other.

They were more spaced-out than Michael had imagined and that was good. "C'mon! It's late and I'm tired!" Michael began untying the rope.

He could hear their footsteps against the concrete as they walked up behind him. Quickly, he grabbed a tall floor lamp from the edge of the truck bed. He spun around, knocking the tallest one in the head.

He dropped like a stone.

Michael looked at the shorter guy. "I'm sorry, I didn't get your name," he said politely.

"Beason. Beason Bates, the third."

Michael stuck out his hand. "Nice to make your acquaintance, Beason. Who's your friend?"

"Mark Simonton. He's my roommate," Beason replied, looking down at Mark.

Michael nodded. "Maybe I should help you get Mark up to bed. Then you can help me move in." Michael slapped Beason's back hard enough to rock him in his shoes.

"Sure. No problem."

Michael took Mark's arms while Beason took his friend's feet and they half dragged, half carried him to the second-floor apartment and into the bedroom. Mark's legs flopped over the side of the unmade bed and refused to budge.

"Guess that's where he's gonna spend the night," Michael said, looking around the room at the stack of textbooks on the desk, on the floor and on the bookshelves. He noticed that most were chemistry and math books. He guessed that one or both of his new neighbors intended to become chemical engineers. He also noticed the bookshelves were antique cherry wood like the kind he'd seen at Phillip Van Buren's mansion. Though the furnishings were sparse, everything from the newly upholstered club chairs to the simple framed mirror on the wall appeared to have come from an old country estate. *Which is no doubt owned by their parents or grandparents*, Michael thought to himself.

These two have no more city-street smarts than I do.

Throwing Beason an accusatory look and imitating his earlier tough attitude, he said, "Where the fuck you from, Beason?"

Beason laughed aloud. "Manhattan, though a bit farther south and thirty stories higher," he replied more soberly. "Mark and me were roommates at boarding school in Virginia and spent our summers together in Europe. My father would shit if he knew I was stoned. It wouldn't look good to the shareholders."

"I'll never tell." Glancing at Mark, Michael shook his head. "Sorry about your friend. I thought you two were going to steal me blind."

"If we don't get back downstairs quick, not only will some of the fine citizens of the Upper West Side be counting their profits, you won't have a truck, either."

"Oh, great," Michael groaned, quickly heading for the front door.

Beason followed behind, chuckling to himself. "Welcome to New York, Michael West."

Michael followed Beason's advice and immediately parked his truck in the one-hundred-year-old "carriage house," which Michael thought should have been condemned eighty years ago. Once his belongings were safe, he decided to survey his new home before unpacking.

Michael didn't tell Beason that though he'd spent his freshman year at Ole Miss, this was the first time he was truly on his own. Unlocking the door, Michael couldn't help smiling broadly as he investigated the apartment Phillip's secretary had found.

The kitchen, living, dining and bedroom were all one giant square room with no division. Overhead were three enormous skylights making the room seem as if it were open to the sky. Where former residents had hung paintings, pockmarks marred the beige paint that covered the old brick walls. The pine floors were stained an ugly walnut color and were in dire need of sanding and waxing. Michael instantly thought of the sand-colored flooring of the old beach houses back home and decided that, as soon as he had time, he'd strip and bleach the floors.

"Hey! You've got some cool stuff, Michael!" Beason said, flopping onto the worn, tufted hunter green leather sofa. "When did you have it delivered?"

Michael was equally surprised at finding an antique mahogany bed, marble-topped nightstand and dark iron candlestick reading lamp in his apartment. Michael knew instantly the furnishings were Phillip's own. He was struck by the similarity of his mentor's furnishings to those of Beason's and Mark's. Michael sensed this was Phillip's way of easing Michael into his new life.

"My benefactor seems to be full of surprises. Guess I won't be needing that moldy old recliner."

"Really? I thought it was kinda funky. If you don't want it, can I have it?"

"That derelict from the salvage store is all yours, Beason, with my blessing."

"Cool! Let's go get it!" Beason sprang tipsily to his feet.

"This isn't one of those decisions you'll regret in the morning once you sober up, is it?"

Beason's eyelids were nearly at half-mast. "No way! That's the ugliest piece of shit I've ever seen. It oughta *really* piss off my mother."

"Why would you want to do that?" Michael asked as they headed out of the room to the carriage house.

Beason roared hilariously. "It's my purpose in life."

It took less than an hour to empty the truck and deposit the recliner, floor lamp and rickety wicker table in

Beason's apartment. Michael kept the boxes of clothes, personal items and books.

By the time he'd thanked Beason and said good-night, Michael was too excited about his new home to sleep. Instead, he unpacked his clothes and hung them in an unexpectedly large closet. Carefully, he placed his socks and underwear in neat stacks on the narrow shelves that lined the far wall. He folded his faded sweatshirts and piled them on the long overhead shelf and placed his tennis shoes and boat shoes next to the pair of black dress shoes Phillip had given him. His tuxedo and pleated shirt hung inside a plastic garment bag to keep them from being contaminated by his old clothes.

His meager supply of jeans, slacks, shirts and T-shirts were a far cry from the abundance of preppy clothes he'd seen draped over the chairs in Beason's apartment. The vastly empty closet looked like a giant black hole. It would take a fortune to fill it with the kind of clothes Michael had envisioned owning ever since the day he'd first met Phillip Van Buren.

Someday I'll fill a closet this size with only the best. Suits in every color, for every season. Silk shirts like Phillip wears and Italian shoes, too. I'll put those cedar shoe trees in every pair and have my butler polish them every week. I'll have a big penthouse in the city and a country home in Connecticut. I'll go to Europe whenever I feel like it. Someday I'll be in the same league as Beason and Mark and maybe even know more about Paris and London than they do!

Someday I'll make it happen. All of it.

Michael awoke the next morning to the sound of someone pounding on the door.

"Michael! Are you in there?" a girl's voice shouted.

"Yes!" he replied as he stumbled from bed, wondering who knew he was in New York. "Kristen?"

"Who did you think it was?" she demanded as he opened the door.

Her scowl instantly transformed into a smile. "Why, Michael. How sweet of you! You're naked."

She rushed into his arms before he said a word. She shut the door with the toe of her foot and dropped her black leather satchel on the floor. "I've waited forever for this moment," she breathed seductively, and kissed him.

He'd never been turned on so much, so fast. He would never really be sure if he flung her halter top across the room or if she did. The Gloria Vanderbilt jeans seemed to drop to the floor of their own volition as she fell on top of him wearing only a pair of pink silk bikini panties.

Michael felt the hard wood under his buttocks as Kristen placed her legs on top of his. Though they were chest to breast, belly to belly and thigh to thigh, Michael wished she were taller or broader only so that he could feel more of her soft skin against his. He slid his hands down the length of her, memorizing the deep inward curve from her hips to her small waist and then out again over her large breasts.

"You missed me," he said, coolly gazing into her limpid blue eyes.

"Not in the least."

"Liar," he said, then licked her top lip and pulled away, making her seek his mouth for satisfaction.

"I had plenty to keep me busy while you were trouncing across those Florida beaches," she said flippantly.

"Is that so?" His hands moved back down her sides to the soft fleshy mounds of her buttocks. He spread his legs apart knowing hers moved along with his. "They must not have been any good. Otherwise—" he slipped his finger inside her "—you wouldn't be so wet."

Kristen's eyes rolled back in her head as Michael teased her bud, forcing her to the edge of the precipice, and then stopped abruptly.

"Are you crazy?" She slapped him angrily on the shoulder. "Don't ever do that to me again!" Her eyes shot fiery sparks but her swollen mouth took his with a vengeance.

He kneaded her buttocks and manipulated every press of his hips, every touch of his fingers until she climaxed.

"I love you," he said.

"Mmm," she replied as if she hadn't heard him.

Raking his tongue with her own, Kristen showed Michael again she not only was an expert kisser, but that she knew what else he would like her to do with her mouth.

"Oh, God, Kristen..." He wove his fingers into her hair and pushed her head down the flat plain of his hard belly. "Are you sure..."

"Just tell me if I hurt you," she murmured, taking him into her mouth.

Michael never questioned her skill and how she'd come by it as she pulled, teased and sucked on him. He was all too happy she liked the same things he did. Michael pressed his head against the floor and clenched his jaw. His muscles stiffened and the thunderous roar in his head was the frantic rhythm of pulsating blood rushing through his veins.

"Oh, Jesus, baby!"

Jerking her mouth away, Kristen watched as Michael exploded onto his belly.

When the pulsation of his climax had subsided, Kristen touched her fingertips to the semen on his abdomen.

"I made you do all that?" she asked with a curious gleam in her eyes. Her laugh was devilishly sensual as she cupped his testicles in one hand and squeezed his penis with the other. "Could I make you do it again?"

"Sure...later," he whispered with the last bit of energy he felt he had.

Gently at first, she pulled, then tugged on him. Then she tightened her grip. "But I want more now," she commanded.

"I don't know if I can," he said, trying to push her away.

Her eyes sparkled with a fire so bright it could have been from hell, he thought. She said nothing but continued playing with him. "I think you can do anything if you put your mind to it, Michael. You told me that yourself. Didn't you?" She pinched the tip of his head.

"Ow! You hurt me!"

"Thank you for telling me that. I need to know these things if I'm going to please you, Michael." Her voice was unemotional and flat like a robot's. "Because you did what I asked, I've decided to reward you."

Michael felt himself grow harder than before. He couldn't believe what was happening to him. "What do I win?"

Kristen pulled herself up to her knees and crouched over him. Then she rammed his full hard erection into herself. She moaned and shivered with ecstasy. "God, you're so big it hurts, Michael."

"I'm sorry," he said, putting his hands on her hips to push her off.

"Don't do that!" She shoved his hands away. "I had

no idea what I was missing. I swear, you're all I'll ever want."

Like a slowly moving ballerina, Kristen danced on Michael until they climaxed together. Though he was exhausted and sweat-covered, Kristen refused to let him rest. She told him she wanted to go sex-exploring with him. She wanted to try every position she'd ever heard about. Over the next six and a half hours they tried the bed, the sofa, the kitchen sink and the shower.

Michael had never been so tired as he was when Kristen kissed him goodbye late that afternoon. Though he was famished and there was nothing to eat, he was too weak to walk three blocks to the corner grocery store. The stocking of his pantry would have to wait until tomorrow, after his first day of classes.

Stumbling wearily back to bed, Michael smiled to himself, thinking it was going to be a great year for him in New York.

What more could a guy want than a great school like Columbia University, sweet, hot Kristen and the chance to make a fortune?

Fleetingly, as his head hit the pillow, he remembered thinking that Kristen had smelled different today. In fact, not since that first night they met had she worn the perfume he loved. He would have to ask her to wear it again.

Drifting slowly to sleep, Michael also remembered that not once had Kristen told him she loved him.

20

━━━●◄━━━

Indianapolis, Indiana
June 7, 1980

Susannah arrived late for her wedding.

The Methodist church on the north side of town was quaintly romantic. Kate and Susannah had created the blue-and-white-floral pew sprays and matching altar flowers themselves, saving money they knew they'd need for the sit-down dinner at The Canterbury after the ceremony. But none of their efforts had turned out the way Susannah expected. Somehow, the candles didn't glow brightly enough, the cloth runner wasn't white enough and her antebellum pearl-encrusted white-peau gown wasn't quite Southern enough. It was stiff when she'd wanted it to be soft and it was too gaudy when she'd wanted understated. However, she'd gotten it on sale at Ayers and it didn't break their budget.

Everything that could go wrong with a wedding and reception did. Susannah was feeling the acute pressure of it all. Although she put on a good front for her parents, there was always one person she could never fool.

"You look incredibly beautiful, Susannah," Marilou gushed. She kissed Susannah's cheek as she swished into the bridal room.

Because she was so late, all the guests, including her

mother, had been seated. She and Marilou had only a few moments while Susannah's father instructed the organist when to begin the wedding march.

Marilou looked utterly stunning in the slender-cut sky blue silk gown Susannah had chosen for her maid of honor. With forget-me-nots and baby's breath in her shimmering blond hair to match her nosegay, Marilou looked like a dream.

"You're as lovely as I'd hoped you'd be. At least one thing is right about this wedding," Susannah whispered to her best friend.

"I'd love to tell you you're full of it, Susannah, but you're right. Greg's mother is about to drive us all nuts. She's changed their family's seating around three times. The guests are about to stone her. That's some dragon lady!"

"I was afraid of this. From the very beginning, when she demanded their family be allowed more guests than ours, it's been war."

"I'm glad you stuck to your guns, keeping the wedding small, I mean. Fifty guests is plenty."

Susannah frowned. "Bettye acts as if everyone has money to throw around. Once she realized I wasn't going to let my father go to the poorhouse for her ego, she backed off. That's why the groom's side is rather sparse," she said, chuckling. "After all was said and done, Bettye wouldn't dream of letting her friends attend a middle-class wedding."

Gasping, Marilou said, "I've never heard you belittle your family like that."

"Those are Bettye's exact words. I overheard her on the phone last night when Greg and I went back to their hotel room for Greg's tux. I can only imagine what she's been telling her friends about me."

"Okay, that's it. I'll give you my new American Express gold card. There's no limit. You can charge anything you want. Plane tickets. Anything."

"What are you talking about?"

"Dragon Bitch, that's who!" Marilou said, pointing toward the interior chapel. "That's not a mother-in-law. That's a life sentence in Sing-Sing."

"At first I thought maybe she was stressed-out, too. But then she started criticizing every choice I'd made. The roses should be chrysanthemums. Your dress was too sophisticated, why wasn't I having flower girls and she wanted a big ballroom for dancing. God! It gives me a headache just thinking about it."

Grimacing, Marilou said, "The gold card is good at medical clinics, too."

"The good thing is that Greg and I have two weeks in the Caymans before we move in with his family."

"Can't he find you a small place in the city? Point out that he'd be closer to his office. That—"

Susannah shook her head. "I've tried all that. I even threw in the fact that he's making plenty of money now to afford our own place, but he says it's 'beneath' him to live in a common apartment. But I think this is all part of Bettye Banning Walton's brainwashing. Do you know why she always introduces herself that way?"

"I figured it was some New York quirk—too many Waltons runnin' around or something." Marilou laughed.

"No. She wants to make damn sure that everyone— especially her husband and son—know precisely where all that money comes from."

"Ugh! Double Dragon Bitch!"

Sighing heavily, Susannah said, "I always dreamed that my first year of married life would be romantically intimate. How can Greg and I make passionate love with two elderly cousins, Nora and Nell, plus Bettye and Jack listening to every breath we take?"

"You can't," Marilou replied sternly. "Face it. You're doomed to a life of silent sex." She wrinkled her nose. "Believe me, it's the worst."

"God! Silent sex." Susannah paused at a vision of Bettye, Nora and Nell crouched at Greg's closed bedroom door listening for every sound they made.

"I'm in real trouble," she gasped.

"Don't worry, you'll have my American Express card," Marilou reassured her. Seeing her friend's still-distraught expression, she took a deep breath. "Susannah, you don't have to go through with the wedding."

Shocked that Marilou would voice her own misgivings, Susannah said, "I can handle Bettye, and besides, Mother and Dad have gone to such expense and we've all worked so hard on the preparations," she rattled off quickly. "It's just prewedding jitters, that's all."

"Hmm." Marilou eyed her friend closely. "I think it's all a bit odd, you know?"

"What is?"

Shrugging her shoulders, Marilou said, "I dunno. Since I haven't gone through one of these and don't intend to for quite some time, I just thought it would be, well, more romantic. I mean, shouldn't Greg be tryin' to sneak peeks at you or sending a choirboy with little love notes or flowers? I just thought it would be a bigger deal than wearing a pretty dress."

"It *is* a bigger deal. What no one tells you is that by the time you spend six months planning, making decorations and settling family arguments, you're too exhausted to think about romance or sex or anything."

Marilou slapped the side of her cheek in astonishment. "You're not thinking about your wedding night? That tears it! When the time comes, I'll elope."

"Good choice."

Just then there was a knock on the door. "Sweetheart," her father said, "they're ready for us."

Marilou performed the honor of opening the door so Stu Parker could see Susannah.

He gasped with appreciation. The midmorning sun spilled through the stained-glass windows behind her. Surrounded by dancing colored lights, Susannah beamed at him.

Pride sparkled in his eyes as he whispered with awe, "Susannah..."

Not even Broadway lights are that bright, she thought as she hugged her father.

"It amazes me every time I look at you that something this beautiful could come from me," he said wistfully.

The last thing Susannah had thought she'd do was cry on her wedding day, but she did. Touching her heartstrings with delicate fingers, her father knew how to say exactly the right thing at the right time. "Oh, Daddy." She flung her arms around his neck, unmindful of her cathedral-length veil or her bouquet of white roses, jasmine and forget-me-nots.

Losing the battle for control of his emotions, Stu's voice cracked when he said, "I don't know why I didn't realize it before, but this time you're not just going away for another semester at school. I won't be seeing you at the homecoming games or parents' weekend. This time, you're really leaving us."

Susannah suddenly felt as if she was being wrenched from his strong arms by a fate she had no control over. "I...hadn't thought of it that way, either."

"I'm going to miss you, sweetheart. I just didn't know how much until right now."

"Daddy," Susannah cried, turning her face into the hollow between his neck and shoulder. At that moment, Susannah felt more like a child than she ever had. Suddenly, she didn't want to leave. She didn't want to spend the rest of her life arguing with Bettye and struggling to stake out her place in life. How easy it was being a child in a caring home with parents who gave love so freely. The juxtaposition of the Walton family's inner clockworks against that of her parents' instantly brought her new life into sharp relief. Shaded with monumental egos and power struggles, Susannah saw the Waltons as disjointed characters searching in vain for the kind of inner peace Susannah had known all her life.

"If you ever need anything, no matter what the circumstances, you just call me, sweetheart."

"I'll be fine. Just don't you worry about me."

Stu hugged her again tightly. "I'm a father. It's my job to worry."

Suddenly the organist began the wedding march.

"Mascara alert!" Marilou pulled out a linen handkerchief. "I was supposed to give you this for 'something old.'"

"Thanks." Susannah blew her nose and wiped her eyes.

Quickly, they left the bridal room and went to the archway that led to the chapel.

Marilou took her position and walked down the aisle, where she was met halfway by the best man, Allan Pendergast, a law-school friend of Greg's. Allan had confessed to Marilou that he didn't know Greg all that well, but that Greg's friends had canceled their trip to Indiana when the hassles with Bettye had gotten to be too much for them and their parents. Allan happened to be free that weekend and had agreed to the trip. He'd told Marilou that once he'd set eyes on her, he was "damn glad" he'd come.

Susannah was barely aware of most of the ceremony, even though their rehearsal the night before had been thorough. She gazed into Greg's eyes at the appropriate time and repeated her vows. She slipped a gold band on his finger and he placed one on hers. As he spoke his vows to her, she heard him as though he were at the far end of a tunnel.

None of this is what I expected. I thought this day would have such tremendous meaning for me. I thought I would remember every facet forever, but I don't even recall walking down the aisle. Is all the family here from Atlanta yet? I don't remember seeing half their faces. Aren't I supposed to be more elated than this? Shouldn't I be feeling complete?

And yet, I know this is the wisest decision I've ever made. Something else inside me is urging me on, as if this is the most necessary step I'll ever take.

I just don't understand...if it's right and I'm supposed to do this, then why aren't I happy?

The minister closed his Bible. "I now pronounce you husband and wife. Mr. Walton, you may kiss your bride."

The organist burst into a joyful refrain the moment Greg's lips met hers. Immersed in thought, Susannah was startled back to the present. She watched as Greg's eyes closed, his arms slipped around her and pulled her politely closer. His kiss was barely a brush of his mouth against hers. She knew he was dreadfully self-conscious about this very public display of affection. How odd it seemed to her that she'd always believed *this* kiss, above all the kisses she'd ever receive in her life, should feel like magic.

Susannah closed her eyes, but it didn't make any difference.

21

New York
June, 1980

Michael strained his eyes as he searched the audience of proud parents and friends for his father. Receiving his undergraduate degree last June and now his master's seemed nothing more consequential to Michael than necessary steps toward achieving his real goal. To his father, such accomplishments were monumental.

Again this year, Don West had turned down Phillip's offer of a first-class airline ticket to New York and a room at the Plaza. He'd told Michael he would fly coach rather than drive this time. Michael booked his father a room at the Stanhope Hotel at Ninety-fifth and Fifth, where Beason knew the head of personnel, and got a corporate rate.

Don had insisted he pay for the postreception party. The reception Phillip gave last year for Michael's graduation was lavish and costly and Michael knew his father could not afford New York prices. Michael suggested he help out with the expenses. Don turned him down flat.

"I know you've made some money on investments these past few years, but I'm still your father and it's my responsibility to entertain your friends."

After arguing with his stubborn father for hours, he compromised. It would be held at Tavern on the Green in Central Park where Beason knew the owner. Michael further insisted that his father take only himself, Phillip and Kristen to dinner. Don agreed.

Their argument had confirmed Michael's suspicion that his father harbored some resentment toward Phillip. He'd sensed it as soon as his father had arrived for last year's reception. Though Michael had told his father about the Van Buren mansion, the servants and lavish lifestyle, he knew his father had been awestruck. More important, it was the first time Don had been forced to face that he'd allowed another man to pay for his son's education. Don graciously hid the blow to his self-esteem, but Michael had seen the hurt in his eyes.

Though the notion was long ago accepted by Michael, for three years Don didn't acknowledge Phillip's part in Michael's decision to leave home. Lacking a college degree had always made Don feel inferior, a fact only Michael knew. It was also one of the reasons that he insisted Michael get his degree, no matter what the sacrifice.

Don had learned long ago to endure disconcerting situations. Proud of his son, he would have walked through fire for him. But nothing had prepared him for the emotional impact Michael's graduation had on him.

At the reception after the ceremony last year, Michael had watched his father's pride crushed by the way his New York friends had offered congratulations. They had smiled politely as Michael introduced them to his father, saying little more than was conventionally expected, then quickly offered their good wishes to Phillip, as if Phillip were Michael's true father.

Added to the fact that this was his first trip to New

York and nothing was familiar, Don had been uncomfortable with all the Van Burens, the Bates and a dozen or more families Michael had come to know through Phillip, Beason, Mark and Kristen. As a group, they'd seemed more concerned with Don's lineage, the lack of style in his clothing and his odd but endearing Southern accent.

One young matron had taken it upon herself to explain to him the positions of every Van Buren family member. She'd fretted and stewed over each detail, nervously wringing her hands. Speaking in a clipped New England manner, she'd had a distinctive habit of sprinkling her conversation with compound descriptions. "Uncle Timmothy, that's with two 'm's,' was our only wayfarer/mariner person. Officially, he was in the navy, but everyone knew he was a rogue/scoundrel. I'm not supposed to talk about him."

After more than half an hour of listening to the young woman detail the entire Van Buren genealogy, Don had finally excused himself by claiming he was in need of the rest room.

Not until he was alone with Michael after the reception did he have a chance to tell his son that he felt like an alien listening to these people. Their attitudes toward life seemed flippant and shallow while, at the same time, they made simple things seem quite complicated.

Michael had laughed with his father as Don had explained, "They seemed obsessed with making sure I wrote down information they gave me correctly. Do you have the correct address, Don? Repeat it to me again, Don. And the phone numbers I've had to repeat! Hell's bells! Then I heard him on the phone telling a guy to put up three million for some investment, like it was nothing!"

"That's Phillip," Michael had agreed. "That's just the way he is."

Don tapped his temple with his forefinger. "Maybe he's on his way to losing it."

Michael had laughed with him. "Not a chance, Dad."

Don watched as Michael scanned the graduation-ceremony audience. When Don's waving arm caught his eye, he clamped his hands together and raised them over his head victoriously. "I made it!"

Don sat between Phillip Van Buren and Kristen Van Buren, his soon-to-be daughter-in-law.

"Do you see him, Dad?" Kristen asked sweetly, following Don's gaze.

"There, standing in line behind that seven-foot Amazon," Don said, chuckling.

Kristen patted Don's hand. "I see him!" She waved at Michael. "I'm here, darling!"

Kristen blew a kiss to Michael with her left hand, causing the three-carat-diamond ring Michael had given her to flash in the light. Don still couldn't get over the size of it.

Phillip leaned his head toward Don and in a low voice said, "The Amazon is a former guard for the Boston Celtics. They say he retired with more than ten million dollars and he's gotten a master's in finance in order to better manage his investments."

"I'm a Jazz fan myself," Don said, trying to keep the conversation going.

"Really? I prefer classical music myself, though my mother is an aficionado of the blues. You would enjoy exchanging viewpoints with her," Phillip assured him.

"You don't follow sports much, do you, Phillip?"

"Oh! You were talking about a professional sports

team! I apologize. Michael often accuses me of being too focused on business."

Don didn't like the way Phillip's voice held the same kind of affectionate parental tone his own did when he spoke of Michael. Phillip's intense gaze focused on Michael with the guarded sense of anticipation Don had seen on the faces of his cronies at the racetrack. Don watched the way Phillip held his body perfectly straight, hands folded calmly in his lap, his legs crossed in such a way that the folds of his expensive slacks did not wrinkle.

He couldn't help wondering if these people ever relaxed. Then suddenly it hit him. "Phillip," he said, turning his back slightly away from Kristen who was busy waving at Michael. "I get the feeling you're uncomfortable around me."

Phillip dropped his eyes to his hands. "It's that obvious?"

Don couldn't believe his hunch was right. Last June, and now all this time preparing for this trip, he'd felt inferior to the Van Buren money and prestige. He'd felt like a country bumpkin, but he'd endured it all because he loved Michael. "Why in Sam Hill, pardon my French, would you be nervous around me?"

Phillip exhaled slowly. "You're his father. I am his mentor. It sounds harmless and quite civilized, doesn't it? But the truth of the matter is, Michael has become my son. To me, anyway. I've come to care a great deal about him. Frankly, more than I thought possible. And I know you love him that way, too. I suppose I'm guilty of being afraid my feelings would show and that you would be hurt. Michael is extremely protective of you, you know."

"I didn't know that."

"He's told me he would lay down his life for you."

Don nodded. "I'd do the same and he knows it."

"I find that amazing. Perhaps it's because I don't have children of my own."

Don watched as Phillip gazed distantly, as if pondering some long-ago memories. He felt inexorably sorry for Phillip who, with all his money and power, had not found a way to fill his life with happiness.

"I wouldn't quite say that, Phillip. You have Michael now."

Astonishment flitted across Phillip's eyes and warm appreciation curved his mouth into a smile. "I can see where Michael gets his generous nature."

"Don't you think that eventually like kinds of people gravitate toward each other?"

"Yes. Provided we've weeded out the impostors, the bloodsuckers."

Don smiled knowingly. "I've met a few of those in my lifetime, as well. You've probably known scores, given your wealth. Since Michael's wealth is not in dollars but in brains and dedication, I hope he won't be as vulnerable."

"Don't be too sure about that, Don. Michael's assets are more rare than mine."

Don regarded Phillip with respect. "Nothing is more precious than a true friend. I'm glad my son took a leap of faith with you back when your car broke down. Who knows what his fate would have been if he hadn't opened his mouth and told you his dreams?"

Phillip nodded appreciatively. "I don't think I've ever met anyone like you, Don West. Wisdom is rare in the world today." He held out his hand to Don. "Thank you."

Don smiled back. "You're welcome."

The band began playing the processional march, quieting all conversations.

Kristen withdrew a new camera from her purse and focused it on Michael. "Doesn't he look handsome with his new robes, Dad?"

"He certainly does," Don replied proudly.

Every move Kristen made around Don was carefully maneuvered to win the older man's approval. Given Michael's close ties with his father, she considered it wise strategy to get on his good side.

When Michael first moved to New York, Kristen had learned quickly that he was nobody's fool. If she wanted to keep her relationship with Michael moving toward marriage, she would have to be very, very careful.

She never told Michael she'd flunked out of Radcliffe after her freshman year. Nor did she breathe a word to anyone that her father had paid her way through Columbia. In fact, other than her father, no one in the family knew the truth about Kristen's lack of academic prowess. She supposed if she'd tried to apply herself, she might have passed the majority of her courses. The truth was, Kristen didn't give a damn. Degrees were something men needed to get better jobs or get ahead in the business world. All she needed was enough brains to marry the right man.

For Kristen, Michael West was Mr. Right in spades.

When Michael moved to New York that first autumn, she suspected Phillip might care for Michael as more than just a charity case. Doling out money for a stranger's education was not unheard of in their circle of friends, but the benefactor's involvement never went beyond that. But when Phillip handed Michael the keys to a brand-new Porsche their first Christmas together, Kristen realized the full extent of her Uncle Phillip's involvement with his protégé.

Until then she'd been halfheartedly playing with Michael, screwing him when she couldn't find anyone better. She'd planned simply to see how things went. Testing her own wits, she got a thrill out of the clandestine meetings she arranged with other boys. She'd used her girlfriends as cover while she plied Michael with a million different excuses. Most of the time, Michael was so focused on his studies, he hadn't complained.

She'd pretended to be upset when he told her he was taking extra classes "to learn all I can while I'm here." She'd thought him a fool.

"We're young. We're supposed to be having fun. Going out and living it up," she'd argued.

"I have all my life to have fun. I've only got this one chance at my education. I'm not going to waste it. And I won't disappoint Phillip. He's counting on me."

"Phillip never counts on anyone but himself," she'd retorted.

"Well, he's counting on *me*," Michael had said confidently and then instantly clammed up.

Little had she realized what Michael had meant.

Time passed and the gifts to Michael increased, the business brunches with Phillip's cronies were now monthly occurrences and the vacations with Phillip and his associates to Grand Cayman Island came to be expected during every school break. Kristen didn't need any other barometer.

She broke off her relationships with everyone she'd dated. She spent time with Michael when he wanted, not when she did. She taught herself how to make a few of his favorite dishes. Although it was nearly impossible to always think about Michael first, she did it. She also made an effort to ensure that Phillip could find no fault with her.

Even though she yearned to pull the outlandish pranks that had always got her parents' attention, she refrained. She gave up pot and flushed her stash of cocaine down the toilet. Studio 54 closed in 1978 and now her wealthy girlfriends hung out with movie stars and rock idols at places she didn't even know the names of. Her friends told her she was missing out, that life was passing her by. She told them she didn't care; she was spending time with Michael.

Between their junior and senior years, when she turned down an invitation to spend the summer in Europe with some friends from the racquet club, they dropped her from the group.

Kristen forced herself to dress the way Michael wanted. Sometimes she thought if she heard the word *conservative* one more time from him, she'd let it all rip and belt him one. But she didn't.

She endured his sickeningly sentimental stories about his dead mother, whom she was certain never had a clue how to dress. She sent his father cards on Valentine's Day and Easter, and was genuinely surprised when she realized how much a stupid thing like that meant to Don...and to Michael.

As the years passed and Michael racked up another perfect grade-point average, Phillip's lavish parties ended. Instead, he invited Michael, who always brought Kristen along, to intimate dinners for eight.

On these occasions, Kristen noticed the guests were not Phillip's old network of friends. They were younger men with new ideas and new companies who talked excitedly and incessantly about "the future." Having grown up in a family who identified their very existence solely by the accomplishments of past generations, Kristen was shocked.

During the summers, Phillip commissioned Michael to investigate new ways to make money. He acted as a private investment consultant for Phillip.

Michael had taken Kristen with him when he drove out to New Jersey to meet with the biggest creep Kristen had ever seen. The nerd had put together a contraption in his garage that he called an invention. The stupid thing had looked like a tape recorder with too many wires. Michael had been pleasant and overly gracious with the man, as he often was with ordinary people, a habit that drove Kristen crazy. When they got back to Long Island, Michael suggested Phillip invest in the man's product.

Three years later, Michael had profited handsomely from the Tel-Auto phone-answering machines that played recorded music and commercials while clients were on "hold." The dividends had paid for Kristen's fifteen-thousand-dollar engagement ring. She'd learned never to call anyone a "creep" or a "nerd" again.

During the course of their college years, Michael promised Kristen that, once he was out on his own, he'd make up for all her sacrifices. He told her that Phillip's plan was for Michael to be more wealthy than all the Van Burens put together. He'd asserted that with his instincts for making money, he could succeed.

She never questioned him once, having overheard Phillip say the same thing.

However, Kristen always made certain that Michael thought she was suffering for his sake alone.

Her martyr act drew lavish promises from Michael. "I'll take you back to Europe and really show you how to have a blast," he'd promise. "We'll dance all night at every disco you can find. We won't just hang out with movie stars, they'll come to our house for a real party. I'll make you the most famous hostess on this continent and Europe, sweetheart. You want jewels? You can have all you want. Cars? Furs? What else? Think of things the Van Burens have never had...they're yours. You just have to be patient with me. It's going to take time."

Kristen would throw her arms around his neck. "I love you, Michael. I'll be patient," she'd say and go down on him just the way he liked.

Kristen even amazed herself with her ability to suppress her true character so effectively to achieve her goals. But then, pursuing Michael at all was unnatural for her to some extent.

Kristen had been taught never to believe in dreamers. But Michael was different. Even though he was talented, determined and personable, Michael had one asset all other dreamers lacked. He had Phillip Van Buren's name and money backing him.

Kristen believed every single promise Michael had made to her. And she was determined he make good on them all.

22

October, 1980

Swirls of Venetian lace, seed pearls and crystals skimmed the hem and cathedral-length train of Kristen's handmade wedding gown. Three shoulder-length tiers of French-silk illusion cascaded from a rhinestone- and pearl-encrusted crown. From the back, she looked every inch the pedigreed princess New York society was expecting. From the front, Kristen looked like a Las Vegas showgirl. For once in her life, she had gotten her way.

Bent over in front of the mirrored wall of her all-white bedroom, Kristen positioned her voluptuous breasts in the shockingly low-cut sweetheart neckline. When she straightened, the four-carat-diamond pendant Michael had given her as her wedding gift sparkled between two suntanned swells of flesh.

Brutally critical of her appearance, she triple-checked the front slit of the gown, making certain the garters on her white stockings did not show. At first she'd hated the idea of wearing something old, borrowed and blue simply because it was the traditional thing to do, which, to her, always translated to boring.

Kristen couldn't help thinking that every wedding she'd ever attended had been dull and uninteresting. Every one of her parents' crowd spent half their lives trying to outdo one another. Weddings were an excuse for hiring the "in" florists, this year's pick of caterers and, of course, a band from a quarter of a century ago because it was "what we've always done."

God! How she hated hearing all that bullshit from her mother and father.

After four years of kowtowing to Michael's needs and sucking up to Phillip, she intended to brand her own initials into every aspect of her wedding. As far as she was concerned, she was going to marry only once and she wanted a wedding New York would never forget.

A knock at the door jolted Kristen out of her thoughts. "Come in," she said, turning to see her sister, Meghan, walk in wearing blue-jean cutoffs and one of Max's Grateful Dead T-shirts.

"Why aren't you dressed?" Kristen demanded with a scowl.

Meghan flopped into a bergère chair and haughtily regarded her sister. "Don't get pissy with me. I've got time. You're the one who's jumping the gun. We've got two hours before we have to leave for the church. Mother, Max and Karl went to the Waldorf to check on things." Meghan picked at her red nail polish as she spoke. "I told her not to bother—she's gonna hate it anyway." Meghan smiled smugly. "Won't she, Krissy?"

Kristen threw her a damning look, then smiled. "That's the idea."

"You know, there are advantages to being younger than you. All the way through high school everyone called me the baby and Karl's little sister, and all that shit. But now that I've graduated and will be going to Radcliffe where I won't fuck up like *you* did, I have to thank all of you for making every mistake in the world.

Mummy and Daddy think I can do no wrong. After all, what would be the point? You've done it all, right?"

Kristen had heard the same soliloquy from Meghan all summer and fall. "Look, when you get married, you do it your way. I'm doing it mine." Kristen picked up a tube of ruby red lipstick and applied a double-thick coat. She pursed her lips and then pouted seductively at herself in the mirror. Then she frowned. The dress wasn't daring enough. Bold wasn't enough, she wanted to look dangerous. She lifted her breasts another inch higher.

"Why don't you let the nipples show?" Meghan suggested.

"Not a bad idea, but if I did, Uncle Phillip would not give us the villa in Saint-Jean-Cap-Ferrat. He has a way of making his point, you know."

Meghan scrutinized her sister's tightly fitting gown. "Can you breathe in that thing?"

"Barely." Kristen fidgeted with the bodice and shoulder pads.

"Does Michael still think your breasts are natural?"

Kristen glared at Meghan. "Yes, and if he ever thinks otherwise I'll know you were the one who told."

Meghan held up her hands defensively. "No way! Mother says I can get mine done over Christmas while she and Daddy are on vacation. Just like she did for you. Father will never be the wiser."

Kristen lifted her bouquet of red roses and white stephanotis. The red of her lipstick and the color of the roses matched perfectly. Convincing her mother that bloodred was a fall color hadn't been as difficult as secretly booking Blondie to play at the reception. However, Kristen had talked her way through that one, too.

She was not having any formal pictures and poses of stupid things like cutting the cake, garter tossing or throwing bouquets. It was bad enough she had to bear up through a formal dinner. And how she was going to make it through the tortures of the receiving line, she didn't know.

"Mother is good about things like that...implants and nose jobs," Kristen said, "but sometimes she makes me nuts. Is she still mad about the Chippendale dancers at the bachelorette party?"

"Yeah, but only because Muffy Pennington told her mother and then the word got around."

"Know what I think? Mother is mad because she wasn't there!"

Meghan grinned mischievously as she hoisted herself off the chair. "I think you're right." She reached into her pocket. "I forgot to give you this." She pulled out a small piece of memo paper and handed it to Kristen. "Guess today is your lucky day. I intercepted that call before anyone else did."

"Who...?" Kristen unfolded the paper.

"I don't think I ever heard you talk about a Greg. He wouldn't give his last name. Just said he heard you were getting married and wanted to wish you well."

When her sister simply gaped at the message, Meghan jumped up and headed for the door. "I guess I'd better get dressed."

Kristen waited until Meghan left to pick up the bedside phone. Her fingers could barely dial Greg's number. She knew she was taking a chance calling him, but in four years she hadn't heard from him or seen him. Not since the bicentennial weekend when he'd shown up at Phillip's party.

What a shock that was! Karl still denies ever having invited him! I don't even remember his girlfriend's name—she van-

ished so quickly. What a fool I was, throwing myself at him.
Just thinking about that night made her cheeks flame.

However, it had been Greg who called her three days
later. He'd told her he had to see her. At least she could
draw comfort from the fact that he'd been just as turned
on as she. Greg had arranged to take his girlfriend to a
modeling studio or some shit, and while she did her
thing, he "did" Kristen.

They'd met at the Plaza and screwed for five hours
straight. No lunch break, no intermission, nothing but a
sex marathon. This time, he'd done everything she
asked and she'd wanted a lot. He left when the call came
from his club that his girlfriend was ready to be picked
up. Greg explained to Kristen that the telephone-service
personnel at the club were well trained in forwarding
calls from wives and girlfriends in a most discriminating
manner.

Insights into the secrets of the male world rarely fell
into one's lap. Kristen tucked this piece of information
away, knowing it could prove quite useful someday. She
couldn't imagine Michael using undercover tactics; he
was too much in love with her. That would always be
her trump card.

"Hello, Kristen," Greg said in a sexy voice.

"How did you know it was me?"

"I always know when it's time for us to connect," he
replied with a half-menacing, half-needy tone that never
failed to send shivers up her spine.

"You're wrong this time. I'm getting married in a few
hours."

"No! You're wrong! You got that? I know you better
than you know yourself and I can prove it."

"How?" She smiled smugly, knowing she held just as
much power over him as he held over her.

"I bet I could even describe what you're wearing."

"That's too easy. My wedding gown," she said lazily.

"But I'd bet it's not just any wedding gown." He paused and breathed seductively into the phone. "It's low-cut. Very low-cut, isn't it, Kristen? So low that your breasts practically fall out of it. You want every man in that church to know what he's passing up by not taking you. But more than that, you want to walk down that aisle pretending I'm there, sitting in a pew, watching you. Wanting to reach out and touch those beautiful breasts. Squeeze them really hard. Bite the nipples till you feel the pinch all the way down inside you."

Kristen closed her eyes as the fantasy invaded her mind. "You like doing that to me."

Greg continued, "It's also my guess that your dress has a slit up the side or in the front... Yeah, in the front. Maybe it's even cut high enough that at the right angle I could see your pussy. You're not wearing panties, are you, Kristen?"

"N-no. Just stockings and garters." She wet her lips with her tongue.

"Are you standing or lying down?"

"Standing."

"Then spread your legs apart, Kristen. Wide enough to open yourself to me. If I were there, I'd lick you, quick and light, then long and hard. Would you be wet, Kristen?"

"I...I..."

"Put your hand between your legs and feel it, Kristen. Tell me if you're wet," he said demandingly.

Kristen did not open her eyes, but did as he ordered. Her fingertips slid along the edge of her vulva. "Yes."

"Now rub yourself off for me."

"No!"

"Do it! Do it or I'll spank you for being a bad girl. You remember how you like me to turn you over my knee, don't you, Kristen? You have the prettiest ass I've ever seen, ever bitten. You like me to slap that round, soft flesh so it stings just before I slip my fingers down to your clit. You like it even better when I rub you and make you come. I like the way you push your pussy into my hand while you pull on your nipples. Tell me that's the way you like it best, don't you, Kristen?"

"Oh, God! I'm coming!" She was panting so fast she was afraid she would hyperventilate. White stars collided behind her eyelids. Perspiration covered her body. Her knees turned to water and she dropped to the floor. The palms of her hands were sweaty and she lost her grip on the telephone receiver. It fell to her lap. The mouthpiece curled over the opening of her skirt. Greg was closer to his wish than he realized, she thought to herself with a breathless chuckle.

She picked up the receiver. "Greg?"

"You did real good, baby. I don't want you ever to forget this day. I know my girl. And I also know this guy will never satisfy you. No one will except me. Don't forget that."

Greg hung up.

Kristen was light-headed and disoriented as she stood and cradled the receiver. Her mouth was dry. Sweat trickled down her forehead and cheeks, ruining her makeup.

Just then, Meghan knocked on the door and opened it, saying, "Ready to rock and roll?"

"Huh?" Kristen felt the room still spinning.

"The limo's here!"

Kristen checked her face in the mirror. "Just a touch of powder and I'll be down."

"Jesus! How can it take you so long? Does Michael realize you require hours of primping time?"

"Michael?" Kristen grabbed her powder brush and dusted her face.

"Yeah, you know, the groom."

"Don't be an ass. Michael is well aware of my habits. Besides, once I'm Mrs. Michael West, what else do I have to do but primp?" Kristen chirped as she picked up her bouquet and went to the door.

"Good point," Meghan agreed, and they both descended the staircase.

Standing on a chair behind his father, Michael struggled with the older man's bow tie. "I learned how to do this for myself, but not for anyone else."

Don watched in the mirror of the church dressing room while Michael completed the task. When Michael finished, he turned to Phillip. "Did he do it right?"

Phillip smiled. "Superbly. As he does everything."

Michael stepped down from the metal chair. "Don't say that, Phillip. I get nervous when you say things like that."

"It was a compliment," Phillip replied.

"Nobody is perfect. I've made my share of mistakes already."

Phillip stuck his forefinger straight in the air. "Ah, but Michael, your successes far exceed your failures. That's what I meant."

"Whew!" Michael theatrically wiped his forehead. When his fingertips came away filled with perspiration, he clasped both hands behind his back. He couldn't let Phillip know how nervous he was about marrying Kristen.

From what he'd observed over his four years as Phillip's protégé, "adopted son" or "little brother," Michael had drawn the conclusion that Kristen was his mentor's favorite niece.

Phillip often complained about Karl and Max, pointing out to Bartholomew in Michael's presence that buying a child's way through college would do more harm than good. Phillip had tried to keep both Karl and Max on the family payroll, but the task was proving to be a full-time job. Because neither of his nephews seemed capable of completing any job through to the end, Phillip was continually redefining their job profiles. Just last week, Phillip had confided to Michael that he was going to tell both boys either to go out on their own and learn about law and business the hard way, or they would be demoted to errand boys.

Phillip had never complained about Kristen. He'd always complimented her on her exacting choice of attire for whatever social engagement they attended. He'd mentioned more than once that she was an expert organizer and if either Karl or Max had such talent, he could at least hire them as clerks.

"Kristen is the only one in that family to show any promise of maturing into an adult," Phillip had stated one afternoon after yet another confrontation with Max. "Frankly, I think Bart owes you a debt of gratitude. If it hadn't been for you, Michael, Kristen would probably still be wild and headstrong."

"Wild? She's always been a perfect lady with me," he'd said. *Except when we're making love. Sometimes she can get really carried away.*

"Perhaps that's not the right word. *Restless* is the word I'm looking for. All youth is restless."

"So am I, sir. My restlessness brought me to New York."

Phillip had slapped him on the back good-naturedly. "Thank God!"

Michael loved Phillip as much as he loved his own father. And he loved both of them more than himself. He could never do anything to upset or disappoint Phillip.

He certainly could never reveal his grave misgivings about Kristen.

Perhaps it would have helped matters if Michael could pinpoint the problem, but he couldn't. Kristen was beautiful, well-mannered and confident, operating in both the social and business worlds with cool assurance and ease. She was never intimidated by White House politicians or billionaire businessmen. She had a way of making his investment clients, some of whom were among the most influential people in the world, fall in love with her.

Kristen went out of her way to make him comfortable and happy. He knew there were times when she'd wanted to visit her friends, and yet, she'd chosen to be with him.

But something was not right between them.

Because his nagging fears went back to the first autumn he'd come to New York, Michael could not attribute his misgivings to prewedding jitters.

Lying in the dark on those nights when he couldn't sleep, sometimes with Kristen by his side, Michael felt an emptiness he could not explain.

Though he had many new friends in New York now, and Kristen, Phillip and his father as family, he felt oddly alone. The very worst was when he was with a group of friends, Kristen at his side. He would be struck with a stinging loneliness. Sometimes, it took days to shake his bad mood.

As crazy as it sounded even to him, it was as if there

was someone waiting for him. Someone who truly needed him. Someone who understood him even better than he did. Someone...who smelled like Southern night jasmine and tea rose.

Phillip watched Michael as he fussed affectionately with Don's tuxedo, boutonniere and bow tie.

How easily they talk to each other, finishing each other's sentences. It's as if they were one mind with two mouths. How I wish my relationship with Michael was so simple...and direct.

Unfortunately, Phillip had discovered that there were certain subjects he could never bring up. Kristen topped the list.

If he were honest with himself, he could discuss just about anything with Michael, but he didn't dare reveal his true feelings about Kristen.

Michael was so smitten with Kristen when they first met, Phillip was afraid he'd run off and marry her before he finished his schooling. Thank God Phillip had Don's support in preaching the importance of postponing marriage until the diplomas were secure.

During the roughest times for the young couple, when Michael had stubbornly decided to double up on his courses, Phillip thought Kristen would surely dump him for one of her more fun-loving friends. He supposed he should have given her credit for sticking it out with Michael. But something in the back of his mind warned him that she was only biding her time.

Kristen had always been wild, wandering around Manhattan till dawn, giving her parents one riveting dose of grief after another. Before she was eighteen, she'd smashed three family cars. Gratefully, no one had been hurt in any of the collisions, including Kristen, who'd been too stoned or drunk to be injured.

Phillip had heard stories from Bart about the reckless boys she'd dated. The long-haired biker with a prison record had made Phillip's nerves jangle. Kristen had met a football player for the Giants at a disco and, fortunately, Bart had caught them just as they drove up to the house. Phillip had suggested sending Kristen to a boarding school. However, he and Bart knew that restraint would only challenge Kristen to rebel even more.

Phillip never understood Kristen's motivation for rebellion. Sometimes he wondered if the problem with Kristen was nothing more than boredom.

If that was so, Michael's life with Kristen could be more difficult than he'd bargained for. At the same time, admittedly, Kristen had shown signs of maturing. Phillip couldn't put a name to his unease, but it was there all the same. The real devil of it was that he loved Michael too much to disturb his happiness.

Just then the minister came into the room. "Well, Michael, the bride has arrived and we're ready if you are."

Michael looked at his father, who winked at him. "Ready as I'll ever be," he said happily.

Michael smiled at Phillip. "I'm ready. How about you?"

Phillip chuckled and moved toward Don, who was to be the best man. "It's your wedding, Michael. This time, I'm following you."

Michael feigned a surprised look. "Why, Phillip, I thought you always followed me."

The three men burst into hearty laughter.

23

Darien, Connecticut
February, 1981

"I can't believe you bought the house without saying a word to me," Susannah said, struggling to keep her anger under control. She held her gloved hands beneath the folds of her new camel-colored cashmere coat, keeping them warm as she and Greg drove out of Manhattan.

"I don't know how else to explain it to you," he said with exasperation. "Ron Prescott's client dropped dead last week. Handling the estate was a breeze, and the daughter wanted the house sold as quickly as possible."

"But I still say I should have been shown a photograph. I should have had some input into this decision."

Greg shook his head. "What you fail to realize is that properties in Darien hardly ever enter the regular housing market. If word about this house got out, I'd have had to pay twice what I did. It was the steal of the century."

"That's another thing. Why didn't this woman wait, put it on the market and make more money?"

Greg rolled his eyes as he looked at Susannah with that "How can you be so stupid?" look she was discovering he used too often with her. "Darien people care about what kind of residents they have. They would never sell to just anyone. Only because I'm a Walton did I have sway with her."

"Sounds rather snobbish to me." Susannah sighed.

Greg laughed so loudly Susannah nearly jumped. "My dear! Darienites wrote the book on snobbery."

She was aghast. "Then what are we doing buying a house there?"

"Because those so-called 'snobs' are going to be my clients someday."

She could hardly believe what she was hearing. "This was a business decision."

"Now you've got the picture," he replied with satisfaction.

Ever since their wedding in Indianapolis, Susannah had watched her dreams disintegrate one by one. Nine months of living in the same house with Bettye had made Susannah feel claustrophobic, inferior and as useless and unwanted as a cockroach. All of which she believed was Bettye's intent.

Though the Walton women did not perch themselves outside Greg's bedroom door, they hovered over Susannah wherever she went. Susannah thought it would have saved all of them a great deal of energy if they'd simply installed security cameras to videotape her activities. For a long time she wasn't certain if they thought she was planning to steal the family silver or having an affair with Marty, the gardener and sometimes chauffeur.

It didn't take Susannah long to discover that Bettye thought her a total country bumpkin and intended to "make her over."

"Society in Indiana is not in the same league as that in New York."

"I'm not familiar with either," Susannah had replied.

"That's obvious," Bettye had answered glacially.

Bettye's shopping foray into the city on the pretext of outfitting Susannah in proper winter attire had never meant to be a friendly gesture. From the outset, when Susannah had said she'd never shopped at Barney's or Henri Bendel's, Bettye was on a tear.

If Susannah showed even the slightest indication that she liked a particular coat or dress, Bettye chided her just loud enough for the saleswomen to overhear. She wouldn't allow Susannah to buy the tasteful, though not-so-extravagant clothes she liked, but rather insisted on items Susannah knew were dreadfully overpriced.

Other times, Bettye would take a saleswoman aside and explain to her that Susannah was from the Midwest, and she required a great deal of tutelage and direction. There was nothing Susannah could do or say in her own defense. If she was paying for the clothes herself, she would have had a bargaining chip. As it was, everything was charged to Greg's account. Susannah's only retaliation was to take the clothes home, keep the receipts and return them at a later date. Beating Bettye at her own game would be sweet revenge, she thought.

As they drove past bare trees frosted with a thick coat of snow, Susannah had to admit that, all things considered, she probably shouldn't be angry with Greg about the house. Once they moved, Bettye would have little say in her life any longer.

It's just that I'd been dreaming about how it would be, buying our first house together. There's only one "first time." I feel...cheated!

Lost in thought, Susannah did not realize they'd turned off the Connecticut Turnpike and were driving down a beautiful tree-lined street of traditional brick and wood homes. A sparkling mantle of fresh snow made the scene look like a Christmas card.

"Let's see...2012. Where the heck..."

Driving slowly, Greg checked the brass numerals on mailboxes.

"You mean the house is near here?" Susannah came to attention as her eyes quickly moved from one fairy-tale house to another.

"It's on this street!"

"Oh, my God!" Susannah's hands flew to her face. "I know what houses cost on Long Island. If it's here, it must have cost a fortune!" Butterflies fluttered in her stomach as she thought of mortgages and taxes.

"That," Greg replied with a bright smile as he turned the car into the driveway at 2012 Whitman Court, "depends on what you mean by a 'fortune.'"

Frozen to her seat, Susannah could do nothing but stare at the two-story redbrick colonial building. Four white Ionic columns soared to the top of the roof on either side of the front door. The house was trimmed in white and Williamsburg blue. Though the plantings were covered in snow, they were tall and thick, making the porch appear to be guarded by marshmallow men.

Greg opened the door and helped her out of the car. "Well, aren't you going to say anything?"

"It's...like a dream come true!" She threw her arms around his neck and kissed his cheek.

Greg took her hand. "Come on. I want to see the interior," he said as they raced through the snow and up the steps to the front door. He fumbled in his coat pocket for the key.

"It looks as if it was just painted," Susannah remarked.

"It was. Just before the holidays, as I understand it. I don't much care for the blue. We can change it later."

"Blue is my favorite color. I wouldn't change a thing," she gushed happily.

Greg kissed her lightly. "I suppose this is a good time to tell you that, based on the pictures I saw, there will be some work required inside."

"What kind of work?"

He opened the door and pushed it wide. The winter-afternoon sun flooded through the opening, illuminating the worn dark walnut floors, the hideously wallpapered entry and the garish lighting fixtures in the dining room.

Susannah swallowed her former excitement as she watched Greg's frown deepen.

The carpeting in the living room was the ugliest celery green Susannah had ever seen. Even her mother had gotten rid of carpets before they were worn this thin. Why, she could see the backing through the remaining thin strands of wool pile. The kitchen was an even worse disaster. But Susannah didn't say a word. She could tell by the way Greg was devouring his bottom lip that he was not happy.

The forty-year-old gold-and-white-speckled Formica countertops reminded her of a drugstore soda fountain. The walls were papered with brilliantly colored tropical birds so lifelike, Susannah kept wanting to put her arms over her face in self-defense. Spanning the length and width of the kitchen, breakfast room, back hall, laundry and mudroom was canary yellow linoleum still bearing so many black heel marks it looked like a giant tiger skin.

The upstairs wasn't much better, she thought as she caught her high heel on the threadbare carpet in the hall.

Four bedrooms and two baths all needed redecorating.

"I hope the plumbing is good," Susannah said.

Greg ground his jaw angrily. "Jesus Christ! Houses like this are not purchased because of plumbing or lighting or whether the appliances work or not. It's the location, Susannah. Location! It means everything in real estate."

Stalking out of the master bedroom, Greg rushed down the stairs and down another flight of stairs to the basement.

Susannah's shoulders slumped as she crossed the room and went to the undraped window seat. Lacy wisps of frost edged the corners of the small windowpanes. The huge backyard was lined with carefully landscaped flower beds. Huge shade trees held the promise of respite from the hot summer sun. Smaller trees at the far end of the yard looked like apple, cherry and pear trees. A magnificent stone fountain and birdbath sat amidst a cluster of tall oaks, where a matching stone bench faced east.

Straight below, the snow had begun melting on the brick terrace, which was ringed with raised brick planters. To the right was a custom-built redbrick barbecue pit.

Susannah couldn't help thinking that for all their bad taste with the interior decor, the former owners had created paradise in their own backyard.

Susannah smiled to herself as she continued investigating the bedrooms.

There's a lot of love in this old house. Someday, my babies will fill these rooms, and they'll play in the pretty yard. Why, I can almost hear their laughter.

Filled once more with her earlier excitement, she raced down the stairs. "Greg! Where did you go?"

"I'm here," he replied, dusting off his hands and closing the basement door. "The plumbing's fine." He sighed as if in relief.

"I love it, Greg. Every inch of it!" She threw her arms around his neck.

He chuckled. "Mother was right, you have no sense of style."

Ordinarily, Susannah would have taken offense at his comment, but not today. Today she was planning her future. Their future and the future of her children. She wasn't about to let Bettye Banning Walton destroy her happiness ever again.

24

Moving into her new home posed less of a problem for Susannah than it did for Greg. Other than her clothes and a few personal items, she possessed no furniture and few keepsakes beyond the seashells she'd collected in Fort Lauderdale when she and Greg had met.

Carefully placing the shells on her closet shelf next to her high-school yearbook and a tattered scrapbook she'd made in grade school, Susannah was imbued with the sensation that these articles belonged to someone else.

It seemed so long ago, her carelessly planned Florida trip. How young she'd been! How silly and foolish she'd been to think a man could walk out of her dreams and into her life.

Thank God I'm over all that...

"Susannah!" Greg yelled up the stairs. "The movers are here with the furniture."

Great! I can't wait to see what Bettye's been up to this time, she thought sarcastically. "I'll be right down," she called back to him.

She raced down the stairs in time to see the movers tracking dirty snow and slush across the ugly carpets. "Good thing I insisted we wait a while before recarpeting, huh?" she pointed out to Greg.

She and Bettye had battled for two weeks over the issue. Bettye had told Greg he'd regret not following her advice when *he* had to move the furniture after the new carpet was installed. Greg had sided with Susannah. But to keep the peace, they'd both agreed to take the ugly Italianate–style table, chairs and sofa from Bettye's attic.

Susannah knew that the friction in the Walton mansion over Greg's moving into his own home went much deeper than the issue of carpets.

Bettye wanted them to delay moving in until every last bit of redecorating was finished. Susannah wanted to pick every color, fabric and flooring material by herself over several years, which would save money and allow the house to evolve.

Bettye shut her ears to Susannah's wants and surreptitiously hired Mr. Chalmers, an expensive designer who was well known for his work on glitzy Miami homes and Manhattan penthouses. Greg had given his mother a key to the house for emergencies. She in turn handed the key to Mr. Chalmers. He went to the house, took measurements and made an extensive proposal.

Triumphantly, Bettye showed the sketches, fabric swatches and cost sheet to Susannah and Greg. Diplomatically, Greg remained silent. Leveling shocked eyes on the suggested green-marble floors with cherry-wood inlays, white- and gold-veined marble bathrooms with gold swan-shaped faucets, mirrored fireplace facades and contemporary wall hangings, Susannah could not hold her temper.

"Why didn't you ask me what kind of decor I wanted?"

Bettye looked down her nose at Susannah. "Mr. Chalmers is the best. He knows what all the young people want."

"Not this young person, he doesn't!" Susannah's

cheeks turned beet red. Greg put his hand on her arm. "I don't need restraining," she said, glowering at him.

"Fine," he said sharply, letting her know he didn't sanction her tact.

Bundling up her courage, she continued, "I want a cozy home, one filled with beautiful English antiques and big overstuffed chairs and sofas that can swallow me up. I adore English cabbage-rose chintz and garden-print cottons. I want my home to look like spring in the middle of winter. I like warm fires glowing in fireplaces surrounded by rich mahogany polished with beeswax, like the antebellum houses in the Old South. More than anything, I want it to be a haven for Greg after working in the city. The landscaping is magnificent and I'm sure I'll find all sorts of wonderful surprises in the spring and summer when everything comes to life. There are ways to bring that beauty indoors and I can do it."

Listening with a condescending ear, Bettye waited until Susannah was completely finished. "Fine," she said flatly as she picked up Mr. Chalmers's sketches. "No harm done. It was just an idea." She tromped out of the room like a general going off to the biggest battle of his military career.

That was too easy and if I know Bettye, I haven't heard the last of this.

Fortunately, it was only a matter of days before Susannah would no longer be Bettye's easy target. Once she was in Darien, life would be so much easier.

"Where do you want this one, lady?" the mover said, breaking into Susannah's reverie.

"Sorry," she replied, regarding a badly gilded cheap imitation Louis XIV dresser. "Upstairs. The guest room."

"Which one is that?"

"The last door on the left."

Greg slapped his forehead. "I swear to you, I've never seen this...this..."

Susannah nodded. "Your mother told me that Nell bought it all in a single afternoon."

"I remember now. It was the last of my great-cousin's bids for independence. She was forever running back to the city."

Who could blame the old woman?

"As bad as all this looks—" he watched askance as the second pair of movers brought in an Italian Renaissance–style distressed pecan-wood dining table "—it's free and I don't have the cash to redecorate and buy new furnishings."

"It's all right," she replied reassuringly. "I'm resourceful. Our home will be everything we ever dreamed."

Greg put his arm around her shoulder. "Sure it will, honey."

Flowering quince and crocus announced the first day of April and the arrival of her first neighbor.

"Hi, I'm Louise Sanders Christian," said the thirtyish, chestnut-haired woman when Susannah answered the front doorbell's ring. She was dressed in a wool pleated skirt with matching boxy jacket and white pearls.

In contrast, Susannah wore paint-splattered jeans, one of Greg's old Harvard T-shirts and not a lick of makeup. Her voice cracked self-consciously as she answered, "I'm Susannah."

The woman stared blankly at her as if waiting for Susannah to finish. "I'm Beatrice Wallington Sanders's daughter."

Susannah returned a blank look.

"My mother is fast friends with your mother-in-law, Bettye..."

"...Banning Walton." Susannah nodded as she completed the sentence for her. She put out her hand. "I'm pleased to meet you. Won't you come in?"

Louise followed Susannah over a minefield of paint cans, rollers, steamers and wallpaper scrapers. "Looks like I've caught you in the thick of things," she said, chuckling, but making no move to leave.

Shrugging, Susannah replied, "It's okay. I'll be doing this for quite some time, I'm sure."

"You can't mean you're doing the work yourself?" Louise gasped with the kind of horrified eyes Susannah saved for Stephen King movies.

"I enjoy it."

Louise fluttered her lips the way elderly Nell did, making Susannah wonder if learning such gestures was part of the initiation into the clique. "Nonsense. Is your husband doing badly?"

"I beg your pardon?"

"In his practice, I mean."

"I don't see how that is any of your business..." Susannah's temper flared hot enough to brand the newly laid rich mahogany floors.

Louise smiled conciliatorily. "Good heavens, we're not only neighbors, we're practically kin. My mother and your mother-in-law grew up together. I don't actually know Bettye like Mother does." She scrunched her nose. "In fact, I've only seen her twice in my life!" She chuckled merrily as if she'd told a witty joke.

Susannah wasn't laughing. She could feel Bettye's hand creeping into her life to stir up trouble. Clouds of suspicion gathered in her head as she let Louise continue.

"However, we keep to our own and we never, ever discuss family business outside of the circle."

"I see," Susannah replied flatly, but offered no other information.

Oblivious to Susannah's stony attitude, Louise blithely carried on. "Mother tells me she played bridge with Bettye just last week. That was how I came to know you were here. I've been suffocating out here with everyone so much older than I. It must be hard on you, being as young as you are. How old..."

"Twenty-four."

Louise smiled sheepishly as she placed her hand on her cheek. "I'm so embarrassed. I had no idea you were *that* young. I apologize for bringing up the *finances.*" She said the last word in a conspiratorial tone.

"It's okay."

"You won't tell Mother, will you? Or Bettye? God! But they'd make an awful row about my manners."

"Believe me, I'll never breathe a word to Bettye."

"I can count on you then?"

Looking like a child in need of assurance, Louise displayed an undercurrent of insecurity that fascinated Susannah. Yet, there was no doubting her neighbor had been assigned as a one-woman search-and-destroy team. "Bettye doesn't approve of me, my styles or tastes. We have little to discuss."

"Funny you should mention that." Louise switched personalities from that of a child back to a spy. "Mother told me Bettye has said as much to everyone at bridge."

Big deal. So, how many is that? Four old women with nothing better to do? Susannah's sarcastic thoughts helped her brush aside a sudden stab of hurt.

"Mother says that you refused Bettye's gift of having Mr. Chalmers redesign your house."

"She was correct."

"God! That took nerve! I've never known anyone to pass him up. I've got friends who tell me his waiting list is so long, they'll be forty, even older, before he can get to them."

"I didn't like his work. Everything was too staged, too chic. He doesn't decorate homes, he designs homes to look like hotel lobbies."

"What's the matter with that? It's the latest thing. Everyone has oodles of money now. I get so tired of the same old thing. Here I am thirty years old and my house looks just like my mother's. I'd love to get rid of everything and start all over. I adore making color decisions, picking out new furniture, having workers coming and going. A project like that would fill up my time."

"Would your husband let you do something like that?"

"Arnold?" She shrugged. "How would I know?"

God! Is the man dead? Did he abandon her? Nice going, Susannah. You've really put your foot in it this time.

Louise's thoughts seemed to sweep out the window and then whip back in. "Does your husband spend the night in the city?"

"Heavens no! Why would he do that? His home is here."

Louise looked away from Susannah. "No reason. It just seems that they all start spending more time in the city after a while. The first time, he tells you the traffic's bad and he's going to wait it out with a friend from the office. He comes home at ten instead of seven or eight. Then he starts building a 'better future' for the both of you. He stays till after midnight, but he still comes home. Then after a year or two of that, he spends a night every now and then. Not often. Just once every few months. Then he stays overnight once a month. Then he makes enough money to rent a small condo or apartment. You never see the place, although he tells you it's badly furnished and only has a twin bed. Meaning there's only room for one. He tells you he's doing all this so he can get ahead."

Louise let out a sudden deep breath, then broke into high-pitched laughter. "Ha! The worst part is that all the wives in Darien are going through the same thing. They think I'm being melodramatic and that I'm in a depression. They want me to be like them, taking Valium and looking the other way. But I c-can't. I happen to love my husband." Quickly, she hugged herself and looked away to hide her tears.

Sympathy filled Susannah's heart for this lonely young woman. "What's her name?"

"I don't know."

Susannah put her arm around Louise and led her to the newly carpeted stairs. They sat on the same step while Susannah rubbed her neighbor's hand. "Do you want to know?"

"Yes. No! I just want things the way they used to be," Louise replied in an achingly sad whisper.

"When was that?"

The practiced facade evaporated from Louise's eyes. "I don't remember. Maybe it's always been this way."

"Maybe you should think about that," Susannah suggested. "Maybe you'll find out he doesn't deserve you."

Louise dabbed her runny nose with her cotton gloves. "How old did you say you were?"

They laughed then and hugged each other.

"Would it be all right if I came to visit from time to time?" Louise asked timidly.

Susannah smiled. "Anytime you like, but just remember, I have a lot of work to do and I won't always be able to stop what I'm doing. You could help me if you want."

"Me?" Louise shook her head furiously. "I couldn't...I don't know how."

"I could teach you."

"You'd do that for me?" Louise's surprise sprang to her face.

"Of course. Isn't that what neighbors...friends are for?"

"I don't know, Susannah. You're the first friend I've ever had."

Susannah channeled her sympathy for Louise into helping her learn how to paint, sew drapes, hang wallpaper, tape and float drywall and use an electric drill to tighten banister railings.

Susannah couldn't pretend to know what it was like to walk in Louise's shoes and didn't think she ever would. That is, until the night three weeks after Louise's confession when Greg called Susannah to inform her that his business meeting would run past midnight and that he'd have to stay over at the Plaza.

25

It never failed to give Michael a thrill to walk through the entrance of the turn-of-the-century Trinity Building at 111 Broadway. Unlike the way he felt about the merciless towers of glass and steel along Wall Street, Michael almost believed he could feel the spirits of J. P. Morgan and Cornelius Vanderbilt blustering through this building's Gothic halls.

Stories about the old world of banking tycoons and railroad titans were his daily inspiration. Michael didn't believe in myths or fairy tales. Real people accomplishing superhuman feats in their lifetimes were his role models. Those were the individuals who could change the shape of the future. Michael knew he was no more or no less than these people. What he wanted was a chance to prove his worth to the world.

Drawing energy from his proximity to Wall Street, Michael pitted his wits daily against the best of the best in the financial world. He always came out smelling like roses.

By the summer of 1981, he concluded a deal with a small family-owned paint company whose elderly owner had invented a coloration technique for latex paint that resulted in deep, rich tones only presently available in oil-based paints. Complete with the mirror gloss of enamel, the new paints would set the design and construction industry on its behind, Michael was certain of it. Personally visiting every major American paint manufacturer and not getting the results he wanted, he sidestepped into a related field and convinced Dunne Chemical Corporation to pay a hundred million dollars for the German technology.

The *Wall Street Journal* lambasted his idea, calling him "Dunne's Dunce." They said the Germans had taken the Americans for a ride. They predicted Michael's demise.

The design industry tested the first samples of paint and fell blissfully in love with Michael, touting his vision in every decorating magazine in the country. Those same magazines sold weekly and monthly to millions of home owners and builders alike. The clamoring for the paint began in New York City and was heard across the continent.

Six months after the paint was in production and distribution, four new manufacturing plants were opened to meet production demands.

While the rest of the investment world was high on the successful launch of the *Columbia* space shuttle, predicting routine flights every two weeks and costs that would far exceed the ten billion already spent on the program, Michael jotted down the names of the leading NASA scientists. He watched newspapers and aeronautics magazines for blips about up-and-coming Einsteins. Maybe he didn't need them today or even five years from now, but someday he might. The future was coming fast and he wanted to be ready.

With each deal he closed, Michael's confidence grew. So did his need to build an even greater financial base for himself.

Someday I'll own my own corporations. I won't need in-

terim financing or funding from Banker's Trust. I'll fund the deals myself. I'll have total control.

He was twenty-four years old and already a millionaire. The first lesson Michael had learned in the world of high finance was that a million dollars was chicken feed. He felt no more secure today than he had when he'd left Fort Walton Beach.

Other days, when his clients hailed him with accolades and Phillip smiled quietly but proudly at Michael's newest idea, he felt invincible. It was a drug more heady than cocaine. He thought nothing could bring him down.

"For the last time, Michael, I don't want to go to the Caymans!" Kristen bellowed angrily over the sound of the Jacuzzi. She turned her hip into the jet and let it pound the sore muscle she'd acquired in aerobics class.

"Why not?" he asked, crossing the pink marble floor from his dressing room to her bathroom.

"I have too much work to do here."

"You can forget the house for a week. You're just as tense as I am, living in the middle of all this construction."

"It was your idea to move in right away. I told you this place needed more than just a new coat of paint. But oh, no. You thought we'd save money. You believed the contractor when he said it would only take three months."

"And it's costing him every nickel of his profit every day he's late. Thanks to the way I negotiated the contract."

"Who cares, Michael? The point is, this is New York. These workers have lists with all our names on them and they purposely fuck up our houses just because we're wealthy."

Michael turned to the mirror and continued to tie his Italian silk tie. "Who told you that?"

"My mother," she replied haughtily. "Ask anybody. They'll tell you."

Michael had asked and Kristen was right. From the day they moved in, it had taken over a month to get extra phone lines installed. The electrician had charged Michael double the going rate and when Michael called the guy on it, he'd laughed in Michael's face and told him that was the rate for people on Fifth Avenue. Michael found a cheaper electrician, but his work was lousy.

Kristen lathered a loofah sponge and scoured her leg. "Mr. Chalmers specifically requested I sit in on the consultation with the floor people. The blue marble for the entrance is critical to the rest of the house, Michael. Critical!"

He turned to face her. "All I know is that I'm paying this guy a fortune for his expertise. So why can't we go away and let him work his magic?"

Suddenly he grinned mischievously as she raised her other leg high in the air. He knelt on the second of the four plushly carpeted white steps that led up to the raised Jacuzzi. "Keep that up and I'll call in sick."

Kristen's eyes narrowed. "Like hell you will."

"Hey! What's that supposed to mean?" He leaned toward her with his lips pursed for a kiss.

She granted him a brush of her lips. "I know you, Michael. You wouldn't miss your one o'clock with that nerd from California."

"Bill is his name, dear. And unfortunately, you're

right." He backed down the steps. "I can't play hooky today."

"I know," she said quietly.

He looked at his watch. "I'm late! And by the way, I'm serious about the Caymans."

"Michael, *why* do we have to go now?"

He stuck his arms through his suit-coat sleeves. "I've got a lead on a fishing yacht. It's a hell of a bargain and it'll be gone by next weekend. I've got to go now."

She folded her arms on the edge of the tub and rested her chin on them. "Michael, darling. I don't know much about fishing boats, but I do know that Miami is the only place to buy any kind of boat."

"This is a Bertram. The best. It's not brokered through a dealer. This is a private transaction."

"What's that supposed to mean?"

"The guy who owns the Bertram was in Grand Cayman while his wife was in New York cleaning out their bank accounts and the house. *She* canceled all the credit cards. Seems all the money was hers. So basically he has no way home. He's gotta sell the boat."

"Hell hath no fury," Kristen said thoughtfully. "Why do you think his wife was so angry?"

Michael smoothed his hair with his hand. "Probably because she found out he was in the islands with his girlfriend," he said coolly.

"That's a good reason! I'd murder you if I caught you with someone else!" she said sharply.

Michael smiled as his eyes watched her round bottom bob up and down in the water. "Don't worry. All I want is you...in the islands with me," he reiterated.

"Michael." She sighed sweetly but with frustration. "What do I have to say that will convince you otherwise? I don't *want* to look at an old smelly boat. The whole thing sounds boring. I would be of absolutely no use to you whatsoever. You go buy your toy. I'll take care of more important things here."

Glancing at his watch again, Michael knew he couldn't waste another second. *Funny, I thought being to-gether was the most important thing to us.*

"Okay." He rushed out of the mirrored bathroom. "Don't forget we're going to the Met with the Hoskins, then late supper at Lutece."

"Yes, Michael. I won't forget," she replied.

Kristen turned off the jets of the Jacuzzi and stood up. Rivulets of water slaked down her shoulders onto her breasts and fell off the high peaks of her nipples. From every angle in the room, the mirrors reflected her perfection.

Placing her hands on her breasts, she caressed them like a lover. No matter how coldly she observed her body, she was perpetually amazed at its lightning-quick response to proper stimulation. She watched as her breasts swelled, her nipples hardened and a passionate red flush covered her skin from head to toe. Almost involuntarily, she parted her legs and made love to herself. The bathwater mingled with her juices as she felt herself swell. Her breath came in deep, heavy pants at first. The more she pinched her nipples and slid her hand back and forth, the more ragged her breathing became.

The pleasure was so intense she had to hold herself up against the mirrored wall. The second climax was even greater than the first. She wondered if she could sustain her ecstasy while going across the room to the closet where she'd hidden her vibrator. Coming for the third time rendered her immobile. Her legs felt as if they'd completely atrophied. She would use the vibrator again some other time.

She lay down on the bath mat and continued manipulating herself to prove this time she could do it. She could go all the way. But after three more climaxes, she'd hit her limit.

"Shit!" She glared at her reflection. "What the fuck is the matter with you, Kristen?"

Try as she might, she'd never been able to extract more than a half-dozen climaxes out of herself.

Michael only does half as well.

But then, she'd never told Michael how she really liked it. She'd never let herself get so carried away with him that she lost control. She could only surrender to one man.

It was odd how she could go months, even years, and never think about him. Never want him. Then, like a thunderbolt, her need for him was killing. She was like an addict too long without a hit.

Now that he'd invaded her psyche again, she knew she wouldn't be able to sleep or eat until he satisfied her. Trying to see him could prove tricky, even dangerous, she thought as she wrapped an Egyptian-cotton robe around herself. Just the soft press of the fabric against her breasts made her insides ache.

This is worse than the last time! Get a grip, girl!

The more she chastised herself, the more she thought about the things she wanted to do to him this time. It had been far, far too long since she'd had a fix.

She didn't care what the risk, she had to have him. But she couldn't allow Michael to have the first inkling about her dark side. Michael was the kind of man who believed in fidelity and that kept him from believing any wife of any man would ever have an affair. It was another ace to add to her hand.

Gazing at her beautiful reflection, she suddenly realized she'd already given herself the perfect alibi. She breezed into Michael's walk-in closet and began flipping through his clothes.

"Too old, too dark, too heavy. None of this will do for my darling's trip to the islands. Of course, shopping for him will require great sacrifices on my part. Let's see, I have to reschedule my manicure. Oh! And lunch with Meghan, but it'll be worth it."

Humming to herself as she dressed for the day, Kristen was confident all she need do was wait until Michael was safely out of town and then she'd call him.

It had been a long time. He would come. Over and over...

26

New York City
September 10, 1981

Kristen drove Michael's car at breakneck speed out to Long Island. Anxiously, she bit her nails between curses.

"Goddammit! Get the fuck out of my way!" She raced around a red BMW, cutting off the approaching Buick she saw in the rearview mirror. "Son of a bitch," she hissed as she wove from one lane to the other.

This just isn't my day.

She stepped on the gas. Her mother was waiting for her.

Frances Sargent Van Buren had never known a day in her life when her blond hair wasn't perfectly colored and coiffed, her clothes precisely pressed and her demeanor calm. Marking her mental notebook with today's date, she vowed to always remember the day that her world, her life as she'd known it, had gone haywire and it was all Kristen's fault.

What bothered her the most was that she'd had no control over these events. It was one thing when Bart stupidly lost money in the stock market or one of the boys had been caught speeding. Such things were inconveniences. Facing her fiftieth birthday this year had been the most traumatic occurrence she'd had to endure. *But this…*

In the last hour she'd had to summon her personal maid twice to help with her hair and then to find her jar of cold cream, which she swore should have been in her makeup drawer.

Sitting on a vanilla-colored damask stool at her Louis XVI vanity table, Frances looked down at the outstretched hand holding the cold-cream jar. "What would I do without you, Hannah?"

"Waste time looking for things."

Frances shook her head. "No, I'd go insane. I know very well I left it on this table."

"But I put it back in the bathroom, like you always have me do when you finish undressing for the night."

Frances patted Hannah's liver-spotted hand. "You're an angel of mercy." She picked up her comb. "And I'll always remember that." *Just as I'll remember what Kristen has done to me.*

Hannah recombed Frances's thinning blond hair just the way Frances had instructed—teased on top to give the illusion of height and swirled softly around her face to cover her recent face-lift scars.

Frances glanced at the clock, then remembered a call she was to return. She half rose from the chair and then sat down when she realized she'd already made the call. Placing her hands on top of the vanity, she noticed she'd woven her fingers together so tightly her knuckles were white.

"Is something the matter, miss?" Hannah addressed Frances in the same manner she'd used since she'd gone to work for the Sargent family in 1931, the year Frances was born.

"No, Hannah. Everything is fine. I was…just a tad nervous about the scars. They seem awfully pink, don't they? I wonder if that's normal."

"I wouldn't know."

"I'll call the doctor again this morning," Frances lied, hoping to throw Hannah off-track.

Hannah lightly tapped Frances's shoulder with the comb. "There you are." Frances barely glanced at the mirror.

The screeching of tires braking in the circular driveway below stole Frances's full attention.

"You don't like the way I did your hair?" Hannah asked.

"Thank you, Hannah. It's just fine," Frances answered as she bolted from the stool.

Grabbing a Hermès silk scarf and placing it around her neck as she rushed out of the bedroom, Frances very uncharacteristically didn't bother to properly dismiss Hannah.

Kristen nearly flew in the front door. "Mother!" she called as she crossed the tortoiseshell-colored marble floor. "Mother!" she shouted again as she was about to mount the curved staircase.

"I'm right here, Kristen," Frances replied in a terse whisper. "Please, keep your voice down."

"Are you ready?"

"Yes," she replied stiffly, picking up a brown crocodile handbag from the needlepoint-covered chair next to the banister.

"I'll drive," Kristen said, glancing surreptitiously into the living and dining rooms. "Does anyone know I'm here?"

"Only Hannah. She saw the car from my bedroom window."

"Good. She'll never say anything."

Frances glared at her daughter. "That's what fifty years of loyalty means to you?"

"I just meant that we have to be careful," Kristen replied, holding the front door open for her mother.

They quickly got into the car.

"Did you bring the money?"

"Yes."

"In cash? Like he said?" Kristen started the engine and drove down the brick driveway.

Frances slammed her eyelids shut. "Yes! And for God's sake, don't speed. You know how nervous I get in fast cars. Sometimes I believe your brothers drive like maniacs just to upset me."

Kristen laughed as she turned into the street. "Of course they do, Mother. It's the only thing you react to."

"What a ridiculous thing to say," Frances retorted.

Kristen bit her thumbnail. "It is not. Think about it. Nothing ever bothers you. You're more than the epitome of serenity. You're...like a statue."

"I see nothing wrong with that. I was raised always to be a lady." Frances tugged on her navy linen skirt so that it covered the crest of her knees.

"Mother," Kristen said patronizingly, "in case you haven't noticed, the world is a tad different today. There's no such thing as black and white. For the first time, people have realized there's only gray. Life throws you a curve and you dodge, weave, maybe even hit the ball back, but you've gotta react!"

Frances touched her tongue to the top of her mouth to keep her jaws from angrily clamping shut. "And is that what you call this mess you're in? Reacting?"

"Shit! I knew you'd see it that way. Look! It happened. Okay! But I can't let one little mistake ruin my life."

"You call getting pregnant and not knowing who the father is a 'little mistake'? And watch your language."

"Sorry. Yeah, I do. It's a glitch. A situation requiring a solution, as Michael always says."

Frances glowered at her daughter. "You can ridicule me all you want, young lady, but I can tell you this...I've never gotten pregnant and needed or even considered an abortion." She couldn't control the increasing volume of her voice. "Perhaps if you'd paid more attention to what I was *trying* in vain to teach you, you might have learned how not to go to bed with someone who isn't your husband!" Frances had screamed out the last few words.

Kristen spoke after a few moments passed. "I don't know if this baby is Michael's or not. But I can't take the risk of it being born without *his* eyes, *his* ears and *his* nose. Men are so macho about shit, excuse me, like that. Michael and I have plenty of time to have a baby...if we decide that's what we want."

Confused, Frances said, "I thought Michael wanted children. I was certain he said as much last Christmas."

"Oh, Mother. Men get sentimental during the holidays. The truth of the matter is, he hasn't mentioned it since. You just watch, he'll probably say something again over the holidays this year and that will be the end of it."

"You really think so?"

"I know Michael. He's hell-bent on becoming the youngest billionaire in history. He hasn't got time for children any more than I have."

Fifty years of perpetually holding her tongue, never commenting on volatile issues and absolutely never voicing her own opinion had only one fruit to bear— Frances had learned to be an expert listener. By decod-

ing body language, voice intonation, pitch and reso-
nance and by understanding double entendres and the
minutiae of phraseology, Frances had never failed to de-
tect a lie. But she didn't think it ladylike to call someone
on a lie once she'd caught them.

Too many times she had noticed that Kristen used that
slightly higher-pitched tone and that casual, almost
heedless attitude when she lied.

That was how Frances discovered that her daughter,
not Michael, didn't want children. The shocking thought
gave rise to myriad questions she wanted to ask Kristen,
but wouldn't. Was there truly another man? Perhaps
Kristen had invented the lover to cover her true motivation. What had ever happened to Kristen that she
wouldn't want children? Even Max, the playboy of the
family, intended to marry and raise a family someday.
Of course, he might wait until he was forty to do it, but
he would.

As far as she knew, their family had been as normal as
anyone else's in their circle. Certainly, their life was devoid of tension and squabbles over money that seemed
to be the cause of so many divorces among the middle
class. Kristen had always been a bit wild, but no more so
than Kitty Ruffingham's daughter who went off one
summer to Paris to study sculpting and refused to return
to New York. That was five years ago. To Frances's
knowledge, Kitty hadn't heard from her daughter to this
day.

Frances had always attributed Kristen's natural exuberance to the fact that she was smarter than her three
siblings.

Frances had never told Kristen she'd scored in the genius percentile when her IQ was tested in grade school.
The teachers had warned Frances that such information

caused children to become lazy. Karl and Max had in-
herited Bart's dim wit and slow brains. Kristen, and to a
lesser extent, Meghan, possessed a brilliant brain like
Frances's father, Ronald Sargent. For the life of her,
Frances couldn't understand what was the matter with
her daughter's thinking.

"Look, Mother, if you're worried about this abortion
thing, don't. The fetus is only six weeks along at most.
It's nothing. It can't breathe, sleep or eat," she explained,
and then suddenly paused. "Are you sure this doctor is
good enough? I don't want any complications," she said,
sounding nervous. "I mean, I'm not scared of pain. I can
handle that. I mean—"

"I *know* what you mean, Kristen. I've never been in
this situation either and it has upset me to no end. I can't
believe the day has come when I, Frances Sargent Van
Buren, would be paying for an illegal abortion."

"Mother...it's legal. You're not some fugitive from the
law. All I'm asking is that the doctor be the best there is
and that he keep his mouth shut!" Kristen bit her lip as
she turned onto Ninety-third Street. Mount Sinai Hospital loomed to the side of them.

"I've never been to a doctor like this...but Aaron
Wiseman is the best."

Kristen chuckled. "How apropos, Mother. He's not a
WASP."

"No, dear, I'm afraid not."

"How did you find out about him? I mean, you didn't
tell anyone it was for me, did you?"

Shooting Kristen an insulting look, she replied, "This
is not your father you're dealing with, Kristen. I may be
upset, but I do have my wits about me. I asked Thelma
Douglas Donnell for a recommendation."

"Not that sweet little old lady in your garden club?" Kristen gasped.

"Just because she's old doesn't mean she didn't carry on when she was young. She's always bragged that she knows everything about everyone and who to see in...er...situations like this, though she never gossips."

"Never?"

"Not ever," Frances said emphatically. "Dr. Wiseman will be discreet, and at his price he should be."

"Oooph! I don't even want to know how much this is costing until it's over. I'll write you a check tomorrow."

"See that you do," Frances said firmly as they parked the car.

Kristen endured the boring blood tests, urine tests, blood-pressure cuff and weight check. She answered all the pertinent information on the printed form the nurse asked her to fill out. She waited in a freezing-cold room on a sterile gurney, wearing a paper smock, paper head covering and paper slippers. Having never experienced anything more than a routine Pap smear and physical, Kristen had not the least idea what to expect.

She didn't like the way they were taking so much time about all this. What was the holdup, anyway? She needed to get this over with, drive her mother back to the Island and be home before Michael returned at seven o'clock.

She stared at the ceiling tiles, getting angrier and more frightened by the minute. Finally, she couldn't handle her anxiety any longer. She bolted off the gurney. Slipping and almost falling on the highly polished linoleum floor, she cursed the paper booties she wore.

"What's taking the doctor so long?" she nearly

shouted at a trio of nurses conversing in the narrow hall between patients' rooms. "I've been here over an hour!"

One of the nurses quickly whisked Kristen back into the room and urged her to lie back down.

"I don't want to lie down until I've talked with—"

"Hello, Mrs. West. I'm Dr. Wiseman," a tall, dark, handsome man about forty years old said as he entered. "I'm sorry for the delay, but there seems to be a problem with your blood tests."

"A...what kind of problem?"

"Your blood is A-negative."

"I know. So?"

"Do you know the father's blood type? Is it negative or positive?"

Blood type? I don't even know who the father is.

"I'm not sure. O-positive, I think. Why?"

"Your blood type is quite rare. If your husband's blood type was negative, there would be no problem. If it's positive, your baby could require a transfusion at birth. Of course, since you wish to terminate this pregnancy, there's no concern with it. It's subsequent pregnancies, should you decide to carry to term, that could be dangerous to both you and the baby."

"So, what are you saying, that we can't do this today? Because I've arranged everything..."

"Oh, no. We'll go through with everything as scheduled. I do suggest we give you a Rhogam injection afterward, however. This should prevent any future problems from occurring. And then, if you wouldn't mind, when you get home, could you please verify your husband's blood type for our records? It could save your baby's life in the future."

"Sure. No problem. I'll do it this evening and call your office in the morning. How's that?"

"Wonderful. Very well. Let's proceed."

Two nurses came into the room with a rolling metal cart filled with all sorts of instruments Kristen couldn't identify and didn't even want to.

"I'm giving you a local anesthetic and an injection that will make you very sleepy, but not put you under. It will last only an hour after the procedure, but you could be groggy for a while. I suggest you don't drive anymore today."

"My mother can drive me home," she lied. *I hope this stuff wears off by the time I have to drive back to the city.*

Just as Dr. Wiseman finished the injection, Kristen looked at him. "I was told you are discreet about these...problems."

"Absolutely."

The last thing Kristen remembered seeing before she slipped into a light slumber was Dr. Wiseman's charming smile.

Sipping hot coffee from a disposable cup on the drive back to Long Island, Kristen couldn't believe the world made such an issue over abortions. She'd had a worse experience three years ago when she'd had her wisdom tooth pulled. But this was nothing. She could remember nothing. She felt next to no pain.

"If people really knew how simple this was, I'd finance a chain of clinics myself and make a fortune."

Having always believed that the abortion issue was a political football tossed around by men whose egos were boosted by controlling women, Kristen could only laugh at their fumbling. To her way of thinking, women were always going to do what the hell they wanted. Men, whether husband or lover, need never be the wiser.

Smiling, Kristen congratulated herself for her quick

thinking. Getting her mother to pay for the operation and be an "accomplice," as it were, was added insurance she could always use. Better still was the fact that, once again, she'd had control over her mother.

Kristen couldn't remember a time when Frances's superciliousness had ever shown the first sign of cracking. Kristen had more than gotten a reaction out of her mother; she'd seen her angry and unsure about her decision to help her daughter.

How strange it was to observe her own relationship with Frances as if they were fruit flies in a scientist's petri dish. Perhaps it was the anesthetic that allowed her to move out of herself and view the dark side of their relationship.

Coldly dispassionate, Frances clutched the powerful Van Buren name, money and social standing to her breast rather than her children or husband. Her friends were always politically or socially famous and she collected them like trophies, framing their photographs in silver and displaying them on top of the unplayed Steinway. Her children fared no better, and Kristen the worst.

Kristen could not remember a single instance when Frances had ever championed one of her children. In response, the boys committed slight aggravations against Frances's sensibilities, but more for the sake of mockery than malicious intent. Kristen's motivational currents ran much deeper. Kristen had wanted to see if her mother could bleed.

Not until today had Kristen ever derived satisfaction from her and her siblings' mental pillaging. This time, she'd put Frances over the top. Fear-struck and with few options, Frances had done exactly as Kristen had wanted.

Relishing her victory over her mother, Kristen

laughed aloud. Then she abruptly stopped. *What would it have been like if Frances had acted out of love and concern today? Would Kristen be feeling this way about the abortion? Would she feel guilty for involving her mother? Would she have gone through with it?*

The unfamiliar pangs of conscience slid quickly from Kristen's thoughts. It was ridiculous to ponder the impossible. Kristen had long ago learned to deal only in realities. In fact, that was one of the few ways in which she and her mother were similar.

Continually reshaping herself over the course of her life, Kristen made certain she'd done just about everything she could to be Frances's polar opposite. Whereas Frances viewed life with pedantic tunnel vision, Kristen wanted to eat the world with a large serving spoon. Maybe Kristen had made some reckless decisions, like sleeping with Greg without protection, but she'd managed to fulfill her own needs and desires.

"I'm an independent woman and no one is going to crowd my style," she said to herself as she neared her apartment building. "Not Mother, not here-again, gone-again Greg and not Michael."

Parking the car in her regular space, Kristen was surprised she felt dizzy when she got out of the car. "The anesthetic must not have worn off completely," she mumbled as she rode the elevator to their floor. Thankfully, she had almost an hour before Michael got home. She'd decant a nice bottle of Bordeaux to go with the steaks she'd pulled out of the freezer that morning. She felt like celebrating. After all, victory over one's lifetime opponent didn't come often.

Unlocking the door, Kristen gasped when she saw Michael standing in the foyer, holding a half-finished glass of wine.

"Where the hell have you been?"

Feeling her nerves turn to steel, Kristen nonchalantly tossed her keys into a silver tray on the console. "I thought you had a meeting this afternoon." She checked her makeup in the gilded mirror.

"I finished early. I thought I'd come home and surprise you," he said in a flat tone.

"That's nice. But I didn't know that, now, did I?"

"I've been calling everywhere trying to find you."

Leveling an apathetic glare at him, Kristen said, "What on earth for? Did you finally make your billion-dollar deal?"

"I got the deal! We're shy of a billion by several hundred million, but it's some serious money. I wanted to celebrate." His face lifted with a proud grin and then instantly collapsed. "I called your mother's and Hannah said you'd driven away from the house as if you'd had the devil at your back."

Taking his wine from him and drinking deeply, Kristen retorted, "Hannah's Irish imagination is going to be her downfall. Mother and I were in a hurry, is all." She handed the glass back to him.

"Well, okay," he said slowly, then suddenly grabbed her and pulled her against him. "I want to celebrate. Let's go out. Le Cirque. Then come back and make love all night. I want it to be like it was when we were in school."

Kristen rolled her eyes. "Michael, you can't keep your mind off business long enough to make me come."

"Oh, yeah?" He kissed her playfully.

Panic raced through Kristen. There was no way she could have sex with Michael. Didn't the doctor say something to her about waiting a week, or was it two? Or three?

The dull pain in her abdomen suddenly sank sharp talons into her. "Ugh!" Kristen grabbed her stomach and folded in half.

"What is it?" Michael's voice rang with concern.

I can't blow this now, not when I'm almost home free! All I need is a night in bed and I'll be fine tomorrow.

Another pain shot through her.

"Kristen? Are you all right?"

She felt another searing wave. It took every ounce of strength to fight back. "God, Michael, what did you put in that wine?"

Holding his wife firmly in his strong arms, Michael led Kristen to the sofa. "There's nothing wrong with the wine, Kristen. You're as white as a sheet. Maybe I should call the doctor."

"No!" she shot back much too quickly. "I mean, don't bother, darling. I didn't want to say anything, but I started today and well, you know, sometimes periods can be rough."

Knitting his eyebrows together, Michael said, "I don't remember that ever being a problem for you."

"I'm quite tolerant to pain, Michael, and I've always tried to keep it from you." Kristen smiled as sweetly as she knew how. "Be a dear and get me that cashmere throw on the chair over there."

"Sure."

Kristen could feel blood rushing through her, and if she didn't get to the bathroom very quickly, Michael was going to figure out this was not normal. "On second thought—" she rose from the sofa "—I need to use the rest room. I'll be back in a minute."

Michael followed her upstairs and stood in the bathroom doorway. "Do you think this will pass? I have dinner reservations."

Kristen hoped she didn't pass out from the intense pain, but that was nothing compared to what her life would be like if Michael even suspected she'd had an abortion. She had to keep her wits about her at all costs. Obviously, all the anesthetic had worn off. She should have gotten that prescription for painkillers the doctor had offered, but she'd been overconfident. Barely able to formulate her thoughts, much less find the energy to speak, she managed to say, "Darling...why not send out for angel hair and maybe...that salmon you love?"

Considering her idea for a moment, he answered, "I'd rather take you dancing all night. But I understand about these things. I'll go down to Mordecai's and get us some Dom, too. How's that?"

The pain was overpowering. Kristen had never experienced anything so intense. She wasn't sure she'd live through this.

Great. Fucking great. "Make it two."

"You know, Kristen, I don't care if it's that time for you...I mean, we could still..." He glanced over at the bed.

Covered in icy sweat, Kristen hugged her naked body as she watched a thick rivulet of blood trickle down her leg. She turned on the shower. "Maybe...you'll get lucky." *Just leave, Michael.*

"Ha! That's what I thought!" he said cheerfully. "I know what my girl wants and I intend to give it to you all night long." Whistling, he turned away from the bathroom door and left.

Kristen's knees buckled and she dropped to the floor. Turning, she saw herself in the mirrored wall. Her skin was ashen, sweat-soaked blond hair was matted in clumps to her face and neck, while her blue eyes appeared sunken in dark-rimmed sockets. It was as if she were looking at her own corpse.

It was the most frightening sight she'd ever seen.

Hysteria burst from her lips. "Of course I should look like this!" she howled to herself between sobs. "Doesn't everyone on their day of reckoning?"

27

Darien, Connecticut
September 10, 1981

As Greg reached the entrance to his home, the new French doors that led to the terrace were suddenly flung open. Susannah greeted him with an exuberant hug and kiss.

"Well! What was that all about?"

"Nothing. Just that I love you and missed you today." She smiled widely like a Cheshire cat.

Greg pulled back, looking at her askance. "Come on. Something's up." He paused. "Don't tell me the plumber dropped the hammer again and broke the marble tub."

"No, he's very careful now," she replied.

"I'll bet! That mistake cost his company a bundle. Oh, I know, the floor guys didn't show up."

"Oh, no. They came." Sheepishly she glanced over her shoulder. "Considering that all they've managed to do is tear up the linoleum, I'm not so sure that was a good thing."

Greg strained his neck to look over her head. "You can't keep me out here forever. Let me see."

Shrugging, she stood aside and let him in.

"Jesus! They're strip-mining my house!" He slapped his forehead with his palm.

"Wait'll you see the living room and dining room."

Greg looked around for a safe place to put his new leather briefcase, but all he found were counterless cabinets, piles of old black adhesive that had held down the linoleum and sawdust everywhere. "This is the worst experience of my life," he said, cuddling his briefcase to his chest and making his way around power saws and drills.

The living-room carpets were gone. In the center of the room, a small section of new mahogany flooring brought hope that their lives would someday be normal again.

"God, that looks great! What do you think, honey?" he asked, putting his arm around Susannah's shoulder.

"I love it."

Greg turned to the dining room where the carpeting was gone but no work had been done. In the middle of the room sat the ugly Italianate dining table and two chairs. Susannah had set two places. In the middle of the table was a prettily arranged vase of flowers, which Greg recognized as coming from their garden, and two burning ivory candles. "I could have sworn that table was in the garage this morning."

"It was. I asked two of the men to bring it back in...just for tonight."

"Tonight? What's tonight?"

Susannah laughed. "You have that 'Did I forget your birthday' look on your face!"

"Well, did I?"

"No, but it is a celebration, all the same," she replied, and kissed his cheek. "You go up and change into your jeans and I'll pour some wine. Supper will only be another fifteen minutes."

"Sounds super," he said, taking his briefcase with him. "You know that brief I was telling you about?" he began as he went up the stairs.

"Yes."

"Two of the partners told me I did a great job," he said. The exaggeration from "good" to "great" wasn't that much of a stretch, he thought.

"That's wonderful. What about the other two partners?"

He stopped at the top of the stairs. "Mr. Wilkins and Mr. Raleigh are out of town." *I can't tell her they thought the brief needed more work.*

Susannah had started toward the kitchen. "Oh, well, they'll read it when they get back."

"Yeah." *And I've only got one more shot to make it right. I'll have to work late in town, so Susannah won't know the truth. Only this time...I'll stay in the office all night if I have to.*

When Greg returned to the kitchen, his mind was cluttered with the problems he was having now that he'd been promoted. He didn't get it. The first year out of law school, he'd been their new young star. Everything he'd touched turned to gold. He couldn't do anything wrong. Ever since June, he hadn't done anything right.

Susannah took the potatoes out of the oven and set them next to the baked chicken. She handed Greg a glass of chardonnay and touched the rim of it with her glass. "Here's to us," she said happily, but Greg was hardly listening.

"What's on your mind?" she asked.

"I dunno," he replied dully. "Yes, I do." He sipped hastily as he spoke. "I think the cases at work are getting tougher. I liked the tax work I did last year and even the civil lawsuits Mr. Raleigh handles, but this estate work is so intricate. So political. Brother! If every *i* isn't dotted and *t* crossed, I get nailed."

"Isn't that what being an attorney is all about?" Susannah asked.

"I didn't ask for more criticism, Susannah!"

His harsh tone jolted her. "I'm sorry. I said it the wrong way. I didn't mean—"

"I get enough shit all day. I thought you of all people would understand what kind of stress I'm under. And then, every night I come home to this..." He gestured around the room with his hand.

"Greg, I'm sorry! I didn't know things weren't going well. You just told me that two of the partners were singing your praises."

He stared blankly at her. "I did. I know. What I meant was, I have another case that's making me nuts. That's all." He went to her and put his arms around her. "I'm sorry, too. Here, let me help you with this," he said, taking the platter of food and carrying it into the dining room.

Susannah followed him with their wine. He held her chair.

Forcing a smile, he sat and raised his glass to her. "I promise I'll be in a better mood. The drive home got to me more than I thought."

"I understand," she said, while he carved the chicken and served her plate.

"Now that I've dumped on your beautiful shoulders, tell me why you arranged this special dinner."

She blushed slightly. "I was planning to tell you after supper. I bought some cognac..."

He shook his head furiously. "You know me, I hate

surprises and guessing games. Tell me now." He smiled again.

Wistfully, she smiled back. "You're going to be a father."

"I what?" He felt his smile slide off his face.

"I'm pregnant."

Christ! This isn't happening. Two in one day? "You can't be. I thought you were on the Pill...or something."

"I can't take the Pill. It was an IUD. A very bad one, I'm afraid, but it's not like we were waiting for any particular reason, is it? I mean, what difference does it make if we have a baby this year or the next or five years from now?"

A big difference to me! I'm not ready to be a father! I don't want to be a father at all, in fact. Not to your baby or to...Kristen's. "Uh, no reason, I suppose." He scratched his head.

"Why, Greg, you look as if you aren't sure about this."

He chuckled, smiled and quickly leaned over to kiss her. "It's not that. It's just that I wasn't prepared for this." *Any of this.* "I'd thought we were taking precautions."

"I did! No contraceptive is foolproof. You know that."

"So I've come to understand." It was a struggle for him to remain cheerful. And he didn't understand it. Throughout his life he'd referred to his future children as heirs. Begetting future generations was his Walton task, his destiny. He'd married Susannah because he knew she would make a good mother to his children. This was what he wanted, he'd told himself.

Now that his goals were reality, he suddenly felt quite differently. He'd never been around small children until he and Susannah had moved to Darien. Now, it seemed everyone in the world was either pregnant or had kids.

All summer long he'd not been able to sleep in on Saturdays for the sound of tricycles screeching down the sidewalks. Once the days grew long, the neighborhood children played hide-and-seek until ten o'clock. Darien was experiencing a baby boom and it scared the shit out of him.

He found he couldn't stand the crying, wailing and runny noses. Some of the mothers were just as bad as the children, complaining too loudly about their husbands who didn't help with the baby, didn't do the dishes and didn't come home. Who could blame the poor guys? These complaints weren't as bad as the other group of mothers who praised their husbands as though they were saints.

This situation was poles apart from the terror he'd just been through with Kristen. Fortunately, she'd been all too ready to get an abortion and forget it. From the time she'd called him three days ago and told him she was pregnant, until last night when she'd called to say that, despite having a rough time of it, she was feeling fine, Greg hadn't known a moment's peace.

Worrying about Kristen had caused him to fuck up that brief. He'd told her point-blank that the baby couldn't be his. After all, they'd only been together once in...how many years was it now? The whole thing sounded like some bizarre trick only Kristen could think up. He'd accused her of trying to jack with him, but she'd sounded sincere and, finally, he'd believed her. She'd admitted the baby could just as easily have been Michael's and probably was. However, if the baby wound up looking like Greg, she could make him pay for their all-night sex Olympics for the rest of his life.

He'd even asked her when the baby was supposed to be due. She'd said April twentieth, which would have coincided with the night they'd been together back in July.

When he pressed her to the wall about the abortion, even offered to give her some money, she'd admitted that she didn't want any kids...ever. At least on that score, they thought alike. She'd told him she didn't need his "damn money."

Oddly, her refusal had hit him to the core, as if this were another time the Van Burens had bested the Waltons.

Now his own wife had told him she was carrying his baby, too.

Goddammit, but women can cause some grief!

Susannah was chatting away about how she intended to decorate the nursery and go to auctions to find an antique cradle, when Greg took her hand.

"So tell me, pretty mama, when is the baby due?"

"April second," she said, beaming.

God! This really isn't happening! It's too much of a coincidence that both babies' birthdays would have been in the same month!

Greg covered his real feelings by offering a toast. "Here's to all three of us," he said. "You're really happy, aren't you, Susannah?"

"Yes, Greg. I really am," she said softly.

He touched her cheek. "I can tell. I've never seen your face as radiant as it is now."

Gently, she placed her hand over his. "We're going to raise a beautiful, healthy family, you and I."

"That's all I want," he said, and kissed his pregnant wife.

28

New York City
December 23, 1981

Michael appeared to be on top of the world, Phillip thought. And so he should. Like a master marksman, everywhere he aimed his sight, he hit another target on the bull's-eye. To help Michael celebrate his recent victories, Phillip had arranged a special lunch at Windows on the World. By one o'clock a light snow that had fallen since early morning had turned to fat, fluffy flakes, transforming New York into a Christmas-card scene.

Michael raised his glass of chardonnay and offered his favorite toast to Phillip. "Here's to your health, wealth and happiness and time to enjoy them."

"*Salut*," Phillip replied, and thoughtfully replaced his glass. "Michael, I don't think I've ever seen you quite this..."

"Happy?"

"*Exuberant* is more the word for your energetic mood today."

Phillip looked at him quizzically. Michael had closed every project they'd slated for the year. Planned for the new year was a half-dozen promising deals that Phillip intended to co-venture with a group of handpicked financiers. However, none of these transactions were even

close to the final phases. What could possibly create
such excitement in Michael? No, this news was something else. Something Michael had wanted, dreamed
about for a long time, and probably never revealed to
anyone.

"You've found the condo in the Caymans you
wanted?" Phillip suggested, knowing Michael loved
prolonging the suspense as much as Phillip enjoyed the
guessing game.

"I'm still thinking it over. In fact, I'll probably need a
larger place. Who knows? I may have to build my own
condos and sell them in order to get what I want."

"Now, don't get greedy, Michael."

"It's not that at all," Michael replied.

"Then what the devil is going on?" Phillip finally fell
prey to Michael's game of cat-and-mouse.

"Kristen's pregnant."

Michael was beaming so widely and his chest was
puffed up so proudly, Phillip could only pray his face
did not betray his shock. *Kristen is pregnant.* It was impossible! Of all the things he knew about his beautiful,
selfish, self-absorbed niece, the fact that she couldn't
stand the idea of babies, much less the reality of them,
had always been obvious.

How many times had Frances stated at family gatherings that she knew grandchildren would have to come
from the boys' wives, because neither of her daughters
were interested in raising families? In fact, Frances's
only lament in life was that she'd obviously done something wrong, missed a turn in the rearing process with
both Kristen and Meghan.

Although neither Karl or Max was exactly a doting
son to their mother, their waywardness had always been
harmless. In contrast, Kristen and Meghan couldn't find

enough ways to rebel. At every family gathering, both girls had continually talked of leaving home. Phillip had never believed either girl, Kristen in particular, yet he sensed there was something deep, something sinister about their intense dislike for their mother.

Phillip hadn't understood the dynamics of his brother's family and probably never would. Perhaps if he'd had children of his own, he might have been more knowledgeable.

Judging by Michael's elation, he had certainly made his wishes clear to Kristen. He could only believe that she, on the other hand, like a knight building a fortress against an enemy, would have used every contraceptive on the market. Warning bells clanged dully in Phillip's mind telling him not to trust the situation. Something was dreadfully wrong.

"I'm thrilled for you, Michael!" Phillip's chest tightened with anxiety, but he tried to act enthusiastic. Michael obviously knew nothing about Kristen's neuroses regarding children.

"Thanks," Michael said buoyantly.

"When is the baby due?" Phillip asked.

"August twenty-second. The doctor says Kristen's healthy. Everything is just fine and he sees no complications we should worry about."

"Really? She's been to the doctor already? Did you go with her?"

"Not yet. I'll go next month. He wants me there," he said proudly. "I want her to take Lamaze classes and I intend to go with her. I want to speak to the doctor about being in the delivery room with her."

"Oh, Michael, are you sure about that? I've thought these new trends quite unsavory for a man."

"Phillip, you're my dearest friend, but you're too old-fashioned sometimes," Michael teased affectionately.

"I suppose I am. I guess that's why I don't have any children."

"I don't believe that for a second! You can hand that bullshit to some people but not to me. You've got a heart bigger than an ocean. If you'd have married that woman you fell in love with way back when you should have, you'd feel the same way I do."

Suddenly, Phillip's eyes darkened with sadness.

"Damn!" Michael said. "I'm sorry, Phillip. I didn't mean to say that."

"Yes, you did."

"I guess I really stuck my foot in it. I'm sorry."

Shaking his head, Phillip replied, "It's not what you said. You must have thought these things for quite some time for them to come out the way they did. No, you're absolutely right. There isn't a day that goes by that I don't think about Gloria and what could have been."

"Gloria? That's her name?"

Phillip looked stunned that he'd actually revealed the name of the woman. "Yes. Gloria Banning. She lived in Westhampton. She and her father were incredibly close after her mother died. She was the sad one back then. I fell in love with those sad eyes. When we were together, her eyes came alive. She breathed life into me."

Michael remembered the scattered pieces of the story Phillip had told him years ago; how Adele had forbid Phillip to marry someone beneath his class and Gloria had gone off to Europe, never to return; the power plays that had strangled Phillip for years and his disastrous marriage to a woman he never loved.

Remembering Phillip's story, it suddenly struck Michael to his core. As incredibly excited and happy as Michael was about the baby, he couldn't honestly say such soul-felt things about Kristen.

There had never been a time when he'd looked in Kristen's eyes and felt the world had just begun. But he loved her, despite her self-centeredness. And now that she was giving him a baby, he loved her even more. Perhaps the baby would bring them together in a way he'd never experienced before.

Phillip's forlorn voice spoke to that hollow feeling deep inside Michael that he'd successfully ignored for years. His heart went out to Phillip. But so did his frustration. "Jesus, Phillip, if she's still alive, why don't you go to her? Tell her what you feel instead of pining away forever. You both could have a wonderful life together."

"I can't do that."

"Why the hell not?"

"I'd feel like a fool. I've wasted so much time already—"

Interrupting Phillip, Michael hit the table with his fist and made the silver service jump. "Pride? You're letting pride stop you from having a life?"

"It's not pride at all."

"What would you call it, then?" Michael pressed him.

Looking sheepishly at his wine, Phillip nodded slowly. "You're right. And for the life of me, I don't know where it comes from."

"Inbreeding," Michael chuckled.

Phillip laughed with him. "You may just be right." Thoughtfully, his eyes grew more serious. "Do you suppose in my own way I've been agreeing with my mother's opinion of Gloria being 'unsuitable' for me? That the Bannings and Waltons were not of our class and social stature? That Gloria had been too old for me? Too...outgoing?"

"It's possible. Maybe she was too independent for you. Going off to Europe and remaining there all these years is a pretty strong statement."

"I've always thought she hated me."

"Did you ask her?"

"No, I was afraid of her answer."

Michael shook his head. "If it were me, I would have asked her. I guess I'm just too curious about things. That's why I ask a lot of questions. I find out a lot by listening to other people."

Phillip's eyes probed Michael's. "It's important to be that way in personal matters, too," Phillip said.

"It's not hard," Michael said, flatly knowing he was guilty of not asking Kristen enough questions about her comings and goings. He had never been the possessive type. She was entitled to see her friends and work on the decorating without constantly reporting to him.

"Well, Michael, with all your good news, I suppose offering a Christmas toast to your first child is hardly sufficient."

"Of course it is..." Michael gazed at Phillip. His friend and mentor had that "I've-got-a-plan-brewing" look. "What are you plotting, Phillip van Buren?"

"Do you remember your first visit to me, Michael?"

"Fourth of July, 1976? I most certainly do."

"What you don't know is that I knew then you would make it through school with ease and grace. I knew instinctively you would excel at everything you do...and you have. You don't know it, but from then until now, I've looked upon you as my own son. And so, Michael, this baby is like my grandchild. My heir. The heir to my fortune."

"Phillip, that's very nice, but Kristen, her brothers and sister are your heirs."

Phillip clutched the sleeve of Michael's suit jacket. As he spoke, his fingers dug almost painfully into Michael's forearm. He was shocked at the older man's strength. "I want your word of honor as a Southern gentleman that you will never breathe a word of what I am about to say to anyone. Especially not to your wife."

"Not to Kristen?" Michael asked, astonishment knitting his eyebrows. *I've never seen Phillip like this.*

"Most definitely not to Kristen. Promise me…on your honor."

"On my honor, sir," Michael said implacably.

"As your Christmas gift, which I give to you and your child, son or daughter, I want you to be my sole heir."

Knocking the breath out of Michael, Phillip's words assaulted his heart and brain simultaneously. Michael's body went rigid then he slowly sank against the back of his chair. "You're not serious!"

"Deadly serious." Phillip laughed at his own joke.

Michael couldn't even crack a smile. "Not only do I think I'm not worthy, but what if I'm not up to the responsibility?"

"Michael, you proved yourself worthy a long time ago."

For years, Michael had wondered if his marriage had anything to do with Phillip's generosity. So many times he'd wanted to know and had backed off. If he were true to himself, true to his pattern of always asking questions to satisfy his curiosity, he couldn't hold himself back this time. "Is it because of Kristen?"

"It's because of you. I can't turn my fortune over to a passel of bumbling fools, Michael. Only you have the kind of business wit and brains I possess. At times, I often wonder if you aren't more gifted than I."

"I doubt that entirely. You're being kind."

"Nonsense. It will be up to you to keep everything running, to ensure the money is properly invested for your children's children. This is the guardianship I was entrusted with by my father."

Reflecting on all Phillip had said and was asking of him, Michael could already feel the weight of responsibility on his shoulders. Something else bore down upon him, but as yet he couldn't pinpoint it. However, it was there all the same.

There was no question about it, Phillip was hiding something from him and it was about Kristen. Phillip didn't make sudden decisions on whims or holiday sentiments. Phillip was as calculating as anyone he'd ever met. He *had* been planning this for quite some time.

Michael was surprised that Phillip didn't want Kristen to know of the gift. It was one thing that she was not to be the executor of Phillip's estate or was not expected to help run his empire, because she was not trained for either. But not to tell her that their child would someday inherit so much wealth was a carefully contrived plan on Phillip's part.

Michael wished he didn't suspect Phillip's motives, but he did. Phillip was telling Michael he didn't trust Kristen.

Like a shooting star, Michael's earlier exuberance burned to cinders when he realized that deep down, Michael agreed with Phillip. Though Michael could not claim fact or data to substantiate his instincts, he agreed that Kristen was not trustworthy.

Michael wished to hell he had reason for feeling the way he did about his wife. Perhaps her selfishness was enough to kindle his misgivings. Maybe he was being unfair. But he couldn't ignore that Phillip agreed with him.

Michael almost wished he hadn't come here today. He wished Phillip hadn't been so generous. How simple it was to remain in his dreamworld, thinking about his baby and his beautiful wife. He'd dreamed of family dinners at Christmas, maybe going to Aspen and staying in one of those fabulous condos with huge windows overlooking the incredible snow-covered mountains. He'd dreamed of taking his child to buy a tree, bringing it home and then stringing cranberries and popcorn the way his mother had taught him. He remembered the smell of fresh pine and his mother's perfume. The feel of her soft arms around him as she held him to her heart.

He wondered if Kristen would do that with their child. Suddenly, he knew she couldn't. Nor would she. Kristen didn't love people the way his mother had.

The revelation shocked him to the core. He loved Kristen...didn't he? Or had he been foolish and fallen in love with a woman in a dream? A woman he'd long believed was Kristen, but wasn't?

Was it possible he, the man who prided himself on his instincts, had made a mistake? And what if he had? There was nothing he could do about it now. His fate was tied to the Van Burens in more ways than just Kristen. It was obvious Phillip was making certain that not only he, but his children and grandchildren, would be part of the Van Burens forever.

There was only one glimmer of hope that might enable Michael to loosen the Van Buren bonds. It would take some effort to work on Phillip's stubborn mind-set and his outrageous sense of pride. But with time, Michael believed he could convince Phillip to take action with his own life.

It was a sketchy plan but it could work. It *had* to work. His hope was Gloria.

29

Greg looked up when he heard the delivery-room doors whoosh open. The handsome young doctor scanned the waiting area with anxious eyes before finding Greg. From the ashen look on the doctor's face, Greg knew things had turned from bad to worse.

"What's wrong now?" Greg said, still holding his breath.

"I'm sorry, Greg. It doesn't look good," Dr. Medvale said to Greg.

"I've told you that I don't care about the baby," Greg said emphatically.

"I'm not talking about the baby. I'm talking about your wife."

"Look, an hour ago you told me my wife was in danger. Why hasn't anyone done anything yet? I thought you were going to do a cesarean section?" *Jesus! Were all these people idiots?*

"I'm not licensed to do a section. I'm only covering for Dr. Sisao and she's been unreachable."

Greg wanted to hit him. "Not licensed? Then how do you know she needs an operation? Maybe you've miscalculated."

"I'm a resident here, sir. I'm fully capable of handling the surgery, but obstetrics is not my field. I've already sent for Dr. Jacobson. I was just told he's in the hospital and is probably washing up now."

Greg wiped nervous sweat from his forehead. "Good. Then there's no cause for alarm."

"Susannah's blood pressure is dropping. She's toxic and exhausted. She's been fighting for over twenty hours now and has lost a great deal of blood. Dr. Jacobson is one of the best obstetricians in Connecticut, but he's not God."

"Really?" Greg sneered cynically. "I thought all you doctors walked on water. Or thought you did."

Dr. Medvale lifted his mask over his face and turned away, saying, "We're doing everything we can." Then he rushed back to the delivery room.

Susannah had insisted on a natural birth for her baby because she was suspicious of the effect drugs could have on a newborn. For months Susannah had read every article and book on birth, nursing and child-rearing she could find. The idea that choices she made out of selfishness or ignorance could harm her baby frightened her immensely.

It was she who had told the doctors not to give her gas and painkillers when they'd discovered that her birth canal was smaller than any of them had realized. Now her baby was stuck in the canal.

The pain was excruciating and constant. She bore down for another long, harsh wave of pushing but knew the futility of her efforts.

She told them to save the baby and not to worry about her. After floating in and out of consciousness many times, she now sought the bliss and peace she found in that other world. Dr. Medvale had told her of Greg's instructions to save her and not the baby. She was appalled at his decision. She'd never wanted anything in her life as much as she wanted this baby to live.

For nine months her baby had grown inside her. She knew his personality, his sleeping patterns and the fact that he tumbled around like an acrobat whenever she played her favorite music. She talked to him every day while working in her gardens or decorating the nursery. She had wanted her baby to live in a perfect world. However, she'd discovered that hers and Greg's world was far from that.

When Susannah insisted she *knew* the baby was a boy, Greg told her that she was only guessing. Only an ultrasound could tell them the truth. Greg had wanted to know the sex of the child from the doctor's own lips. Susannah had refused the information, believing her inner voice knew just as well as technology.

Greg not only stated he wanted a full-time nanny to care for their baby, but had actually interviewed several women for the job before Susannah called a halt. Greg told her that he would be mortified if any of his friends discovered he did not employ a nanny. She was shocked that appearances and his stature as a wealthy Walton were higher on his priority list than she and the baby.

It was after that argument that Susannah noticed Greg stopped calling her by her name, only referring to her in conversations with others as "she" or "my wife." Even when he called for her at home, he never used her name. When she'd confronted him about his behavior, he denied knowing what she was talking about.

By the time Susannah reached the end of her pregnancy, Greg used every occasion when she asked for his help with a chore or errand to bring up his nanny argument.

"Why must I always be the one to wait on you hand and foot?" he'd say. "What's it going to be like after the baby comes and I'm not around to help? What will you do then? You don't know anything about raising children! We're too young to be parents."

Susannah realized that while she wanted this child, Greg could have cared less. He was selfishly angry that Susannah's world did not revolve around him anymore. Susannah turned to the only person who knew them both well enough to give her stable advice—Aunt Gloria.

Too ashamed to reveal her misgivings to her mother, who still believed Greg hung the moon, Susannah wrote to Gloria in Monaco. Her first letter was answered promptly. Gloria had been equally stunned by Greg's actions. She suggested long heart-to-heart talks in which Susannah openly expressed her feelings to Greg. Susannah decided to try Gloria's advice.

Greg's reaction was silence. He refused to discuss any matters concerning the baby. Then he let it slip that Susannah had gotten pregnant without his consent. He said he felt as if he hadn't had any part in the decision.

When Susannah wrote to Gloria explaining Greg's latest stance, Gloria finally admitted that she'd seen signs of self-centeredness in Greg when he was a child, but she had loved him so much, she thought he would outgrow such childishness. His current behavior confirmed her fears. Though always the practical one in the family, Gloria finally told Susannah all they could do now was pray Greg would come to his senses once the baby was born.

Swirling like banshees in her mind, Susannah's fears tortured her as she bore down again to push.

"Hold your breath, Susannah," the nurse said. "Don't go with the contraction so much. You've used too much energy already."

"I...can't stop!" She was strong enough for this. She had to be. She couldn't leave the baby now. After all, who would care for it? Not Greg...

"Susannah, the doctor is nearly ready," Dr. Medvale said, bending down to her ear. "We're going to transfer you to another gurney and take you to surgery."

Susannah didn't understand everything that was happening. "Dr. Sisao is here?"

"I told you, we couldn't find her. Dr. Jacobson is the best there is with cases like yours. Everything is going to be fine."

She opened her eyes and stared at him. With more strength than she thought she had, she grabbed the shoulder of Dr. Medvale's surgical greens. "You make sure nothing happens to my baby!"

"We'll do everything we can."

She nearly hissed through her teeth. "Save my baby! You got that?"

"Yes, Susannah," he said, and gave the signal to the orderlies to lift her to the other gurney.

Susannah remembered seeing ceiling tiles and overhead lights whiz past her as if an invisible hand had smeared them together. She remembered how her teeth chattered in the cold surgery room. Like the low drone of a dying fly, the voices around her faded out as she slipped into oblivion.

Susannah didn't hear the doctor's triumphant announcement that she'd given birth to a perfectly healthy, beautiful blond baby boy.

New York City
August 22, 1982

"You son of a bitch! I can't believe I let you do this to me!" Kristen screamed at the top of her lungs.

"Do what, honey?" Michael wiped a thin film of perspiration from Kristen's forehead with a sterile cloth.

"Get me pregnant!" She hurled her words at him like poisoned daggers.

Michael chuckled. "That's usually the case between husbands and wives." He glanced over his shoulder, looking for the doctor to arrive.

"Not for this wife..." Suddenly, Kristen stopped and her face contorted with pain. "Oh, Jesus! Here it comes again! I don't know how much more of this I can stand!"

Kristen clutched Michael's forearm, digging her nails into his flesh. She held her breath as the pain rumbled through her like an earthquake splitting her insides apart.

"Breathe, Kristen! Like they taught us in class," he urged her.

Kristen felt as if she'd been gutted. As far as she was concerned, childbirth was the most barbaric, disgusting, humiliating experience of her life. It was bad enough she had to submit to monthly obstetrical examinations. But she should have known by the denigrating attention from her family and friends, who suddenly treated her as if her mind had turned to mush, that life as she'd wanted to live it was over. She could still hear their voices:

"How sweet, Kristen's having a baby!"

"We must watch her diet for her and make certain she doesn't overexert herself."

"We'll decorate the nursery for her since she knows nothing about such things."

Kristen realized she'd become a nonentity. No one asked her opinion about anything anymore. It was as if nothing else was happening in her life except this asinine pregnancy. It was hard to believe so many people actually cared about the state of her health. "How are you feeling?" "Did you vomit again today?" "How much weight have you gained?" "Are your ankles still swollen?"

But the worst was the daily "How is the baby?," as if it were alive. By the end of her seventh month, when her breasts and stomach had grown to mammoth proportions, her frustration had gotten the better of her and she'd yelled at her grandmother, Adele, "How should I know how the baby is? It's not alive yet! It can't talk! But if it could, it would tell everybody to bug off!"

Adele had nearly choked on her tea right in the middle of Phillip's living room where she and Kristen had met to make plans for a baby shower. Phillip had not only offered his house as the setting, but insisted upon paying for the catered champagne luncheon, as well. "Since when have you developed a sassy tongue?" Adele asked once she'd recovered her decorum.

"Since the day I found out I was born into this heartless family!" Kristen had blurted out.

"What a terrible thing to say," Adele replied solicitously. "Do you really mean that, dear?"

"Yes," Kristen said flatly, and turned away from the old woman's remarkably clear, probing eyes.

"We Van Burens have prided ourselves on our closeness, our—"

"Yeah? Well, maybe a little less pride might have done everyone some good." Kristen crossed to the fireplace. Odd how specters of the night when she'd first met Michael came back to haunt her. She'd been sitting on this very sofa, crying over Greg's chilling treatment of her. She'd wanted to toy with Michael's naive Southern ways. She'd wanted to teach him how a real woman liked sex.

God! What a fool she'd been! Greg was still the only man who could satisfy her. Being pregnant hadn't curbed her sexual needs an iota. She still dreamed of Greg, and even tried to meet him over the holidays but it hadn't worked out. She'd given up trying to find another lover. No one else would do. Instead, she'd contented herself with fantasizing about Greg. When Michael complained that all she wanted on weekends was hours of sex, she'd almost told him that once a day would never be enough for her. Twice a day was simply adequate. Four times a day, every day, that's what she craved. Perhaps she could live with less if Michael were more adventurous.

Humph! Michael's too rigid with his sexuality. I'll bet he's never come close to having the fantasies I do! Excitement! That's what I need.

"What or who has made you feel this way, Kristen?" Adele asked.

"Mother," Kristen replied without thinking.

Adele folded her thin, delicate hands in her lap and waited.

Staring blankly at the vase of summer flowers on the marble mantel, Kristen wandered through scattered memories. "I hated being a child. I remember Mother always saying I was 'useless.' Not that I was singled out, because she said the same about Max and Karl. Even Meghan, her favorite. I always remember Mother's face when she inspected us before we went out. She had a funny way of holding her nose as if we smelled like..."

"Like what?" Adele urged softly.

"Like we had dirty diapers." Kristen's surroundings faded out as she peered into her own long-ago past. "I remember her coming to the nursery after my nap once, dressed in beautiful clothes. I couldn't have been even two years old then. She snarled at the nanny and told her to clean the 'piss' smell out of the crib linens. Then she fired the nanny on the spot. I was scared and I wanted desperately for Mother to come and hold me. I was so cold in my wet clothes. But she never picked me up. I screamed bloody murder wanting Mother to just touch my head or hold my hand. But she didn't.

"Mother always had someplace she had to go. Luncheons, the opera, parties. I distinctly remember that. I would scream, or later when I was older, I broke things or pulled Meghan's hair to make her cry, but Mother still wouldn't pick me up. Sometimes, she'd even have the nanny pull down my pants and spank me while she watched. Sometimes, I'd really piss her off by refusing to cry. Then I learned to turn away. Just like she did."

"Your mother was only following the rules we all raised our children by," Adele said stoically.

Kristen's mind slowly returned to her body as she faced Adele. "Then the rule maker was a fool."

"I had nannies for both boys when they were young," Adele told her. "They went to the best schools. They always seemed quite well adjusted."

Flashing like a strobe in her mind, Kristen's memories grew uglier. She couldn't remember anyone ever taking time to play with her, read to her, hold her, caress her. She remembered her father turning her away because of business calls, client golf games and innumerable meetings. Even Adele had spent very little time with her. However, when she had, Kristen admitted that her grandmother had spoken to her as if she were truly interested. Adele had taught her how to choose two contrasting pieces of fabric for their texture, not simply color. She distinctly remembered three or four outings when Adele had taken her into the city to shop or to see the musical plays she loved.

Kristen had often heard her grandmother state that she valued her sharp wits, keen mind and ability to see the world objectively. Terse in speech and brusque in manner, Adele considered herself to be "efficient" and "cordial." She prided herself on never succumbing to useless sentiments. She detested romantics and idealists. They had no place in the modern world. Adele wanted her sons to be just like her. Her grandchildren, as well.

Unable to withstand close scrutiny, the Van Buren family, in Kristen's opinion, was and would remain heartless. Sadly, the only person who even came close to loving Kristen had been Adele. The only trouble was, Adele was very, very old. The odds against Adele seeing Kristen's baby grow to adulthood were infinitesimal.

"I'm not criticizing you, Grandmother Adele," Kristen replied diplomatically. "I was telling you about Mother and how she did not give me the attention I should have had." Kristen sat next to Adele on the sofa. She took the old woman's hand in her own. "After all, my mother is not a Van Buren. Perhaps she just didn't know any better."

"My point exactly, Kristen. There is a difference, isn't there, dear?"

"Oh, yes, Grandmother. An unmistakable difference."

Adele smiled. "You know you've always been my favorite, don't you, Kristen?"

"I always hoped so," she replied.

Adele gently laid her hand on Kristen's distended belly. "I promise you on the Van Buren blood that runs in your child's veins that I will provide for you and this child for the rest of your lives. If you need anything, you come to me. Not your mother. Not your father."

Not daring to let her surprise show, Kristen dropped her eyes and lowered her head when she spoke. "You're the only one in this family who would say that to me."

Adele smoothed Kristen's hair once, then abruptly pulled her hand away. "I know, dear. I know."

Kristen was wheeled into the delivery room only two hours and twenty minutes after her first contraction. Kristen screamed for drugs and got them. With four long, hard pushes, her son was born. The doctor laid the baby on her aching stomach while he cut the umbilical cord.

When Michael had told her in sickeningly sweet tones how proud he was, how joyous he was about the baby, Kristen had moaned, rolled her head to the side and vomited.

All she wanted was for this nightmare of pain to stop.

The doctor and nurses praised Michael for coming into the delivery room and staying out of the way. They told Kristen her baby was the most beautiful they'd seen in years. They commented on his full head of blond hair, his long-lashed blue eyes, his barrel chest and strong grip. They told her his skin was exceptionally clear and evenly pink. They told him he didn't look like a newborn at all.

Kristen looked at the cross-eyed, prune-faced baby

and was terror-stricken. It was so tiny and odd-looking she was reminded of aliens she'd seen in movies. How could anything so hideous come out of her? Worst of all, it looked pathetically dependent. It couldn't talk, see or eat on its own. What the hell was she going to do with it?

It was the first time Kristen had ever felt compassion for her own mother. Kristen felt her future dry up before her eyes.

My life is over!

She felt incredibly weak as she closed her eyes. A buzzing in her ears was the sound of Michael's happiness mingling with clashing steel surgical instruments and the nurses' coos as they tended to the crying newborn.

Then she heard the doctor ask her a question. She tried to move her lips, but they were as heavy as concrete. Her mind told her it was an important question and she should answer him. Then she heard a droning sound come to her from far away. Or was it close? The drugs were taking her out of the conscious world into the unknown. She couldn't answer the doctor, he was on the other side of awareness.

Dr. Slater turned to Michael who was standing next to the scale where his son, Robin, was being weighed and measured. "He's twenty and a quarter inches long?" Michael turned to Dr. Slater. "Is that normal?"

"He's going to be tall like his father, but it's quite normal."

Michael was so excited he couldn't stop talking. "And he's just over seven pounds, not as much as I thought he'd be. I thought because Kristen was having such a hard time of it—" Michael paused upon seeing one of the nurses roll her eyes "—that Robin was much larger."

With a quizzical expression on his face, he turned to Dr. Slater.

"Kristen had a very easy time of it, Michael," the doctor said. "Most first pregnancies result in a very long labor. Fourteen hours or more."

"But she was in so much pain." Michael glanced over at his sleeping wife.

Dr. Slater took off his surgical gloves and motioned for Michael to walk toward the doors. "Childbirth isn't easy for any woman, Michael. Kristen told me that she has a low pain threshold. I'm not certain about that—it's not my place to judge another's tolerance. However, after working with your wife over the past nine months of her pregnancy, I and others in my office do believe your wife is given to a bit of…theatrics, shall we say."

Michael smiled. "I've noticed that."

"Have you? Well, then please take my advice, and when you get home don't let Kristen spend too much time in bed or allow her to become inactive. I've seen this kind of behavior before and, generally, it runs a certain pattern. My concern, Michael, is not so much for her as it is for you."

"For me?"

"You're the kind of new father whose excitement over the baby could cause you to become run-down. Juggling your career, caring for a new baby and thinking your social life should remain the same as before will only end up creating frustration."

"I don't think you have to worry about me. I can handle it."

"Kristen has told me how busy you are…"

"She complained about my work?" Michael was surprised, though he knew he shouldn't have been.

Dr. Slater nodded. "Yes. When she first came to my office, we were talking about the importance of the Rhogam injection..."

"The what injection?" Michael was confused.

"It's vital to your future children since you have O-positive blood and Kristen has A-negative blood..." Dr. Slater scratched his head. "I could have sworn Kristen said she'd discussed all this with you: Of course, I know you've been overseas quite a bit these past months."

"You were saying, Doctor." Michael couldn't for the life of him figure out why Kristen didn't tell him about this procedure.

"The reason little Robbie is so healthy and didn't need a transfusion immediately after his birth—"

"Jesus! A transfusion?" Michael interrupted.

Dr. Slater continued, "...was because Kristen received a Rhogam injection after her first pregnancy."

Michael was stunned. *First pregnancy? When had Kristen been pregnant? She's never told me about a baby. Any baby. Had she gotten pregnant in high school before she met me? Yes, that had to be it. Kristen would have told me about something this important to our lives.*

Michael could tell from the way Dr. Slater was eyeing him that Michael's face may have betrayed his thoughts. Women and their doctors were notorious for keeping secrets, he thought. If he wanted the truth, he needed to be sharp. "I'm sorry, Doctor, between jet lag and thinking about my business overseas, by all rights I should have lost my mind long ago..."

I was with Phillip when he finally went to see Gloria in Monaco. I'd planned for Phillip to fall in love with Gloria all over again, make her his wife and heir. With Gloria in Phillip's life again, the Van Buren bonds would loosen.

But Gloria wasn't there. We just missed her. But Phillip

still hasn't given up hope. We'll be going back to Monaco again.

Michael saw the doctor studying his face and realized his voice had trailed off. He focused his attention back on what he was saying. "It's just that I honestly didn't remember her telling me anything about this Rhogam thing. Maybe she thought she was protecting me. Didn't want me to worry and all that. Kristen is like that." *Keeping things from me.*

"I understand. My brother is an investment banker. Hell, his wife doesn't even know what country he's in half the time. She runs the house and three kids like an admiral, though. And when John gets home, she lets him believe her work is a snap."

Michael chuckled good-naturedly, but his heart was slamming anxiously against his chest. "Yeah, that's how Kristen is." He paused. "Did you give her the Rhogam last time?"

"No, I wasn't her obstetrician. As I recall, it was Dr. Wiseman. A friend of the family, she said."

Michael nodded placidly as if he knew everything he was being told. "Kristen's family. I'm from Florida originally.

"I wonder why she didn't go back to Dr. Wiseman this time. It wasn't that long ago..." Michael deliberately baited him.

"Yeah. Last September."

September? Michael's blood turned to ice. His stomach lurched. He felt as if he'd been disemboweled. *Last September? Just eleven months ago? How was that possible? Kristen told me she was pregnant in...December. Yes. That's when it was.*

My God! I'm losing my mind! How could my wife, the woman I love, have done this? Why would she do this? Why would she get rid of my baby? And why did she keep this baby?

Was there something wrong with the other baby? Was the baby diseased? And if it had been, what had caused the disease? Why wouldn't the same disease have threatened Robbie's life?

Christ! I need answers. Lots of answers. But I can't ask Slater. He wasn't her doctor. He wouldn't know what was going on then.

But Frances does.

Dr. Slater continued explaining. "I asked Kristen the same question. After all, Dr. Wiseman's office isn't that far from mine. She said several of her friends were coming to me and that they wanted to plan their luncheons together after their morning visits. That's a pretty common practice." He smiled winningly at Michael.

"Yes, it is," Michael replied. *Except no one in Kristen's crowd is pregnant. If I ask him for the names of her friends, he'll think I'm totally out of touch with Kristen's life. And...maybe I am.*

"There's a shower for the fathers across the hall, Michael. The nurses will have Robbie bathed and dressed shortly. Feel free to go to the nursery and see him. I suppose your families are waiting for the good news, huh?"

"Yes, my father is in Florida. I'll call him right away."

Dr. Slater left as two orderlies came into the delivery room. Silently, they strapped Kristen to the gurney and wheeled her out the doors on the opposite side of the room.

Michael watched numbly as his sleeping wife was taken away. Only moments ago, he'd felt closer to her than he'd ever felt to another human being since his mother.

Now his life had been transformed into a surrealistic

nightmare. He didn't know Kristen any better than he knew the strangers who worked in this hospital.

Dragging his leaden feet across the hall to the men's bathroom, he peeled off the surgical greens he wore.

Allowing logic to rule his destiny in business had made Michael "a young man to be watched," the *Wall Street Journal* had stated last month. Until this moment, Michael had not employed logic in his relationship with Kristen. Had he done so last year, or the year before, or certainly the day they'd met, he might have seen this guillotine coming. But he hadn't. He'd been a fool in love. He'd believed in his dreams. He'd always made them come true before.

Now he looked reality dead in the face.

Why, he asked himself, would Kristen get an abortion? One reason could be that she didn't want his children.

The only other reason a woman in Kristen's situation would have had an abortion was...that she was pregnant with another man's baby.

The first reason would not be logical for Kristen. Even if she didn't want children, and he now doubted seriously she did, their child would stand a chance to inherit a great deal of money. Besides her own endowments from Bart, Frances and Adele, their son would eventually gain the majority of Phillip's estate, though Kristen still knew nothing about Phillip's new will. All totaled, it was more than a sizable sum of money. It was enough money to keep even Kristen's selfish, spend-thrift heart singing for the rest of her life.

That left only one reason that Kristen would have had an abortion. *It wasn't his baby!*

Michael dropped his head against the tiled shower wall and cried. He thought about his newborn baby and how much he loved his son already. He pounded his fist against the hard wall as his mind screamed a million obscenities.

It wasn't fair that Michael be born to a loving and good mother and that his son be denied an equal chance at happiness. After his mother had died, Michael's father had told Michael life was never fair.

Michael was learning that lesson all over again. And this time, he would beat life at its own game. This time, he had Robbie to love. He would insulate his son from Kristen's angst and give him all the love Kristen had shunned. He would make certain that Robbie never suffered because of his mother's indiscretion and his father's foolishness.

Michael would also make certain he never gave his heart away again. He wouldn't care if people called him a cynic as they did Phillip.

He would do everything in his power to keep his heart and his son safe.

30

➤━━◆━━

Darien, Connecticut
April, 1986

Inviting twenty neighborhood children for her son, Travis's, fourth birthday party was a clear sign to Susannah that motherhood had caused her brain to dysfunction.

Because Greg had told her they needed to cut back on all their expenses, which included scrapping the new swimming-pool plans as well as the new minivan, she thought having an old-fashioned kind of party devoid of magicians, ponies, merry-go-rounds and clowns would still delight the children. She was dead wrong.

Without something to amuse them, the boys and girls spent the afternoon complaining about the heat, the "stupid" pin-the-tail-on-the-donkey game and blatantly told her that the homemade cake she made was too "plain" and "booorrrring."

One seven-year-old red-haired boy told Susannah that the reason the ice cream melted too fast was that she'd bought a cheap brand that had too much air. If she'd bought Häagen-Dazs, the way his mother always did, it would have kept longer because it had more butterfat.

"I'll bet you're going to be a scientist when you grow up," Susannah had commented sarcastically.

"I already am," he replied, and stomped away.

She'd wanted the day to be joyous for her son, who had brought her more joy than she had ever imagined. Travis was bright, happy, well-adjusted and beautiful, although he didn't like his angelic-looking face because most people thought he was a girl. He wanted to be friends with everyone. He had that same puppy-dog "here I am world, don't you just love me?" attitude Susannah had had when she was a child, which caused his feelings to be easily hurt.

When Susannah learned that Greg had been passed over again for a promotion, she'd finally admitted to herself that her husband was not the brilliant attorney he believed himself to be. Greg was already living beyond his means trying to keep up with their Darien friends. The payments on his new BMW, the Ralph Lauren wardrobe he insisted was essential to his success and the fifty-thousand-dollar country-club membership caused Susannah to cut more than a few corners for herself and Travis.

She told herself she didn't mind. The sacrifices were worth the time she spent at home with Travis. There would be chance enough for her to work again when Travis entered school.

Ironically, today's birthday party brought the inequities of her life with Greg into sharp relief and, sadly, Travis was paying a heavy price for his father's selfishness.

Susannah heard her son's young guests' cruelties just as Travis did.

"How can you have a proper party without Mrs. Eastley's decorations, Travis? My mother says it's very important to have the proper setting," pretty Jennifer Wallington said while smoothing the skirt of her Laura Ashley dress.

Confusion contorted Travis's bright smile into a corkscrew grimace. "My mommy doesn't know that lady."

"That's why I'm telling you about her, Travis. I don't expect you to know these things. I'm four years older than you. Just remember that."

"Okay." Travis sighed heavily under Jennifer's dour tone, stuck his little hands in his shorts' pockets and trundled away.

Susannah's heart went out to her son and as she turned back into the kitchen, she watched Penelope Lindstrom push a wooden kitchen chair up to the wall phone, climb up and telephone her mother.

"Come get me, Mommy," the five-year-old, dark-haired little girl said. "No, she doesn't, Mommy. No, I won't, Mommy. Okay, Mommy. Bye."

The party was only twenty minutes old when Susannah felt her rage explode. These children were the fruits of their parents' prejudices and snobbery and she was damned if she was going to let their cruelties sear even the thinnest edge of Travis's feelings.

She knew she had to think fast.

Quickly, she gathered sheets from the linen closet, string from the toolbox, scissors and tape. She moved all the furniture in the living room away from the fireplace and lined up the dining-room chairs to form rows. She stuck popcorn in the microwave to pop while she went to Greg's office and typed up a short playbill. She made copies on the home copier Greg had bought last year. She chuckled to herself thinking how furious Greg would be if he knew she was "snooping" in his office. She used Travis's crayons to make a cover for the playbill and copied it. While the copies were being made, she popped more microwave popcorn and placed the bags on every other chair.

Going back to Greg's study, she stapled the playbills together and placed them on each chair and sofa seat-cushion.

Digging in her closet, she found the zippered plastic bag that contained the *magic* dress she'd worn to the Van Buren Fourth of July party ten years ago. Gloria had given her the dress on her first wedding anniversary, telling her that maybe the dress would bring her luck one day.

She piled her long flaming hair on top of her head and inserted dried roses from her preserved wedding bouquet that she'd had stashed in a hatbox. Twisting three ropes of cheap pearls around her neck, then grabbing the brass French horn off the wall on the landing, she dashed down the stairs.

She went to the French doors and blew the horn. The children immediately looked up. She didn't miss Travis's brilliant blue eyes as he listened to his mother.

"Hear ye! Hear ye! The Queen of Walton Wonderland invites all of her subjects to witness a tale of amusement and drama inside the Walton Theatre! Will Prince Travis Walton please come forward?"

She held out her hand to Travis as he approached her with both curiosity and admiration in his eyes. Halfway across the lawn he broke into a run, rushed up to her and threw his arms around her legs. He was only three feet four inches tall and the top of his head did not yet reach her waist. He hugged Susannah with all his might then tilted his head back and looked up at her adoringly as she smoothed his hair.

"Oh, thank you, Mommy! Thank you for bringing all my friends here. I love you so much, Mommy!"

Never in her life had anyone touched Susannah as deeply as her little son had at that moment. Knowing she would treasure this moment for the rest of her life, she replied, "I love you more."

In unison, the children cheered and rushed forward like a tidal wave.

They scrambled into the living room and fought each other for the best seats. All except for Jennifer, who calmly walked up to Susannah, her hands held primly in front of her.

"Your gown is quite beautiful, Mrs. Walton."

"Thank you, Jennifer."

"I don't think my mommy knows where to buy a dress like you have. Would you mind telling her so she will know?"

"This is a very special dress, Jennifer. There are no others like it in the world anymore."

Suddenly the little girl's haughty facade slipped. She looked on the verge of tears, but she fought them back valiantly. "Are you very sure? My mommy *needs* a dress like that."

Susannah smiled at Jennifer. "I call this my magic dress, Jennifer. Actually, I'm sure your mother has a special dress, too."

Jennifer shook her head sadly. "I know she doesn't. She doesn't believe in magic. She told me fairy tales and make-believe aren't good for my development."

"I'm sorry to hear that, Jennifer." Feeling terribly guilty for thinking ill of Jennifer and her family, Susannah now felt only pity. "Why don't you sit over there on that big chair?"

Jennifer left Susannah, sat in the chair and shoved a handful of popcorn into her mouth.

Sliding behind her makeshift curtain, Susannah noticed that now all the children were crowded around Travis, each of them vying for his attention. Finally, her birthday boy was the center of attention. All was as it should be.

Susannah began a one-woman rendition of "Rapunzel." The younger children adored the story, she judged by their rapt attention. Not until she began describing the White Knight's dangerous sword fight with the Black Knight who then transformed himself into an alien winged-monkey monster with computerized laser eyes did the older children become equally spellbound.

Embellishing the story with enough contemporary terms, technology and gore to leave little of the original story remaining, she kept the children entertained.

So immersed in her acting and her interaction with her young audience, Susannah was startled when the doorbell rang. The first of the mothers had come to retrieve her child.

Groaning with disappointment, the children filed out of the house complaining that they hadn't eaten all of their cake, hadn't watched Travis open his presents and, most emphatically hadn't been able to ask Mrs. Walton to tell them another wonderful story.

Travis held a plastic bag for his mother while she cleaned up the discarded popcorn bags. "This was the best party I've ever been to, Mommy!"

"I'm glad you liked my surprise, sweetheart."

"Oh, I did! And the kids want you to give them another show next week! Could we do that?"

"Well, that may be a bit soon, but maybe for special

occasions." She smiled as she returned the last chair to its place.

"I didn't know you could be all those people. How come we didn't do this before?"

"I used to tell you stories. Don't you remember them?"

Travis's bottom lip pouted. "I was a baby then!"

Smiling again, she pulled him into her arms. "I forgot. You're four now and grown-up."

"I'm not all grown-up. I don't want to be all the way grown-up."

"Why not?" she asked.

"Because I'd be like Daddy and have to leave you alone all the time." He threw his arms around her waist. "I want to stay here so you don't get lonely."

Lonely. The way he says it makes it sound agonizing.

"When you go to school in a few years, I may decide to go back to work, but I'd be home every night to be with you and Daddy."

"What did you used to work at?"

"I was going to be a teacher, but I never actually taught. Once your father and I got married, there didn't seem to be any point." *I wish I had gotten my teaching certificate and saved all the money I earned so that I could give you the kind of birthday party you deserve, my little darling. I wish...I'd done a lot of things differently. You are the best decision I've ever made.*

Travis slapped his small palm on the kitchen table. "I think you should be a movie star instead! You're the most special mommy in the world. You should be somebody special!" he exclaimed gleefully.

Susannah laughed. "I'm afraid that will never happen, sweetheart. I thought about it once." *Half my youth I*

thought only about being an actress. I couldn't even cut it as
a model. What chance would I ever possibly have?

"Just once? But you told me if I wanted something I
had to think a long time about it and then work hard and
think some more. Then I could make it happen. Didn't
you tell me that?"

"Yes, I did."

"So, how come you don't try that?" Travis asked, his
big blue eyes demanding an answer.

"You're so silly." She tickled him. "How could I do
that and take care of you, too?"

Travis grabbed his tummy and giggled. "You're the
silly one!" he squealed. "If you can teach school and take
care of me, you can be a movie star and take care of me!"

Susannah was stunned as Travis's words reverber-
ated in her head. They continued to echo loudly as she
cleaned up the kitchen and Travis went to the living
room to open the last of his presents and play with his
new toys.

How do I know? Will I ever know? Where would I start?
Who would I call?

Susannah's thoughts weighed heavily as she cleaned
the yard, took out the trash and went to the mailbox. Absentmindedly, she shuffled quickly through the usual
bills, advertisements and magazines. Going back into
the house, she was still preoccupied with a dozen different ways she could go about building her acting skills.

As close as Darien was to New York, she would have
no trouble at all finding acting workshops and classes.
For years she'd wondered if she truly had any talent.
High-school plays were hardly Broadway. Why, she'd
have to be nuts to throw herself into the New York
arena.

Penny, the young maid she'd met at Bettye's house

when she'd first come to New York, had wanted to act far more than Susannah had. To her knowledge, Susannah had never seen Penny on television or read about her on Broadway. She'd disappeared from all their lives over seven years ago.

Even Marilou had gone to Los Angeles after graduation to find a producer to marry, but as yet had not done anything more than open a health-food bakery. Marilou wrote to her at Christmas and always called on Susannah's birthday.

Marilou never forgets Travis's birthday, either! she realized.

Picking up the stack of mail, she carefully flipped the envelopes behind each other. Then she stopped.

"Look, sweetheart! There's a card from Auntie Marilou!"

"Oh, goodie!" Travis jumped up from the floor and raced to Susannah. He grabbed the envelope and looked at the stamp, a habit he'd formed on his own. Susannah had no idea why he was so particular about stamps, and whenever she asked him, he always replied that he was "just checking."

Travis had several similar little quirks that made his personality all the more endearing. When he removed the card, money dropped out. "Look, Mommy! A dollar!" He pretended to read the card, which he could not.

Susannah picked up the money and realized it was a fifty-dollar bill. Travis shoved the card in his mother's face.

"Read me what it says!" Then he scrambled into his mother's lap.

"Goodness! She wrote all over this thing, didn't she?" Susannah examined the tightly crammed card and the words that formed a wreath around the borders.

Dear Susannah,

Don't faint! I'm an actress! I got a part on a soap out here. Mostly I wear a bathing suit or low-cut dresses and act sullen, which isn't hard for me to do. Grab the newest copy of *People*—I'm featured toward the back. The show is called "L.A. Love." It's on at two o'clock EST.

Happy Birthday, Travis! Buy your mom some chocolate. As I remember, she can't get enough of the stuff. Or maybe that was me when we were at school.

Still no husband. Guys out here are such jerks. Nothing like lovey-dovey Greg, right, Susannah? Call me, babe!

Ciao,
Marilou

Travis closed the card and looked up at his mother. "See? Auntie Marilou is an actress. You can do it, too."

Dazed over Marilou's news, Susannah let Travis take his money and card to his room and put them in his "secret place" inside a battered metal box in the back corner of his closet.

Then she remembered that one of the magazines in her lap was *People*. Quickly, she thumbed through it and found the article on Marilou.

The photo was taken at a small Spanish bungalow surrounded by tropical plants and blooming flowers. Marilou must have moved since they'd last spoken. Saltillo tile encompassed an elliptical-shaped swimming pool by which Marilou reclined in a bikini smaller than the one she'd bought in Brazil when they were in college.

Impossible as it seemed, Susannah swore Marilou's breasts were even larger and she couldn't help wondering if she'd had implants. Her waist was smaller and her hips trim and fit. Her hair was expertly arranged to look as if she'd sun-dried it after a dip. Knowing Marilou the way she did, Susannah knew a half-dozen hairdressers probably hadn't been enough to please her finicky friend.

Sitting on the wrought-iron lounge chair padded with black-and-white-striped canvas was a German shepherd larger than Marilou. The dog stared at Marilou with its tongue hanging out, which was precisely the effect her wacky friend would have wanted, Susannah thought.

She probably paid a fortune to hire a dog trainer...if she even owns it! I wouldn't put anything past that nut!

Thinking about the paths her and Marilou's lives had taken, Susannah couldn't help laughing at the irony.

When they were in college, all Marilou ever wanted was a rich husband. She'd gone to Los Angeles, not to become an actress, but to chase rich, old men.

Susannah had dreamed of acting for much of her young life, but by the time she met Marilou, she'd given up hope.

Yet today, Susannah had been forced to rely on her own talents to save the party for Travis. Enthralling the toughest audience possible had been surprisingly thrilling. She'd wanted to give all the credit to the magic dress, but she no longer believed in fairy tales any more than little Jennifer did. Susannah had to wonder if she didn't actually have some real talent.

She had buried her desire to explore this creative side of her for much too long.

Marilou had taken a chance and won.

That realization was all Susannah needed to kindle her own hopes. If Marilou could do it, so could she!

Susannah rose from the chair and raced up the stairs

to Travis's room. He had just pinned Marilou's card to his cork bulletin board.

"Sweetheart, let me see that card. Did Aunt Marilou write her phone number anywhere?"

"I don't think so. I kept the envelope. It's in my secret place. Do you want it?"

"Yes," she replied while Travis went to the closet and closed the door behind him, as was his habit. While waiting for him, Susannah looked at the card and found there was indeed no phone number.

Travis emerged from the closet. "You didn't see, did you, Mommy?" he said, handing her the envelope.

"No, honey. Is it all right if I take this downstairs and copy it into my address book?"

"Sure."

Susannah went to the kitchen drawer where she kept her address book and found it missing.

Rifling through every drawer in the kitchen served only to frustrate her. Because she kept her emergency numbers and a long list of dependable baby-sitters in the front, Susannah never moved her address book from the drawer by the phone.

Believing she'd misplaced it during the rush to prepare the house for the birthday party, she checked the laundry room, the cabinet under the sink in the half bath, the living-room end-table drawers and even the drawers in the hunt table in the dining room. As a last resort, she went to Greg's office, where she knew it would *not* be and found it.

"What on earth is it doing in here?"

Her only conclusion was that Travis must have put it in there thinking he was helping. As she picked up the leather book, a piece of stationery stuck to the back of it.

The heavy ivory embossed paper was not Greg's

usual gray with burgundy ink he always ordered. It was too small to be business stationery. It was more like a...woman's personal note card.

Thoughts of Marilou and acting were obliterated from Susannah's mind as she carefully turned the card over. There was no monogram to identify the sender. Whoever she was, she knew Greg...intimately.

Darling,
   I'm going insane! I need your hot tongue

Susannah couldn't read any further. Shaking violently, her hands blurred the words. Rage flushed her face and her eyes swam in hot tears.

This isn't happening! It can't be!

Greg? With another woman?

She forced herself to read the entire note. The language was lewd and intentionally arousing. The woman, whoever she was, had clearly performed sexual acts with Greg that bordered on violence. Susannah didn't recognize the man this woman was addressing, but when she described his genitals, Susannah knew the note could only be for Greg.

Twice the sender used the phrase, "all these years." For Susannah those three words cut more deeply than all the rest.

This wasn't a one-night stand or a weekend fling. This was an on-going affair, revealing a dark and evil side of her husband she could hardly believe existed.

Susannah's intestines felt as if they'd shriveled. Her skin turned icy cold as shock burrowed deep inside her. It was as if, for the first time in her life, Susannah learned that hate was hard and brittle.

Unable to move, Susannah's eyes read the note again.

And again. She wanted—no, *needed* to remember every line, every word. Memorizing the curve of the woman's handwriting in case it might someday be important to her.

After an inordinately long period of time, she replaced the horrible note and closed the drawer, making certain everything looked untouched.

Woodenly, she walked to the kitchen and picked up the phone. She punched out the number Marilou had last given her. A computerized recording told her that Marilou's number had been changed. Then it repeated the number twice while Susannah copied it into her address book.

The phone rang four times before the recorder picked up.

"Marilou, this is Susannah. Travis thanks you for the birthday card. Your article was fantastic. I just wanted to let you know that I'm going to take you up on your offer to use your credit card. If it's not valid, please call me. I suppose you know me well enough to realize, I'd never take advantage of you. But the time has come."

She bit her lip to keep from crying. *I must escape.*

31

Monaco
April 1986

Gloria Banning was leaning quite ungracefully over the Tuscan-style granite balustrade of her cliffside-apartment balcony when Susannah saw her.

After opening the door, Gloria's chauffeur had pointed upward past the soaring ancient cypress trees and climbing clematis and flowering bougainvillea, directing Susannah's gaze to Gloria.

Susannah shielded her eyes from the midday sun and waved to her friend. "Hello!" She mouthed the words so as not to disturb the stoic-faced doorman dressed in blue-and-gold livery.

Gloria's smile covered her face, but when she saw Susannah reach back into the twenty-year-old black Mercedes and take her little boy's hand, she burst into joyful tears. "Travis," Susannah heard her murmur as the older woman placed her hand over her heart.

Susannah and Travis waited for the doorman to open the glass, art nouveau brass door.

Travis smiled up at the stony-faced man and said, "You must be very important to wear so much gold!"

The man's expression melted instantly. Suddenly, he couldn't do enough for Susannah. He escorted them to the elevator and punched the button numbered with a brass "2." And once the antique wrought-iron doors closed over the open elevator cage and they began to ascend, he waved to Travis.

Gloria came rushing out of her apartment just as the elevator stopped. "My darlings! How wonderful to see you!" she gushed happily as she and Susannah embraced.

She leaned down to Travis, who was dressed in navy pants and a white sailor's shirt edged with navy braid. A replica of a sea captain's cap sat on his head. "You're even more handsome than your mother said in her letters. Except for your blond hair, you're the image of her. I'm so very happy to finally meet you."

Smiling, Travis pulled off his cap and put it under his arm with such stiff formality he looked as if he'd been at sea since birth. He shook her hand. "Thank you for my birthday postcards. I've kept all the stamps and postcards in my secret place."

Gloria beamed. "I had a feeling you might enjoy my special stamps. I collect them, you know."

He nodded excitely. "Me, too. Yours are the best!"

Susannah rolled her eyes. She'd asked Travis the significance of his obsession with stamps and the mail. Now she knew the answer to the riddle. Travis had been looking for letters and cards from Gloria. Without ever having met, Travis and Gloria had bonded. The thought pleased her immensely.

"Rinaldo will bring up your luggage while we visit. I've made a light luncheon for us, and my favorite Tuscan pastry shop made *profiteroles* just for you, Travis."

"Profit rolls?" he repeated uncertainly.

"Don't tell me you don't like cookies, Travis," Gloria said. "*Profiteroles* are cookies."

Instantly he jerked his head back to look up at his mother. "How many can I have?"

"Two, but after lunch."

"Aw." He trudged across the sea blue and white marble foyer, through the delicately appointed French-style living room and out to the terrace where a round table was covered with snowy white linens and set with gold-and-pink bone china. The table was piled with all kinds of fruits, a tray of cheeses, a bottle of wine and a three-tiered server filled with dozens of cookies and pastries.

Susannah and Gloria had followed Travis and watched as he looked through the stone-carved balusters to the Mediterranean Sea. Glittering sun rays pirouetted on the royal blue surface. Hundred-foot-long sailing yachts with masts so tall they looked as if they could pierce the sky were lined up in rows like soldiers. Squatting like fat dowager geese, luxurious power yachts filled the rest of the yacht basin. Gold-and-pink villas and houses perched on the seaside cliffs. Potted flowers and expertly pruned trees lined the streets below, where pretty people, dressed in cool summer clothes, laughed and smiled.

Travis whirled to look at his mother.

"Mommy, are we going to live here forever?"

Taken aback, Susannah wondered how much Travis had overheard when she'd phoned Gloria and asked if they could come for a visit. "Why do you ask that?"

He grinned so widely, his cheeks bunched up and nearly closed his eyes. "Because it's so beautiful! I wanna buy a boat like one of those and never go back!" Without waiting for her answer, he spun around and looked back out at the azure water.

Glancing at Susannah worriedly, Gloria went to Travis and put her hands on his small shoulders. "You can stay here as long as you want and come back anytime you want. All you have to do is ask."

He looked up at her and nodded.

"Come. Let's have something to eat," Gloria urged. "You've had a long night of it traveling, haven't you?"

Travis walked with Gloria to the table and sat down. Politely, he waited until his mother was seated and then followed her lead, putting the white lace-edged napkin in his lap.

"I'm afraid I don't eat many hamburgers and pizza like you probably do, Travis, but I hope you like what I've prepared," Gloria said apologetically.

Travis's eyes grew larger as he surveyed stacks of petits fours and chocolate-iced cookies.

"It's okay, Aunt Gloria. I think I like your food better."

It was nearly five o'clock when they finished eating and then unpacked. The long travel had exhausted Travis, who fell asleep on a chaise lounge next to the balustrade. Susannah carried him into their room and laid him on the large antique white four-poster bed.

When Susannah returned to the living room, Gloria had poured them each a cup of steaming English tea. Looking at Susannah, she said, "I realize you must be just as tired as Travis. Perhaps we should wait until later to talk."

"No," Susannah replied, taking the dainty china teacup and saucer from Gloria. "I don't think I'll ever be able to sleep again."

"Sure you will," Gloria assured her. "Tell me what happened."

Susannah explained how she'd come to find the note and recited the message she'd read, verbatim. The fact that the affair had been ongoing hurt Susannah deeply. She left out none of the details, including that the woman didn't sign the note.

Gloria wasn't in the least bit shocked, which bothered Susannah even more. "I called my friend Marilou and told her I needed to use the credit card she'd given me as a wedding present. She phoned me back that night and said it was still valid and so was the offer to use it. There was no way I could go home and tell my mother and father all this. They think the world of Greg. Not that they'd think any less of me—it's just that I don't want them to worry. You see, my mother is different. She's from a very protective Southern family. She raised me like that, too. She taught me always to look for the good in people, and to trust in myself. Things like that. Honestly, I don't think she's strong enough to handle this kind of sordid truth. I'm not so sure I am, either."

"Of course you are, dear."

Susannah shook her head. "You were my only hope. I wanted to get as far away from him as I could. So, I called you, booked our flights and well...here we are."

"Did you see an envelope? A return address? Maybe the note wasn't meant for Greg."

"Please, Aunt Gloria. I may be naive, but I know when someone else is describing my husband's penis."

"You're right," Gloria replied in her unflappable manner. She patted Susannah's hand.

"What did you say to Greg when you confronted him?"

"I didn't."

Gloria's perfectly shaped eyebrow arched. "What excuse did you give him for coming to see me?"

Gloria's seemingly logical and simple questions bore down on Susannah like steel anvils. She felt as if she were being interrogated. How could she tell Gloria that she'd been too frightened of the truth? Too unsure of his loyalty and love to believe the excuses she knew he'd give? Just hearing Gloria's sensible questions caused Susannah to doubt her actions. Should she have demanded an explanation? Panic had overwhelmed her and she'd jumped to a conclusion. All she'd wanted was to flee. She'd wanted to find a haven where she could quiet the harpies in her head.

"I left him a note on the kitchen table. I told him I'd discovered he was having an affair. I told him I would call him today...after I was calm."

Gloria's expression was thoughtful, not judgmental. Susannah loved her for it. "Interesting."

Susannah didn't understand. "What is?"

"All of it. Two things are blatantly suspicious to me. The first is that Greg hasn't called here."

"But I didn't tell him where I was going."

Gloria rose and went to the window. "An innocent man would be frantic. He'd call your mother and every friend he's got. He'd call Bettye, who would call me, if only to gloat and say something derogatory about you because she knows I pushed for this marriage. She'd claim you were unbalanced or something to that effect. Then she'd urge Greg to call the police since you had Travis with you. That would give him two points in his favor."

She turned to face Susannah. "Bettye's big on keeping score. Greg would have called here early this morning if he loved you deeply. He, of all people, would know you'd come to me and that I would take you and Travis in. It's not that difficult to figure out. So, why isn't my phone ringing?"

"What's the second thing?" Susannah asked.

"Only you can answer that one."

"Me? What did I do that's suspicious?"

Sitting again on the sofa, Gloria said, "You ran away. A woman who trusts her husband implicitly would have shown the note to him, had a good laugh and asked him if he knew anything about it. He would have told her it was part of an office joke or something like that. They would have made fun of it, thrown it away and never given it another thought."

"I...ran away because I knew it was the truth."

Gloria nodded. "And because of that little voice in your head that has been trying to be heard for a long, long time. And you've chosen not to listen to."

Susannah placed her cup and saucer on the coffee table. "That's ridiculous. I have never suspected Greg was having an affair. He's always been loving and thoughtful..."

Folding her arms across her chest, Gloria leaned back against the sofa. "Really? Do you want to read your letters to me over the years? I can show you instances where his actions have proved that's not the case."

Her head aching from trying to make sense of what Gloria was saying, Susannah combed her fingers through her long hair. Her heart pounded rapidly as flashes of the past edited themselves into an insightful cinema of her life.

She saw the elaborate party Greg's mother had thrown for them in New York after their wedding. It had been filled with the people who would later become Greg's clients and his connections for club memberships. Even then she'd thought fleetingly that Greg had few friends outside of a fraternity brother or two.

She remembered how his buddies kidded him about the "wild" night they'd had before he'd left for the wedding in Indianapolis. At the time, Susannah thought they were referring to how much they'd had to drink. She even suspected a porno movie or a stripper. Though she didn't like it, she thought such things were "normal" at a bachelor party. But as she skewered her mind to the details of the conversation, she realized they had implied that Greg had performed oral sex with the stripper. How could she have disregarded something like that? Unless she'd wanted to.

She remembered the pressure she'd felt at the time. Kate had been thrilled by the big society party. Susannah thought she'd never seen her mother so happy. She remembered feeling guilty every time Kate hugged her, telling Susannah she was living the life of a fairy princess.

Susannah had turned her back on the truth for her mother's sake.

The way Greg had bought the house without her consent had told her he did not consider her his equal.

Greg had always been indifferent to her pregnancy and even made more physical demands on her at the time. More than once his lovemaking had been so harsh, so painful, he'd bruised her. She'd wondered at the time why he wasn't more gentle, more concerned that he could hurt the baby. But again, she'd pushed the thought out of her mind.

After Travis was born, Susannah cared for her son. Not once did Greg walk the floor when the baby was sick or needed his two o'clock bottle. Not once did he try to play with the baby. Even now, Greg only referred to Travis as "he"...a pronoun...a nonentity, just as he did her.

Then there were the darker, more sinister signs of infidelity she'd never wanted to acknowledge.

Greg's work patterns changed, just as she'd been warned they would. He called at seven to tell her he'd be staying overnight in the city. He was working hard to get the promotion he'd coveted. As the months became years, the overnights increased and Greg never got promoted. For someone who worked so hard, Greg was going nowhere.

She remembered smelling a woman's perfume on his shirt one time. Another time, she'd found odd charges on his credit-card bill. Still another, she'd found a bottle of perfume in his briefcase when he'd asked her to bring him the small calculator he kept there.

The evidence against him mounted as she thought of the stinging feeling she got in her stomach every time she noticed him watching other women with a kind of lust in his eyes he'd never had for her. He thought she wasn't aware of his seductive glances or the way he licked the corner of his mouth when he saw a woman he wanted. Unknowingly, she'd given him a great deal of rope. In restaurants, when his eyes lingered too long on a leggy brunette, Susannah excused herself and went to the bathroom. At parties in New York, when he jokingly hugged the sexiest woman in the room and followed it with a pat on her hip, Susannah engaged herself in conversation with one of the partners' wives.

The blanket she'd thrown over her head for years was heavy and had successfully cut out the light.

She'd told herself it was easy to pass off such things. Unconsciously, she'd spent their time together making excuses for him. But her heart had known. That was why she'd run away.

"I don't need to see my letters," Susannah said, swallowing a lump in her throat.

Gloria propped her elbows on her knees and leaned

forward. "You haven't done anything wrong, Susannah."

"I wasn't thinking that."

"You're berating yourself for being stupid. For not seeing the truth."

Susannah glanced at the Louis XV gilded wall clock. "Am I that easy to read?"

"You've always carried your emotions on your face...and in your eyes. That's what makes you so endearing to me. That same guilelessness makes you easy prey to those who want to use and manipulate you."

"Use? Is that what he's been doing?"

"I don't know what else to call it. None of us ever really knows another person. All we ever have is our perception of the truth. Greg probably thinks he's been a good provider, done the right thing by having a beautiful, capable wife to show off to his colleagues. After all, in Greg's world, it wouldn't do for a man to be single."

"Why not?"

Shrugging, Gloria replied, "People might think he wasn't stable. They wouldn't trust him with their legal lives, so to speak."

Susannah felt incredibly uncomfortable. She rose and began pacing the room. "I can't ever trust him again. And yet I don't know how to end it. I don't know what I'd do! What about Travis? How would I raise him by myself?"

Gloria went to her and put her hands on her shoulders. She stared deeply into Susannah's turquoise eyes. "The way I see it, you've done a damn good job raising him by yourself. Greg hasn't been much of a father. Travis told me that himself."

"When?"

"Just today." She motioned with her head toward the

balcony terrace. "He said he never wanted to go back. That should tell you that his life, as far as he's concerned, is with you."

"Oh, God!" Susannah dropped her face into her hands and began to sob.

Gloria pulled her into her arms and comforted her. "I warned you before about guilt, Susannah. Don't give in to it. It makes a terrible mess."

Susannah spent the next three hours telling Gloria her innermost thoughts. She reminisced about her childhood, her dreams of becoming an actress, her love of Southern homes and the gentle O'Shea family in Atlanta she adored. She even told Gloria her silly dreams about the sea king. She refrained from telling her how much she'd believed in him a long time ago. Susannah didn't want Gloria to know she'd ever been that illogical.

Susannah slept for eleven hours before waking the next day. In some ways, she felt as if she'd died and been born again. In others, she knew nothing had been resolved.

Gloria told her Greg had called. She'd informed him that Susannah and Travis were with her and all was fine...for the moment. When he cross-examined her and asked why Susannah thought he'd been having an affair, Gloria did what she knew was a senseless act.

She meddled.

While they walked on the seawall for Travis to get a closer look at the yachts, Gloria gave Susannah an exact account of her phone conversation with Greg.

"What excuse did he have?" Susannah asked.

"None. He knew I would never abide bullshit," Gloria said, and chuckled. "He neither confirmed nor denied anything. All he asked was what he had to do to get you back."

"I'm not going back...ever."

Gloria adjusted her sunglasses as she watched Travis run from boat to boat proclaiming each better than the last.

"Yes, you are going back, Susannah."

She gasped. "I—I can't imagine even being in the same room...much less the same bed..."

Gloria grasped her arm tightly. "Last night you told me a great deal about yourself, not so much in your stories but in the way you told them to me. I felt as if I were there in pre–Civil War Atlanta with your family. Susannah, you have promise as an actress."

Susannah laughed and looked out over the azure sea. "I'd better forget all that! Especially now."

"Wrong, Susannah. This is the time you've got to use every bit of acting talent you've ever had. When you see Greg, you'll either give the performance of a lifetime, or you'll lose your son," Gloria said.

Susannah's focus shot back to Gloria. "You're serious."

"Dead right I am. If you pull this off, you won't need acting lessons." She motioned to Travis with her head. "That little boy needs you. I know Bettye and Jack will back Greg all the way if you go in there battling for a divorce. It would kill you if you lost Travis."

A chilling wind blew through Susannah's heart. "He wouldn't dare! He doesn't care about Travis."

"I believe you. But Bettye isn't going to let her grandson out of her sight. You can take that to the bank. Bettye's need to control everyone in her life is obsessive. Why do you think I live over here?"

Susannah clamped her hand over her mouth as tears filled her eyes. "What am I going to do?"

Gloria smiled confidently. "Beat them at their own game."

"How can I? I don't know what the game is."

"Why, my dear, I thought surely you would have figured that one out. Power is the game. And I know how you can defeat them."

Susannah's trembling stopped as she probed Gloria's determined eyes. "But when you played their game, they ran you off."

"Precisely. Because I lost back then, I learned their strategy. Until now, I simply haven't felt like participating. Now I do."

That night while they drank Napoleon brandy in whisper-thin crystal glasses, Gloria enlisted herself as Susannah's general.

After a brief vacation with Gloria, Susannah was to return home and tell Greg that not only did she forgive him for whatever he'd done, she hoped he would forgive her for running away. They were to promise each other never to discuss his indiscretions again. Gloria assured Susannah that Greg wouldn't be able to agree fast enough.

Susannah would then act as normally as possible. If that meant being kind and thoughtful to Greg as she'd always been, then it was imperative her manner with him didn't change. Because of his affair, it was only natural Susannah would not want to have sex with Greg. Gloria insisted she sleep with him. There were to be no separate bedrooms. When he wanted intimacy, Susannah was to grit her teeth and bear it, remembering that every distasteful moment ensured her position later in court.

Once she'd accomplished all this, hopefully within the first month, she was to explain to him that she wanted their lives to be different. Telling him, not asking, that she intended to enroll in acting classes was the first order of business. She would arrange for Travis's care when she was gone and Greg was not to worry. What she would not tell Greg was that she was going back to Magda's agency. Magda's girls were becoming actresses and she'd have all the connections Susannah would need. Besides, Magda believed in Susannah. She needed that kind of support system now. When she started getting jobs, which Gloria assured Susannah she most certainly would, she wouldn't tell Greg about them until the time came when she could no longer avoid the inevitable.

Gloria told her how to stash money from her household account and from any income she made acting.

She was to take Travis to a child therapist so there was a record of Travis's malcontent about his father. Gloria not only gave her the name of the best divorce attorney in New York, she phoned him herself and set up an appointment. Harold Winslow even agreed that Susannah's charges would be nearly gratis. He'd owed Gloria an enormous favor for a very long time, she'd explained.

Susannah was to go overboard for family birthdays and holidays, making certain Bettye and Jack saw Susannah as the perfect wife and mother. Even though Bettye would become suspicious, her ego was so strong Susannah's performance would trick her into believing she'd won control over her daughter-in-law.

Once Susannah's career was on track and she'd accomplished some visibility, Bettye would blow up. She would demand Susannah stop at once.

"That's when you lower the boom," Gloria said. "You tell them about the note you found. You tell them you will declare Greg unfit to be a father. Bettye will offer you money to get out of acting and stay married. By then, you'll have an income and the promise of more money to come. You won't need a dime from them. That will diminish their power. Then, you tell them you'll drag the whole family through court if they fight you for Travis. Or, you'll go away quietly and they'll keep their money and reputations. Bettye will demand Greg give you the divorce."

"How...long do you think this will take?"

"It could be as little as a year, but might drag on forever. It depends on how good an actress you are and how much you believe in yourself."

"I've never tested myself," Susannah replied hesitantly. "But I love my son more than anything." She met Gloria's gaze squarely. "I'll never let them take him from me!"

Gloria nodded. "They never will."

32

———➤◀———

After two exhausting weeks in London, Phillip met Michael in Paris. At Michael's insistence, they flew to Nice, rented a car and drove to Monaco.

"You deserve a rest, Phillip." *And so do I.*

"But I like Paris. Love it," Phillip argued as he rubbed his weary eyes.

"Paris is a city. We live in New York and work in big cities all over the world. I'm tired. I want a change of scene." *I want to stay away from home as long as I can. In fact, if it weren't for Robin, I'd never go back.*

"All right, but this isn't another of your crazy schemes to get me to see Gloria, is it?"

"You deserve to be happy, Phillip. I told you before that ever since you told me the truth about her...I've had this feeling. I can't help it. I think you should at least try to see her."

"I did."

"First time doesn't count," Michael bantered good-naturedly about their attempt four years earlier.

"This is nuts," Phillip argued.

"Why do you make it so difficult for someone to do something nice for you? Try to understand...I want..."

Phillip smiled affectionately and put his hand gently on Michael's sleeve. Michael realized he was grasping the steering wheel more forcefully than necessary. Phillip cocked an eyebrow. "This is important to you, isn't it, Michael?"

"Yes. It is."

"Why?"

"I told you, because I...you mean a great deal to me." *Jesus! One of us should be happy.* Suddenly, Michael's thoughts radiated with new light as he looked more deeply at himself and his life.

Odd as it sounded, Michael realized he was living vicariously through Phillip. Michael's relationship with Kristen had broken down so abominably, he was looking everywhere for love. To ease the pain of his own unhappiness, he'd become obsessed with bringing Phillip and his true love together again.

If Michael could prove to himself that someplace in this crazy world there was real love, then perhaps he could find hope for himself again.

For too long, Michael told himself that if Phillip were married to Gloria and found happiness, he would be less inclined to continually bestow gifts upon Michael, which still made Michael uneasy and which Kristen had come to expect.

In his heart, Michael didn't think it right that Phillip leave the majority of his estate to him. Last year, they'd gone to the mat arguing over the issue. Phillip had insisted once more that he only trusted Michael to preserve the Van Buren fortune. Sadly, Michael had to agree that none of the heirs was capable of more than squandering it.

Kristen alone could go through half a million a year and have nothing to show for it. He was aware of where she spent the money. In addition to the hairdressers, manicurists, facialists and her personal trainer she claimed she needed to be "presentable," there was the cost of her clothes, shoes and jewels; her piano lessons, riding lessons, foreign-language lessons, art and sculpture lessons and the Saturday-morning ballet class. It amazed him how much it cost to keep her "amused."

No matter how much he shelled out month after month, year after year, he honestly didn't care. Kristen was so busy and preoccupied with herself, she'd left the majority of Robin's care to him.

Michael didn't want it any other way.

Though Robin's nanny stayed with him all day and even on nights when Michael was traveling, Michael had been the one to choose Sarah Armstrong. She was forty-seven, childless, creative and loving. Sarah was the antithesis of Kristen and that was just how he wanted it.

Sarah was a simple woman of average height and weight who wore her salt-and-pepper hair in a neat French twist. She wore very little makeup because she didn't need it. Her green eyes sparkled merrily every time she held Robin. Her cheeks and lips had a natural glow about them, probably from the energetic manner in which she scrubbed both her face and Robin's with soft terry cloths at the end of the day.

Sarah was as identical to Michael's mother as he could find for his son. Kristen couldn't understand someone like Sarah because the woman didn't covet owning beautiful clothes or socializing with only the "right" people.

Sarah only cared about Robin.

Michael always made sure to call Robin and Sarah, if not every night he was away, then every other night. Just hearing his precious little boy say, "I love you, Daddy," made Michael's ridiculous life seem sane.

Divorcing Kristen was a dream Michael only wished he could fulfill. Since the day Robin was born and he'd learned about Kristen's abortion, Michael had walked into Jake O'Shaunnesy's office a dozen times. And he'd walked out again without doing a thing.

Fighting the Van Buren name in a court of law for custody of his son would be the most foolhardy thing he'd ever done because, as Jake assured him, he would lose despite Michael's closeness to Phillip.

Kristen's reputation as a charity fund-raiser in New York grew every year. Though Michael knew she farmed out even the smallest chairmanships assigned her to wannabes, Kristen was unbelievably well connected and possessed an incredible ability to coerce her wealthy friends into donating huge sums of money. No charity board would ever cast a stone at Kristen. She was Ivana Trump and Mother Teresa rolled into one.

Jake suggested Michael hire a private investigator to follow Kristen, but the idea was so unsavory it made him ill. Bringing up Kristen's affairs would cause a media frenzy. Paparazzi would follow them everywhere. In the end, the person who would be hurt most was Robin.

Michael loved his son too much to allow that to happen.

Because Michael loved Robin more than himself, he remained married to Kristen. He seldom slept with her and then only when he needed release, paid her bills and lived vicariously through the dream of happiness he'd conjured up for Phillip.

"Does she know I'm going to be in Monaco?" Phillip asked, swallowing hard.

"Yes. I telephoned and she said she had some visitors leaving today. She asked if we would come around for cocktails at six. She wants very much to see you, Phillip."

"I know Gloria. She doesn't break down easily. What did you say to her?"

Michael smiled as they curved around the ocean-view road. "She's got a way of speaking her mind without you knowing what hit you, doesn't she?"

Phillip laughed and slapped his knee with his hand. "By God, she's just the same! That's my girl."

Glancing at Phillip's shining eyes, Michael's hopes for victory rose. "She wanted to know what took us so long to reschedule our last appointment."

"What else did she say?"

"You do know her well." Michael grinned. "She asked if you paid me enough to act as your John Alden."

Phillip roared with laughter. "What did you say?"

"I told her it would take a lifetime to count my commission...but that I would never take money for what I'm doing."

Phillip's laughter died as he solemnly peered at Michael. "You said that?"

"I did. And I meant it."

"I know you did, son."

Pulling the rented Mercedes to a stop in front of Gloria's apartment building, Michael handed the car keys to the doorman and asked that he announce them.

"Miss Banning is expecting you, Mr. Van Buren." The doorman led them to the elevator and assisted them just as he did all visitors to the building.

Observing the blanched expression on Phillip's face, Michael realized his friend had not believed Gloria would be waiting for him. Phillip licked his lips, but his intense anxiety kept them parched.

"Would you rather I wait downstairs or at the little café..."

"Absolutely not. At least not right away," Phillip replied with a nervous crack in a voice reminding Michael of a schoolboy on his first date.

At that moment, Phillip did look younger. Anticipation cast a gleam in his eyes and a glow to his skin and smile. As always, Phillip was impeccably, though casually, dressed in dark navy Giorgio Armani slacks and sport jacket, with an ivory silk shirt, no tie and Ferragamo loafers with no socks. His dark hair was fringed with silver around his face and over the ears, but was so perfectly cut and styled it looked as if nature's artist had purposefully colored and blended each strand. He didn't look a day over sixty though Michael knew he was seventy-seven.

Because Phillip had finally confessed that Gloria had been twenty-one and he only eighteen when he'd wanted to marry her, Michael suddenly realized he'd frozen his own vision of Gloria back in the past. She was seventy-nine now and would turn eighty soon. The shock of seeing each other in the flesh could be disastrous.

I should have left them to their fantasies about each other. I should have left well enough alone. What if Gloria is sick? What if she's still bitter about the affair? What if she blames him for Adele's meddling? Oh, God! What if she's planned to use today to vent her anger at him? Phillip would never forgive me. I'd never forgive myself!

Instantly, Michael looked around for an escape route and found none.

Glancing at Michael, Phillip chuckled as the elevator jerked to a stop. He pulled back the collapsible metal grate and opened the wrought-iron doors. "Don't look so terrified, Michael. I've prepared myself for all eventualities."

"All?" Michael asked dubiously.

Phillip regarded him. "If things go badly, perhaps that café might not be a bad idea," Phillip teased.

"I understand," he replied, standing behind and slightly to the side of Phillip when they stopped at the door marked B3.

The door to Gloria's apartment was answered only seconds after Phillip rang the bell.

Her hair was more blond than silver and it fell in soft fingertip waves to her chin, a style Michael recognized as belonging to the thirties. She was shorter and more petite than he'd imagined Phillip's dream woman to be, making her look more like a child than an adult. The expensive blue-silk print dress she wore fell gracefully over her hips, hiding her slightly age-thickened waist. Her shoes were chosen more for comfort than looks and he noticed that their nearly nude color matched her stockings, making her legs look longer and leaner than they were.

But it was her face that captured his attention. Though lined with sorrow and happiness, she wore the years beautifully. Her smile was magnetic and drew him in. Her clear blue eyes were fringed with heavily mascaraed long brown lashes, though the rest of her makeup was subtly applied, giving her a rosy glow.

Gloria was as beautiful in her late seventies as she must have been at twenty-one.

"Phillip, darling! How I've missed you," she said softly while taking his hand. Imbued with profound emotion, her words sent tremors through Michael's world.

Blatantly shocked at the warmth of her welcome, Phillip burst into a smile bright enough to rival the sun.

"Gloria, dearest!" He took her hand and swept it to his lips, kissing her palm.

She lowered her eyes like a schoolgirl.

Michael felt like an intruder, yet he was spellbound by the interchange. Though he'd nominated himself as the catalyst to bring them together, he suddenly realized there was a deeper, more personal reason that he was here. He was struck with the thought that perhaps destiny had moved them all to this place in time and he hadn't had a thing to do with any of these machinations.

Michael felt the sharp pangs of emptiness in his own life, having never experienced the kind of love Gloria and Phillip obviously shared.

Though he was happy for Phillip, the revelation suddenly made him horrendously jealous. He turned his eyes away and stared at the gold-and-white-striped wallpapered hall.

Why not me? Have I not done something I should have? Am I not seeing something I should? What if I never find love?

He looked back at the couple, and seeing the raw emotion that passed between them, he stepped backward a few steps, hoping to slip out silently.

"You must be Michael, the young man who arranged this meeting," she said, stopping him in his tracks.

"Yes, ma'am."

"I'm pleased to meet a fellow sentimentalist." She smiled with serene trust, making him once again conjure up visions of her in her youth.

"I suppose I am," he replied.

"And thank God for you!" she said boisterously, pulling Phillip into the foyer. "If not for your persistence, I might have gone to my grave never seeing Phillip again." She laughed.

Michael thought of all the practiced and forced laughs he'd heard over the years: laughter from both social and business phonies who thought to dupe him; guffaws from superiors who feared his energy and brains; and chuckles used to mask secrets and treachery. Nothing in his life, not even Robin's giggling, had ever sounded like the ebullient sounds coming straight from Gloria's soul.

Suddenly, he knew how it was that she'd captured Phillip's love for a lifetime.

Michael was too awestruck to speak, but Phillip was not. "Darling, I did have *something* to do with this."

"Really, Phillip?" she cooed. "Why don't you come inside and tell me about it?"

"Gladly," Phillip replied almost breathlessly.

Michael took another step backward. "I think I'll be going...er, to that café."

"I apologize for my lack of manners, Michael," she said. "You've been traveling all day and must surely want to freshen up. Please join us for a glass of wine. I've prepared some light sandwiches and fruit."

"I..." He looked at Phillip who hadn't taken his eyes off Gloria for an instant.

She reached out for Michael's hand. "I won't hear another word about it." She urged him inside and shut the door. "Phillip will uncork the wine. The bath is straight through there." She motioned to the closed door to the right.

"Thank you," he said, taking the hint.

"You'll find everything you need should you want to bathe. Towels, soap, razors and shampoo."

"Sounds wonderful," he said, and left them alone.

The blue-, white- and gold-tiled bathroom was wonderfully opulent. In the center of the ceiling hung an antique Austrian-crystal chandelier. A white marble tub large enough for two was flanked by four white Corinthian columns with gilded capitals. Diaphanous white silk curtains covered an eight-foot-high window that overlooked the most beautiful view of Monaco and the harbor he'd ever seen.

Little had he realized Gloria was giving him the best room in the house, he thought as he rubbed the aching muscles at the back of his neck.

Come to think of it, a hot bath sounds darn good.

Only three steps inside, Michael stumbled over a child's toy boat at the corner of a patterned blue-and-white rug. "What is a child's toy doing in Gloria's bathroom?"

Assuming she probably had plenty of friends in Monaco with young children or grandchildren, he picked up the toy and recalled that Robin often played with a similar bathtub boat. He remembered hundreds of baths he'd given Robin, how they'd splashed water all over the bathroom, both giggling so loudly even he couldn't tell whose laugh he heard. He had a sudden urge to pick up the phone and call his son, but Robin would have been asleep for hours now.

Sighing, he wiped his hand down his face. "God, I miss you, Robin." With two major meetings yet to attend, it would be almost a week before he returned to New York. Only once before had he been away from Robin more than four days at a time. This upcoming merger was an especially important one. If Michael could close this deal, he'd make enough money to finally feel safe, he thought as he hung his jacket and shirt on the china wall hook.

"Safe?" he said aloud, looking at his reflection in the mirror. *From what?*

He sat in a Louis XV chair while taking off his shoes

and socks, then stepped out of his pants and underwear and hung them on a second hook.

Letting the tub fill with steaming hot water, he placed the toy boat on the chair. Slowly, he lowered himself into the water. He wet a thick washcloth and placed the steaming cloth on his neck to soothe the pain.

Feeling his tensions ease, his thoughts came into clearer focus.

You'll only be safe, Michael, once you and Robin are away from Kristen.

Splashing his face with water, he almost hoped to wash away the truth. As always, it could not be avoided.

Money—his money, not Van Buren money—would free him. It would take a lot of money to convince Kristen she could live just as well without him. He'd made a sizable fortune for someone his age. His instincts told him it still wasn't enough for Kristen.

Always used to having money, never knowing what it was like not to have everything she wanted, Kristen would demand plenty.

Michael didn't care. He wanted to be away from her. He wanted to know what it was like to allow himself to dream his dreams again...like Phillip did.

What was it like to think, even for a millisecond, that there might be someone out there waiting for him?

Closing his eyes, he slid deeper into the comforting water. *Just seeing Gloria and Phillip look at each other like that, as if there was no one else on earth but them, told me what I've always wanted to know. Maybe that's why I never gave up hope of bringing them together. Maybe it was my own experiment I was conducting and they were the guinea pigs.*

I hope to God I didn't screw up their lives. Still, I had to know if it can happen.

Sadly, he also now knew that kind of spiritual union would never happen between himself and Kristen.

She didn't have it in her.

Frustration and anger swirled inside him, creating a whirlpool of self-recrimination. He slammed his fist into his palm. "By God! I won't live like this anymore! It's time I take my own destiny into my own damn hands and make something happen!"

Propping his elbow on the side of the tub, he laid his head in his hand. "It's taken so long, just to get this far."

But it took Phillip a lifetime. I'm not that patient.

For the next twenty minutes, Michael planned the steps he would take. First, he'd confront Kristen and make his offer. If she refused the money or threatened to fight him in court, he believed he had enough money saved in offshore accounts to fight her and win. He knew three top divorce attorneys with Cayman Island bank accounts who would gladly accept his nontaxable funds.

The time had come to fight. And when the fight was over...

God! When it's over. Then what? Look for love again? Get hurt again? Be more miserable than I am now?

From what he'd seen recently, nobody believed in much anymore. Not marriage, not fidelity and certainly not love.

Maybe he'd been born too late, he thought blithely, and then sat bolt upright as the realization hit him. *That's exactly what had happened!*

Truth was, he was only comfortable with Phillip. Men and women of Phillip's generation were less cavalier with their morals and hearts. They *believed* in something.

Maybe that's where he'd been screwing up. His life was so hollow, he hadn't believed in much of anything except his ability to make money...and his love for Robin. That had to count for something, didn't it?

Michael wasn't exactly sure how he should go about finding out what he believed in. Was he supposed to go to church? Pray? Toss a coin in a fountain? Wish on a star? Beg the gods for a sign?

Distress and confusion muddled Michael's mind. Shaking his head, hoping to clear his thoughts, he snapped his neck.

"Goddammit!"

Pain shot through his neck like hot lightning. Reaching for the terry cloth, he let blistering hot water run over it. Then he put the compress on his neck. Still the pain persisted.

He'd had stiff muscles from plenty of plane flights, lumpy hotel beds and roller-skate-size European rental cars, but this pain was due to tension. He felt as if he had an ax embedded in his neck.

He remembered his father used to use a strong-smelling liniment oil for his lower back that he swore was better than any of the new sports rubs. However, his father was in Florida and he was on the other side of the world.

Massaging his neck with his thumbs helped somewhat.

What I wouldn't give for a bottle of Dad's old...

Just then Michael glanced to the right corner of the tub and there behind a huge natural sponge was a brown pharmaceutical bottle like the kind he remembered from his childhood. His mother used to pour huge tablespoonsful of bitter-tasting cough medicine from bottles just like this one. It was the same kind that contained his father's back rub.

"Aw, this is nuts!"

He picked up the bottle, unscrewed the cap and poured a bit of the liquid onto his fingertips. It *was* an oil!

I believe! I believe!

He'd been asking for a sign, but this was ridiculous. At this point he didn't care if the liniment came from the devil himself; he needed relief.

He poured a goodly amount into his hand, put the bottle back and began massaging the oil into his neck. His fingers slid smoothly up and down his knotted muscles, easing his pain. His nerves calmed and he began taking deep breaths.

He kept waiting for the liniment to get hot like the sports rubs he'd used in the past, but it remained cool.

He took another deep breath.

Then he knew...and it nearly stopped his heart.

Southern night jasmine and tea rose. It's Mother's perfumed bath oil!

He looked around the bathroom, but of course his mother wasn't there. It had been a long time since he'd thought about the woman in the dream he'd had that first weekend at Phillip's house. That magical Fourth of July when everything in his life altered its course. He'd never had the dream again, though this past year he'd thought about the woman several times. He'd turned her into the embodiment of all his wishful thinking. She was a figment of his imagination and nothing more.

This, however, was Gloria's house and the perfume must have been a popular blend when she was young. Somehow, she'd managed to obtain the bath oil from a local perfumery or pharmacist, he reasoned.

Michael looked at the bottle.

It could still be a sign.

Maybe it's time I believe that anything can happen if I want it to.

33

Greg met Susannah at the airport with a bouquet of pink roses and a tentative smile. After giving her a bone-crushing hug, he lifted Travis in his arm and handed him a stuffed animal in a shopping bag from the airport gift shop.

Susannah tried to convince herself that Greg's gift to Travis was not an afterthought, but she couldn't. His inability to accept Travis's presence in their lives was at the core of their deep-seated problems.

Susannah put Travis to bed that night and headed downstairs to join Greg, who was waiting for her on the terrace. During her last days in Monaco, she'd told herself—and promised Gloria, too—that she would *act* her way through the difficult months ahead. But now that she was back, she knew she had to say what was on her mind. This was her *life*, not make-believe. She would, though, be mindful of all she had at stake and not push things too far. Unfortunately, about *that* Gloria was right; she didn't have the luxury of leaving the consequences to later.

Susannah steadied herself on the staircase railing as she descended. She felt as if her stomach acids would burn straight through her skin. Whether her physical condition was a product of nerves, anger or both, she wasn't certain. She wished now she'd stayed in Monaco rather than endure this confrontation. For Travis's sake, she continued on her way out the kitchen door rather than retreating to her room.

Greg was biting his thumbnail between taking sips of straight scotch. He stood when she walked onto the terrace, a social gesture he used only when in the presence of his mother or someone he feared or revered.

Susannah instantly felt her position solidify. She even smiled at him when she sat down in a wrought-iron chair.

Greg glanced at the night clouds scudding the sky, then, "I don't know what to say."

"Try an apology."

"Look, Susannah, I don't know where you got these ridiculous ideas about me and some—"

Susannah burst into laughter. She howled. She grabbed her sides as she looked at his startled face. She wished she could remain calm and play out this chess game, but it was just too funny. Booming screeches and guffaws escaped her mouth. Her eyes teared as she bent double. Then her laughter turned to sobs. Drops spilled down her cheeks and she gasped for breath.

Greg appeared stunned at her behavior. He sat dumbly watching her. "Shall I get you a drink?"

She nodded frantically. "Wa... Water."

Greg raced to the kitchen. He returned, shoving the glass in her face. "Here."

Susannah drank deeply and soon regained her composure. Calmly, she leaned back in the chair and looked at the empty glass in her hand. Her fingers were wrapped around the base of it so tightly she knew her anger could crush it. "Don't bullshit me, Greg."

"I don't know what you're talking about," he mumbled.

She leveled heartless eyes at him. "If you don't want to admit your affair, fine. The point is, I'm on to your game. I came back because I want to put our lives back together. But the rules are different now. This time I won't be so gullible. You opened my eyes for me, Greg. I see the world much differently than I ever did before. For that, I thank you. However, there's a dark side to my newfound perspective."

"Dark side?"

"Yes. Every time you set foot out the door, I will always be wondering who you're screwing today. Will it be today? Tomorrow? Next month, maybe? I'll be looking for notes again...like the last time. I'll check your pants' pockets and wallet for hotel receipts."

"Jesus! You make it sound like hell! Why would I want that?"

Susannah didn't know she was capable of a malevolent smile, but she was. "That's your choice. You rearranged our lives to fit someone else in. I didn't. So I won't give you my trust again until the day you can prove to me that you deserve it."

"How long will that take?"

She glanced away to the flowering rosebushes she'd planted years ago. "I don't know. But we *are* a family. I'm willing to try if you are."

Greg reached out to touch Susannah's hand. She knew her fingers were icy cold, just like her heart. "I think we can make it."

She looked back, offering him only a placid grin. "Your mother would think that a wise choice on your part."

Gaping at her, Greg asked, "Did you talk to my mother about this?"

She nodded. "Enough to know you lied through your

teeth to them. Telling them I was having some kind of personal crisis was not a good move on your part, Greg."

He blanched.

"Don't worry, I won't say anything to Bettye unless she pushes me too far," she warned as his face bleached white under the moonlight. "Don't think I believe for a minute that Bettye isn't the reason you're pressing for reconciliation. I can just see her now, up there on her soapbox about the holy and unblemished Waltons and how your career will collapse if we divorce."

Placing his hand across his eyes, Greg tried to hide his startled look. "I swear, Travis is right. You do know everything."

"Bettye is so transparent she's invisible, Greg. If you'd only open your own eyes, you'd see what I mean."

He got up and walked to the edge of the terrace. Shoving his hands in his pockets, he faced Susannah. "I never thought we'd be like this."

"Neither did I," she replied icily.

As if avoiding the slap of her anger, he turned his face away. "I don't know if I can do this. Before, it was so..."

"What? Easy?" She folded her arms over her chest. "I'm not stupid anymore."

"Damn it, Susannah, you were never stupid! Quit making this harder than it already is."

"You're the one making it difficult!" she blasted.

"I am?"

"Yes." She paused, and with barely a whisper she said, "By not admitting your guilt, you also have no reason to offer an apology."

"Fine! I'm sorry! Is that better?" He ground his jaw as he glared at her.

"Immensely," she said.

"I'm glad," he replied dully. Then he looked at her.

She stared blankly at her husband, wondering who he was, this person who should have sheltered her from all harm. Instead, he'd been the cause of the most intense anguish she'd ever felt in her heart.

"Is that it?" Greg asked.

"I don't have some kind of plan, if that's what you're asking. I've never been in this position before. I only know that from now on I need to think a bit more for myself. Perhaps I've been guilty of relying on you too much. Maybe it's all too much for you." She gestured with her arms to the house and gardens. "It's no secret you haven't been doing all that well at the firm. Maybe this house, our child, our marriage is too stressful for you. It could be you're just not cut out to be a family man, Greg. Did you ever think of that?"

"No. Even hearing it sounds like heresy."

She bit her lower lip trying to stop herself from speaking her mind. But she gave in to her impulse. "Or so your mother would have you think."

His blue eyes probed hers for the first time in a very, very long time. "I never thought about it in quite that way."

"I'll bet not. Bettye would be the first to brand you a traitor. Think about it."

"I will," he agreed. "But what will you be thinking about, Susannah?"

"Me? Nothing." She looked up at the stars. "And everything."

A chilling night breeze raced through the trees.

"Storm's coming," Greg said. "I'm going in." He paused thoughtfully. "I don't suppose you'd want to..." His eyes traveled up to their bedroom window.

"No." She looked at a cluster of fluttering pink rose petals the wind had plucked from their blooms.

"I guess now's as good a time as any to ask about the sleeping arrangements. Will you...will we..."

"I don't believe this!"

"Well, Jesus, Susannah! It's a valid concern."

"Sex is what caused all these problems. I should think you'd had enough for a while."

"I take it that means no," he said.

"You take it right."

She shook her head. *Marilou was right. Men are concerned with the condition of their dick, first, last and always.*

"I can't have you sleeping on the couch, Greg. I told Travis we were coming home. He doesn't have any idea that anything happened between us."

What happened to my loving husband? Maybe I was mistaken. Maybe I never had one to begin with. How can you be so apathetic about our marriage? Why aren't you taking me in your arms and telling me you'll never do it again? Or telling me you're genuinely sorry? If you did, maybe there would be a chance for us. Maybe we could make love and I'd believe in forever again.

Why do I feel I'm the only one in pain here?

If only you'd try, Greg, I would do the same. But I can't make love to someone whose heart isn't in it with me. Not now. Not ever. I deserve better. I deserve the best.

Susannah forced her thoughts away from herself and back to Travis. "As far as Travis is concerned, he believes I took him on a holiday. He was thrilled with Monaco. He told me he wants to live there the rest of his life. I suppose it was all the yachts—"

"Yachts?" Greg interrupted. "Whose yacht did you go on?" he asked suspiciously.

"You really don't know anything about us at all, do

you, Greg?" she asked, without masking her frustration. "Travis loves boats of any kind. He's like you in that regard, though it seems ages since we went sailing."

"I thought it was a kid's phase or something. He hasn't asked me to take him sailing that I remember."

"Have you offered?"

"I've been busy at work. This last court case has—"

Holding up her hand to stop his argument, Susannah expelled a heavy sigh. "I don't want to hear it. Besides, it's not me you should be talking to about this."

Greg nodded. "I see what you mean."

I hope you really do, Greg, for Travis's sake.

Another blast of cold air wafted across the terrace. Greg hugged himself. "I think I'll go in." He looked at her tentatively.

"It's okay. I want to sit out here for a while yet."

"Suit yourself," he said, and went inside.

Susannah didn't feel the least bit cold now that Greg had gone upstairs. She'd always liked looking at the stars, but now they seemed different somehow.

She closed her eyes and her head spun with hundreds of emotions. She seemed to rise out of her body into the night sky and look down at her life from an angel's perspective. Sadly, she wondered if she'd ever unscramble her own inner puzzles.

Tonight was the first time she'd ever recalled not jumping at Greg's whim or need. She'd actually allowed herself to say what she felt and, in the process, she'd discovered self-respect.

She hadn't planned to be harsh or cold. Caught somewhere in the remaining fragile gossamer threads of her naiveté, she'd believed they could put their lives together again. Now she realized almost too fully what Gloria had been trying to explain to her.

Susannah would have to do more than act over the following months. She would have to lie to Greg, to Travis and perhaps even to herself in order to rebuild her life. From this distant perspective, Susannah could see ragged gorges and twisted highways in her fundamental ways of thinking. It was going to take a lot more than a bank account and an acting course to make herself into the kind of self-reliant person she wanted to become.

Traveling down paths she hadn't known existed frightened her more than staying with Greg, and certainly more than the idea of divorce. She knew she would figure out some way to survive. She knew she was capable of caring for and nurturing Travis properly and that someday he would become a responsible adult.

And she knew she was smart. She knew she was hardworking, determined and energetic. She knew she was a good friend to people with whom she felt an affinity.

What she didn't know was what she believed in anymore.

The last time she'd started out on life, she'd believed in dreams. She'd childishly believed Greg was her sea king. She'd believed that if she wished and hoped and prayed, the angels or God or fate would guide her.

Now she knew none of those things existed.

She felt terribly alone and incredibly afraid.

34

New York City
1986

Bettye Banning Walton marched into Harold Winslow's office like a drill sergeant eager to intimidate a new set of recruits. Following her like recalcitrant ducklings were Greg and Jack Walton.

Leaning over the monstrous desk, she glared at the attorney with eyes so filled with anger the irises had turned white. "I want my grandson away from that bitch!"

"Jesus." Jack grabbed his wife's elbow and physically pulled her away from Harold's desk. "I apologize for my wife's ill-mannered outburst, Harold. I was hoping to stop her from all this."

Harold nodded coolly at Jack. "I've spoken to Greg's attorney, if you remember, Mrs. Walton."

Greg blushed as he shoved his hands in his pockets.

Jack glared at his wife.

Bettye seemed barely aware that anyone was in the room with her. "He says there's nothing I can do and *that* is the most ridiculous thing I've ever heard."

Harold leaned his portly physique back against his high-backed leather desk chair. He tugged on his black-wool vest and chuckled faintly. "James Willstone lied."

"What?" Jack's eyes flew open, then quickly narrowed suspiciously. He folded his arms over his chest and waited for Harold to elaborate.

"Shit," Greg muttered to himself, slumping into a couch against the wall. He could care less what his mother wanted and even less what Susannah wanted. He was sick of therapists and marriage counselors and attorneys. He wanted Susannah to pay for the hell she was putting him through. He wanted her to beg him to take her back. He wanted to hear her voice pleading with him to take care of her. He wanted her to say she was sorry.

Then he'd lead her on to think they'd be together forever, and then he'd dump her. He'd let her know what it was like to explain to all her goddamn friends that she'd been tossed out on her ear, as he'd been.

Jesus! Showing that note from Kristen to his mother and father had been the lowest. Never mind he'd dared her to do it. Never mind he'd promised to watch her day and night, tap the phones and personally get her fired from the frigging commercial she'd gotten!

And after he dumped her, he'd call the fucking shots. Then things would be fair.

Self-satisfaction perched on Bettye's lips. "I knew it!"

Harold peered at Bettye with detached, cool eyes. "You can bring any kind of charges you want against your daughter-in-law. You can say she's an unfit mother. Hire someone to say that she'd sold them drugs or been their lover. Get a neighbor to state that Susannah's left Travis in the house alone for hours on end. Overnight would be better. You can say anything you want. With your kind of money, you can buy any kind of justice you want, Mrs. Walton.

"However, the first thing I will do is call every national media contact I've ever had over the years. Why, I've got a granddaughter just graduated from Vassar who works over at some fancy PR firm on Fifth Avenue who'd love to come to your house, take pictures of you and Greg there. Send them out to wire services. Why, the Waltons will be the talk of the town...Europe, too. There won't be anywhere in this world you could go that people won't stop, stare and point at you. 'There go the New York Waltons,' they'll say. And everyone will read those shocking headlines that after a certain time simply become boorish." Harold paused theatrically. "You know what I'm talking about, don't you, Bettye?"

Gasping for air like a drowning woman, Bettye finally said, "I don't want the newspapers involved."

"But that's the only way I'll let Susannah play your game, Bettye," Harold said with quiet arrogance.

"But she can't do this! Waltons don't divorce! It's unseemly."

"Yes," Harold replied, crimping his mouth in the corners, "it is."

Deflated, Bettye turned to her husband. "What are we going to do, Jack?"

Taking Bettye's arm in his, Jack replied, "We're going to let Harold handle Susannah's divorce from Greg. We're going to let the laws decide what kind of visiting rights Greg will have. And we'll do what we should have done a long time ago."

"What's that?" she asked as Jack led the way toward the door.

Jack turned toward Greg and motioned with his head that it was time to leave. "Tell our son to keep his dick in his pants where it belongs."

Darien, Connecticut
1987

Kate Parker flew to New York to accompany her daughter to court and to help move both Susannah and Travis out of Greg Walton's house.

Susannah met her mother's plane and, after locating Kate's luggage, they drove to the Fairfield County Courthouse where Susannah was to be granted her divorce.

"You really didn't have to do this, Mother."

"Nonsense." Kate squeezed Susannah's hand. "It's a mother's place to be with her child during difficult times."

"Mom, it's not so bad now. The worst part was when I came back from Monte Carlo. Pretending to live together like we were a family when we were clearly not. Gloria had told me I'd have to be the best actress I could be. I just had no idea how difficult it was going to be.

"There were times I'd even convinced myself our life could be glued together somehow. But Greg didn't want to make a relationship. He just wanted his wife back, like I was a baseball glove he'd left overnight at a friend's house. I had no concept of how juvenile he is. Travis has more wherewithal about him than Greg. Why is it that I couldn't see it before?"

"I don't know," Kate replied sheepishly. "I've been thinking a lot of this was my fault. The way that you met in Fort Lauderdale really did seem like fate to me."

"I've thought a great deal about that, Mom. I wonder if maybe we're *supposed* to go down some roads that don't work out the way everyone around us thinks they should. Maybe divorce isn't wrong, after all. Maybe it's something I came here to do. If I hadn't married Greg, I wouldn't have had Travis. And after all that's happened, that little boy is the world to me."

"You've been a good mother to him, Susannah. I know that even if Bettye doesn't."

Chewing her bottom lip thoughtfully, Susannah replied, "Deep down, I know Bettye believes the same thing. That's why she went after me using the custody issue. She knew it was my Achilles' heel and she was right."

Kate shook her head regretfully. "Still, I was the one who wanted you to marry into a good family."

Susannah smiled calmly. "Please don't do this to yourself, Mom. I knew exactly what I was doing when I married Greg. You know, even on our wedding day, I felt something wasn't quite right."

"Well, my God! Then why didn't you say something? We could have stopped everything right then and there!" Kate said.

Shaking her head as they turned off the turnpike, Susannah said, "It wasn't that strong of a feeling then. It was just this little nagging thing, like a persistent tickle. Something I didn't recognize or understand, but now I do."

"That little nagging was your heart trying to be heard," Kate replied thoughtfully.

Nodding in assent, Susannah parked the car in the courthouse parking lot. "I never thought of it that way, Mom."

Kate looked out the window. "I should have told you."

Susannah slipped her arm around her mother's shoulders comfortingly. "Mom, it's not your job to teach me everything." She paused and then turned off the engine. "It's nearly time."

The courtroom was sparsely scattered with somberly dressed attorneys and their distressed-looking clients. Susannah was not the only woman with a parent. One young man was accompanied by an entourage of two-dozen relatives, including infant nephews and nieces.

Thank God I don't have to face Bettye, Nell and Nora today. I could handle Jack because he'd be fair, but not the women. They'd want me to try again. Take Greg back again. Keep the good family name from being scandalized.

Susannah saw her attorney, Harold Winslow, discussing something with the judge. She didn't like the way the judge kept shaking his head as if he wasn't going to hear her case or grant the divorce.

Kate clutched Susannah's arm. "Can you hear what they're saying?" Kate said, sounding worried. "You don't think Greg is going to try to take Travis after all, do you?"

Susannah held her mother's hands in her own. Suddenly, she'd become the parent and Kate the child in need of reassurance. "Nothing like that is going to happen, Mom. Greg is a master at taking a person's every fear, voicing it, manipulating it and using it to his advantage. Every dirty trick he could pull, he did. And none of it was to keep me because he loved me. He wanted to own me. Right from the beginning, that's all it was with him. Possession. He wanted a beautiful wife. He didn't want to be a father, though he wanted Walton heirs. Seems he miscalculated, and once he discovered children are real human beings with feelings and needs, he turned his back."

"He's an asshole," Kate blurted out, then appeared shocked at her own words.

"Precisely."

Just then, Harold Winslow came over and sat next to

Susannah on the pewlike bench. Susannah introduced Kate to Harold.

"Thank you so much for watching out for Susannah's interests, Mr. Winslow," Kate said.

Harold nodded his freckled balding head and pushed his bifocals back up the bridge of his nose. "We had some tough battles there for a while, Mrs. Parker." Harold chuckled. "Bettye Banning Walton would still be pecking at our heels if Jack hadn't made her back off. I told Susannah all along that justice would be served."

"Yes, you did, Harold. Thank you for everything."

"It was a pleasure."

At that moment, Susannah's case was called and she, along with Harold, approached the bench. The judge asked Harold a few questions and Susannah took the stand. The standard litany of questions Harold asked her barely registered in her head. Susannah couldn't help thinking how oddly numb she felt. This was supposed to be one of those life-altering days and yet, just as her wedding to Greg had been, she felt removed from it all, as if it were happening to someone else.

Observing oneself is nearly impossible during times of crisis. When she'd first found Greg's note from his lover, Susannah had felt gutted. Her life had revolved around Greg and the illusory cocoon she'd spun around herself and Travis. She'd forced herself to believe they were the perfect family with only minor worries about bills, Travis's winter colds and her ongoing personality clashes with Bettye. They'd argued at times over where to go on vacation and she'd harbored secret dreams of becoming an actress, yet she'd never realized how her disappointments and unfulfilled ambitions had eaten away at that cocoon.

Perhaps Greg hadn't been as guilty as it seemed. Perhaps she'd been just as much at fault. True, she hadn't driven him into another woman's arms with shrewish ways, but if she hadn't been true to herself, then how could she build a solid marriage with any man?

Susannah refused to cast all the blame on Greg, though if she'd tried to explain that to her mother, Kate would never have understood. Kate had been raised in a world where people were either rich or poor, good or bad.

Just as Kate would have called off the wedding had Susannah told her that "something wasn't quite right," Susannah would never be able to explain that today was not tragic at all. The decisions of her life had led Susannah to this spot. Everything was as it should be. It was *right*.

35

➤━◄

New York City
1990

Coaxing quince, redbud and pear blossoms out of their winter's sleep, spring brought the promise of new life to the city. Susannah rose each morning with the dawn, packing Travis's lunch, running a load of laundry and tidying up the Greenwich Village first-floor brownstone they'd lived in since her divorce two years ago.

"Mom! Quick!" Travis shouted while stuffing his mouth with another spoonful of cereal. "You're on TV!"

Rushing into the kitchen with her hair half set in electric rollers and an old terry-cloth robe tied around her, Susannah's face was filled with anticipation. "Magda said it wouldn't run for another week."

Susannah's plunge into the world of modeling and advertising had been haphazard at first. Though she'd desperately needed experience, she'd hidden her activities from Greg.

Magda had taken Susannah with such enthusiasm, she felt as if they hadn't been apart a moment since the summer of 1976. With Magda's help, Susannah landed jobs as a model for local department-store catalogs and Sunday-newspaper supplements, but the pay was not enough to support Susannah and Travis once she was divorced. Susannah's goal was still to become an actress.

Following Gloria's advice to take acting lessons, Susannah enrolled in an actor's workshop on Tuesday and Thursday mornings while Greg worked and Travis was in school. Neither of them knew about her successes while in training. Susannah felt she couldn't risk telling Travis anything. Should he slip one day and blurt out the truth to Greg, her plan would fail. She stockpiled her small paychecks along with her awards for "Best Sense of Comedic Timing," "Best Dramatic Actress," "Best Supporting Actress" and "Overall Best of the Class." The workshop's mini-Tonys and mini-Oscars were nothing more than cut-out paper dolls, but they represented her first steps toward the real thing.

Helen, the agent she'd found through Magda, booked Susannah's first television commercial for a New Jersey heating and air-conditioning company. It was the kind of local advertising Greg would pay little attention to, she thought correctly. Though the job paid very little, Susannah wanted the experience.

The egocentric owner had written a horrendous, sexually exploitative script and had personally chosen Susannah from a stack of fifty models' photographs because of her long legs and voluminous hair. Within ten minutes of dealing with the bullheaded man, Susannah turned the tables on him.

He'd wanted Susannah to be lying naked under a red satin sheet in a king-size bed, writhing and sweating in discomfort because the air conditioner was broken. Then she would sit bolt upright, holding the sheet low enough to make the censors go nuts, and scream out the name of the air-conditioning company.

Susannah agreed to make the commercial just as he'd

wanted. Then she asked to tape another commercial, played for laughs, run them both and see which one brought more customers. If she was accurate in her assumption that women called for service repairs more often than men, he would pay her ten percent of the total sales resulting from her commercial. She further thumped his ego when she lied to him, telling him her best friend was a CPA who would help her track her winnings.

Cocksure his idea was foolproof, the owner agreed to the bet.

In her version, Susannah sat in a rocking chair, her back to the camera, her damp, long hair hanging down over the edge of the chair with only a pair of bare legs to be seen. Then she turned around, her face covered with sweat, to reveal a very pregnant body profile and said, "Tired of waiting for relief?"

A month later, the owner called Helen and told her that Susannah's idea had resulted in four times as many sales-and-service calls than his commercial. The crowning blow to him had been that Susannah's slogan had already become a catchphrase with his New Jersey customers.

He sent Susannah's first winnings to Helen's office by messenger.

During the twenty months it took for Susannah to work out the details of her separation, custody of Travis and the final divorce, Susannah determinedly kept herself focused on her future. Gloria's advice to see a therapist had helped her over the roughest spots. She learned how to look inside herself and rediscover her own desires and needs. Though she'd been shocked to discover she was guilty of demanding too little for herself from Greg, she also realized she'd fallen into the guilt-trap of living Kate's fantasies for her. The therapist had told her it was a common disease and not to berate herself for any mistakes.

"Mistakes are our lessons in the classroom of life," he'd told her. "There are no mistakes with God."

Simple words had seen her through many a seemingly endless day. Above all, she'd waged a personal battle against bitterness, anger and feelings of betrayal, and learned how to turn them into *positive* actions. Those actions had taken the form of acting, and her painful emotions were the qualities that gave her acting depth and sincerity. Incredibly, the heartache she'd experienced over Greg was bringing her closer to her dream of becoming a great actress. For that reason, Greg had served a purpose in her life.

Now that Susannah no longer needed to hide her career from Greg and her offers were moving steadily up the pay scale, she left Helen, who gave her blessing, recognizing she didn't have the clout Susannah deserved. So Susannah returned to work with Magda full time. Her next segue would be to real acting parts. For that, she and Magda agreed she needed a talent agency. Today, Magda had arranged for her to meet Robert Vane, the top agent at ICM.

Suspecting that Robert Vane might be watching the very commercial Travis just called her to watch, critiquing her talent and looks down to the last eyelash, Susannah placed her hand on Travis's shoulder for moral support.

Analyzing every movement and sound bite, Susannah held her breath until the commercial's end.

"Whaddaya think, Mom?" Travis asked.

"I've still got work to do on my eye contact with the camera."

"That looked fine to me, Mom. But there're shadows on your face."

"You know, I complained about the lighting."

"See? You're better than they are."

"I think you're right. Hopefully, I'll get this new agent today and then I'll have more clout to make suggestions."

Travis finished the last of his cereal, grabbed his lunch sack and got up from the table. "I think you should be making your own movies like Steven Spielberg."

Susannah pulled the rollers out of her hair as she talked. "Sweetheart, I have no interest in producing movies."

Travis stuck his arms through the sleeves of his uniform sweater, adjusting the crest of the Methodist school over his heart. One of the stipulations in the divorce had been that Greg would pay for Travis's education through graduate school, should he decide to go to law school like his father. Travis was proud of his new school and actually liked his city friends more than Susannah had expected. Not until after they'd left Darien and moved into their new flat did Travis reveal the problems he'd had fitting in with Darienites. She'd been shocked to discover that most of Travis's friends' parents had considered Susannah "odd." He told her that they thought her to be too "artsy," too creative and much too energetic. They didn't like that she insisted upon doing most major projects around the house herself. Frowning on her "obsession" with the yard, one mother had told her daughter that Mrs. Walton was "probably one of those New Age earth people, and such people should never expect to be accepted in Darien."

Susannah would have laughed if Travis hadn't defended her so fiercely to his friends. He'd taken their prejudices to heart, thinking not that *she* had been the misfit, but that *he* was.

All that was behind them now. Travis was showing great promise in school. Each semester she noticed that not only did his grades improve but that his ability to grasp new concepts and ideas was keen.

Travis followed Susannah into her bedroom, pulled out her Nikes and a pair of black pumps from the closet and placed them next to the simple black suit she planned to wear to lunch. Then he opened the dresser drawer where she kept her scarves. He selected the black-and-gold square he'd seen her wear with the suit and shoes to every interview and audition she'd gone to.

Susannah could never get over how thoughtful and helpful—and unlike his father—Travis was growing up to be. "Listen to me, Mom," he chattered as he assisted her. "This is important. Lizzie Mannering's father is an independent film producer. He says that all the big studios are going to get bigger and bigger. And unless you're already a star, you'll never make it. He says there's lots of room for people with good ideas to start their own companies."

Susannah walked back into the bedroom from the minuscule bathroom and grabbed her suit off the bed. Carrying it back to the bathroom to change, she said, "Lizzie Mannering's father is the heir to an oil fortune from Oklahoma or Texas. I forget which. He can do anything he wants with his money because he doesn't have to work like I do."

"But Dad gives us money," Travis said.

"It's not enough," she replied. Greg had pressed her to the wall financially when she'd asked for the divorce.

Deluding himself into thinking she would back down if he refused to give her more than the mandatory child support of a thousand dollars a month, Greg had remained obdurate and rigid. Throwing caution aside, Susannah had accepted his terms. She knew this was her chance to make her own destiny. She was determined to *make* something happen or die trying.

Susannah shoved her feet into her shoes and grabbed her purse, scarf and house keys. She glanced at the clock. "We're late!"

Travis smiled and raced to the front door. "*We're* not late...you are!"

Susannah met with a photographer for a preliminary meeting on a fashion layout Magda had set up for her. Then on her way to Le Cirque, she stopped at an automatic teller machine and withdrew the last twenty dollars in her checking account.

When she'd left Darien, Greg had remained in the house, saying he would put it on the market. Once the house sold, they would divide the profits in half. The only problem was, Greg was in no hurry to move. He'd placed an exorbitantly high price on the house and, when she'd protested, her lawyer had informed her that he would be glad to continue fighting Greg for her but couldn't spare the time to grant her any more favors. He advised her to handle Greg herself. "Eventually, he'll come around," Harold had said.

So far, Greg showed no signs of budging. The only money she could count on was the child support Greg paid and her infrequent checks for modeling and commercials. But now that Magda had taken over her career, things were looking up. She had two new assignments that would pay her handsomely. The only problem was surviving the interim.

Above all, she promised herself never to go to Greg or her parents for a loan unless it was absolutely, positively necessary. She hoped that day would never come.

Turning away from the money machine, she quickly stuffed the cash into her purse and raced to make the next light. Since her first days of living in the city, she'd discovered that carrying her pumps in a canvas bag and wearing running shoes not only saved money on cab fares, the exercise kept her in great shape.

Jogging down Fifth Avenue past the Metropolitan Museum of Art, then east on Sixty-fifth, Susannah wove through the oncoming crowd. She arrived at Le Cirque five minutes early, which left her enough time to change shoes and freshen her makeup in the ladies' room.

Looking as if she didn't have a care in the world, she crossed to the maître d's podium and found Magda just as she was about to be shown to their table.

"Ah, there you are, sweetness! You haven't been waiting long, have you?" Magda said to Susannah while breezing past the first tables in the dining room. One of Magda's personality quirks was that she often asked questions but never expected a reply, usually because she would provide the answer. "Of course you haven't. I know you too, too well, Susannah. Now, stay behind me until I give you the signal."

Though it had been more than thirteen years since Susannah first met Magda, she often marveled that her agent did not look a day older. Dressed in a French-couture suit made by an unknown designer, Magda still turned heads when she walked into a room. As far as Susannah could tell, Magda's only concession to age was that she'd acquiesced to simpler lines and subtler colors in her attire. But she had not toned down her flamboyant mannerisms or energy. If anything, Susannah thought she'd turned up the wattage.

"Robert! Darling!" Magda exclaimed as she swooped toward an elegantly dressed figure. The handsome older man smiled charmingly as he rose to greet them.

"Magda." He kissed her cheek and held both her hands. "You look wonderful."

Magda waved off his comment. "I look like a hundred pounds of dog meat and you know it. What a week this has been. However, I'm thrilled you are finally meeting my Susannah!"

Magda stepped out of the way, as if she were a theater curtain hiding the main act. Susannah stepped up to the table, smiled and held out her hand. "I'm pleased to meet you, Mr. Vane. Magda has sung your praises for weeks. Thank you for taking the time to meet with us."

Robert Vane took one look at Susannah and plopped down in his chair as if he'd been pushed. His eyes were as big as saucers as he fumbled in his breast pocket for a pair of tortoiseshell glasses.

"You can't be," he finally said.

Magda began laughing as she seated herself. "I never thought I'd see the day that I'd rattle you, Robert." She placed her small kid-leather purse on the table next to the floral centerpiece. "Close your mouth, Robert, it's quite indelicate of you."

As Robert continued to gape at her through the lenses of his glasses, Susannah nearly felt like squirming he made her feel so uncomfortable. "Is something the matter?"

"Matter?" Robert finally came to his senses. "No." He took off his glasses and replaced them in his pocket. "It's just that Magda has trooped some, rather, er..." He glanced at Magda for help.

"Untalented boobs," she finished. "And the pun was intentional. Unlike Robert, who prides himself too much on diplomacy and tact, if you happen to piss me off...at least you know where you stand with me. I've told him for years he's too nice," she teased him and then shrugged her shoulders. "However, he gets such great roles for his clients."

"However, your description is apt, Magda," Robert explained. "In the last ten years, maybe it's fifteen, I've seen enough cleavage to last me for the next three lifetimes. No one seems to be interested in talent anymore. That is why I don't accept new clients, Miss..."

"Parker," Susannah said. "If you aren't considering any new clients, then perhaps I'm wasting my time."

Magda's hand clamped down on Susannah's wrist so fast she nearly jumped. "Let's not be hasty," she urged through clenched teeth. "Even God makes exceptions. Don't you, Robert?"

He turned back to Susannah. "Can you really act?"

"I like to think... Yes, Mr. Vane, I can act quite well. I realize I don't have years of off-Broadway experience and I've only done a few commercials here and there, but I swear to you that if you get me a role, drama or comedy, I'll not only give it everything I've got, but I will surprise you."

Robert crossed his arms over his chest, glanced at Magda, who remained silent, and then turned back to Susannah. "Which do you prefer? Drama or comedy?"

"Which one has an opening right now?"

Robert's lips curved upward with only the slightest indication of pleasure. "Aptly put, my dear." He turned to Magda. "If she can do what she says..."

"She can," Magda said firmly.

"Then I'll owe you one."

Magda grinned mischievously. "I look forward to collecting, Robert."

Three days later, Robert accompanied Susannah when she read for a one-month fill-in role for the leading lady in a television soap opera. She got the part. Robert told Susannah that the brunette star had eloped with a wealthy financier from San Francisco without warning the producers. Her actions had put everyone in a spot. Because there was no time to write the star out of the involved plot the show had recently undertaken, the producers were scrambling.

Susannah read three different scenes. All her performances were exceptional. The director commented to Robert that Susannah was too good an actress for daytime television. Several cast members told her that taking the job would be the kiss of death for her career because the star was so well loved by the fans of the number one soap, she didn't have a prayer of impressing a soul.

Susannah took the challenge in stride. By the end of the first week, phone calls and cards began trickling into the station praising Susannah.

By the end of the second week, Robert had lined up a Broadway-play reading and a screen test for an action-romance movie in Hollywood. Robert sent three-dozen white roses to Magda and personally paid for a limousine to drive Susannah to the studio every morning. He intended to take very good care of his star.

36

━━━━◆━━━

New York City
New Year's Eve, 1991

Michael drummed his fingers on the computer desk next to his telephone, waiting for an answer at the other end. "Please be there, Phillip." *I need you.*

Letting the phone ring eight times, it was finally picked up by an answering service. *"Bonsoir, monsieur,"* the operator answered.

"En anglais, s'il vous plaît," Michael replied. "I'm looking for Mr. Van Buren. Did he leave any messages for Michael West?"

"Yes. He asked that I inform you he contacted Mr. Dwight Blair and that all is in order."

"Thank God," Michael replied with great relief. "Did he say when he would be back?"

"Monsieur and Madame Van Buren will return at the end of January, but other than the Imperial Hotel in Hong Kong, he left no forwarding number. He collects his messages once a week on Fridays."

"Thank you so much. You've been an enormous help!" Michael said gratefully. *You can't imagine how you've helped.* He hung up the phone and immediately dialed Dwight Blair's number in New York.

Nervously biting off a hangnail, Michael waited impatiently for Dwight's line to be picked up.

"Hello?" Dwight's gruff elderly voice answered.

"Michael West, Dwight. How are you today?"

"Fine. What can I do for you, Michael?"

"I spoke with Phillip Van Buren and I understand that you've had an opportunity to discuss with him the business plan and investment proposal I sent you on Comp-Scape."

"Yes, I spoke with him as he was leaving for Hong Kong. Sounds like a lovely trip, doesn't it?"

"Yes, sir, it does."

"Gad! How I envy Phillip. Getting married to Gloria after all these years. Then moving to Monte Carlo and turning his back on all the headaches back here. My wife is constantly complaining that we never go anywhere anymore. 'Course, Phillip's in a better position than I am these days. That damn savings-and-loan debacle hacked the crap out of my investments." Dwight began laughing. "But hell, Michael, you know all about that, don't you?"

"Can't say that I do, sir."

"So sorry. That's right. Now I remember, it was the crash of '87 that wiped you out. Jesus, that stung like hell for the longest time, didn't it? I didn't get burned too bad that time around. I saw it coming. Told all my investors to get out once the Japanese bond market sank through the floor. But did they listen to me? No, sir! They all thought they knew more than the old man. Ha! I covered myself on that one. Did you put some money in an offshore account like I did?"

"I sure wish I could say that I did, sir." Michael wiped a thick film of perspiration off his forehead. One of the things he'd learned in all his years dealing with the

wealthy was that they lived life by their own agenda,
and nothing, not even acts of God, would change them.
Listening to their life stories was simply part of making
the deal. Sometimes Michael believed the only reason
most of his clients had worked with him years ago was
that he was such a good listener. Easily a third of them
had so much wealth, they didn't care whether they
made a thousand dollars or a billion dollars. Just as long
as they didn't lose their capital, they were happy to play
the game.

Michael remembered how at one time in his life making money had been an amusement. But not anymore.
Not since he divorced Kristen.

"Phillip tells me you lost quite a bit, Michael. So what
was it?"

"The IRS."

Dwight gasped, the air rattling loudly in his old lungs.
"Jesus! The IRS is enough to scare the hell out of anyone.
And once they've got you, they never let go. What the
hell did you do, boy?"

"I asked my wife for a divorce. She gathered up every
file, record, receipt, tax return and canceled check I had
for the past ten years. Not to mention my clothes, photographs of my son and me, plus my high-school scrap-
books. Then she hired two guys to haul it all off to the
dump and gave them each two hundred bucks apiece to
bring back photographs of the bonfire they made with
my things. Then she called the IRS and told them,
anonymously, of course, that she had worked in my office for a decade and that she knew I had not reported
hundreds of thousands of dollars in income. I couldn't
prove a single deduction I'd claimed for five years."

*I'll never forget the meeting with that smug-looking thirty-
thousand-dollar-a-year IRS accountant. Robots. The IRS*

hired robots who went around the country annihilating people's lives over shit like this. The asshole had no sympathy for my situation. It was as if he really did believe Kristen's accusations that I'd been stealing from the government! Any idiot should have realized that such vindictiveness from a soon-to-be ex-wife could only be lies.

Michael continued. "They slammed me with a two-million-dollar tax lien forcing me to sell my cars, boat, watch, furniture. Hell, by the time I'd sold everything, I still had over a million left to pay. I filed bankruptcy to keep them from going after me for a while. Without credit cards, a checking account and the ability to get a bank loan, it's been a little difficult to keep my head above water, sir."

"I should say so! Did she give you the divorce?"

"Yes. And then proceeded to tell everyone that Phillip was on her side."

"Christ! I'd say that woman was pissed off!"

"I believe you're right, sir." Michael paused. *Kristen was born pissed off. Pissed off at her mother, at the Van Buren name and at life for expecting her to grow up. She hates herself and is miserable, and she wants everyone around her to be just as miserable. She'll never change because she thinks she's right and the world is wrong. She casts blame on me, Robin, her family and anyone else within shouting distance. I may be broke, but now I'm happier with myself than I ever was with Kristen.*

Shaking himself out of his reverie, Michael said, "I was hoping you might be interested in this dynamic new company I've found. I believe Comp-Scape will be right up there with Microsoft, given the right kind of backing. And I further—"

Dwight interrupted with a cough and a bark. "I'm aware of all that, Michael, but since I've known Phillip for a long time, I feel I should be just as honest with you as I was with him."

"By all means, sir. I wouldn't want anything less than the truth."

"It's like this, Michael. I know you've done well by Phillip and most of his cronies in the past. But things were different a few years ago, before the investment world went haywire. And well, hell, boy, I'm having a difficult time believing Phillip on this one. He says you were the genius behind his big landslide deals. I'm not saying he's lying or even stretching the truth a bit, but I know how loyal he's been to you. Phillip and I go a long way back. To our boyhoods. Phillip was a genius when we were kids and no one, not even Phillip, can tell me he suddenly lost his talent when you walked into the picture. It's no reflection on you, Michael, but I believe I'm going to pass on Comp-Scape."

"I'm sorry to hear that, sir." Michael had to control his breathing while he spoke in order not to scream with frustration. This man had not only insulted him, but in his own way had said he never wanted to do business with Michael.

He's telling me I'm a loser.

"I won't be taking any more of your time, Dwight. It was good speaking with you," Michael said courteously, and hung up.

Michael looked out the frost-covered window of his Chelsea apartment at the wintery city streets still decorated for the holidays. In the 1880s and 1890s, this row of town houses was fashionable to high society when Twenty-third Street was a blossoming new theater district. Once Hollywood lured the bohemian actors away, the area became public housing. For the past twenty years, the town-house rehabilitation had been excruciatingly slow. The only reason Michael was able to rent this apartment was that he'd agreed to refurbish the interior for Jesse Cavanaugh, one of his former clients.

For nearly a year, Michael had spent his weekends plastering, painting, scraping and learning the fine trade of carpentry. After eliminating the wall between the dining room and library, creating a single open space, Michael had replaced the rotten floorboards with new pine planks. Though Michael saw his mistakes glare at him from their uneven corners, Jesse praised him and gave him a check for the materials to redesign the kitchen.

The work had been a godsend, keeping Michael physically and mentally occupied during a time when his business ventures continued to vanish at an alarming rate. Here it was the end of another year, and again he'd barely skimmed by financially. His prospects for the future had never looked so dim. Even the Christmas wreath on the lamppost failed to cheer him.

Michael glanced at his watch. It was nearly five o'clock, and since most everyone in the neighborhood worked, it wouldn't be long before the dark buildings across the street would light up. They would prepare their dinner, play with their kids, go on about their lives. He would do the same.

He rose from the wooden chair, stuck his hands in his four-year-old wool slacks pockets to warm them. He walked to the galley kitchen he'd yet to renovate. Opening the cabinet door, he stared at three cans of generic-brand soup, a box of instant rice, a box of cereal and a jar of peanut butter. Suddenly, he began to laugh. His laughter rose in pitch, then rolled to a low, husky belly laugh. He grabbed his sides trying to keep his ribs from cracking under the pressure. He propped himself up against the counter with his arm as he fought for self-control.

Lunacy! That's what his life had become.

All Michael had wanted was to be loved. Instead, he'd chosen a wife who not only cheated on him, but who had an abortion without his consent—and God only knew what else she had done. But because *her* family had wealth and influence, they'd tried to discredit him, they'd taken his son away and stripped him of his wealth, possessions and connections. They'd tried to take his soul, but he'd clung to it. He managed to survive, but only barely.

Daily, Kristen, her mother and father tried their damnedest to make Robin believe that Michael was not a good father. No matter how much they lied and tried to bribe his son, Robin loved Michael. And it drove them all crazy.

Phillip had sided with Michael through the court battles, but now that he and Gloria were together, Michael urged him to live his life. Michael didn't feel right about leaning on Phillip anymore. Phillip had coddled Michael through college and, for all Michael knew, Phillip may have coerced his colleagues to work with Michael. It was also time Michael learned to stand on his own two feet. Though his recent failure to close business deals was debilitating, he was learning the true depth of his talent, his courage and his energy. Plunging into the dark abyss of his soul, Michael was coming to know who he was and what he wanted.

It was Phillip's turn to have the kind of life and love he deserved. He and Gloria had waited their whole lives to be together. Though Michael didn't want to think about it, he was all too aware that Phillip didn't have that many years left to enjoy happiness.

Being Phillip's only friend to urge him to move to Europe, Michael hadn't counted on the fact that the rest of those friends and former clients would turn away from him in droves. Almost from the day Phillip left New York, Michael began receiving one cancellation after another as investment counselor to Phillip's colleagues.

The shock of their dismissal had pierced Michael to the core. All those years, with all the millions of dollars he'd made for them, obviously not one of them had truly believed in him. They thought much the same as Dwight: that Phillip spoon-fed Michael and allowed Michael to take credit. They believed they'd been appeasing Phillip.

In the end, only Michael believed he had talent, and most days, like this one with its disappointing call to Dwight, even Michael's faith cracked.

Struggling for financial survival after the bankruptcy was hell. Without credit cards or the ability to obtain a loan, Michael couldn't buy or lease a car. He needed new shirts and underwear, but even those necessities would have to wait. What little cash he got for giving tax advice to his former secretary, his barber and their friends had gone into paying the phone bills and cab fares that kept his business dreams going.

The worst part of his new life had been not seeing Robin every day. Though the court ruled that Michael could have Robin every other weekend, every other holiday and supper on Wednesday nights, it still wasn't enough.

Irony of ironies to Michael was that when he'd had millions, he'd been forced by work demands to travel overseas, which cut into his time with Robin. Now that he had no money, he still wasn't free to see Robin whenever he chose. Somehow, he was determined to find a balance.

When the doorbell rang, Michael was still caught in a web of memories. Rousing himself, he went to open the door.

A diminutive Chinese woman with arrestingly dark eyes and hair so thick, black and shiny it seemed to fall down the length of her back in sheets smiled at him. "Hello, Michael! Happy New Year!" Mai Chu, Michael's neighbor from across the hall, said as she darted past him on her black spike heels into his living room. She was wearing a black miniskirt that looked as if it was made out of some kind of rubber. No fabric he knew of could be *that* tight. With it she wore a gold metallic blouse with a neckline so low he could see most of her perfectly rounded breasts. She dragged a fake leopard coat behind her. As always, she moved into the room swathed in a cloud of orange-blossom-scented perfume.

For weeks Mai had pleaded with him to take her to a New Year's Eve party and he'd emphatically declined. He hated being around drunks on any holiday and he especially despised the kind of phony, plastic people Kristen had foisted upon him at such times. He wanted to stay home and pretend tonight was anything but a holiday.

Mai had come baited to hook him, he thought as she opened her mouth to speak.

"No, Mai. I'm not going," Michael said, preempting her question.

"Why not?" She glanced around the apartment. "You got another girl here? Is she cuter than me?" Mai clamped her hands on her tiny rounded hips and shot him a provocative smile. "She doesn't dress like me, either, I can bet. Do you like my design? I just sold it to Saks today!"

Michael slapped his forehead with his hand. "Your presentation was today! I'm sorry I forgot!"

She drew her bow-shaped mouth into a pout. "You know how hard I've worked for this! If my clothes sell, then I can quit that disgusting job!"

"Listen to you. Do you know how many people would kill to be designing costumes for the theater? And your pay is pretty darn good, if you ask me."

Mai stomped her foot like a spoiled child. "Money? Is that all you think of? I am an artist...a creative person. I have to express my talent," she defended herself fiercely.

"Don't forget the part about the fame," he added.

"That, too," she replied sheepishly.

Michael remembered how many times they'd sat on the front steps of the apartment building sharing dreams about the future. He wanted his security back for himself and his son, Robin. She wanted to see her initials monogrammed on clothes, shoes, purses, scarves and even luggage someday. She had all kinds of dreams for herself.

He knew she wanted to become his lover, but he wasn't interested. One night they'd gotten drunk on tequila shooters and Michael had told her the truth. "I don't want just a lover, Mai. You're a good friend, but that's all it can ever be. And it's not because I love my ex-wife, because I don't. And it's not because I have someone else."

He smiled, wondering if he sounded crazy. "I'm looking for this woman. I don't know her name or where she lives or even what she looks like, but when I find her...or she finds me...I'll know. She'll know."

"What if...you never find her?" Mai asked quietly.

Michael's eyes had begun to tear. "I'll find her," he'd breathed heavily. "I have to."

It had been over a year since their tequila night, and still Michael hadn't found what he was looking for and Mai was still trying to seduce him.

"Michael, you promised me if I got the order for my designs, you would take me out to celebrate."

"I did, didn't I?"

"Yes. And I want to go to Le Cirque and be with all the rich and beautiful people like you used to," she said.

Michael tried not to react to the stabbing pain of loss he felt every time he remembered his "other" life. "Mai, I can't even offer you a glass of distilled water, much less dinner at Le Cirque."

"I know that. I'll take a rain check. But you owe me, okay?"

She moved seductively toward him and stood close enough that her breasts touched his chest. She tilted her head back in such a way that made the light fall on the high plains of her face.

Michael swallowed hard. It would be so easy to take Mai here, right now. And God knew it had been a long time since he'd had sex...too long. But something told him Mai wanted more than one night of passion. He sensed that Mai wanted his business and social contacts from his Van Buren days. She wanted sex from him, all right, there was no mistaking that, but eventually she would plead with him to marry her. Michael was not going to marry anyone ever again unless...

Michael pushed the faint memory of dreams and the lingering scent of Southern night jasmine and tea rose out of his mind. *This is reality, Michael. Deal with it.*

"Since Le Cirque is out of the question," she said,

"won't you please take me to Tracy's party? You know his parties are always great."

Michael put his hands on her shoulders and shook her playfully. "You know I hate parties, especially New Year's Eve parties. You set me up, didn't you?"

"Yes," she answered mirthfully. "You don't even have to change," she said, sliding her hands over the six-year-old navy cashmere pullover he wore.

Michael smiled. "C'mon, you minx. I'll get my coat."

Mai clapped her hands together as he left the room. "It'll be fun, really. He's one of the hottest producers in New York. There'll be interesting people, important people, champagne, music..."

Michael came back to the living room buttoning his coat. "But will there be food?"

"Prime-rib dinner at midnight and garlic mashed potatoes," she said, beaming.

"Well, why didn't you say so before?" He immediately took her arm and put it through his.

Glimmering brighter than Broadway lights, the highly polished marble floors, brass crown moldings and crystal chandeliers of Tracy Dodd's Fifth Avenue penthouse dazed Mai and depressed Michael. He could remember too easily when he'd owned apartments and condos in Hyde Park, Grand Cayman and Aspen to rival Tracy's. The waiters poured oceans of 1988 Cristal champagne, which Michael knew cost over a hundred dollars a bottle. The hors d'oeuvre table was uniquely designed. The trays were displayed on stone risers between which water was pumped to create waterfalls that flowed into a long narrow "stream" filled with goldfish. Chunks of pineapple, papaya, mangoes and bananas sat next to dipping pools of melted chocolate, rum coconut cream and lemon-flavored yogurt sauces. Smoked salmon, spicy boiled shrimp, garlic- and basil-marinated crab claws and sherry-soaked lobster flowed down a bread "volcano" like lava.

Michael recognized the caterer as Behan Wolfe, the same chef he'd employed numerous times over the years for parties he and Kristen had given. He picked up a hunk of lobster and reveled in the taste.

Appreciatively, he took in the fourteen-foot-high natural spruce tree, decorated in Renaissance papier-mâché royal blue-and-gold angels. He also admired the tasteful blend of Russian antiques and 1920s reproduction upholstered chairs and sofas and the vast collection of objets d'art from the owner's worldwide travels. With no more than thirty beautifully dressed guests, most of whom were actors, writers, producers and theater directors, Michael realized that he was probably the only stranger in Tracy Dodd's home.

Suddenly, an eerie sense of foreboding slipped over him. He felt out of sync with time, as if he had just stepped into the future. It was the kind of feeling he used to have when he was about to close a huge deal. It was the kind of *knowing* that moved heroes to bravery.

"Timing is everything," Phillip had told him incessantly. Michael sensed that the right time was now. Something was going to happen tonight; something so important and critical to his future that he doubted he'd had a hand in his being here at all.

Over these past difficult years with his divorce and bankruptcy, Michael's soul-searching had taught him that his talent would never abandon him. Though he'd lost his pride, his money and his home, he'd never lost faith that *eventually* he would find his way back. He believed he was being led to his destiny.

There was no doubt in Michael's mind that he was here at Tracy Dodd's opulent party for a reason.

"Tell me you're not dressed yet. Tell me the hairdresser didn't show up, but of all things, don't tell me you have a fever, Susannah!" Tracy Dodd barked into the telephone.

"Okay. I'm healthy as a horse. But the doctor said my hundred-and-two-degree temperature has to stay in bed."

"Of all the times for you to get sick!"

"I didn't plan it, Tracy. It just happened. Travis was sick last week and I—"

"Never mind!" Tracy yelled and then instantly stopped himself. "I'm sorry, too. It's just that in all my life, I've never wanted to make anyone a star as much as you. I planned this entire party around you being here. I've got Abe Bateman from Los Angeles here. He wants to meet you before he casts Demi Moore in his next movie."

"Tracy, you're a darling, but I'll bet Abe Bateman hasn't even seen a head shot of me yet. Your expectations are running higher than my fever!"

"I'm trying to raise money for Charlie's play, you know."

"Yes, and you and Charlie Klein have been friends forever, and I love his play as much as you do," Susannah said, realizing that, despite the fact that she was sick, she was being the nurturer, which always seemed to happen when she had differences with Tracy. However, not since Magda had she met anyone who believed in her talent and potential as much as Tracy. It upset her a great deal that she'd gotten the flu, today of all days.

"How can I make you famous when you're not here?"

"Tracy...I look like shit."

"Say no more. I do understand, darling. I do," he replied with plenty of self-pity. "I'll call you tomorrow to check on you. Get lots of rest and take all your medications."

"I will. Maybe I can meet with Abe in a few days when I'm better."

"He's flying back to the coast in the morning, remember?"

"Damn!"

"Precisely."

Considering the option of going to the party even for a half hour weighed heavily on Susannah's mind. Her cardinal rule had been that if she could not make a sterling first impression, it was better not to be seen or heard from at all. Thus far, her rule had kept her employed and steadily on an upwardly mobile track. She was ready to make the leap to a large Broadway production where she'd pit herself against actresses like Anne Bancroft and Chita Rivera. Tracy's plans for her were even larger. He wanted to take her to Hollywood.

"I'll let you know what happens, Susannah. Happy New Year," Tracy said, his disappointment lowering his voice an octave.

"Happy New Year, Tracy," Susannah replied, and hung up.

Tracy Dodd straightened his tie, wondering if a noose was any tighter, and walked down the hall to the open living-dining area where his guests awaited him. Using acting skills even Dustin Hoffman would admire, Tracy smiled and greeted the young actors who had made a critical success, though not necessarily a financial landslide, out of *Dreamstalker*, Tracy's current play at the

Shubert. There were former backers who'd all made money, agents, Charlie Klein and, of course, Abe Bateman.

Standing next to Abe was the tiny Asian girl who'd made such smashing costumes for *Dreamstalker*. Insiders gossiped that she'd be up for a Tony this year, but he could never remember her name. She was ogling a tall, good-looking stockbroker type and didn't notice Abe, whose eyeballs couldn't get any higher up her tight miniskirt.

This is good, Tracy thought as he walked over to Abe, still trying to remember the designer's name. *Mary... starts with an M, but Asian...Me? No, that's not it. My! Mai! Mai Chu! That's it! If Mai turns Abe on, then maybe I can buy some time for Susannah.*

Holding his hand out, Tracy walked up to Mai and planted a kiss on her cheek. "Darling, you look good enough to eat."

Before Mai could respond, Tracy turned toward Abe and winked. "Abe, have you met the most incredible costumer since Edith Head?"

"Why, no, Tracy. But I would love to."

Seeing that Abe was practically drooling over Mai, Tracy knew his plan would work. "Abe Bateman, I'd like you to meet Mai Chu." Tracy almost ducked to avoid the sexual sparks that shot between Mai and Abe. He continued his introductions. "Abe is one of the few maverick producers in Hollywood, Mai. He's here to talk to me about Charlie's new play. If he likes it, maybe he'll back it for a movie."

Mai suddenly seemed to become even more interested in Abe. She took a deep breath so that her breasts swelled over the low-cut cowl neckline and sensually parted her legs just enough to give more curve to her derriere. Tracy had no doubt Mai knew *exactly* what she was doing when she licked her bottom lip and smiled at Abe.

Abe puffed out his middle-aged chest. "I'm pleased to meet you," he said gallantly, his dark brown eyes gleaming.

Mai lifted her hand to Abe, who took it and planted a very wet, very sensual kiss on her delicate skin. Tracy felt like a voyeur.

Without taking her eyes off Abe, Mai introduced Michael to Tracy and Abe. "I'd like you to meet my neighbor, Michael West."

After shaking hands with them both, Michael turned his attention toward Tracy.

"I'd like to compliment you on your party, Tracy," Michael said. "Would you give my regards to Behan Wolfe when you see him? He's done a marvelous job this evening and I'd like to pass along my congratulations."

Tracy turned away from the scene he'd created between Mai and Abe and looked at Michael. "You know Behan?"

"Quite well. Actually, it's my recipe for the sherried lobster your guests are enjoying."

"No shit?" Tracy laughed.

"No shit," Michael replied.

Tracy slapped Michael on the back. "West? Do I know you?"

"Not unless you're interested in putting big deals together. I used to be a private investment counselor for Phillip Van Buren—"

"Jesus Christ! I *have* heard of you!"

"No kidding?"

"Yeah, you got a buddy of mine, William Mitford, to

put his money into some cockamamy computer company instead of my new play back in '85 or '86..."

"It was early '87 and he quadrupled his money while the market was crashing that September."

"Yeah. I hated your guts," Tracy grumbled. "My play never got off the ground."

"I'm sorry about that," Michael said good-naturedly.

"Don't be. The play was a dud and I knew it. Instead, a few months later, Charlie Klein wrote one of his best plays ever. *Deep Winter* ran for two years."

Michael laughed. "Glad I was part of your good fortune."

Clasping his hands behind his back, Tracy stopped and eyed Michael critically. "Funny thing the way that all worked out. And now here I am meeting the man who I thought at the time was the Antichrist." Tracy paused. "What havoc are you wreaking upon me now, Michael West?"

"What's your new play about, Tracy?"

"It's a little premature to say I have a new play. I was hoping to put Abe Bateman together with my leading lady tonight, but she's got the flu. I figured they'd hit it off, Abe would fall in love—everyone falls in love with Susannah...I did. Then I figured Abe would either give me a strong enough endorsement so I could raise the five million I need to produce the play, or he would announce he was taking the production to film, which would bring me plenty of backers. Either way, I'd win." Tracy shrugged.

"Instead, Abe's taking my date and you're still at square one," Michael surmised.

"You got it."

Michael's eyes sparkled when he looked at Tracy. "Why don't you hire me to raise the money for you?

Give me a salary for sixty days plus a ten-percent commission. I'll put your play on Broadway."

"I've been trying to raise money for six months. Everybody in this town wants to buy what you're selling...high-tech, computers. Stuff like that. You can't do shit with entertainment these days, much less raise it in sixty days!"

Michael rocked back on his heels confidently. He cocked an eyebrow and grinned mischievously. "Try me. All I need is some expense money and a salary to pay my phone bills."

Tracy smiled appreciatively. "You're a cocky bastard, aren't you?"

"Only when I know I'm right." Michael held out his hand. "I'm from the Old South, Tracy. I was taught that a man's word is his bond. If we shake on it, then you've got a deal. I'll go to work for you tomorrow morning. So, what do you say? Do we have a deal?"

Tracy laughed and shook Michael's hand. "My lawyer would kill me if he knew I was doing this. No paperwork, no contract. Just your word. Christ, you're either nuts or the smartest son of a bitch I've ever met."

Michael smiled. "I've always been a little bit of both."

37

If Tracy Dodd had taken five minutes to think about what he'd told Michael that New Year's Eve night, he would have realized that raising the money for his play was only a phone call away.

It took Michael less than a week to schedule a meeting with William Mitford after he'd refreshed William's memory about the computer stock he'd urged him to buy in 1987.

He greeted Michael warmly as he ushered him into his conservative and expensively decorated office.

An erudite-looking man in his late fifties, tall, slender, with a thick crop of expertly colored and styled dark brown hair, William steepled his fingers as he stared over his gold-rimmed glasses at Michael.

"You're Tracy Dodd's *personal* counselor now, hmm?" he asked with the kind of New England accent that sounded as if each word were being chipped off blocks of ice.

"Yes, I am."

"I didn't know you were doing that sort of thing now, Michael. Exclusive, I mean," he said condescendingly.

Had Michael not worked with William previously, he would have been put off by William's extraordinary need for acceptance that he hid behind a haughty facade. In 1987, Michael used William's Achilles' heel to manipulate the meeting and, ultimately, win the deal. He intended to do the same this time.

"I won't beat around the bush with you, William. I know you are well aware of my divorce. Unfortunately, many of my former clients decided to believe my ex-wife's side of the story that I had fallen out of favor with Phillip, when nothing could be further from the truth."

Michael watched as William blanched. Purposefully directing his comment toward what he knew were William's sentiments, Michael sought to disarm his opponent and end any hope of confrontation.

"You...speak with Phillip, then?" William appeared to be so unsettled he'd begun tapping his forefinger against the tooled-leather desktop.

"I not only speak with him, I still advise him. How do you think he is able to travel for months on end and not tend to business?"

"But Bart handles all the stateside family funds. He told me so himself!"

Michael nodded. "That's true. But I'm talking about Phillip's *personal* money."

"Ahh...personal..." William nodded appreciatively. The room fairly hummed with energy. After a few moments of contemplation, William continued, "And Tracy is doing well, hmm?"

"Very well. Which is why I'm here today, William." Michael leaned back in the tapestry-upholstered wing chair. "Correct me if I'm wrong, but did I not make you more money with TechComp than you've ever made on a single investment?"

"I've made a great deal more on my investments, Michael," William said haughtily.

"But not on a *single, one-time-only* deal."

Hesitantly, William answered, "No. It was incredible."

Inwardly, Michael was already popping champagne corks. "I want to do that for you again, William. I have that feeling—" he pointed to his solar plexus "—that I've had in the past, which I know I've told you about, William."

William's eyes grew larger, but he remained silent.

"Tracy Dodd wants to produce a play that Charles Klein has written. He needs five million to bring it to Broadway. That's not much these days for a hit, William. The cost of production is very low. There are only three members in the cast and the sets are nothing. The play will succeed on the strength of the script and the acting. The bulk of the money is needed for publicity."

Michael paused to build his own level of suspense. "I realize that the last time I came to you, I told you that entertainment was not a good investment. Computer software was on the rise and, granted, it still is. I've got another company I could tell you about, but to be frank, William, I don't have this gut feeling about any of them."

"You don't?"

"No, sir. Not at all. In the next few years, as the world gets more and more technical with new communications devices, faxes, fiber-optic networks and such, I believe the need for any kind of fantasy—anything that makes an ordinary person feel extraordinary—is going to make a great deal of money."

William was unmoved. He considered Michael with brutally calculating eyes. "For years the financial community said you were a wunderkind. They said you had a sixth sense for investments, but when you brought TechComp to me, you had mountains of backup material. I know you, Michael, you don't leap without a safety net."

Looking conspiratorially at William, Michael leaned forward in his chair. "I've been through every bit of Tracy Dodd's background. To date, he has never lost a dime on a play in his life. True, some have not made much money, but he's always paid back his investors. This particular play is a comedy suspense."

"I never heard of such a thing."

"That's why Tracy thinks he's got a winner. This is different, but does not attack some political or topical issue. Therefore, it has mass appeal. He's got Dustin Hoffman sewed up for the male lead. Charles Durning is all but signed. The newcomer is Susannah Parker, who Tracy claims is so good he's trying to get Abe Bateman to sign her for the movie version."

"Tracy's got an Abe Bateman movie deal already? Can you verify that for me?"

"I won't let you put your money into this without it," Michael replied firmly. "It's the film connection that gives the play investment some teeth."

William shook his head. "I don't like the idea of an unknown actress. I'm not usually this crass, but is she Tracy's girlfriend?"

"Don't apologize at all. I asked Tracy the same question. According to him, this girl is as pure as the driven snow. He says she's had parts on several soap operas, done numerous bit parts and supporting roles on Broadway and gotten rave reviews." He shrugged. "I've always been too busy making or spending money to have time to go to plays or movies and I certainly never watch soap operas, so I don't know anything about Susannah."

"But you have met her, hmm?"

"No, I haven't. Tracy's word is good enough for me.

All the remaining elements for a good investment seem in order," he said thoughtfully. "I tell you what. We'll put in a clause that if the play falters due to Susannah Parker's acting or lack of name recognition, then she must be immediately replaced by an actress of stature, say, Bernadette Peters."

"I like that idea," William said with the first show of enthusiasm all afternoon.

"Good." Michael folded his hands in his lap. He glanced down at them momentarily, thinking it had been a long time since he'd executed this unconscious gesture of conclusion. "I'll have the contracts drawn up immediately and sent over, and you amend them if necessary. Then I'll set up the contract signing for a week from today. How will that be, William?"

"Fine." He smiled placidly as he rose.

Just as Michael reached the office door, William stopped him. "By the way, Michael, do you have any other investments I should look at? You mentioned another high-tech company. A computer company, wasn't it?"

Michael knew he had William's confidence again. With the nod of his head he could sell Comp-Scape to William, take the man's check and make Dwight Blair eat his dust.

He *could* pull off a double hit...

Suddenly, Michael realized why he hadn't been able to finalize the Comp-Scape deal all this time, not even with Phillip's friend, Dwight Blair.

My intuition should have been zinging. But it wasn't. Not like it does now over Tracy's play. Jesus! My timing was off. Way off!

He'd been so preoccupied scrambling for money, for work, for anything to get his career back on track that he'd overlooked the one thing that had never failed him. His intuition.

Though he'd had faith in it, for a long time he'd wondered if he'd lost it or given it away. Now he knew that Phillip didn't teach him that, nor had Kristen stolen it. Rather, Michael had buried it beneath anxiety, self-pity and mountains of fear.

It had been there all along, waiting for him to remember it.

"That's not the right deal for you, William. I believe this is better."

"That's all I needed to hear," William said trustingly.

As he left, Michael couldn't help thinking that William's confidence in him was one of the greatest gifts he'd ever received.

On the Fourth of July, Abe Bateman announced he intended to start preproduction for *Sweet Sinner* within two weeks. Though Demi Moore, Meg Ryan and Julia Roberts had all expressed interest in playing the lead, he'd been impressed with Susannah Parker's performance on Broadway and had given the part to her.

Hollywood laughed behind their copies of *Variety* and the *Hollywood Reporter*, knowing a rookie Broadway actress seldom, if ever, made the transition to film. They called Abe Bateman a fool.

He squirmed. He sweat. He got drunk. But he stuck by his decision, hoping not only to prove them all wrong, but someday to be credited as a starmaker.

Within days, Susannah Parker's name was on everyone's lips. The theater world adored her and the critics raved over her lightly comical yet sensitive portrayal of the young married socialite who is convinced her new husband is trying to kill her.

Susannah spent her days posing for magazine covers and her nights on the stage of the Wintergarden Theater. Joan Lunden interviewed Susannah on "Good Morning America" and Oprah Winfrey's production company beat out Phil Donahue's bid for a one-hour special.

Fan mail arrived by the sackful. On the weekends, Travis and Susannah opened the letters, read them aloud and organized them into neat stacks for Susannah's new secretary, Annie Peace, to attack on Monday.

Though Susannah's financial position was finally secure and she no longer felt as if she were falling without a parachute, the media attention she received drastically cut into her time with Travis. Often she felt guilty for not being at home to help with his homework or listen to his stories about his day at school or his frustrations with his peewee baseball team.

It was Travis who handled their life changes with aplomb and maturity.

"Mom! You've got to take these requests for interviews!"

"If I do the article for *Good Housekeeping*, then I can't see your game on Wednesday. If I agree to the lady from *People* magazine, I'll miss your science fair. Enough is enough!"

Travis shoved his hand in his baseball mitt and smacked the heart of it with his palm. "See this?"

She nodded, wondering what he was up to. "It's a baseball glove."

"Right. This glove and I are going to be together a long time. I'm not very good right now, cuz I'm little. I'm just startin' out, like you did. Right?"

Susannah smiled in agreement.

"You've worked really hard and all this time you never got upset when you had a late audition or when they had to retape a commercial or one of the soaps. You said you had to work because we *needed* the money."

Smiling at Travis, she ruffled his blond hair. "I get it! And now I've got to do these things so that we never go back to *needing* the money again."

"Right!" He squealed as Susannah rolled him back on the bed and tickled him. Finally catching his breath, Travis sat up. "That was a whole lot harder than it is now, Mom. Honest."

"I know, sweetheart. And thanks for not telling me back then how hard it was. Everything really is getting better for us, isn't it?"

Travis kissed her on the cheek and then flung his arms around her neck. "Oh, Mom. I just wish you were happy like you used to be when I was really little."

It was a false happiness, Travis. I was just making it up. I was acting even then. "Truthfully, sweetheart, I'm happier now than I've ever been. I'm doing the work I've always wanted to do. Serious work. Not just commercials. And I have you. What more could I want?"

Travis shrugged his small shoulders and kissed her cheek again. "I dunno, Mom. I guess you're just tired, huh?"

She held him close, her hand on the back of his head pressing his face into the crook of her neck, where she could feel his breath on her skin. Glancing at the mirror on the wall over Travis's dresser, she saw the faint lines he'd attributed to tiredness.

She'd been so busy for so long she hadn't noticed their emergence, but Travis had. She couldn't understand why they were there; her life was running as smoothly as anyone could expect.

She had new friends like Tracy Dodd, who was generously giving her and Travis the use of his condominium near Destin, Florida, for a summer break over Labor Day weekend before she was to begin filming the movie version of *Sweet Sinner*. She had enough money now to fly her parents to New York every other month or so, just for a visit. She could even afford to telephone Marilou in Los Angeles rather than rely on letters. On the cheap late-night weekend rates, she'd even called Gloria in Monaco when she and her new husband, Phillip Van Buren, returned from China.

Between work, Travis's schedule, her friends and her parents, Susannah couldn't imagine why she should feel the slightest bit dissatisfied. But she did.

It made no sense to her and, as she put Travis to bed that night, she promised herself she would at least take the time to think about it.

Susannah arranged to meet Marilou in Destin, Florida, on the Thursday before Labor Day weekend. Because she was flying commercial class and this month every magazine in the country seemed to be running an article on her, Susannah disguised herself with a blond wig, sunglasses, Versace scarf and a two-sizes-too-big yellow cotton dress.

Travis carried his own backpack filled with snorkel, diving mask, baseball, three bathing suits, four T-shirts, one fluorescent cap, toothbrush, toothpaste and a brand-new autograph book in which he intended to get Marilou's signature.

They changed planes in Atlanta and took a smaller plane to Eglin Air Force Base near Niceville, Florida, where Marilou would be meeting them a half hour after their landing.

Tracy Dodd had arranged for a driver to pick them up and take them all to the condo in Destin. He'd told Susannah that the management had filled the refrigerator with everything they'd need for breakfast in the morning, along with soft drinks and white wine. He gave her detailed maps of the area, and even the names and phone numbers of his neighbors.

Because Susannah had wanted to travel incognito, Tracy had not told anyone her real name nor the length of her stay. He wanted her rested and ready to work when she flew to Los Angeles on the tenth of the month.

Marilou's plane was late due to bad weather over Texas. While Susannah and Travis waited, two more small planes landed, filling the little airport with dozens of beach-bound travelers.

She noticed a burly elderly man standing at the window watching both small commercial jets and expensive air-force jets roll past. She didn't know why she was fascinated with him, but she was.

She guessed him to be in his seventies. He was dressed in simple jeans, a short-sleeve cotton shirt and old leather boat shoes. He was tanned and the many lines in his face and neck told her that he'd been in the sun most of his life.

He held his hands folded in front of him as a child does at Sunday school and, with that same childlike air, he watched the planes arrive and depart. He seemed to marvel at the wonder of humans rising into the air like birds.

She wanted to go up to him, ask his name and, at least for a few moments, see the world through his eyes. Without thinking how her request would sound to a total stranger, she rose from the plastic chair.

Suddenly, the loudspeaker announcer read off the information about Marilou's incoming flight. Travis jumped to his feet and shouted gleefully, "She's here!" He rammed his cap backward onto his head. "Mom, come on! Let's go meet her!" He grabbed her arm and looped the straps of her leather shoulder bag onto it.

"Okay," she replied, briefly looking back at the elderly man who was now greeting a man and a boy who had just entered through the glass doors. The blond boy looked to be about Travis's age, but his baseball cap was pulled down so low on his forehead she couldn't clearly see his features.

The handsome man, whom she believed to be the old man's son, held his father in a long and very emotional embrace. Unabashed tears of joy slid down the older man's face as he put his gnarled hand on the little boy's head and pulled him into their circle. Because the younger man's face was hidden from view by his father's, she couldn't tell if he was crying, as well. She guessed from the slight shudder of his wide shoulders that he was.

Immersed in the strangers' reunion, Susannah did not feel the tears in her own eyes until the scene wavered before her like a mirage. She closed her eyes and glanced away for a brief moment. When she looked up, the trio had vanished.

"Susannah Parker! Even under that ridiculous wig, I'd know you. I can't believe you're really here!" Marilou's Southern drawl had not been diminished by time, distance or voice training.

Marilou flung arms filled with totes, purse and carryons around Susannah, who felt as if she was being bodyslammed. "God, you feel wonderful, child!" Marilou gushed, and then stepped back to look at her old friend. "I hate your guts, Susannah! Nobody looks that good without a little nip and tuck, except you. It's not fair! You're comin' to L.A. and, boy, is that town gonna find its fanny or what?''

Susannah howled with laughter. "You haven't changed a bit, Marilou.'' Then she took Travis's hand. "I'd like you to meet Travis.''

Marilou looked down at the ten-year-old and beamed. "Lord almighty! Is it possible he's more beautiful than you?''

Travis's mouth was agape. He watched Marilou play a rookie nurse every Wednesday night on "County General Hospital.'' Without taking his eyes off her, he pinched his arm as though to check if he was dreaming.

Marilou held out her hand. "I'm pleased to meet you, Travis.''

He swallowed hard and tentatively took her hand. "Me, too.''

Marilou gave Travis a hug, then stood and put her arm around Susannah's waist. "Can you believe it, pretty soon we'll all be neighbors.''

"What?'' Travis looked anxiously at his mother. "Are we moving to Los Angeles?''

"No, not permanently. Marilou is just getting ahead of herself, is all. Once I go out to film the movie, I thought I'd fly you out to see me on weekends, rather than me coming back to New York. All that travel would wear me down after a while.''

Travis nodded. "I definitely think I should come to see you, Mom. Definitely.''

Marilou clapped her hands together. "Good! That's settled.'' She looked around the waiting area at the number of stares they'd been receiving. Recognition had begun to dawn in one too many pairs of eyes. "Where's our driver?''

"Out front waiting in the gray Olds," Susannah explained.

"Not a limo?" She shook her head as she began walking toward the door with Susannah. "Honest, darling. You New Yorkers take this anonymity bit much too seriously."

As they drove away from Eglin, Susannah scanned the area for any sign of the elderly man and his family, but they were long gone. She didn't know what she would say if she found them, but she felt she should apologize for looking when their hearts were open.

38

Destin, Florida
Labor Day, 1992

Tracy Dodd's twentieth-floor, two-story penthouse shimmered with every bit of Broadway glitz he was known for. Standing on the outdoor terrace looking out on the Gulf waters, Susannah viewed the crowded beach below. Her vantage point made her feel as removed from the world as an angel. Tracy had gone to great lengths to ensure both security and privacy for his leading lady. Every staff member had been instructed to answer Susannah's requests promptly and without question, but above all, they were to keep silent about her and Marilou's presence in the building.

Still, she and Travis finally were made aware of the kind of paparazzi frenzy her fame had created by their second day in Florida. As he walked between Susannah and Marilou down to the beach, Susannah saw him turn his head at the whispering of the security guards and doorman. A cluster of maids and janitors slipped pocket cameras out of uniform pockets and from beneath stacks of towels. After being photographed for the seventh time, Travis stuck his tongue out at the gardener who frightened him when he popped up from behind a ligustrum hedge.

Susannah immediately stepped between her son and the camera lens. "Pretend he doesn't exist," she counseled.

"You'd think you were some kinda CIA agent," Travis grumbled as he hoisted his fluorescent green fins under his arm.

"Nah." Marilou waved aside his misgivings. "Spies would crumble under our kind of pressure."

Travis was still frowning as they crossed the startlingly white sugar sand. "Are they always gonna gawk at us like this?"

"No," Marilou replied flatly. "These bozos are amateurs. By the end of next week, the pros will hone in on us. Then the games really begin."

"But it's not like Mom's a rapper or on TV like you."

Susannah walked over to the umbrella and two lounge chairs that the condo management had set up for them. "Travis, this is one of the consequences of all those magazine articles. All my publicity has been geared to come out at the same time. This weekend. That's why I wanted to come here. It's not Lake Tahoe or Aspen where most movie stars will be found this weekend. I wanted a bit of quiet time for us."

Travis yanked his mask and snorkel over his head and began adjusting the headstrap. "It's just that I never thought of you as famous, Mom. Being in a play isn't the same as being in a movie." With the mask in place, his lips bulged out like two sausages, making him sound like Daffy Duck. "Tho, Mum. I jwust want you ta know, I can take it. I won't sthick my tongue out anymore."

Awkwardly turning around, his flippers throwing sand into the women's faces, Travis flip-flopped into the water.

Marilou roared with laughter, but Susannah stared

solemnly at her son. "Our lives are going to change so much, Marilou. I hope to God Travis is not affected by all this. If this movie takes off, I know everyone is going to want me to move to California and I don't want to do it. Greg would throw a fit and use my career demands to try to gain custody of Travis. But if I keep residency in New York, when I'm filming I'll be away from my son too much...I'd miss him terribly." Tears formed behind her sunglasses.

Marilou reached over and placed her hand on her friend's arm. "Don't you dare give Greg another thought. I've got the best attorneys money can buy. I'll show you how to protect yourself legally. Besides, you're forgetting one thing."

"What's that?"

"Your relationship with Travis is strong and based on unconditional love. That child is your child, Susannah. He always was and always will be. He's old enough now to understand his father's shenanigans if Greg tries to pull anything. Travis will defend you to the death. Greg wouldn't dare take you back to court because he knows, as I do, that all that judge would have to do is interview Travis and the case would be closed. In four years he'll be fourteen and permitted to decide with whom he wants to live anyway. Even if Greg demands to see him, once he's fourteen, Travis doesn't have to go."

"God, that's right. I'd forgotten that. Say, how do you know so much about all this?"

Marilou smiled smugly. "It was the plotline in a soap I did for a couple years. You wouldn't believe all the trivia about law and medicine I've got packed in this brain," she quipped, tapping her temple.

Susannah glanced toward the water, making certain she could still see Travis's bright green snorkel bobbing in the waves. "Life's so complex, isn't it? All these years I've fought like a cat to get this break and now that it's here, it scares the shit out of me. Not that I'm backing away from it, mind you, just that there are so many pitfalls."

"Be careful what you pray for, you just might get it, huh?"

"Something like that." Susannah sighed.

Marilou rolled over and propped her elbow on the chaise longue, resting her head in her hand. "It's weird, you know. Us being in Florida after all this time. I remember when we took off that weekend for Fort Lauderdale. You were lookin' for that dream guy..."

Susannah pulled off her sunglasses and stuck them on top of her head. Looking out to the sea, she could almost feel herself inside the dream again.

"Do you still have that dream, Susannah?" Marilou asked sincerely.

"Not for a very long time. I don't believe in that kind of dream anymore," she replied sadly. *Though I wish I could.*

"You're getting older, you know. Maybe you had the dream and don't remember it."

"Alzheimer's doesn't run in my family, Marilou. I'd remember."

Marilou sat up and gazed blankly out to sea. "Too bad. I always liked that story."

Once again, Susannah felt a vast emptiness inside her. Closing her eyes, she probed her mind, searching out its cause. Like gnarled tree roots of indeterminate beginnings and endings, her feeling of hollowness could not be sorted out. It wasn't sadness or loneliness, nor bitterness, anger or pain. All she sensed was a vast, barren territory. Instantly she recognized it as her life. Something was drastically lacking, something that she knew must be fulfilled.

What could be missing?

Susannah pushed her thoughts away with frustration. She didn't have the luxury of time to think about personal fulfillment.

Tracy's high expectations of her talent for the camera tied her stomach in knots. She'd hired an acting coach to help her sharpen her skills and a voice coach to perfect her delivery. Though Susannah loved challenges, too many film people were already predicting her downfall. She wanted to prove them all wrong. Tracy, as well as Abe Bateman, was depending on her. At the same time, she wanted her life with her son to remain as unchanged as possible.

"Marilou, you're just the same as you always were. How have you managed to be unaffected by all the bullshit out there?" Susannah asked honestly.

Without looking at her friend, Marilou answered, "You just think that because you don't know the truth."

Susannah's voice registered surprise. "Truth?"

"I earned my fame the good old-fashioned way—I slept my way to the top," she joked with carefree aplomb. "Seriously, I planned it that way." She glanced at Susannah's shocked expression. "See, it's like this. A person has to take stock of their assets and faults. Me? I have no talent, at least nothing like you've got. I have a photogenic face, a great bod and I'm scathingly honest with everyone, includin' myself."

Taking a deep breath, she continued. "Sure, when I was young and stupid and first went to L.A., I thought I'd be a great actress. I fell for the most romantic sweet-talkin' guy I'd ever met. Believe me when I say that my Southern upbringing had never prepared me for anyone so devious. I hate the fact that my story is so ordinary, yet it happens to naive girls every day. Anyway, he said everything I wanted to hear. That I was talented and beautiful. He promised me a part in a movie. Fortunately, I discovered that all he really wanted was Daddy's money to fund his movie. He broke my heart. I dumped him and wised up."

"How so?"

"I went to the toughest acting class I could find and had the coach tell me the truth. I was pretty enough to get in the soaps, but that was all. All the acting classes in the world will never help me, because I frankly don't give a shit."

"You don't mean that."

"Sorry, Susannah, but I'm not dedicated like you. Anyway, I made sure I went to all the premieres, got my butt in the tabloids and moved from one soap to another, gettin' my face seen all over the place. I dated only producers and directors of prime-time shows. One movie-of-the-week led to another. Then the series came along and ta-da! That's my story."

Susannah listened for sharp edges of bitterness, but found none. "And that's all you want?"

Marilou lowered her sunglasses and peered at Susannah over the rims. "We're both thirty-five years old. Not exactly ancient. I work out two hours a day, put my money in secure Treasury Bills and keep my nose clean—meaning, no drugs. I've met enough creeps, jerks, assholes and users to fill ten lifetimes. But someday, I'm going to meet the right guy who'll take one look at me and know we were meant to be. Then we'll move to a ranch in Montana and raise horses and kids and I'll never look back."

Gaping at her friend, Susannah said, "You're kidding?"

Marilou smiled affectionately as she shook her head. "Maybe you gave up on your dream man, Susannah, but I didn't." She turned her face back to the sea.

Following Marilou's gaze, Susannah watched her son playing in the surf. Perhaps she'd been wrong to forget her dreams. Without them, she never would have given birth to Travis.

Marilou was right. They were still quite young. She'd almost forgotten what it was like to think of herself like that.

Sounding like locusts, the clicking noise of camera shutters crept toward Susannah, interrupting her thoughts. She neither flinched nor acknowledged their presence. Keeping her eyes closed, she pretended she was Susannah Parker from Indianapolis with her friend Marilou on spring break from college. They were just two normal young girls filled with fanciful dreams, their lives still very much ahead of them.

For the Labor Day weekend, Michael had rented a two-bedroom beach house at the Sandestin resort in Destin. He'd intended to play golf with his father and son, maybe a game of tennis now that Robin was proving to be an even better athlete than himself. But for the most part, he wanted simply to spend relaxing time with his family.

By Saturday morning the temperature had soared to the upper nineties and the heat proved too much for Don, who was unable to complete the first nine holes of their golf game. Fortunately, Michael had rented an electric cart with a surrey, which kept the blistering sun off his profusely perspiring father.

"Grandpa, are you all right?" Robin asked after sinking a birdie putt on the eighth hole.

"I'll be fine, son," Don replied in weak, gasping breaths.

Michael put his putter back in the rented golf bag and signaled to Robin to sit next to him in the cart. Michael turned on the electric ignition. "I think we'll call it quits for today, Dad."

Don's lids hung heavily over his dazed-looking eyes. "I'm sorry." He languorously patted Robin's knee. "I'm not up to these vigorous sports anymore."

Michael's insides felt as if they were being squeezed in a vise. He drove the cart as carefully, yet as quickly, as he could toward the clubhouse.

Robin didn't know what was happening to his grandfather, but from the concerned look on his father's face, he knew it was serious. For weeks, Michael had talked to Robin about the fun they'd have in Florida, playing golf and tennis. Robin knew how important this trip was to his father because his mother had been fiercely determined to keep Robin at home to spite him.

Eavesdropping on his mother's telephone conversations, Robin had heard her swear to Michael she'd never let Robin go to Florida. When he hid behind the potted palms on the terrace at his grandmother Frances's house and heard his mother explain her scheme to spoil Michael's plans, Robin had confronted her that moment with the truth.

Ever since his parents' divorce, Robin had noticed that his grandmother did not always side with his mother. Though the Van Burens were defensive of the family name, he'd watched several battles in which his Aunt Meghan and his Uncles Max and Karl attacked his mother. He didn't understand what the fights were about, but he did know his mother never won.

He recalled confronting his mother about the trip to Florida. Keeping his hand on his grandmother's shoulder, Robin had asked pointedly, "What's so bad about me going to Florida with Dad?"

Kristen's heavily mascaraed eyes narrowed. "It's my turn to have you for Labor Day."

"No, it's not," Robin replied, feeling his grandmother's body stiffen.

"Is that true, Kristen?" Frances asked.

His mother hesitated. She glanced away and then folded her arms across her chest. Then she rubbed her upper arms with her palms. "Well...I'm not sure. Maybe it is. I don't know."

Frances's lips thinned. "It either is or isn't. Robin certainly seems to remember. Why can't you?"

Kristen directed a glare at him. "I suppose he can go." She waved him away. "But I want a full account of all your activities, young man."

Robin didn't budge. "No."

"What?" His mother nearly came out of her seat.

Frances calmly placed her hand over Robin's, letting him know she was on his side. "He's right, Kristen. It wasn't your weekend, to begin with. He can do any damn thing he wants."

"What's gotten into you, Mother?" she demanded. "Have you suddenly sided with the enemy? Letting Michael get away with his tricks is tantamount to giving the devil a pack of matches!"

Frances stood slowly, holding Robin's hand. "My grandson is ten years old. He's not a baby. According to his teachers, with whom I've kept in close contact, he's not only top of his class, he's gifted in math and science.

From the surprise on your face, I can see you were not aware of this. Robin is mature for his age, has better manners than you and displays a caring attitude toward most people he knows. In other words, Kristen, my grandson is not stupid. He's figured out your games. From this point forward, I doubt you can ever use him as a pawn against Michael again."

Robin didn't want to remember all the swearwords his mother used to describe himself and his grandmother. He didn't think his father would approve.

"Grandpa, I dunked my towel in the ice cooler. Maybe if you put this on your face, it would cool you off," Robin said, handing the icy cloth to Don.

"Thanks," Don replied gratefully.

"Robin, get Dad a piece of ice to chew on."

With a mirthful cluck of his tongue, Don looked at his grandson. "No need for that. I'm just overheated, that's all."

Michael clutched the steering wheel as they pulled up to the front door of the snack shop. "No pain in your left arm or in your chest? No shortness of breath?"

"No, son. I'm out of shape, but I'm not dying." Don handed the wet towel back to Robin and got out of the golf cart. "Lord almighty, I may be almost seventy and need to slow down a bit, but I'm sure not ready to quit. And don't be giving me your arm to hold on to like I was some kind of invalid. I can make it on my own just fine."

Michael glanced at Robin, whose eyebrows were knitted with confusion. Grumpy behavior had never been one of Don West's patterns. "We're right behind you, Dad," Michael said as he and Robin followed Don inside to the snack shop.

Michael watched his father like a hawk as they sipped

icy drinks at a window-side table. Don's normal happy spirits returned while he talked with Robin about his grandson's plans for the upcoming school year.

Draping him like a shroud, a sense of foreboding caused Michael to overreact to his father's every move. "Maybe you should be drinking water instead of that tea, Dad. Too much caffeine isn't good for you. I'll get the waitress. Maybe some juice, huh?"

"I'm fine, Michael," Don answered good-naturedly, and winked at Robin.

"We should order something to eat. A chicken sandwich. That's light, no fat, no cholesterol. On wheat bread. Yeah," he said, scanning the room anxiously.

"I'm not hungry, son."

"Why can't I find a waitress when I need one?" he grumbled, finally rising from the table.

"Michael, you're getting upset over nothing," Don insisted.

Nothing? You and Robin are all I have. You're my family. Family is not "nothing"…it's everything. "I don't think so," was all Michael said before heading toward the hostess's podium where he knew he'd get assistance.

Don looked at Robin. "Is he always like this?"

"Pretty much. You should see him when I get a cold. When he was rich, one little sneeze and I had to go to the doctor. Mom said he was overly protective."

"Do you think he is?"

"No. I think he loves me," Robin replied earnestly.

"Does it bother you that he's not rich anymore?"

"No. Dad always told me we were just 'temporarily poor.' And pretty much he was right. I can tell things are better for him now because he got some new underwear last week."

His grandfather let out a chuckle then, sobering, said, "It's a hard lesson your father has learned...that money doesn't buy happiness."

Robin shrugged. "I guess. But Dad's always seemed the same to me. 'Cept now he's real sad-looking sometimes."

"That's because he wishes you lived with him," Don offered.

"Nah. He gets that look when he thinks I don't see it. I think he needs a girlfriend," Robin said bluntly while leaning over to sip his cola from a straw.

Don swallowed his tea the wrong way and coughed. "What?"

"I've got a girlfriend. We pass notes in the hall at school and she comes to my soccer games. Her name's Jessica. She's cute and really smart. She lives with her dad."

"She sounds wonderful, Robin. Do you think Michael misses your mother?" His grandfather watched him intently, waiting for his response.

"No way! I'm glad they don't live together." He leaned conspiratorially toward his grandfather. "As soon as I'm old enough, I wanna live with Dad. Mom's just not real...motherly. You know?"

Don nodded. "Yes."

"Dad dates a lot of different girls, I think. But it's kinda weird cuz he can never remember their names. I asked him about it and he said he only goes to fancy parties for business. He just doesn't like anybody. He says they aren't like Grandma Emmy."

"There's never been another woman like her."

Robin sighed heavily. "I wish there was."

"I had no idea he'd cut himself off so much. He's too young to be alone."

Rolling his eyes, Robin said, "Grandpa, Dad will be thirty-six this month!"

Don smiled and ruffled Robin's hair. "That old? I guess I'd forgotten."

"Good thing I reminded you," Robin replied.

Don looked up to see Michael approaching with their waitress. "We'll talk about this later. Florence Nightingale's back."

Robin looked at the name tag on the waitress's uniform that clearly read Wendy. His grandfather needed better glasses.

Michael's concerns over his father's health did not abate until after an uneventful supper later that night. Once he was convinced that his father was comfortably resting in the air-conditioned bedroom of the little beach house, Michael joined Robin, who was sitting on the front steps looking at the stars.

Robin sat next to Michael and said, "Grandpa's going to be all right, Dad."

Michael put his arm around Robin's shoulders and pulled him to his side. "I know, but I worry about him just like I sometimes worry about you." *Still, I can't get rid of this feeling that something's wrong. It's almost like somebody needs me, but I don't know who. It's so strong and so very strange.*

"Tell me a story about the stars, Dad, like you used to when I was little. And not the usual ones I already know like Cassiopeia," he said, pointing upward. "And look, there's Orion's belt and Pegasus." He glanced at Michael. "Tell me a new story."

"Hmm. A new story." He glanced upward and saw two twinkling objects that glittered red and green lights. Michael pointed to the satellites. "See those stars there?"

"Yeah."

"We'll call them the wandering stars. They're older than any stars in all the galaxies. Billions of light-years ago, the red star met the green star and they fell in love. They were so much in love they shared their lights, which gave them even more power to shine in both red and green colors. They promised each other they would never be apart.

"Then an evil black, mighty meteor thundered through time and space seeking them out to destroy them because he was jealous of their colorful lights. He sent one star spinning off to another galaxy and left one here near earth where he could only wait."

"How long did he have to wait?" Robin asked anxiously.

"Eternities, but he always believed they would come back together. He never gave up hope. And when enough time passed to test his belief, the other star came back to him. And there they are in the sky, still happy, still together."

Robin kept his eyes riveted on the two satellites. "We have to give them names, Dad."

"Oh, they have names. Phillip and Gloria." Michael had no sooner said the names aloud when suddenly he sensed why he'd been filled with dread. It wasn't his father who was in danger this weekend, but Phillip. Quickly, he glanced at his watch. It was nearly midnight, which meant it was early morning in Monaco.

Michael kissed the top of Robin's head. "I've got to make a phone call, son."

"Okay. I'll wait out here for you."

Michael placed an overseas call to Phillip's number in Monaco. He let the phone ring nearly twenty times, but there was no answer. He hung up and dialed again, hoping he'd simply called the wrong number. The phone was left unanswered and the answering machine didn't pick up.

Only once before had Michael's intuition rattled him this forcefully. It was the day his mother died. His hand was shaking when he dialed his own number at his New York apartment. The answering machine picked up and Michael entered his code to retrieve his messages.

It's a long shot, but...

The machine gave the date and time as Thursday, only an hour after Michael and Robin had left for the airport.

Then he heard Phillip's voice on the tape.

"Michael, I have terrible news. Gloria...died tonight. She was perfectly all right when we went to dinner with our friends." Phillip's voice cracked. He cleared his throat. Then, sobbing, he continued. "She just looked at me, spoke my name, then clutched her heart and dropped into my arms. It was all so fast. So very fast. I...I don't know who to call...I don't know anyone who ever really cared about us the way you did. Please, call me, Michael. I don't think I want to live without her." He hung up.

Frantically, Michael dialed Monaco again and again. There was no answer.

Realizing his father was spending an awfully long time on the telephone, Robin walked into the house in time to hear him dictating a message.

"Received news of Gloria. Stop. Am in Destin, Florida, for the holiday. Stop. Call me at 555-678-9090. Stop. Returning New York on Tuesday. Stop. Will fly to Monaco immediately. Stop. Love, Michael."

Robin sat on the couch next to his father and waited

patiently until he finished his call. When Michael turned to Robin, there were tears in his eyes.

"Aunt Gloria's dead, isn't she?" he asked.

Michael hugged Robin so tightly he thought his father's arms would crush him.

Silently, Robin held his father as he thought about his Great-Uncle Phillip and Aunt Gloria, whom he'd never met. Though he knew his dad's star story was make-believe, he couldn't help wondering if Gloria's spirit hadn't winked at him from heaven tonight.

39

New York City
Labor Day night, 1992

Arriving at home shortly before midnight, Susannah and Travis had not yet unpacked their bags when Magda telephoned.

"You're back. I was planning to leave a message on your machine. Susannah, I'm afraid I have bad news," Magda said, and went on to explain that she'd received a call from Phillip Van Buren's secretary about Gloria's death on Saturday night.

"When and where is the funeral?" Susannah asked, stunned.

"Tomorrow morning at ten in Monte Carlo. The name of the funeral chapel is Viaponte House. I thought you'd want to send flowers or a wire."

The loss of her mentor and dear friend ripped through Susannah's heart and she was deeply saddened. "I'm going."

"Where?"

"To Monte Carlo. If I can catch a red-eye tonight, I can be there in time for the service and then I'll fly right back. Would you be a doll and look after Travis for me?"

"Hold on. Shouldn't you think about your work

schedule? I thought you had meetings with a publicist this week. And what about—"

"You hold on, Magda," Susannah replied a bit angrily. "Gloria was the one who saw me through the most difficult days of my life. We had a bond that doesn't come around very often in life and..." Susannah started to cry.

"I'm coming over to help you pack," Magda replied, and hung up.

Michael arrived the day before the service, doing everything he could to give Phillip the moral support, courage and comfort he needed. He walked with Phillip through the crowded city streets, sat in a hotel bar and shared old times with him over a brandy. Michael knew this was not the time to talk about himself. It was Phillip's turn and Michael was there to listen.

"She would have liked to have seen you again, Michael. It's so funny." He chuckled to himself. "When she met you for the first time, she told me she had the eeriest feeling she'd met you before or known you before."

"I don't recall when it would have been, Phillip."

Phillip smiled down at the brandy. "You have to know Gloria like I do. She wasn't referring to having known you in New York. She meant from a previous life all three of us lived together."

"Oh," Michael replied, not fully understanding.

"I think Gloria was right about that kind of thing. As we get older—and hopefully wiser—about the machinations of this world and those we can't see or hear, we come to believe that there's coherence behind the apparently crazy patchwork of our lives.

"I had so many business associates tell me I was insane to let you guide so many of my investments. Ha!

You were only in your twenties. And you were eating their egos for breakfast. The best part was you didn't know a thing about it."

Laughing with Phillip, Michael said, "I don't understand what all that has to do with you and I knowing each other from another time."

"Simple," Phillip began. "Talent like that can't be learned in school nor from thirty years in the business world. Like Gloria said, you were an investment adviser before."

Curiosity filled Michael's face. "When?"

"Crash of '29, of course."

Chills blanketed Michael's body, but rather than being alarmed, Michael was reassured. As Phillip continued, Michael felt the familiarity of the twenties in New York as if he'd actually been there riding out to Long Island in Phillip's Bugatti. He could smell the brand-new leather-bound books in Phillip's library and the richly cured aroma of fine Havana cigars. Amazingly, the picture of life back then came into sharp relief for Michael; he could even feel the tension in the air the day Phillip read the stock-exchange reports from his private ticker tape.

Phillip chuckled under his breath and said, "Odd, isn't it, that in this day of faxes and overnight mail, I had instant communications with my colleagues through transatlantic cables, telephones, ticker tape and wire services. The business world has been fast paced for a very long time. Perhaps things haven't changed so much after all." He paused and his face turned somber again.

"Michael, I've told you before that you're like a son to me. That's why I'm saying all these things to you. I want you to be prepared for your future on all levels."

"I understand. I'm not sure I grasp your metaphysics, but I promise you, I won't forget what you've told me."

Placing his hand on Michael's shoulder, Phillip's eyes delved deeply into his. "Wisdom isn't always profound, Michael. Sometimes it's quite simple."

Whether or not Phillip's rendition of life was the truth didn't really matter to Michael right now. Maybe years from now he'd have the luxury of enough time to contemplate it all. Knowing that Phillip was the one who needed reassurances about life and the changes he'd be undergoing without Gloria, Michael remained silent and listened. It was all he could do.

Cupping his hands around his glass, Phillip said, "I've discovered from Dwight and some of my other friends that things haven't been all that good for you since the divorce, Michael. You never told me about your problems with the IRS. I knew Kristen was a bitch, but I didn't realize she tried to destroy you. I'd like to know why you didn't come to me. I would have helped you. Didn't you trust me?"

Michael was stunned by Phillip's question. "My God, Phillip, if for one moment I thought my actions had caused you the slightest pain or doubt... No, Phillip. I wanted you to have a life with Gloria without my stresses or problems. It was your turn for happiness. To be honest, I also used that time to discover things about myself. I realized I had leaned on your reputation and network to make my fortune. I'd never really been out there on my own, facing my fears. I believed in myself, sure. I knew I had talent, but what I didn't know was if the rest of the world would ever recognize it."

"You were proving something to yourself."

"Precisely. I discovered I have the intuition you always believed in, but now I know it for myself. Comebacks are tough in any business. Some worse than others. But I've started recovering. Contracts and commissions are coming in. I'm working with honest, productive people and I feel good about myself." Michael paused. "That's more than I knew six years ago."

Phillip inhaled deeply and sat a bit straighter. "I'm very proud of you."

Beaming, Michael absorbed his mentor's praise. This time he'd earned it. "Thanks."

"Do you remember the conversation I had with you years ago about my will?"

"That you were leaving everything to me and Robin? Yes."

Phillip's face was rigid with concern. "Because of the divorce, Kristen is going to raise holy hell when I die. Like her brothers and sister, they're all counting the days with exuberant anticipation. I know they'll contest the will and throw it into court. I've contacted my attorneys in New York and moved some things around a bit. It may take a few months, but I'm selling the Long Island house."

"My God! That's your home!"

Phillip shook his head. "That's what I've discovered about life, Michael. Home is within yourself and the person you share your life with. Home is the love I had with Gloria. That house is a white elephant. I've got an interested buyer and then I'll place the proceeds in a trust account in Grand Cayman for Robin. I have a few other shenanigans up my sleeve, but what I want you to know is that you won't have to worry about Robin's education or the schooling of his children if you just leave the money in the account."

"Are you sure about all this? I can provide for Robin."

"Handsomely, too, I'm sure," Phillip replied. "That's not my point. I'm leaving the bulk of my estate to charity, research and a scholarship fund to help young men like you. But I'll be damned if I'm going to let one single cent go to Kristen or my greedy, lazy brother, Bart. He can go screw himself."

Chuckling, Michael said, "You sure don't beat around the bush, do you, Phillip?"

"Not when it's about something that means this much to me, son," he replied, and smiled warmly.

Glittering in the morning sun, the baroque-inspired chapel in Viaponte House was filled with Phillip and Gloria's American and European friends. Marcello Viaponte, the curator of the funeral home, was in a dither as to what to do with the continuous stream of people. Like the six generations of Viapontes before him who had built the original chapel in the side of this cliff, Marcello spoke softly and gently urged everyone to pay their respects and then quickly leave.

The Europeans knew what to do and how to conduct themselves; it was the Americans who lingered so long. He wondered if they thought their lengthy meditations were going to raise the dead.

"Please, if you don't mind," Marcello urged the tall, slender woman wearing a Hermés scarf on her head and dark sunglasses. "You must move along." He hadn't the slightest idea where she'd come from since he'd just spied her in the crowd. Usually he was able to see newcomers coming through the front door. She must have found the vine-covered side door.

"I've come a long way," Susannah replied.

"So have all these people," he said, waving his hand to indicate the dozens of people jamming the doorways and brushing perilously close to the extravagant bouquets of orchids, roses and rhuberum lilies. He was flustered over the lack of airflow in the chapel, which was designed for small gatherings. This Van Buren affair was more work than a royal funeral. *If only Phillip Van Buren had warned me the lady had been so popular, I could have moved everything to the rotunda. Now it's too late!*

"I understand," the graceful voice said to him. "I don't know any of these people. I only knew Gloria. I came for her. Not for them."

Marcello was taken aback by the deep sincerity he heard in her voice. Though her appearance was hidden by the accessories, he admired the confident yet unassertive way she stood. Delicately using her hands only to punctuate her words, she regally held her head high, like a swan. Her mystery intrigued him immensely.

"I'm sorry to report the eulogy was over fifteen minutes ago. Mr. Van Buren will be leaving shortly, but we intend to keep Mrs. Van Buren's ashes here in the chapel till the end of the day for those like yourself who couldn't get here in time."

"Oh," Susannah replied sadly. "I missed it…"

"I'm afraid so," Marcello said, noting her trembling bottom lip and the way she bit it to control her emotions. "You were obviously very close to Mrs. Van Buren," he probed.

"Yes," she replied as a soft smile born of memories curved her lips.

"Then you would want to pay your respects to Mr. Van Buren."

"I won't take long, I promise," she assured him.

Marcello bowed his head apologetically. "I was wrong to rush you. Take all the time you need."

Susannah thanked Marcello and slowly shouldered her way through the groups of people in search of Phillip Van Buren. She'd only met him once at the Fourth of

July party at his home in 1976, and wondered if she'd recognize him. Suddenly she remembered the intense foreboding feelings she'd had that night sixteen years ago. Ironic that she would remember that night as if she were back there in time, going through those fears and anticipations all over again.

Shivering with chills, Susannah felt as if she'd left her body and come back. Once again, she heard that clicking sound in her brain as if her life had just switched onto another train track.

What could possibly happen in this place? I don't know a soul here. Gloria isn't here to guide me. The eulogy is over. All I can do is pay my condolences to Phillip and leave.

Shaking off her thoughts, she continued to scan the crowd for Gloria's widower.

"Phillip, you're exhausted," Michael said. "I know you want to see everyone, but I think it would be wise if I invited your friends to the house now. You need something to eat."

Nodding, Phillip said, "I never dreamed so many would come. These past years I'd lost contact with nearly everyone."

"Marcello's refreshments are fine," Michael said, "but some of these people have flown all night to be here. I've already called the caterer and ordered more food."

Phillip's eyes filled with tears. He wiped them with a linen handkerchief. "My home has vanished, Michael. Gloria's not here anymore."

Michael could feel his heart breaking for Phillip. *To have loved only one person for so long and shared so little time isn't fair.* Michael wanted to say a thousand things to Phillip, but all he could put into words was, "I know, Phillip. I know."

Just then, the Escalantes from Madrid walked up and began speaking with Phillip. They turned and thanked Michael for the "inspiring" eulogy and left.

"I'm going to ask the driver to bring the car around to the chapel door. While he takes you home, I'll have time to spend a moment with everyone and ask them personally to come to the apartment."

Wearily, Phillip nodded. "I suppose you're right. Make sure you invite everyone."

"I will." Michael squeezed Phillip's shoulder affectionately and then worked his way to the chapel door to find the driver.

Susannah saw that Phillip was finally alone and she approached him. "Hello, Mr. Van Buren." She extended her hand. "I'm Susannah Parker, a friend of Gloria's."

Phillip stared at her blankly. "You're very young," he said as she took off her sunglasses.

"I know you don't remember me, but I met you at a Fourth of July party that you had at your house on Long Island in 1976."

"Really? You're right, I don't recall." He bowed his head. "I'm not quite myself right now."

"Please, I don't mean to intrude. But I wanted you to know how much I dearly loved her. She was my ex-husband's great-aunt."

"You're a Walton?"

"I'm divorced. Gloria was my salvation during those terrible times. Greg, my ex-husband, wasn't anything like Gloria. She opened her heart to me the first time she met me. She even let me wear a fabulous crepe gown she'd worn at one of her father's Fourth of July parties in the twenties."

"I proposed that night," Phillip said, and began relating how much in love they'd been and how his own mother had deceived him to get her way.

Susannah thought she'd never heard a story more tragic than Phillip's. Gloria had always related her side with a sense of unfulfilled destiny, as if she was waiting for the right time.

By the time Phillip finished his story, he was thoroughly drained. "I apologize. I'm quite tired. Won't you join the others and come to our house for something to eat?"

The last thing Susannah wanted was to be with strangers who would distract her from her memories of Gloria. This was a time for Susannah to be with her friend in heart and mind, not with people she didn't know. "I didn't mean to take so much of your time, Mr. Van Buren. I just wanted you to know I will miss Gloria very much."

"Thank you" was all Phillip said as he shook Susannah's hand.

Susannah left through the front door this time so that she could thank Marcello for his assistance. She'd asked the cabdriver to wait for her and then take her back to the Grand Hotel. She'd call Magda and then rest for a few hours before flying back to New York. She had a monstrous schedule to face after taking this time off, but she didn't care. She'd been with Gloria today and that was all that mattered.

Michael walked up to Phillip. "I'll help you out to the car."

"Oh, I'm fine, Michael. I just had an interesting conversation with the most beautiful girl."

Suddenly, Michael was surrounded by the scent of

Southern night jasmine and tea rose. His senses went on alert. "What girl? What was her name?"

"Name? Sharon something. I think it was Sharon. No, Susan. That's it. Susan. She's a cousin of Gloria's, at least that's what I think she said." Phillip paused. "Perhaps I will let you walk me out, Michael. I don't seem to be doing as well as I expected."

Michael was undeterred as he took Phillip's elbow. "Tell me more about this woman," he urged as he walked through a cloud of her perfume.

"I don't remember. She was wearing a beautiful Hermés scarf... She said she came to my Fourth of July party in 1976."

Christ! I was there! I smelled that perfume, had that dream. God in heaven! Is it possible that I was supposed to meet this Sharon or Susan or whoever she is? That I mistook Kristen for this mystery woman? Can that be?

Michael's mind whirled with possibilities. On the one hand, it was too ludicrous to believe and, on the other, in some mystical way, it made perfect sense. Now he wished he'd paid more attention to all what Phillip had said yesterday. Was the key to his own destiny locked somewhere in Phillip's words?

Perhaps it wasn't too late. She was here somewhere in this chapel. Once he'd gotten Phillip to the car, he'd make sure he talked with every person here. There was still a chance he'd see her at the house.

Feeling his adrenaline rocket through his body, Michael vowed he'd find her.

Watching the driver leave with Phillip, Michael quickly turned and began his search for a lone woman wearing the scarf Phillip had described. However, after twenty minutes, he came up empty-handed.

Even Marcello had little information. He told Michael

that before she left she'd told him she was from New York City and had planned to fly back that afternoon. Though he wanted to race to the airport and search for her, he'd promised Phillip he'd stay for a few more days to help with settling Gloria's affairs.

Perhaps Phillip could help shed some light on this strange occurrence. Most people would say Michael was nuts for thinking only one woman could be his destiny. It sounded like something out of a romantic movie. Thankfully, Phillip was wiser than most people.

40

New York City
March, 1996

"I can't believe the only time I'm able to see you is sitting in a goddamn limousine on the way to the airport!" Tracy Dodd complained as he pulled down the burled wooden door of the hidden bar.

Michael laughed. "It's *your* goddamn limo and I'm going to Los Angeles on your behalf. Which, by the way, is totally unnecessary since you've been on a winning streak for the past four years. You need me like you need a hole in the head."

"Shut up. You're my lucky charm," Tracy grumbled, and poured himself a glass of perfectly chilled chardonnay. He handed the glass to Michael.

"Thanks," he said, glancing at the Cakebread label. Tracy stocked one of the better private wine cellars in the city. Still, Michael thought he was a puppy compared to Phillip Van Buren. Just thinking about his good friend saddened Michael immensely.

He remembered returning to New York to find the interim investor for Intelligence Communications ready to sign the next day. Michael had been forced to delay his return trip to Monaco for three days. By the time he arrived, Phillip had been hospitalized after suffering a massive coronary. The housemaid and Gloria's companion told him that Phillip had cried incessantly since Gloria died. It was her opinion that he'd died of grief.

Michael had remained by Phillip's side in ICU until he died. When the nurse asked him to witness a legal statement regarding the circumstances of Phillip's death, she'd asked Michael, "What relation are you to the deceased?"

"I'm the only son he ever knew."

Four years later, Phillip's estate was still entangled in legalities, with the Van Burens at loggerheads over who was to inherit which dinner fork. Michael couldn't help thinking how apropos their situation was. He envisioned them like a passel of greedy cats, clawing and hissing at each other over a bowl of milk, when their own bowls were filled to the brim.

Phillip's passing had taught Michael to live every minute of his life to the fullest. In January of 1993, he'd pressed Kristen for custody of Robin. Once Robin told Frances and Bart he wanted to live with Michael, they convinced Kristen that a court battle was not in the family's best interests while Phillip's estate was being settled.

Marveling at the twists fate handed out, Michael thought of Phillip every day and thanked him, wherever he was, for giving Robin back to him.

Tracy slipped a long Havana cigar out of his breast pocket. "Look what I smuggled into the country from Quinvaca last week."

Michael grinned mischievously. "You devil. For me?"

"It's your favorite," Tracy replied. "See? I take care of my friends."

Michael studied the cigar and handed it back to Tracy. "I can't be bribed."

"Would I do that to you?"

Shaking his head emphatically, Michael replied in a stern tone, "For the umpteenth time, I'm not going to the Oscars as somebody's escort. Hire one of those young pretty boys you've got working in that god-awful thing at the Cherry Street Theater."

Tracy frowned. "I'm closing the play this week."

"I told you it wouldn't make you any money."

Balling his fist, Tracy pounded his knee. "Goddammit, Michael. You still don't know anything about the entertainment business, do you?"

"I try to avoid that part at all costs," Michael bantered good-naturedly as he clipped off the end of the cigar and slid it under his nose.

"Why? If it weren't for me giving you that break back in '92, you wouldn't have the hordes of clients you've got now. Who, by the way, are all too much into that boring high-tech crap for me."

"That crap just made one of my twenty-six-year-old software geniuses a billionaire this month. You'll be glad to know it was one of your friends who funded his company last year."

Gasping, Tracy nearly spilled his wine. "Billions?"

"Doesn't sound so boring anymore, does it?" Michael goaded his friend.

"Okay! So I never looked into that shit when I should have. But Jesus, can you blame me? With all the entertainment mergers going on, my plays being made into movies with budgets getting close to a hundred million to produce, I've been a little busy myself."

Michael patted Tracy's shoulder affectionately. "Now you understand my viewpoint."

"Susannah Parker is not some starlet. She's a big star now and I've talked her into coming back to Broadway next fall to do my new play. We're already working on the screenplay she'll star in for Paramount." Tracy glanced at Michael's intractable expression. "Goddammit, Michael! Being nominated for Best Actress is not small potatoes. If she wins, I could even go back and revive *Sweet Sinner*. She was great in that, wasn't she?"

"I don't know. I never saw it."

Stunned, Tracy jerked his head toward Michael. "The play or the movie?"

"Neither one," Michael replied. "In fact, I've never seen any of her movies."

"You raised the money for that play. You made her a star."

"No, you made her a star. I made a connection with William Mitford who introduced me to his friends. And now I'm in the process of making serious money for quite a few of them."

"Don't rub it in. I'm a creative person. My parents were in vaudeville when they were young. I don't know any other kind of life than the theater. So, when you get out there, don't tell these investors about one of your billion-dollar computer babies. Just tell them about me. That I've never lost a dime of capital investment. At the very least, I've always broken even."

Michael blew out a puff of smoke. "You worry too much. I know how to handle it."

Tracy glanced out the window as they pulled into the airport, thinking that Michael was the one person he knew who was as good as his word. Michael would get the deal, and once again, Tracy would be grateful. He should do something special for Michael. He reached in his pocket and pulled out his key ring. He untwisted a brass key. "Here's the key to my condo in Destin. I don't use it as much as I used to. I was thinking about selling it. Feel free to use it anytime. And let me know if you know anyone who might want to buy it." He handed Michael the key with a smile.

"Thanks. Maybe I could take Robin once school's out. You know I grew up near there. My dad's still there."

Tracy feigned ignorance. "You don't say." He lit a cigar. "Anytime's fine with me."

The limousine pulled up to the American Airlines terminal.

Tracy shook Michael's hand. "Now listen, once you sew up this deal, I'd like you to think about taking Susannah to the Oscars. She refuses to go with another actor and, being loyal to me, certainly no other producer."

They waited while the driver retrieved Michael's suede hanging bag from the trunk. "Why's that?"

Tracy lifted his palms heavenward. "She's an actress and they all have the craziest notions sometimes."

When the driver opened the door, Michael got out of the limousine, then leaned back in to ask, "What notion would keep her from taking a date to the Oscars?"

"She says she hasn't met the 'right' one yet. Said she'll go it alone until he shows up." Chuckling to himself, Tracy shook his head. "Can you believe it? In this day and age?"

Michael seemed to mull over Tracy's words for a moment. "Yeah, pretty hard to believe, all right," he replied vaguely. Michael hesitated, then asked, "Where'd you say I'd find Susannah?"

"She's staying at the Beverly Wilshire this weekend."

"She doesn't own a house out there?"

"Nope. She lives here in New York most of the time.

She's refused to move her son to La-La Land. He's in a private school here."

"I know how she feels."

Tracy glanced at his watch. "You better get going or you'll miss that plane."

"Yeah, sure. Well, thanks for the lift. I'll call you tomorrow and let you know how it's going."

"Fine," he replied, and waved Michael off.

The driver closed the passenger door, got back into the car and eased it away from the curb.

Puffing on his cigar, Tracy suddenly remembered that Susannah's son was about the same age as Robin. Then he pushed the thought aside. "It's just a coincidence."

41

Michael finished his third day of nonstop meetings by placing a triumphant phone call to Tracy Dodd in New York. Not only had Michael funded the Broadway production of *Silent Indiscretions*, but he'd put together a two-movie deal, as well. Although Michael had a signed letter of intent from Susannah Parker that she would star in both the play and the movie productions of *Silent Indiscretions*, all Michael needed to finalize everything was another statement from her that she would star in Tracy's second production.

"But I don't have another play in mind," Tracy told Michael.

"Then find one. It's only good business for Keynes and Broad to spread their investment over three projects. Give me something that's on your back burner. You can find someone to rewrite it, can't you?"

"Sure, but Susannah is picky. That's why she's Oscar material. You'll have to talk to her."

"Okay. Where is she again?"

"The Beverly Wilshire. Let me know what she says."

Clucking his tongue, Michael quipped, "She'll say yes, of course!"

Michael talked to Susannah's secretary and scheduled a meeting with the star for four o'clock that same after-oon. After showering and changing into a banded silk hirt and wool slacks, he called his apartment in New 'ork. There was no answer. It was well past six on the ast Coast and he knew Robin should have been home rom his tennis lessons by now. It was possible that Robn had coerced Sarah, his childhood nanny, who still remained in Michael's employ, into taking him out for a izza. Michael left a message on the answering machine ;iving both the phone and room numbers at L'Hermiage, in case they'd misplaced them, and the number at he Beverly Wilshire Hotel where he was to meet Susan-ah Parker.

Michael arrived at Susannah's hotel and went straight o the front desk where a tall woman in her mid-twenties miled at him.

"Would you ring Susannah Parker's suite and tell her hat Michael West is here."

The woman nodded and then suddenly stopped her-elf. "Excuse me, Mr. West. A call came in for you just a ew moments ago. It's from New York." She handed im a sealed envelope.

He opened it and read the message from Robin. 'Where are the pay phones? I need to make a long-distance call."

"Over there," she replied, pointing to a small hallway with a bank of phones.

"Thank you," Michael replied, and quickly crossed he lobby.

He dialed direct, and the phone on the other end was nstantly picked up. "Robin? What's wrong? Your mes-age said urgent. Are you all right?"

"I'm fine, Dad." Robin's voice cracked as it often did

now that he was fourteen. "It's Grandpa, Dad. He's in the hospital."

"Dad..."

"The doctor called and said Grandpa had had a heart attack. He's in ICU in Fort Walton Beach. Sarah's on the other phone booking a flight out for you and one for me. I can get there by midnight."

"He's still...alive?" Michael felt the marble floor under his feet shift. His stomach turned to ice water.

"Yes, Dad. He's been asking for us."

"Jesus..."

"Dad, here's Sarah. She wants to talk to you."

Michael lifted his hand to his forehead and felt droplets of cold fear on his skin. "Yes, Sarah?"

"Sir, I've got a flight booked for you out of LAX one hour from now. Can you make that?"

"Make it?" Dazed by the shock, he barely understood what Sarah was saying. "I'll have to get a cab..." He looked back toward the front desk. The young woman was staring quizzically at him.

"You'll fly direct to Houston. Then take a puddle jumper from Intercontinental to Ellington Air Force Base. There's a late-night flight going to Eglin Field. I'll call and have a driver pick you up at Eglin and take you directly to the hospital."

"What about Robin?"

"He'll be at the hospital by the time you get there, sir."

"My God...Dad." Michael's voice quaked.

"Sir? I have to hang up in order to drive Robin to Kennedy. You must get a cab immediately. I know how everyone talks about the traffic at rush hour in L.A. It's worse than here."

"Yes. Of course." Numbly, Michael hung up the phone and walked quickly to the front desk.

"Is everything all right, sir? You're not ill, are you?" the young woman asked, looking at Michael's ashen face.

"Call a cab for me, would you please? I have to get to the airport. My father is dying."

He turned and mechanically walked toward the front doors. Halfway across the lobby, he stopped and turned back toward the woman at the front desk who was already placing his call to the bell captain for a cab. "Tell Ms. Parker I'll see her some other time."

Michael had always known his father was a stubborn old mule.

Standing next to Don's bed, Dr. Peltgrin told Michael and Robin they were amazed the man was still alive.

"We lost him twice between the station and here. The paramedics said he was DOA, but they revived him. I've never seen anything like it," the doctor said with admiration in his eyes.

"He told me he'd passed his exam last month," Michael said. "What happened between then and now?"

"What exam? I didn't give him any tests. Does he have another cardiologist?"

Michael was confused as he looked down at his unconscious father who was hooked up to a bevy of machines, tubes and television screens. Computers registered heartbeats and brain waves. He was reminded of the helplessness he'd felt when Phillip was dying. This time he realized that some of the computer equipment in the room was manufactured in part by a small company he'd helped to fund more than ten years before. Without realizing it then, he might have been instrumental in providing the technology that was buying his father another hour on earth.

It was the first time in Michael's life he'd understood the meaning behind the words *We're all in this together.*

"You're Dad's only doctor." He looked down at his father again. "You never went to a doctor at all, did you?"

Just then Don's eyes fluttered. He opened his mouth to speak, but only air rushed out. Michael felt the pressure of his father's fingers in his hand. He leaned his ear close to his father's lips.

"Don't...be mad...about the doctor. I was just tired of waiting to see your mother."

Michael's heart clutched. "Oh, Dad."

Robin moved to the other side of the gurney and bent over to hear his grandfather's words. When Robin held his hand, Don opened his eyes to look at him.

"You never got to see her...but your grandma's here..."

Robin glanced questioningly at his father. Michael shook his head.

Don's eyes focused on the far corner of the ceiling. "She's here...I can smell..."

Suddenly, Don's eyes opened wide. His lungs took a shallow breath.

"Dad...please," Michael pleaded.

Computerized sounds filled the room. The monitors no longer displayed rhythmic squiggles, only a flat line.

Michael frantically clamped his hand over his father's wrist feeling for a pulse, but there was none. Michael felt as if the world had stopped. He'd just lost the man who had given him life and who had loved him unconditionally. Believing it impossible for anyone ever to love him that much again, Michael had never felt so desperately alone.

"Grandpa?" Robin's voice cracked not from adolescence, but with emotion. His face was wet with tears and his nose was running. He held his grandfather's hand to his mouth to stifle a painful sob.

A nurse pulled a turquoise curtain around them, co-cooning them in a circle of grief. Dr. Peltgrin waited solemnly for ten minutes before personally unhooking the unnecessary lifesaving tubes. Finally, the doctor told Michael it was time for them to leave.

As Michael looked back one last time at his father's still body, he was certain, if only for a fraction of a moment, that the scent of Southern night jasmine and tea rose filled the air.

42

➤ ◄

Beverly Hills, California

"Tracy, forget it," Susannah said emphatically into the receiver. "I'm packing up and going to Destin. I waited all afternoon for your friend to show and he canceled on me from the lobby!"

"I'm sure I'll hear from Michael soon. He's the most conscientious guy I know. It's not like him to drop off the face of the earth for no good reason."

"I'm sure he's a prince. But Travis only has this weekend left of his spring break and I'm taking him and the dog as far away from Los Angeles as possible. You can talk to me all you want once I get to Florida."

"But what about the Oscars?"

"Whatever happens, happens," she answered, and hung up.

She turned around and found Travis had packed all their luggage and was helping the bellman place the bags on a brass cart. Sitting patiently next to the door was their two-year-old golden retriever, Rebel.

"Your car is waiting outside, madam," the bellman informed her, looking askance at the dog.

Susannah smiled. "Didn't the manager tell you about Rebel? This is his favorite hotel. Isn't that right, Rebel?"

The dog barked in agreement as Travis clipped the leash onto Rebel's collar.

"We're going to have a great time in Florida, Rebel," Travis said, following his mother out of the room. "Just as soon as Mom chills out."

"What's that supposed to mean?" she asked Travis.

Condescendingly patting her shoulder, he said, "Face it, Mom, this Oscar nomination is making you nuts."

"Is it?"

"Uh-huh. I'll be glad when it's over and our lives will be back to normal."

Normal? What's that?

She sighed heavily. "Me, too."

After an uneventful flight and the drive from Eglin Field to Tracy's condo at Destin, Susannah's first truly calming moment was when she gazed out on the water the next morning.

It was a pristine day with a sky so clear and blue it looked artificial. The shallow waves glistened with twinkling sun rays as they lapped onto the white sand.

Travis walked out of his bedroom dressed in bathing trunks, a Smashing Pumpkins T-shirt and running shoes. He grabbed a banana out of the fruit basket Tracy had ordered for her.

"I'm going for a run with Rebel," he said, picking up the leash.

"Wait a minute and I'll go with you."

Travis dropped his chin to his chest, a favorite sign of exasperation. "By myself, please."

"The string-bikini crowd won't hit the beach until ten, Travis. I'll wear very demure shorts and a really cruddy T-shirt and no one will recognize me. Give me that Knicks hat to wear."

"Oh, all right," he acquiesced as she darted into her

room to change. "But hurry up! Rebel has to go." He bent down to pet the dog. "Don'tcha have to go really bad, right now, boy?"

Susannah dressed in record time and rushed out of the penthouse with Travis and Rebel.

They walked down the beach talking about the chances of Travis's baseball team that summer while Rebel raced ahead of them and then came racing back when he knew he'd gone too far.

They joked and laughed and kept walking, not minding the time or distance. With every step, Susannah felt her tensions over the upcoming Oscars fade.

"Will it be so terrible if you don't win, Mom?" Travis asked.

Susannah burst into laughter at his question. "Sweetheart! I'm not afraid of losing. I'm afraid of winning!"

His face scrunching into a look of utter dismay, Travis threw his arms up in the air. "I give up! I'll never understand you."

She tossed her arms around him and hugged him quickly, then continued walking. "It's hard to explain," she said as her mind wandered into her past, stopping thoughtfully along the way.

"Try me," he urged.

"Something so very awesome as an Academy Award should be shared with someone very, very special," she said musingly. Clasping her hands behind her back, she looked down at the sand shifting under her feet as they walked a bit more slowly. "I came to Florida when I was very young thinking I'd find someone that special."

Haltingly, Travis interjected, "You met Dad in Fort Lauderdale."

"I know. But he wasn't the one I was looking for. It was just a dream I had. And it's not important now."

"But, Mom, it must have been for you to think about it now. C'mon, tell me."

"I don't want to bore you, but maybe you should know my story." For the first time, Susannah told her son the dream about the sea king. She didn't tell him that she'd mistaken Greg for the sea king. Nor did she include her misgivings about Greg from the beginning of their relationship and marriage. She only told him about the dream and how it came back to her from time to time.

"How long has it been since you had the dream?"

"So long I can't remember. I don't believe it anymore, so I suppose it went the way of Santa Claus and the Easter Bunny."

"Oh," Travis replied a bit sadly. After a thoughtful pause, he asked, "Am I the reason you've never remarried?"

Cranking her head around to stare at him, she crinkled her nose. "Good God, no! Whatever gave you that idea?"

"Well, you never go out with anyone other than a time or two...at least in New York."

"And there's no one in Los Angeles, if that's what you're wondering." She pulled up to a halt. "I guess I haven't given anyone a chance to find out if they were special, have I?"

He shook his head. "'Fraid not."

"Well, it doesn't matter. I'll know it instantly when it does happen."

"Think so?" he asked sincerely.

She placed her hand on his shoulder, suddenly realizing he must have grown another two inches overnight. He was taller than she. *When did that happen? God! They grow so fast at this age. Change so much. Yesterday he was buying toys. Today, he's my only confidant.*

"Yeah, I'll know." From a forgotten distant corner of her mind, she heard her mother's voice. She repeated the words. "It will be kismet."

"What's that?"

"Meant to be." She smiled and took off to run after Rebel.

Destin Pass Bridge
Destin, Florida

In the last will and testament of Don West, the instructions for cremation and dispersal of ashes were very precise and for Michael and Robin, deeply moving.

Standing next to Robin on the Destin Pass Bridge shortly after daybreak, his father held a simple wooden box filled with his grandfather's ashes over the water.

Robin slipped his arm around his father's waist as he scattered the remains. "Do you really think they're together, Dad?"

Swallowing, he answered with emotion, "Yeah. I'm sure of it."

Robin held on to his father while they prayed silently. Robin promised himself he'd try to be the kind of patient and thoughtful man toward his grandchildren that his grandfather had been to him. His only regret was that his mother had been able to keep him in New York all those times when he'd wanted to see his grandfather. Now that Robin was older, he felt more in control of his life. He was all the family his father had left and that worried him.

Someday, he'd have to go off to college, and eventually he'd get married and have kids of his own. Of all the goals in his life, the one thing Robin wanted was to be a good father. He didn't care if he was super-rich like his mother's family or not. He wanted to be happy and spend time with his kids.

Even though his father was able to spend more time with him, Robin wished Michael didn't feel that he had to pretend he was happy. But that was just the way his father was.

From beneath the bridge, Robin heard a dog barking. He looked down at a boy about his age, he guessed, maybe older since he looked taller, playing with his girl-friend and the dog.

"I always wanted a golden," Robin mused aloud.

"What did you say?" His father roused out of his reveries.

"That kid down there has a golden retriever. I always wanted a dog like that, but Mom wouldn't let me have any animals at all."

"You're kidding? You never told me that," Michael said with amazement.

"You never got a dog, so I figured you didn't like them."

Michael scratched his head. "I guess I never thought about it."

"You mean, I could get a dog? Not just any dog, mind you. It's got to be a golden...like that one." He pointed excitedly to the dog far below them.

Michael smiled and hugged his son. "Yeah?" Suddenly leaning over the railing, Michael called, "Hey! You there! Can we buy your dog?"

"Dad! Have you gone nuts?"

Michael grinned mischievously. "You want a dog? You're getting a dog!" He cupped his mouth with his hands. "I want to buy your dog!"

Robin watched for the young couple's reaction, but they didn't look up and kept walking.

"I don't think they heard me," Michael said.

"Me, neither," Robin replied a bit sadly.

Michael put his arm around Robin's shoulder. "Let's drop off our luggage at the beach house, get changed and go for a swim, and then we'll find a pet store."

"Today?" Robin opened the door of the rental car.

"Sure. The way I see it, we haven't a minute to waste."

Michael used the key Tracy Dodd had given him to unlock the penthouse door and then walked into the marble-floored foyer with Robin behind him.

Robin whistled. "Wow! Some beach house." He carried his duffel bag into the large living room with its wall of glass overlooking the water. "This is incredible!"

Michael bent over and picked up a woman's silk robe that was draped over the back of a chair. "This is occupied."

"What?" Robin spun around.

Michael felt the hairs on the back of his neck stand on end as he lifted the gossamer-thin silk to his face. "It can't be…"

"Can't be what?" Robin started toward him.

"This perfume is…"

Suddenly, the front door burst open as Travis and Rebel bounded across the foyer and into the living room. "I beat you, Mom…"

Travis came to a dead stop.

Southern night jasmine and tea rose, Michael finished his thought.

From the hallway came the sound of a woman's laughter. It was full-voiced, yet lilting and mellow, Michael thought as the scent of her perfume filled his nostrils and then his head.

"You only won, Travis, because Rebel pulled you out of the elevator!" The woman laughed as she sprinted through the open door, holding sunglasses in one hand and a cluster of tiny seashells in the other.

Michael dropped his arm to his side and let the robe flutter to the floor. He held his breath.

When she removed her cap, cascades of tumbling auburn hair obscured her face momentarily. Sunlight from the window bounced off her hair and lit the most beautiful turquoise eyes Michael had ever seen. Mesmerized by her tentative smile, he walked toward her.

The intense sunbeams backlit the three figures in front of Susannah. She squinted, thinking the hazy form coming toward her was some kind of mirage or phantom from a dream. He was dressed in blue—a very dark blue suit and a lapis lazuli–colored tie with a gold pattern. The sun struck his straight hair and, though it had begun to gray at the temples, she could see it was a sandy color.

Susannah's heart stopped and then pounded rapidly, making her feel delirious.

He kept moving toward her.

Then she heard Travis's voice. "Who are you?"

From behind the phantom she saw another figure move toward Travis. He was the same height, the same size and frame as her son, with the same blond hair and bright blue eyes. The silhouettes of the boys' shadows moved slowly together; Susannah couldn't help thinking she was seeing double.

"My name is Michael," he said with a smooth Southern drawl. "I'm sorry we have intruded upon you."

Chills raced down her spine, the backs of her legs to the tips of her toes. She wanted him never to stop speaking. His voice was like liquid velvet covering her, making her believe in dreams again.

Unable to tear her eyes off his still-obscured face, she scrambled for a reply to his remark. She couldn't think of anything to say that would make sense to this total stranger who knew nothing about her dreams.

"I'm afraid there's been a mistake," he said, taking the last step before coming to a stop in front of her. "You see, I thought I'd be alone here."

His eyes were honey brown! Not blue or green or violet. Honey brown with flecks of gold the way she'd known they would be since childhood. God in heaven, she'd found him! At last, he'd found her!

Susannah's lips moved, but no words were spoken.

Michael didn't take his gaze from hers. "Your eyes...they're the color of the Caribbean where the blue swirls with green."

Susannah smiled with wonder.

Piecing together fragments of information, Susannah realized that there was only one person this Michael could be. He was Michael West, Tracy Dodd's friend. Michael, the man who'd miraculously found the funding for *Sweet Sinner*. The man whom she was supposed to have met in Los Angeles. She couldn't help wondering how many times in the past they'd missed each other.

We're together now and that's all that matters.

Michael recognized her from the photographs in Tracy's office. Not one had done her justice. Dressed as she was, without makeup and her spirit radiating with vitality, she looked younger than he'd expected.

Without touching her, Michael knew he'd found what he'd been waiting for all his life. He didn't want to frighten her by telling her that he knew they would spend the rest of their lives together. Someone as famous as Susannah Parker had probably heard that line a hundred times from more men than he'd ever want to know about. Besides, most people would think such foolish announcements were ridiculous.

He saw a warmth in her smile that seemed to come straight from her heart, encouraging him, reassuring him. When he smiled at her, he didn't mind giving his heart in return.

"I don't think there's been a mistake at all, do you?" Susannah said.

"Not this time," Michael replied.

He reached out for her hand. She gave it willingly.

We hope you enjoyed *Elusive Love*. For those readers who collect Catherine Lanigan's recipes, she will be sharing two autographed recipes with this publication. The sherried lobster is second only to a fabulous marinade for filet mignon everyone will want to try immediately. For these recipes and an autographed bookmark, send a self-addressed stamped envelope to: 5644 Westheimer, P.O. Box 110, Houston, Texas 77056-4002.

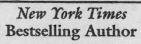

Take 3 of "The Best of the Best™" Novels FREE
Plus get a FREE surprise gift!

Special Limited-time Offer

Mail to The Best of the Best™

3010 Walden Avenue
P.O. Box 1867
Buffalo, N.Y. 14240-1867

YES! Please send me 3 free novels and my free surprise gift. Then send me 3 of "The Best of the Best™" novels each month. I'll receive the best books by the world's hottest romance authors. Bill me at the low price of $3.99 each plus 25¢ delivery per book and applicable sales tax, if any.* That's the complete price and a savings of over 20% off the cover prices—quite a bargain! I understand that accepting the books and gift places me under no obligation ever to buy any books. I can always return a shipment and cancel at any time. Even if I never buy another book, the 3 free books and the surprise gift are mine to keep forever.

183 BPA A4V9

Name	(PLEASE PRINT)
Address	Apt. No.
City	State	Zip

This offer is limited to one order per household and not valid to current subscribers.
*Terms and prices are subject to change without notice. Sales tax applicable in N.Y.
All orders subject to approval.

UBOB-197   ©1996 MIRA BOOKS

National Bestselling Author

MARY LYNN BAXTER

"Ms. Baxter's writing…strikes every chord within the
female spirit." —Sandra Brown

LONE STAR
Heat

SHE is Juliana Reed, a prominent broadcast journalist whose
television show is about to be syndicated. Until the murder…

HE is Gates O'Brien, a high-ranking member of the
Texas Rangers, determined to forget about his ex-wife. He's
onto something bad….

Juliana and Gates are ex-spouses, unwillingly involved in an
explosive circle of political corruption, blackmail and murder.

In order to survive, they must overcome the pain of the past…and
the very demons that drove them apart.

Available in September 1997 at your favorite retail outlet.

From the bestselling author of
THIS MATTER OF MARRIAGE

DEBBIE MACOMBER

Their dreams were different and their life-styles clashed, but their love was anything but mismatched!

Chase Brown offered Letty Ellison love and a life with him on his ranch. She chose Hollywood instead. Now, nine years later, she's come back with her young daughter—another man's child—and as the past confronts Letty and Chase, they must learn that some things are more important than pride.

DENIM AND DIAMONDS

Available August 1997
at your favorite retail outlet.

"Debbie Macomber is the queen of laughter and love."
—Elizabeth Lowell

 MIRA The brightest star in women's fiction